THE PRETENDERS OF COPPER COUNTY

COPPER COUNTY
BOOK 1

MAY ARCHER

Copyright © 2024 by May Archer
All rights reserved.

No part of this book may be reproduced in any form or by any electronic or mechanical means, including information storage and retrieval systems, without written permission from the author, except for the use of brief quotations in a book review.

This book was not written with AI. This author does not give permission for any portion of this book to be used to train AI.

Cover Art: Natasha Snow Designs
Editing: One Love Editing
Proofreading: Jodi Duggan

All the good bits are theirs, and any mistakes are my own!

THE PRETENDERS OF COPPER COUNTY

It was supposed to be a straightforward protection job. Remove the target from Vermont, get him to the safehouse, keep him there until his mafia uncle testifies, get back in my employer's good graces.

Boom, done. Easy.

But it turns out things get complicated real fast when your target is an adorkable, accident-prone cutie with a shockingly low sense of self-preservation, zero clue that he's related to the Fromadgio crime boss, and 100% too much inclination to chat happily with strangers.

When Chris compromises our safehouse (and accidentally starts a "lowkey, unavoidable" bar fight), our only option is to go undercover... pretending to be campground hosts in Copper County, New York.

Make that *married* campground hosts. (Long story.)

Now I'm hiding out with a guy who's obsessed with action-adventure shows and hand-knit sweaters, and whose most fearsome talent is arranging charcuterie boards, all of which is far less helpful in a gunfight than you might think.

And worst of all... the sweet little virgin I rescued is growing on me.

Somehow I find myself listening to his happy chatter when I should be watching the woods, trying to figure out how his mind works when I should be getting us out of this predicament, and appreciating the way he looks in my shirts when I should be focused on getting my career back on track.

But when the Fromadgios' enemies finally find us, protecting Chris is no longer just a job. I'll do anything to protect what's mine... and there's nothing *pretend* about it.

CHAPTER ONE

CHRIS

Some days, I was really freaking tired of being boring Chris Winowski.

"Hey, Chris? Can you swap out the Heady? It's running slow." Van set the pint he'd just pulled in front of Norm Avery. "Crowd after the town meeting must've cleaned us out last night."

I straightened from where I'd been unloading a bunch of freshly washed glasses onto a rack under the bar, wiped my damp hands on the leg of my baggy jeans, and pushed up my glasses. "Me? Heck yeah. I'll do it right now!"

Was it ridiculous that my pulse leapt at being asked to change out a keg—a messy job that meant yanking around a container nearly as heavy as me and arguably the worst of all the tasks involved in being a barback?

Low-key yes.

But I'd been working at the Bugle, the centuries-old tavern in Little Pippin Hollow, Vermont, for almost half a year now, and after one teeny, tiny, barely memorable keg-changing incident last spring, I hadn't been asked again, so this almost felt like—

Van put his gnarled hand on my thin shoulder and squeezed lightly. "I didn't mean you, kiddo."

"Oh." I frowned at him. "But—"

Crys—aka Crystal, aka Original-Crys, even though she hadn't lived in the Hollow much longer than I had— slouched in from the back room wearing thick boots, cargo pants, and a flannel shirt she'd cropped herself last week with her pocket knife, not to purposely show off her amazing abs but because the extra material was "freaking killing my range of motion, man." Her messy hair, which looked like it had been hacked off with the same knife, framed a pretty face, a friendly smile, and dark eyes that reminded me of a caged tiger I'd seen at the zoo as a kid.

"On it." Crys's voice was confident as she clomped back off to get her tools.

My shoulders slumped, but I could hardly complain. I mean, of the two of us, I'd have given her the job, too.

"Guessing Van doesn't want a repeat of the Great Beer Baptism." Norm gave me a wink. "You remember that, Chris?"

"Yes, sir." I tried to muster a polite smile. "Yep. I was there, so…"

"I thought we were calling it the Keg-tastrophe," old Mrs. Graber teased. "It was like a geyser of beer erupted right here in the bar. Lord, I never saw such a sight in all my born days."

That covers a lot of days, I thought uncharitably, my fingers toying with the frayed blue cuff of my sweater, but I nodded along and kept my smile plastered in place. Nothing worse than a man who can't take a joke, Uncle Danny always said.

"You talking about the Ale-pocalypse?" A man I'd never met before set his empty glass on the edge of the bar and rubbed a hand over his bald head. "I heard about that. The way they tell it over in Keltyville, beer ran down the sidewalk in a wave."

I leaned a hip against the bar and closed my eyes with a sigh. It had taken me less than six months in Vermont to become a small-town urban legend. That had to be some kind of record.

I was fairly certain this wasn't what Uncle Danny had in mind when he'd sent me north to stay with Van to "relax awhile" and "find myself" while helping his old army buddy out.

"Not quite," Van said dryly. He darted a glance at the bright white section of new plaster on the ceiling and patted my shoulder again. "It was a hell of a mess, but it could have happened to anyone. Besides, Ernie's been meaning to replace that ceiling nearly as long as he's owned the place."

I wasn't sure about that. Norm didn't look convinced either.

"I didn't mean to get distracted. I disconnected the old keg, like you showed me," I explained. I could feel my cheeks heating, and though Uncle Danny's voice in my head reminded me that uncontrollable babbling was a really inconvenient stress response, the words kept pouring out. "A-and I started screwing the coupler into the new one. But then the Sunday family came into the bar, and everyone was making toasts to Webb and Luke, and someone was asking if it was true that they'd gotten married, and then... well. It just sort of happened," I finished lamely.

"Sure. Like I said." Van shook my shoulder gently one last time before wandering off to help Crys with the keg.

Mrs. Graber leaned toward me over the bar. "You were thinking about making 'em one of your charcoochie boards, weren't you, sweetheart?" she asked in a sympathetic voice.

To the bald stranger, she confided, "Chris does the boards for the Little Pippin Hookers Knit-Ins, you know. They're *magnificent*. All different themes. So colorful. And so pretty, too! Meats, and cheese balls, and even those... whatjacall'em? Edible flowers? This man does amazing things with a salami."

I felt my face go even hotter and gave her a genuine smile. "Thanks, Mrs. Graber." I felt a little guilty for my unkind thoughts about her earlier, so I picked up her mostly empty glass of seltzer and lime and grabbed the soda nozzle to refill it.

Unfortunately, I couldn't blame charcuterie boards for my distraction the day of the keg incident. It hadn't even been the horde of Sundays that distracted me—though lord knew they were difficult to ignore, especially when gathered in multiples. According to town gossip, four out of the five brothers were gorgeous, green-eyed, gargantuan lumberjacks, even the one who worked in Washington as an accountant or something. I hadn't met them all, but I could say for sure that the ones I *had* met were capable, kind, and devoted to their family. Webb Sunday in particular gave off a total John Ruffian vibe... and that was *not* a compliment I gave lightly since I'd been a *John Ruffian: Pretender* fan since the day the show first aired and could quote nearly every one of its seventy-two episodes from start to finish.

In fact, the day of the incident, I'd seen Webb grin down at his brand-new husband, wrap him up in his beefy arms, and give him a kiss so pure and loving that all my breath had left my body in a sigh... and *that* had gotten me thinking about the episode where John pretended to run an ice cream factory to save a woman's dairy farm from financial ruin.

After the dairy lady had given him a tearful thank-you,

John Ruffian had said, "No need to thank me, baby," in his deep, gruff voice. Then, he'd wrapped one huge hand behind her neck and bent her backward—literally, no kidding, *backward*—and kissed her like she was the only other human in the universe, a lot like the way Webb had kissed Luke.

Since this was in my top seven all-time *John Ruffian* kisses, naturally, I'd replayed the whole scene in my head… and then I may possibly have started imagining what it might be like one of these days when I found someone of my own to kiss and wondering whether he'd call me—

"Chris!" Van yelled a second before I felt a distinct dampness around my ankles.

"Huh?" I blinked down to find that I'd overfilled Mrs. Graber's glass by an ounce or two… or twenty… and the excess had run all over the bar and down my jeans. "Oh, shoot. Oh, *frick*. Oh, mother-clucking cluckballs. I'm so sorry, Van." I mopped off the lower counter of the bar with a rag and then crouched to mop at the floor. "I, uh… I…"

"Got distracted?" Mrs. Graber suggested from somewhere above me. "Again?"

"Yeah," I admitted.

"Never mind," Van said. "We'll clean it up later."

I continued mopping aggressively.

"Chris," Van sighed in the fond but slightly despairing tone I'd become familiar with. "Leave it. In fact, come on back to the office with me. I need to talk to you."

I stood and swallowed hard, not meeting anyone's eyes as I followed Van through the swinging door to the stockroom and then to his office.

Was I being fired? I'd never been fired before. Of course, that might have been because my only paying job had been working for Uncle Danny at the Cellar—the wine and cheese shop that had once belonged to my nonna.

Danny hadn't seemed too upset that I was occasionally —not often, swear to gosh, just on one or two teeny, tiny, inconsequential occasions—distracted or unobservant. I was a hard worker, he often said. A *very* hard worker.

Then again, when Uncle Danny had retired last spring, he'd decided to sell the shop rather than let me run it, which wasn't exactly a vote of confidence, so—

"Lord, I have never needed a vacation more than I do right now," Van muttered. He closed the office door behind us, dropped into the desk chair with a groan, and motioned toward the spindly chair in front of the desk. "Take a load off."

"Please don't fire me, Van," I said in a rush. "I know I get distracted sometimes. I can do better. I *will* do better. I—"

"Relax, kiddo. I'm not firing you," Van said.

"You're not?" Relief had me collapsing into the chair.

"Hell no. For one thing, I like you. Customers love you. You're a hoot."

I wasn't sure how to take that, so I nodded.

"For another," Van went on, "your uncle would use my balls as bait if I fired his precious nephew while he was on his fishing sabbatical." Wrinkles creased his tanned face as he smiled. "Don't suppose you've heard from him recently?"

I shook my head and pushed up my glasses. "Not once since he left. I mean, not on the phone or anything. He's sent me a couple postcards, though. Remember I showed you the one with the bluefin tuna, maybe a week and a half ago? He, uh, he did warn me that he wouldn't have any cell service where he was going, and he can only get the postcards out when the resupply planes come by, so…" I shrugged. "I still post pictures a couple times a week on my private Instagram. Someday, when he gets service, he'll be able to catch up on all the stuff I'm doing."

"All the stuff," Van agreed with a little smile. He linked his hands behind his head. "You still worry about him, don't you? I'm sure he's fine, kiddo."

"Yeah! No, yeah, of course he is. Uncle Danny's really strong, and the doctor cleared him to travel almost right away after his heart procedure. I bet he's having a ton of fun. But I, ah… I guess I didn't know he'd be gone quite this long? He didn't really specify, and you know how much he hates it when I ask him a bunch of questions, and I… I miss him, that's all." I rubbed my palms over my jeans and joked, "I'm feeling a little short in the family department temporarily." Even my cousin Nicky had gone radio silent since I left New Jersey.

Not that I'd expected him to call—or even particularly wanted him to, all things considered— but still.

For half a second, when Van inhaled, he looked almost angry, but his expression cleared so quickly I was sure I'd imagined it. "Well, the good news is you're welcome to stay with me for as long as you like." He sat forward. "In fact, you've got the house to yourself for the next couple weeks. I'm heading to Portland for the Brew Fest, and then I'm taking a quick camping trip before leaf-peeping season really gets going around here. I took you off the schedule, too." He nodded to the paper spreadsheet taped to the wall.

"You did?" I blinked. "But… why? Is it because of the spill? Because I really will clean it—"

Van waved my words away. "It's not that. It's that… Chris, how long have you been on your own since Danny left? And how many places have you explored?"

"Around here?" I frowned. "I guess not a lot? But I'm here to work, Van—"

"And you do, kiddo. You do. But did you ever think maybe part of the reason you're so distracted is 'cause you... well, you ain't got much of a life outside of work and home?"

"Uh." I pondered this for a second. "No? I also make charcuterie boards for the Hookers and the PTA meetings sometimes, and I helped out at the orchard a couple times too. I know lots about apple varietals—Uncle Danny taught me a lot about gardening, and pollinators like butterflies and bees, and hybridization—and it turns out keeping an orchard's not *so* different from gardening. Oh, and I helped decorate for the town fair. Ms. Fortnum said I was really good at hanging bunting—"

Van shook his head. "This is worse than I thought. Kiddo, what have you done that's *fun*? You're young. You need to get out and see the world. Run with the wrong crowd for a while. Let folks get to know you. Make some friends."

"I have friends," I protested. But that wasn't really true. I'd made a lot of acquaintances in the Hollow, but no one I really hung out with. No one who called me up and asked me over for dinner. To be honest, I'd never really been good at having those kinds of friends—the couple of times I'd thought I'd found one in the past, they'd sort of drifted away, and Uncle Danny said family was more important than friends, anyway.

"Tell me." Van scratched his cheek. "When was the last time you hooked up with a hot, uh... guy?" he guessed.

I nodded, then shook my head, then pressed a hand to my stomach, where a bunch of pygmy blues were fluttering their wings as if trying to escape. "Guy," I agreed in a small voice. "And it's, um, been a while." I refused to admit that I hadn't dated a guy, let alone hooked up with one, in... let's see, it was a couple weeks until my twenty-fifth birthday, so if I did the math correctly, that meant it had been approximately... twenty-five years?

"Well, there you go. Plenty of hot single guys in this town." He winked broadly. "Have an adventure! Be like the dude in that stup—uh, that really interesting show you're always watching. Hasn't Crys asked you to go out with her crew a couple times now?"

"Oh, well..." I rubbed the back of my neck with the cuff of my sweater. One time, Crys had invited me to go ax throwing. Another time, she'd invited me gorge jumping, which, to my shock, involved *jumping into actual gorges.* "She might be a little too adventurous for me? And I... you know. I'll be going home once Uncle Danny's ready to come back, so I don't know if I want to put down roots here—"

"Who said roots? I said sow wild oats," Van said reasonably. "It'll be good for you. You're young. You're sweet. You're a looker, too, underneath those sweaters your nonna knit you back in the day—that's an objective observation, mind you," he added quickly. "Ya ain't *my* type."

I snorted and tugged the cuffs of my sweater—which, yes, *had* been hand-knitted by my nonna—further down my hands. "Thanks, Van."

"But be honest: would you even notice if someone tried flirting with you?" Van lifted one bushy eyebrow. "Just yesterday, I heard someone asking Ernie about you—who you hung out with, whether you were dating anyone, and so forth—so it stands to reason—"

"Someone asked about me? Wait, really? Was it a guy? Do I know them? Were they cute?" The tiny fluttering butterflies became a whole kaleidoscope of giant swallow-tails. "What did Ernie say?"

Van scowled. "Jesus, kiddo, I didn't stand around eavesdropping, and I ain't the damn Matchmaker of Little Pippin Hollow. The point is, open your eyes and open your mind." He tapped his temple aggressively. "I know Danny raised you to keep your head down and be responsible and all that. He wasn't wrong... to a point. But your Uncle Danny was also so stressed about work and... other stuff, his heart went wonky at fifty-nine. Part of the reason he sent you here was to figure out what you want your life to look like, right? So next time you get asked to do something—I don't care if it's joining a bread-baking club, or going on a date, or doing one of them psychedelic retreats in Peru—if you're even the smallest bit interested, promise me you'll do it. Don't overthink. Don't ask yourself what Danny would say. Throw caution out the window and leap before you look. Okay?"

"Sure," I agreed. And because it meant so much to me that he cared, I nodded a bit more enthusiastically and promised, "Yes. I'll do that."

"Good man," Van said with a nod. "Now, get outta here. Go home and change. Nobody's adventure ever started with damp jeans, ya feel me?"

Because he was right, when I left the office, I ducked under the pass-through and called a cheery "See you later" to Crys, who was working the bar.

I was surprised when the bald man from earlier stopped me as I headed for the door. "Hey. Chris, right? I wanted to ask you about those, ah, charcuterie things? My wife's a sucker for 'em. Don't suppose you have a business card?" He gave me a hopeful little smile.

"Me? Oh." I shook my head. "No. I only do it for fun.

Nobody's gonna pay somebody to arrange their cheese into —" I stopped.

That was cautious Uncle Danny talking, right there, after I'd promised Van I wouldn't second-guess myself that way. And after all, what was the harm in making a little cash on the side and helping this man do a nice thing for his wife?

I cleared my throat. "You know what? I'm going to print up some business cards." I grinned. "If you're around tomorrow, I'll give you one."

"I'll be here," he agreed.

It *did* feel good to do something a little... risky, I realized as I stepped out onto the sidewalk and pulled my jacket tight against the chilly twilight air. Really, refreshingly good. Maybe Van had a point about the whole adventure thing. Maybe he was right that good things would happen if I went a little wild.

So when a sporty little black car pulled up alongside me halfway down the block and the passenger's window rolled down, I didn't ignore it or walk faster the way I might usually have done.

"Chris?" The driver of the car had a voice so deep—so *John Ruffian* deep—I stopped in my tracks, sure I hadn't heard right.

"Um. Yes?" I peered into the open window

In the weak, golden glow of the dome light, I saw that he was tall and broad and bearded and plaid-flannel-shirted and—holy shoot, holy *freaking* shoot—he had the same bright green eyes as the Sunday brothers.

"Thank fuck," the missing Sunday said in a voice that— pinky swear—was the sexiest single sound I'd ever heard. "Get in. I've been waiting for you."

"Get in," I repeated inanely. "In..." I swallowed hard. "...your car?"

"Yeah." He frowned like this should be obvious, and probably, it was.

I pushed my glasses up, then ran my hand through my hair, hoping that for the first time in my existence, I could pull off "effortlessly cool," but it was no use. The idea that this man—this lumberjack, this *Sunday*—had been waiting for me had dumped my brain into a blender and hit the smoothie button. I could barely make my mouth form words.

"Oh. Um. Does Webb need something at the orchard? Or..." My voice trailed off as I sifted through the slurry of my brain, trying and failing to come up with any other plausible reason why this gorgeous man would be looking for me. "Does someone need an emergency charcuterie?"

"What the hell is an emergency char—? Never mind." He glanced up and down the mostly deserted street, seeming agitated. Almost kind of... nervous? It made my chest go warm in sympathy, which somehow reconnected my brain to my mouth.

"Try taking a deep breath," I suggested. "That sometimes helps me."

"I think what would help is not doing this here," he muttered. "Where the trees have eyes and every busybody has an opinion. But here we are."

The poor guy didn't seem any better at making sense when he was nervous than I was, but I nodded encouragingly.

He pushed an impatient hand through his hair, managing to look far sexier than I did with that move. "Let's start over. I'm *Sunday*." He gave me a meaningful look.

"I figured." I gestured from my own dull, brown eyes to his gorgeous ones. "Dead giveaway."

"Right. Okay. So?" He nodded toward the car.

I still wasn't sure what he wanted, and I hated to presume. "So...?"

He huffed out a frustrated breath. "This isn't my usual MO, okay? When I'm picking someone up, I like to arrange things in advance. But the Powers that Be threw you into my path with zero warning—"

My jaw dropped. Had he... had he really said *when I'm picking someone up?*

Did that mean...?

Was I the *someone?*

I'd never been picked up before. I didn't go to bars and clubs much—or, okay, *ever*—since they weren't my scene, and when I'd tried Grindr just to see how it worked, I hadn't even uploaded a profile picture before five messages popped up, four demanding dick pics and one inviting me to a nearby stranger's home to "rail his horny ass through the mattress." I'd panic-deleted the app instantly.

But now, unless I was very much mistaken—always a possibility—this bristly-jawed man with forearms of pure muscle was standing in front of me and honest to gosh talking about picking me up because the Powers that Be had thrown me into his path.

My lungs worked, but I wasn't sure they were actually sucking in air. Could a person drown on their own lust?

"Yup. I didn't even know what you looked like until this time yesterday—" His wry grin obliterated my past, present, and future composure.

Yesterday? Where had I been this time yesterday? How had I not noticed him noticing me? Oh, man, what had I been wearing? Because that was now going to be my forever-and-ever favorite outfit—

"—and, in fact, it's only thanks to Ernie York that I even knew where to find you—"

"Ernie," I breathed, the facts slotting together in my mind.

Oh my gosh. Oh my flipping gosh.

This hottest of all the incredibly hot Sundays had been the person asking Ernie about me? I was suddenly, wildly glad Van hadn't divulged this information, or I might have melted into a pile of incredulous goo back in his office and missed this whole interaction.

"Yeah. Ernie mentioned you'd be working tonight." He rolled his eyes. "Small towns, man. Everybody knows everything. On the one hand, useful for finding the guy you're looking for. On the other..." He darted another glance up and down the street, then shrugged. "Anyway. I usually prefer things done in a more controlled and orderly fashion—"

I nodded like a bobblehead. I loved things to be neat and orderly, too! Gosh, we had so much in common already.

"—but that doesn't mean I'm not a hundred percent committed here." He pressed one large hand to his dazzlingly thick pectoral and said earnestly, "I am."

"Oh. Well. Th-thank you?" I bit my lip.

Was I hallucinating? Was I misinterpreting what he was saying? There was nothing worse than thinking someone liked you and wanted to get to know you, only to realize, when they stopped talking to you at school or stopped coming in to the Cellar during your shift, that you must have been wrong about them. I'd been wrong like that both as a kid *and* as an adult, and I really, desperately didn't want to be wrong now.

But... what else *could* he mean? He'd said he was trying to pick me up. And he was a Sunday—a member of the kindest, friendliest, most upstanding family in all of Little Pippin Hollow—which meant he had to be sincere... didn't he?

"Now that all that's out of the way." He leaned over the passenger's seat and popped the door open. "You ready to go?"

My heart rate kicked up, and then up again. I could hear Van's voice in my head telling me not to overthink, to sow my oats or whatever, but there was going wild and there was going *wild*. I was barely ready for the adventure bunny slope, still reciting, "French fry, pizza slice," to remember how to navigate on my adventure skis. Meanwhile, this man —this sexy, sexy man with his intense eyes and his serious expression and his shirt rolled up to his elbows—had triple black-diamond-level adventure written all over him.

"Just so I'm clear, exactly what's going to happen after I get in the car?" I asked because I needed to be sure.

He sighed impatiently, and I cursed myself for asking.

What if he thought I was being too difficult? What if I was too much trouble? What if he had the same philosophy as Uncle Danny? *You ask too many questions, Christoforo, and you ruin life's surprises. Don't argue. Be calm.*

"I've got a place—a house—that's private and secure. Once we get there..." He shrugged. "What happens then is really up to you. But you'll be safe, that much I can promise." He dropped his voice so it was warm and liquid, like sliding into a bubble bath. "I don't blame you for being nervous, but you can trust me to take care of you, Chris. I swear it."

My jaw dropped. How could someone I'd never met before know exactly, *exactly*, what I hadn't known I needed to hear? I didn't even mind—or, okay, not much—that he seemed to realize I was an utter, absolute, never-been-kissed, twenty-four-year-old virgin in need of reassurance. The way he looked at me, the way my name sounded on his lips, made it impossible for me to be embarrassed or worried in the slightest.

It was no John Ruffian calling me "baby"... It was even *better*.

I was getting picked up by the hottest man I'd ever seen.

So I didn't overthink it. Heck, from that moment on, I didn't think at all. I slid my ass into the passenger's seat, shut the door, and bid boring old Chris Winowski goodbye forever.

And as the car peeled away from the curb, my first thought was that Van had been wrong. Apparently, some adventures *did* start with damp jeans.

CHAPTER TWO

REED

Some days, being Agent Sunday wasn't all it was cracked up to be.

Twenty-four short hours ago, I'd been chilling with my family, distracting myself from some unwanted time off work. And even though I was maybe the one human being in the universe who didn't seem to love spending time in tiny Little Pippin Hollow, I'd actually been enjoying myself.

Don't get me wrong, I loved my family *always*. Those fuckers were impossible not to love. We hadn't had the easiest childhood, what with my mom dying young and Dad's second wife bolting out of the Hollow when Emma was still a toddler, but we'd all moved on. I had my career now, Knox and Webb were busy running the orchard and being in love, Porter and Emma were grown and mature (mature being a relative term in Porter's case), and even sweet Hawklet had found himself a purpose and a boyfriend—one who'd calmly accepted my death stare and reminder (not that Jack needed it) to treat Hawk like the precious being he was.

All of that family goodness, I was totally here for.

But the other shit that came with a visit to the Hollow—the parade of nosy neighbors who remembered me from my motherless, paste-eating elementary school days, the parade of weird celebrations, the endless fucking apples—was usually a hard, *hard* pass.

This time around, it hadn't been so bad. I hadn't gotten itchy and started anticipating my departure five minutes after arriving. Maybe that was because the farmhouse rang with laughter. Maybe because folks in town finally seemed to understand that I had zero interest in meeting a nice boy or moving "home." But most likely, it was because, for the first time in fifteen years, I hadn't had an active assignment for the Division calling my attention back to Washington.

In fact, due to my forced administrative leave, the future of my job was tenuous at best—a situation so stressful that last night, I'd happily (well, happy-ish-ly) agreed to dress up like a Regency gentleman for the town's latest ridiculous event rather than sit at the farmhouse contemplating it.

But just as my breeches and I had been on our way out the door, my boss had contacted me for the first time in weeks.

"They're calling you back in, Sunday." Janissey had sounded more tired and stressed than usual, and in the background, I'd heard the familiar shuffling and zipping of someone trying to pack their life in a bag for an unknown period of time. "Got a new protectee for you. How much do you know about the Fromadgio crime organization?"

"Not much." I'd quickly shuffled through my mental files. I hadn't heard any specifics on the investigation, but I'd gotten bits and pieces. "The head of the family was under investigation, right? And shocked everyone by turning himself in a few months ago, saying he wanted to make a deal? I assume he's in witness protection now if he's sharing information that could make him a target—"

"Yep. The US Marshals are handling that while the Department of Justice is hammering out details of his plea. The DOJ's planning to use some of Dante's information to seal up its case against Robert Evanovich, which is headed to trial in November."

"So what do you need me for?"

"A couple days ago, Dante told the DOJ he had credible information that someone—likely an Evanovich—is threatening his nephew. He's refusing to finish negotiations and sign the deal unless the kid is protected twenty-four seven until the trial. *He* is your protectee."

"Dante's nephew? You mean Nicky... what's his name?" I'd demanded. "Since when does the Division protect criminals? If he's agreed to cooperate, shouldn't the Marshals be handling that too?"

While our roles overlapped sometimes, the US Marshals Service was involved in all sorts of shit—apprehending fugitives, coordinating prisoner transport, and providing witness protection, just to name a few—while the Division was focused solely on the protection and relocation of innocent witnesses. It was one of many reasons I was glad I'd chosen to join the Division.

"Puh-lease. I don't think Nicky Costello's ever cooperated with anyone. I'm talking about Dante's other nephew, Chris."

I'd shaken my head. "Never heard of him."

"Well, no, you wouldn't. *This* one is supposedly innocent as a lamb. Of course, that's what Dante said about Nicky, too—he's refused to implicate Nicky in any of the shit the DOJ could have pinned on him—but both boys got the hell out of Dodge the second their uncle turned himself in, so I have my doubts."

So had I. Innocent often meant "not someone the government can make a case against" rather than truly blameless.

"You wanna tell me how Dante Fromadgio got this information? How is he in contact with his former associates while he's in protective custody?"

"This is what I like about you, Sunday," Janissey had approved. "You ask good questions. The answer is... who the fuck knows? You know how it goes. Coulda been one of Dante's lawyers, passing notes. Could be one of the Marshals protecting him has been getting a little lax—in which case, we'll never get the details. Personally, I think it's bullshit that they're still entertaining Dante's demands at all. The man's been stringing out this deal for six fucking months, and Evanovich's trial is coming up quick. I say, you sign on the dotted line or you serve your time, buddy. But the Powers that Be continually remind me I'm not paid to give my—*fuck. Hang on, Sunday. Yes, Eloise? Five minutes. Tell them I'm coming... Then they can fucking wait for me, can't they? Give me five goddamn minutes.* Sorry, Sunday, what was I saying?"

"What's going on over there?" I'd never heard him talk to his assistant that way.

He'd made a noise halfway between a groan and a sigh. "All hell's breaking loose, that's what. You're literally the only agent on the books in this office without an assignment, which is why the guys upstairs are willing to overlook your recent failure and reinstate you without a hearing. Must be your lucky day."

Janissey's words had struck a spot in my chest that had been sore for weeks. "I didn't *fail*. I know the guys upstairs think so, but I thought *you* understood I was trying to do the right thing—"

"Yeah, I read the report," Janissey had said wearily. "But nobody gives a shit what you think is right, any more than they give a shit what I think. You went rogue and disobeyed a direct order. You wanna get up in front of the review board next month and explain that your conscience told you to do it, and blah blah? You think that'll fix this? Or do you wanna keep quiet, take the golden ticket you've been handed, and show everyone you're the excellent agent they thought you were?"

I'd fumed at this response... but silently. Because when it came down to it, I fucking lived for my job. I loved protecting people. Loved that I was always in motion—new people, new places, sometimes even new identities. It was the big, wild life I'd always wanted, and I loved the thrill of it. It was never, ever dull.

Janissey had snorted. "Smart man. I've got eleven —*eleven*—cases that have all gone hot at once, Sunday, and only nine agents who aren't on leave or already assigned. I asked the director to pull in folks from other agencies and got a giant 'hell no,' so I've been forced to assign my *own* ass to fieldwork for the first time in ten years. This whole situation is my nightmare—I'm missing my daughter's ballet recital, my wife's probably going to withhold sex until the next millennium, and someone far above my pay grade has decided that Margot from Accounts is qualified to handle asset coordination while I'm out, which, yes, is likely to cause a series of epic and far-reaching clusterfucks I'm gonna have to un-fuck one by one later on, thanks for asking. But for you, this situation is a ticket to redemption. Your way back into the Division's good graces. So don't fuck it up. Do *not* listen to whatever sob story your protectee's gonna give you. Do *not* question your orders. Do *not* let him out of your sight. Do your job."

"I will." I'd clenched my teeth, burning with the need to prove myself. "Send me the files on the nephew. Arrest warrants, mug shots, whatever you've got."

Another snort. "Yeah, I've got none of that."

"What?" How was that possible?

"Kid looks squeaky clean. No arrests, no investigations, no unpaid parking tickets. Of course, when you're dealing with a family like that..."

"There's no such thing as innocent," I'd finished.

"You know it. I'll send you over what we have—a driver's license photo and some bank records. Margot'll be arranging your safe house. No time for new IDs or elaborate cover stories, and you shouldn't need them anyway since this is temporary and whatever happens to the guy after trial isn't up to us. Unfortunately, you're on this twenty-four seven for the duration. If you need support, call—*Eloise, I'm right in the middle of... Yeah, I know. Jesus. One more minute.* Sunday, you still there?"

"I'm here. I need some more information—"

"Gotta go. Margot will send you safe house coordinates. I expect you to send her regular reports."

"Wait! Which agent briefed my protectee? I'll need to follow up with them and get the protectee's contact info so I can arrange a meet. I'm gonna need to arrange a plane ticket and a rental car—"

"Not sure who Margot tasked with that. Hawley, maybe, but she's already in Texas on a different assignment to cover Shane, who's down with a broken leg." He made an impatient noise. "But you're not gonna need a plane ticket. Can't believe I forgot to mention where the kid's been staying. You're gonna love this—"

I had not, in fact, loved hearing that the potential heir to a crime syndicate was hiding in the Hollow, right down the street from my family. *Livid* had been closer to accurate. But Janissey had stopped taking my calls once he left on his own assignment, and no one else seemed to have had a clue how this had happened... especially not Margot, who might or might not be amazing at Accounts but was comprehensively shitty in her temporary role of asset coordination.

"Uh-oh," a gentle voice said. "Muscle spasm?"

"What?" Startled out of my thoughts, I glanced over at the man I'd been assigned to protect.

I'd avoided looking at the guy since he'd climbed in, even though every time he fidgeted in his seat, a burst of cologne—subtle, musky vanilla weirdly overlaid with the strong scent of lime soda—floated across the car.

Christ, he was a tiny thing. Maybe five seven, a hundred and twenty pounds, all slender muscles beneath an over-sized yellow-and-blue-striped sweater, with fine-boned features and big, dark eyes poorly concealed by enormous, thick-rimmed glasses.

I had to admit, his getup did the job of making Dante's nephew look innocent as fuck, but if he was trying to make himself ugly or unnoticeable, it was working about as well as Clark Kent slapping on a pair of nerdy Ray-Bans and trying to pretend he wasn't the hottest thing in Metropolis. Whoever had approved his "disguise" should be fired imme-diately. The man didn't just look sweet; he looked down-right *edible.* Any human with even the slightest potential attraction to adorably goofy men would be drawn to him like a bee to honey.

"Do you, you know, rub it?" The man slow-blinked at me with doe eyes that would put Bambi to shame.

Unfortunately, I had more than a *potential* attraction to

men like him. Sweet, pretty twinks were my catnip. Even knowing this was most likely all an act—a part of the legend that went along with whatever cover the man had been living under in my hometown—it was having an effect on me.

"What?" I asked again, trying to remember what the fuck he'd been saying.

"Oh, um, it's just that y-you were clenching your jaw a second ago. You looked a little bit... disgruntled? So I figured maybe you were having a muscle spasm. I don't get them myself. I'm not a clenchy sort of person, even though *technically* I'm a Virgo, and Virgos are supposed to be very meticulous. Sometimes I wish I could ask my mom if I'm really a laid-back Libra who was born a couple weeks early, but she died, so I guess it'll remain a mystery."

"*What?*" I spoke three languages fluently, but none of them were... whatever nonsense he was speaking.

"My nonna, though, she was a slave to the spasms," he continued, undaunted. "Capricorn through and through. And when her jaw got tight, she did this thing like... Here, it's better if I show you." He turned toward me, opened his jaw, and ran his finger back and forth along the inside of his mouth until his finger was spit-shiny and his cheek bulged obscenely. "*Mmmnnnghkuh?*"

I made a garbled, high-pitched noise of my own.

His face crumpled with sympathy. "Aw. You poor thing. It sounds so painful. Let me do it for you. Sometimes it's better when someone else rubs it." He leaned toward me with one hand outstretched.

"No!" I said firmly, leaning away so abruptly my head almost smacked the window. "I'm... I'm fine."

I *had* been fine until that unexpectedly erotic display.

I clenched my hands on the steering wheel. *He's your*

protectee, Sunday. The nephew of a criminal mastermind. Get it together.

"Sorry! Sorry. I'm sorry." Chris—the *protectee*—fluttered his hands, then dropped them to the seat and trapped them under his thighs. "One thing to know about me is that I tend to talk a lot when I'm nervous, and this whole situation is like... *whoa.* Unexpected, you know?"

"Yeah," I gritted out. "I know."

"But not unwelcome! I'm actually really excited that you, um, picked me up. It was perfect timing. Like fate, maybe, if you believe in that kind of thing." He smiled warmly and adjusted his glasses. "I... oh! Hey, this is the lane for the highway. You might want to move over if—"

"I know where I'm going," I assured him.

"Oh." He paused, considered, and nodded. "Okay."

He went quiet for a moment, and the car rang with beautiful silence. But we hadn't gotten more than two exits down the highway when his toes began tapping the floor mats, and he burst out, "Um, I figure you probably don't want me calling you Mr. Sunday while we're, uh... you know. So we should exchange first names. Unless you'd rather that I called you something else? Like... like... *sir?* Because I could do that." His forehead puckered. "Probably."

"Was there an actual question in there?" I demanded.

He sighed. "Who am I kidding? I could totally *sir* you, if you really wanted me to. I'm an agreeable person by nature, and I'm, ah, pretty motivated here." He laughed nervously, and his hands made a desperate bid for freedom, emerging to flit around some more as though the flapping powered some internal engine that forced his words out. "N-not that I'm making assumptions about what you might want! Gosh, no. We don't know each other yet, and if you're not ready to get that intimate, that would be fine. *Better*, even. For me. To take it slow. But... but... I think I'd feel more comfortable with this whole thing if I knew your first name."

It took a minute for my brain to sift through the veritable haystack of speech and nervous gestures, and when I did, I looked at him in disbelief. "Hold up. No one told you my name? You know nothing about me at all?"

"Uh." Another way-too-adorable frown. "N-no? Someone might have mentioned it, but..." He shook his head. "I think I'd have remembered."

"God." I stretched my neck from side to side, fighting annoyance at Janissey, at Margot, at the Division in general and this assignment in particular.

Standard operating procedure for a protective detail like this one involved a shit ton of briefings, often beginning weeks in advance. Briefings for the agents, briefings for the protectees, briefings about the situation that put the protectee in danger, and briefings about how we'd remove them from the threat. For all that the Division claimed that operating outside of the government's alphabet soup bureaucracy gave us a unique flexibility other agencies didn't have, I'd swear nothing got Janissey harder than a team Zoom where we could "deep dive" and "pivot" and "leverage our assets" and "circle back" to whatever or whoever needed circling.

The upside of this was that long before the protectee and I were in the same zip code, I usually had a huge-ass background file that included everything from their dental records to their Hinge profiles, and the protectee knew about me, too—at least the parts I needed them to know, like my qualifications and my freaking *name*.

But in the clusterfuck I was now assigned to, my protectee didn't have a file. He didn't have a legal address in the Hollow. He didn't even have a phone number on record. In fact, the only way I'd managed to find my protectee so quickly was thanks to a chance conversation with my little brother last night. Hawk had let slip that "Chris" who moved to town "a few months ago" was some kind of weapons expert and worked at the Bugle. This had led me to make a few inquiries of Ernie York, the town mayor and the Bugle's owner, who confirmed that Chris was "short and wiry and strong as fuck" and "frankly, a little scary." One look at a picture from the Bugle's staff barbecue last summer on Ernie's phone had shown me the very man from the driver's license photo Janissey had sent over, and I was sure I had the right person.

I glanced at the passenger's seat. So far, the guy seemed about as scary as Webb's golden retriever puppy, but as the man himself had said—and it might have been the only sensible thing he *had* said—we didn't know each other. Beneath the cute-and-innocent schtick he seemed determined to cling to, he was still a Fromadgio. Still dangerous.

"Reed," I said belatedly. "You should call me Reed."

"Reed," he repeated. Then again, like he was tasting the word on his tongue, "*Reed.* I like it. It's not unusual, but not common either. If someone says, 'Hey, Reed,' I bet you know they mean you." He sighed a little. "So... what's your middle name?"

I glanced at him again. His act was solid, I'd give him that much. If I didn't know better, I might think the man actually spoke every thought in his brain out loud.

"Reed is my middle name," I admitted gruffly. "Nobody calls me by my first name."

"Oh. That's handy. I don't have a middle name, which is too bad because I'd totally go by that. Chris is so common." He pushed those ridiculous glasses up his nose.

"So you're the third Sunday, right? The one who's an accountant for a Washington think tank?"

Annoyed as I was at this reminder that he knew my family, I still found myself laughing a bit at his joke as I took the exit for Route 91. "Yep. That's me, alright."

I'd invented the "think tank" job back when the Division recruited me after college, before I'd learned how impossible it was to keep the details straight when you tried to keep a secret like that for any length of time. These days, I didn't spend much time with my family, which sucked on the one hand because I felt more disconnected from them as the years passed, but was also ideal since it kept the danger of my work life away from them and drastically reduced the number of lies I needed to keep track of.

They were so far from knowing who I really was or what I really did, my brother Porter actually *joked* that I was a "secret-agent super-spy" because he knew no one would believe it.

"Um, Reed?" Chris piped up, because two seconds of silence was apparently two seconds too long. "I don't mean to be a nag, but how far are we going? Because this highway goes to Connecticut." His laughter sounded forced. "Your place isn't all the way in Connecticut, is it?"

"Of course not." I flipped on my blinker. "It's in Massachusetts."

A glance at the rearview mirror showed a car with New Jersey plates following us off the exit. Had they been following us long? *Damn it*. I wasn't sure.

"Massachusetts," he repeated faintly. "Oh. Okay. Yeah. That's..." He fumbled a tin from the pocket of his jeans and pushed it in my direction. "Uh... mint?"

"No." The New Jersey car sped up, too, keeping pace, so I switched lanes, pulling around a lumber truck that was having a hard time chugging up one of the hills south of town. I unceremoniously pushed the tin of mints away and pushed the gas pedal to the floor. "Fucking *fuck*."

"Fresh breath means you won't use fresh language, Nonna used to say." His voice had gone helium-high in the last two minutes. "N-not that I'm complaining about your language! Not at all. I use fresh language, too! All the... all the hecking time. And frankly, many of my nonna's sayings weren't entirely accurate. L-like, she said the louder you sneeze, the longer you'll live. But there was this episode of *John Ruffian* where John is in a ghost town and the bad guys are looking for him, and one loud sneeze would've given him away—"

From the corner of my eye, I saw his hands flapping again, fast as hummingbird wings.

"And Nonna always said to carry cash in your shoe for emergencies, but that seems really uncomfortable and potentially unhygienic, especially if you were to, say, spill soda all over yourself because you were temporarily but unavoidably distracted—"

"Chris," I began calmly. "Take a deep breath and stay calm."

His voice rose in speed and pitch like he was stuck in fast-forward. "And she also used to say," he went on, "you can't fight gravity, sweetheart. Which I guess is true in a way, but, um, the existence of the aviation industry would suggest that sometimes you *can* cooperate with it for a little while, so—"

"Chris," I said in the firm voice that had calmed dozens of protectees over the years. "*Chill*."

"I'm chill! I'm on an adventure with Reed Sunday, and we're going to Massachusetts! *I've never been chiller in my life!*" Chris pressed a hand to his stomach. "Is it possible to be allergic to wild oats, do you know?"

"Easy now. Remember what I told you before?" I asked in the same soothing tone my dad always used to calm his livestock. "I've got this. I'm taking care of you. You're gonna be fine."

"I remember you saying that, Reed. I do. But I also remembered that I didn't actually tell Van I was leaving, and he might worry if I don't come back, and you're driving like we're in a high-speed chase, and I can't help but notice that you're talking to me the way Webb talks to Stella at milking time."

Despite the seriousness of the situation, I felt my lips twitch up in a smile before I restrained it. The way his panic was edging into annoyance, making him look like an angry, near-sighted kitten, was not adorable, damn it.

Once we passed the lumber truck, I pulled back into the right lane, and the suspicious car sped past harmlessly.

"See that?" I pointed toward the taillights of the New Jersey car. "Not a high-speed chase at all. They're gone."

"They?" His eyes widened. "Who's *they?*"

"The car I thought was tailing us. False alarm."

"You thought..." Chris exhaled a breath that sounded more like a whistle. "Reed, I'm sure you've realized I'm new to this sort of thing, and I admit that I should have asked more questions before getting in the car, but I didn't expect tonight to involve you performing an impromptu audition for some Green Mountains revival of *The Fast and the Furious.*"

"Breathe," I suggested again.

His nose curled up like a grumpy bunny's. "I *am* breathing. I'm definitely breathing. And I know that because if I weren't breathing, I'd be unconscious, and if I were unconscious, I wouldn't be so d-dang nervous."

"We'll be there soon," I lied. By my estimation, it was at least an hour to the coordinates Margot had sent. "I know this might seem scary, but you're doing great. And you might be a newbie, but I'm not."

He sank down in his seat and pushed up his glasses. "Yeah, it's obvious that you're, um..." He swallowed. "Way more experienced than I am at this sort of thing."

I couldn't lie, his words made me puff up a little bit. "Yup. I've taken care of dozens of men and women like you over the years." I did some quick mental math. "Maybe even ten dozen. You're in good hands."

"You..." He gave me a look of mingled intrigue and horror. "You've done this with over a hundred people?" He shot me a look I couldn't read. "And you're, what, forty?"

I scowled. "Thirty-five." I'd started young, and I'd had a very successful career... until recently. "I'm good at what I do."

He squirmed a little. "Kind of a, um, strange thing for you to brag about, especially since you're, like, with me, but okay."

"I'm not bragging, I'm reassuring you." I frowned. "I'm trying to say, none of those people knew what they were doing either, and not a single one was killed or even injured while they were with me. They all—well, almost all—shook my hand and *thanked* me when we said goodbye, okay?"

He stared at me, mouth open and lip curled. "*Killed?*" His eyes flared wide. "Wait. Wait, wait, wait. Everyone you've done this with was a *newbie?*" he whispered. "All *hundred twenty* of them?"

"Well... yeah." I shrugged. I didn't understand where his surprise was coming from. Most people went their whole lives without going into protective custody, let alone more than once. But maybe things were different when you were born into a crime family. "I'd argue that if I do my job right, nobody has to go through this more than once."

"*Go through it?*" He wrinkled his nose further, and his glasses slid down. "Not trying to be critical here, Reed, but you are really not selling this experience."

The man's confusion was strangely appealing, just like his fidgeting and his cologne and his glasses and his stammering... and not only were *none* of those things I had ever found attractive before, but the last thing I needed was to be distracted by a protectee—a *Fromadgio* protectee—less than twenty-four hours after being reinstated to the job I'd nearly lost a couple of months ago.

What the hell was wrong with me today?

Eyes firmly on the road, I took another deep breath and said, "It's perfectly normal to be nervous, Chris. But if you do what I say, everything will be fine. The problem here is that you weren't briefed on the procedure." When he looked confused, I added, "You don't know what to expect."

"That obvious, huh?" He groaned and put his hands over his face. When he spoke again, his words were muffled. "You're not wrong, though. And I'm sure books and movies have given me some unrealistic ideas about, um, how it all works—"

"Don't get me started," I scoffed. The unrealistic portrayals of protectors on television were a pet peeve of mine. "But most people are in the same boat, and it's not your fault. Ideally, someone should have sat you down and explained all this to you. Answered your questions."

"I guess. It's not like I could ask anyone in my life about it, though. My uncle would rather die. My parents are gone. I don't have a lot of c-close friends, really. And Mrs. Rose—

that's our next-door neighbor who used to babysit me—she's really sweet, but everything she knows comes from novels. So, you know, I've asked around, a little bit, and researched it on the internet, as you do, but some of the information I found made me even *more* nervous—"

My jaw dropped. He'd researched this on the internet? No. He couldn't possibly have been that foolish.

"Hold up." I pulled his hand down so I could see his face. "You *asked around?* You did *internet research?*" I envisioned him talking to people in town about me and googling "Agent Sunday, Division, witness protection." Anyone who'd overheard him, who'd checked his search history, could potentially threaten my family. "You're joking, right?"

"No. Of course not." Chris seemed confused by my anger... which only made my temper rise. "I mean, I used a private browser and everything." He dug into his pocket and pulled out a phone as if to demonstrate. "See, I— ohmigosh, Reed, could you please watch the road?"

"You brought a *phone?*" I roared. "A traceable, trackable phone? Are you insane?"

I tried to calm myself. It wasn't the protectee's fault that he hadn't been thoroughly briefed. It was at least partially *my* fault because I'd assumed he had, and I should have verified before he climbed into my car. But holy shit, the one thing movies and books got *right* was that you had to leave all traces of your old life behind when you went into protective custody, especially your goddamn phone.

Did the man have no concept of self-preservation? Did he not understand that he could, at this very moment, be tipping off the people who wanted to hurt him in order to get at his uncle? Or was he a spoiled mafia heir who thought his sweet-and-innocent act meant the rules didn't apply to him?

"Give me your phone," I demanded. "Hand it over."

"N-no." Eyes round, he pulled back, clutching his phone protectively. "No, thank you. You're scaring me a little right now, Reed, and I think I'd rather—"

I didn't care what he'd *rather*. Not when he was endangering both of us. Opening my window, I reached over and grabbed the phone from his hand, then tossed it out onto the pavement. With any luck, the lumber truck would be along shortly to finish the job.

I immediately felt better. Calmer.

Chris did not.

"Hey!" He lunged like he was trying to follow his phone out the window, and it took me a few seconds to wrestle him back onto his own side while maintaining control of the vehicle and definitely not noticing the vanilla-lime scent of him.

He sat upright in his seat, red-faced and breathing hard, and pushed up the glasses he'd nearly lost in the scuffle.

He folded his arms over his chest and glared at me, hair wild and cheeks red. "What in the hecking *heck balls* was that? Turn around right now and get that back."

I glanced sideways, tightened my grip on the wheel, and said as firmly as possible, "No."

"Look, Reed, I like you." He paused like he was rethinking that statement. "I liked the *idea* of you, at least. You've got nice eyes, a-and nice shoulders, and... flannel. I thought you had a John Ruffian vibe—"

"Who the fuck is John Ruffian?"

He gaped at me like this was the most mind-blowing thing I'd said yet. "You've never heard of *John Ruffian: Pretender?*"

"That's... a show?" I guessed. "No. I don't watch television." I didn't have time.

"Is it a show? *Pfft*. It's not *a* show, it's *the* show. The best show in the history of... of... shows. It's about a guy who—" He shook his head angrily. "No, you know what? Never mind. You don't deserve to know. Because I was wrong. You're *nothing* like John Ruffian. John Ruffian would *never* have thrown away the phone my uncle bought me right before I left for Vermont. It was special to me." His lip quivered, but he firmed it and added in what I could only imagine was an impression of the grandmother he kept mentioning, "I don't like your attitude, mister."

"My attitude?" I shot back. "Jesus Christ, I'm trying to *help* you here—"

He lifted his chin. "Well, I don't want your *help*. Not anymore. My pants are damp, you're a terrible driver, and I don't like this adventure. I... I would like you to take me home now." He folded his arms over his chest, but after a moment, like he couldn't help himself, he added a small, polite "Please."

"*Please*," I scoffed. His prim manners and big, solemn eyes were making me feel like a villain when I was only doing my job.

But it didn't matter what the protectee wanted as long as I was doing my job and keeping them safe. It was a lesson I'd nearly forgotten back in August, but I wouldn't forget again.

I hardened my voice. "You won't be going home, Chris. Not until I say. This ride goes one way, and it doesn't stop until we get there. Understand?"

His eyes were so comically wide they took up half his face, and guilt twisted my gut. But learning to follow my lead might be the thing that saved his life eventually, so I didn't back down.

"Sit still and stop distracting me, and let's get this over with," I muttered. "Okay?"

He huffed and curled his arms tightly around himself, leaning against the passenger door, but he kept his mouth shut for once. So I turned up the radio and told myself I didn't miss his babbling as the car rolled through the night.

But if I'd known the kind of trouble I'd be in once we got to the safe house, I might have noticed that he hadn't actually agreed with me.

CHAPTER THREE

CHRIS

I was being kidnapped.

That was the only possible explanation.

Admittedly, it was a slow and mostly uneventful kidnapping, but even that made sense in a way.

It was *my* kidnapping, after all.

As Reed drove us down the highway, I ran through our conversation on a loop—well, the parts I could remember, anyway—trying to make sense of it all. He'd been grumpy the whole time we'd been in the car, but that hadn't been a red flag. I'd been nervous-babbling, even though I'd tried my hardest not to, and I'd figured he'd been regretting his choice of "pickup." I wouldn't have blamed him.

But then he'd started talking about his de-virginizing fetish with a body count in the hundreds and mentioned where we were heading—in retrospect, *secure* probably wasn't a word people used when talking about their homes with potential bed partners, was it?—and thrown my freaking phone out the window before refusing to take me home, and the conclusion was unignorable, as well as mortifying and high-key disappointing.

What I'd thought was my first date was actually an abduction.

Fortunately, Reed hadn't tied me up or dumped me in his trunk like the vigilantes did to John Ruffian in season five, and he hadn't actively attempted to murder or torture me either, unless you considered his totally off-key butchering of classic '80s songs to be a form of torture. Even when I'd broken my silence and demanded in a quavering voice to know what he planned to do with me, Reed had only given me a hard, angry look, told me to "*drop the innocent act and stop with the drama*"... and then offered me a granola bar and a bottle of water from his backpack, which might have been thoughtful under other circumstances, but which I'd refused on principle.

None of this made the situation feel any less fraught, though... it just meant that Reed was really bad at kidnapping.

If he'd been better at it, he'd have picked someone who had, like, access to nuclear launch codes, or friends in powerful places, or more than $267 in his bank account to ransom himself with. As it was, Reed was going to learn pretty soon that he'd kidnapped the absolute wrong guy, and once he did... well, I had no idea what he'd do. The idea of being killed or held captive was truly frightening.

Scarier than the time I'd walked in on Uncle Danny and his theater group reenacting a scene from Sweeney Todd in his garage and thought the blood was real.

Scarier than the time Nicky let his pet rat, Pickles, sit on my chest because he'd claimed it would cure my phobia of rodents.

Scarier than the time I'd cannonballed into the YMCA pool because Nonna assured me that my "swimming instincts" would kick in "just in time," only to find out when

I was already in the water that my instincts had a really bad sense of timing.

But greater than my fear for myself was my fear of what Uncle Danny would do when he got home from his fishing expedition and learned I'd been kidnapped and/or killed. His face would probably go all red, he'd grab his chest and deep-breathe like he did whenever he got emotional, and he might even end up having another cardiac event like the one that had landed him in the hospital last winter. And it would all be because I'd been foolish enough to think someone as beautiful as Reed Sunday might actually want to hook up with me.

I couldn't let that happen. So I had to escape.

Think, Chris. WWJRD?

But when I tried to imagine what John Ruffian would do if he was being abducted in slow motion by a frustratingly gorgeous lumberjack-presenting accountant from Washington who'd lured him into his car with false promises of sexual gratification, I honestly couldn't say.

In episode twelve of season three, John Ruffian had pretended to be a mild-mannered assistant pastry chef while on the trail of a serial killer, when he'd eaten a coconut lime cupcake dosed with sleeping potion. He'd come to in a kidnap shack down by the railroad tracks in time to grab a wooden board, whack the lead pastry chef into unconsciousness, and save the beautiful Giselle from a grisly death.

Then, in episode three of season seven, he'd been impersonating a clown in a circus school when he was abducted by a mysterious scientist who called herself the Ringmaster. In that case, though, it had all been a misunderstanding—she'd thought John was an evil rival scientist and had kidnapped him to save the world, so in the end, they'd joined forces and done it together... before, erm, *doing it together*.

Since I had neither a handy wooden whacking board nor the ability to cobble together a plutonium death ray from a stack of gum wrappers, I knew I'd have to figure out something a little more Chris-Winowski-appropriate.

So I fell asleep.

Or at least I *pretended* to.

I leaned my head against the window, closed my eyes, and let my breath go deep and even, not even stirring when Reed slaughtered the lyrics to "Livin' on a Prayer"—*Doesn't make a difference if we're* naked *or not?* Did he even hear himself? It was *not* endearing. Not even a little—though I did allow myself to make a discontented, sleepy sound like I was experiencing a nightmare because I sort of thought I was.

Gosh, I really hated that I'd been so wrong about Reed Sunday.

Sometime later, Reed slowed the car, and I could tell we were pulling off the highway. Streetlights flashed brightly through the car windows at regular intervals, and I tried to memorize every turn we took and how many seconds passed between each, in the unlikely event that I was able to steal his keys and make a getaway. By the fourteenth (or was it sixteenth?) turn, I was hopelessly confused and convinced he was driving us in circles.

And then we stopped, and the engine shut off.

A shiver ran through my body. This was it. We were there... wherever *there* was. Now was the time when he'd tie me up or throw me in a pit or...

"What in the seven fucking hells," Reed muttered like he was talking to himself. But since the only other sound in the world was the *tick tick tick* of the car's engine as it cooled, every word carried like a gunshot. "I am going to kill Janissey."

I didn't know who Janissey was, but I figured if Reed was busy killing them, he'd be too busy to worry about little old me.

I cracked my eyes open and peered out the side window through my lashes. We seemed to be in a quiet, middle-class suburban neighborhood, not too different from the one where I'd lived with my dad as a kid. The houses were old and a bit run-down—*lived-in*, Nonna would say—but with tidy yards and flowers on the stoops. Television light glowed through the thin curtains of the house next door. I didn't see a single thing that could have made Reed so cranky...

Until I turned my head slightly and caught a glimpse of the house directly in front of us.

The *bright pink* house in front of us.

It was a two-story, older home with an enclosed porch and no shutters, giving the house a weirdly wide-eyed, unhappy look, and the pink color—which, seriously, not even kidding, *glowed in the dark*—made it seem like the house was vaguely embarrassed about something.

If I had to guess, that something was probably the flamingoes.

Fake plastic birds were staked across the entire front yard in tidy rows, like a strange crop ready for harvesting. Another flock climbed the trellis on the left side of the house. And one lone bird perched on the roof like it was surveying the neighborhood.

Despite my anxiety about what was supposed to happen now, I found myself fighting the urge to laugh. Weren't kidnap shacks supposed to be... unobtrusive?

Reed Sunday was definitely a terrible kidnapper.

Beside me, Reed snorted. "You can stop pretending to be asleep now."

Shoot. I'd forgotten for a moment that I was at least as bad at lying as Reed was at kidnapping. Nicky used to say that he couldn't tell me anything because I'd tattle without saying a word. But it was annoying that Reed had caught on so quickly. This didn't bode well for my escape plans.

I groaned loud and long like I was emerging from a deep sleep and stretched out in the seat. I blinked my eyes open innocently. "Oh. Hello." I pretended to glance around for the first time. "This is quite a place. I can, um, see why you made the effort to bring me all this way."

Reed shook his head, popped the latch on the door, and stood. I tried and failed not to notice how his shirt rode up when he stretched his arms above his head or how glimpsing the trail of hair there made my blood thrum with something that should have been fear but wasn't.

"Let's go."

"Sure," I agreed. "Or... wouldn't it be better if we stay out here? It's a nice night, and the view is—" I gestured toward the lawn. "Colorful?"

"Stop messing around." He closed his door, darted a glance around the neighborhood, then pulled a backpack and a large duffel from the back seat. "Get inside. You'll be safe there."

Would I, though? Reed kept saying things like that—that I was safe, that I'd be fine, that he'd take care of me—and I hated to admit it, but some part of me seemed to believe it, otherwise I knew I'd be a heck of a lot more panicked than I was. Nonna always said I was too trusting. I had to keep reminding myself that if I were really safe, he would've turned around and let me go when I asked him to.

Reed pulled open my door impatiently, leaned in to

unbuckle my seat belt—good gravy, the man smelled like forests and fresh breezes, which didn't seem fair at all—then firmly (but surprisingly gently) hauled me out by the elbow. He shut the door, locked the car, and dragged me around the side of the house before I had a chance to take more than a single breath of cool night air.

I licked my lips. Wasn't there some saying about not allowing your kidnapper to take you into their lair? Actually, I was pretty sure it was actually about not allowing them to get you inside their car, but I'd failed the fudge out of that.

I could practically hear John Ruffian in my head, yelling, *Run! Go! This is your chance!* in his deep, growly voice. But I was nearly as bad at running as I was at swimming and lying, and I had no doubt Reed would catch me before I made the sidewalk, so I needed to bide my time. To make it seem like I was going along with him and lull him into a false sense of security while I executed a flawless getaway.

Somehow.

"Nice place you've got here," I said politely as Reed located a box on the side of the door and scanned his fingerprint. "I know some people might be concerned about your flamingo obsession, but I think it's quirky, and quirky things are the best things—"

"I don't have a flamingo obsession." The door lock clicked, and Reed pulled me into the kitchen. He flipped on the light and propelled me into a corner of the kitchen while he made a quick tour of the house, turning on more lights as he went.

It wasn't until later that I'd realize I could have left then, while he was distracted, but in the moment, I was a little too distracted myself.

There were ducks *everywhere*.

Ducks danced across the floral border near the ceiling and the curtains that covered the single window. A duck teapot sat on the old-fashioned stove. Ceramic ducks held napkins, salt, and pepper on the warm pine table. From atop the upper cabinets, a phalanx of wooden ducks with bright blue and pink bows around their necks stared down at us accusingly.

"S-so, not a flamingo obsession," I said faintly when Reed came back into the kitchen, tucking something into the back of his jeans under the hem of his flannel. "But more of an obsession with birds in general? That's great. *Like what you like*, that's what I say. It's not creepy at all!"

"Huh?" Reed glanced around like he'd never seen the room before, then ran both hands over his face, digging the meat of his palms into his eyes. "Janissey," he muttered like an oath. Then he dropped his hands and said forcefully, "Ignore the decor. It's no big deal. What's important is the house is clear. High-quality door locks with biometrics. Easily defensible. Unbreakable glass on the windows." He gave the ducks a dubious glance and added, "Though I'm planning to check the whole place over more thoroughly, just to be sure."

My eyes went wide. Biometric locks? Unbreakable glass? That was... concerning. Okay, more than concerning. It was... low-key psychopathic. Nothing good happened behind biometric locks, I was sure.

And why was he telling me all of this? Did he know I'd try to escape? Was that what his other kidnappees had done?

"No need," I assured him quickly, trying to sound like the most enthusiastic abductee who'd ever been abducted, despite my racing heart. "I'm sure it's very secure. And I'm really—" I managed a huge fake yawn and gestured aimlessly with my hands. "—gosh, just exhausted. You know the kind of exhausted where you can barely move a muscle? That kind of exhausted. So, so exhausted I can barely stand. It's been a long day, what with all the—" *Kidnapping.* "—driving. Besides, I'm much more cooperative and docile when I've had a good sleep," I said earnestly.

Reed frowned. "Okay. But you should eat something first. The kitchen's always stocked. We've got—" He threw open a tall pantry cabinet. Every single shelf, floor to ceiling, all the way to the back, seemed to be filled with red-and-white cans of soup, and all of them appeared to be chicken noodle. He moved to the next cabinet and threw it open to find... more soup.

And then more in the next.

And the next.

I pulled my cuffs down over my hands and pushed up my glasses. With each cabinet he opened, Reed seemed more agitated, and I felt the bizarre urge to comfort him before I reminded myself that we were definitely not on the same side here.

"How fun and not at all strange!" I said brightly. "Who doesn't love soup? So... moist. But could I rest first? I know it's only eight o'clock, but I really am tired."

"Yeah." Reed rubbed the back of his neck wearily. "Same. Let's head upstairs."

"T-together?" I squeaked.

He grabbed his bags and gave me a strange look before turning me and giving me a little push toward the stairs in the center of the house. "Of course. I'm going to check out the bedrooms again. Lesson one in my line of work is trust but verify, and since every aspect of this day has been fucked, I'm not feeling super trusting."

"In your line of work," I repeated. Reed made it sound like kidnapping was a career. Like he had a LinkedIn profile. "Have you been, um, doing this long?"

"You could say that. Thirteen... no, fourteen years now."

Halfway up the stairs, I paused, turned, and blinked at him. "And you've never been caught?"

"Caught?" He looked equally puzzled. "You mean, have I ever had a job go wrong? Sometimes plans get fucked-up, and I have to roll with it." He shrugged. "Sometimes—*once* —I fucked the plans up." His face went granite hard. "But that's not going to happen this time."

The words were a threat—they had to be, right?—but they didn't feel threatening. Instead, they made my insides go warm and gooey, which was even more concerning than the biometric locks.

Was this early onset Stockholm syndrome? Or had I gotten my mental wires crossed earlier, thinking Reed was unbearably hot and possibly interested in me, and now they were having trouble un-crossing? It suddenly seemed even more imperative to get out of here before this got worse.

I faced forward again, marched up to the landing, and deliberately turned right, toward the first bedroom. "Your family has no idea what you really do, do they? Webb always sounds so proud when he mentions you—"

Reed's bags hit the floor with a thud, and a pair of strong hands gripped my shoulders, stopping me before I could take another step. "You don't get to talk about my family," Reed growled. "Understand?" For the first time since we got here... for the first time all night, really... Reed's green eyes were cold, and he looked truly threatening.

I nodded. "Definitely, yes. I mean, definitely *no*. I mean, who's Webb? Never heard of him."

Reed passed me into the bedroom while I stood

frozen in the doorway. The room was sparsely furnished —only a twin bed and a chair—but otherwise looked normal. No chains, no bars on the windows, no instruments of torture. He checked the empty closet—maybe looking for weapons I could use?—and beneath the bed. He bypassed the uncomfortable-looking wingback chair and headed for the window, doing something complicated to the latch before yanking to make sure it was locked tight.

"You should be fine here," he said shortly.

"Yes. Yup. I'll be fine. Sleeping here. Alone and by myself." I nodded. "Good plan, Reed. You're doing great."

He gave me a narrow-eyed look. "Bathroom's down the hall. You can shower and... *fuck*. You don't even have a change of clothes, do you? And naturally, there's nothing in this house for you to wear unless we knit something out of fucking soup can labels or go all *Sound of Music* on the curtains."

I pressed my lips together, fighting a smile—which was a totally inappropriate reaction, but you just don't expect your grumpy kidnapper to blindside you with a snarky musical reference, do you?

Reed threw his head back and glanced at the ceiling as if praying for patience, then demanded, "Strip."

My smile disappeared, and my breath caught. "P-pardon?"

"Strip. Jeans off. Now. I'll take your clothes and wash them."

I blinked. "Y-you're gonna do my laundry? Really?" Needless to say, this had *never* happened in a *John Ruffian* episode.

Reed folded his arms over his chest and watched me stonily. "Didn't you mention your jeans were wet earlier?"

He cocked his head to one side. "Do I need to repeat myself?"

"Yes? I mean, *no*. I mean... Okay." My hands shook as I moved them to my waistband and undid the button.

I'd thought about this, when I'd first gotten into his car tonight. Imagined doing a sexy striptease for him, if I could get up the nerve. And obviously—*obviously!*—I had no interest in doing that anymore, but those dang crossed wires, and, yes, okay, the way Reed was watching me with total absorption made it hard to remember why not.

I slowly undid my zipper... and my baggy jeans fell to my ankles in an utterly un-seductive *whoomp*, leaving me in my boxers and my stretched-out and slightly worn striped sweater.

Reed stared at me, and his eyes flared with something—impatience, maybe? Probably impatience—that made my stomach flutter and my mind go blank.

What next? Too late, I remembered that I hadn't taken my shoes off first, so I turned and bent to ease the pants over them—

Behind me, Reed made a garbled noise, and when I turned with my pants in hand, he grabbed them and quickly backed away. "Never mind. I have to do things. Security things. Right after I take a shower. So... here." His duffel sailed across the room and landed heavily on the bed. "Borrow whatever you want for now."

Then he stalked out of the room, clutching my jeans in one large fist, and slammed the door closed behind him.

I blinked. Was that it? No stern warnings that I was his prisoner? No threats about what might happen if I tried to escape? It felt strangely anticlimactic.

I sat down on the bed uncertainly. Something in Reed's

bag made a soft, metallic *clink* at the movement. Frowning at the closed door, I opened the zipper.

It was mostly filled with clothes—large, soft, good-smelling sweatshirts, T-shirts, jeans, and a pair of sweatpants so big that even when I tugged a pair on, rolled them up, and cinched the waist as tight as possible, I probably still looked like a kid playing dress-up. Beneath the top layer of sweatshirts, I found the source of the noise: a multitool, two boxes of bullets, and a small holstered gun that looked exactly like Uncle Danny's.

Holy, holy crap.

I wouldn't—couldn't—use a gun. Uncle Danny had insisted on taking me to target practice as a teenager so I could learn to protect myself, but as much as I'd wanted to please him, I could barely make myself hold a weapon, let alone fire it. Something about feeling the hunk of metal in my hand, knowing that it had the power to hurt and maim and kill, felt too wrong. After the third or fourth time, I'd told Danny very seriously that I thought I might be allergic to gunpowder, and he'd never taken me to the range again.

But Reed didn't know any of that.

I mentally downgraded Reed from "bad at kidnapping" to "worst kidnapper ever." And while I should have been thanking my lucky stars, I actually felt a little bit... sorry for him? I knew what it was like to try your hardest, to be determined, and to never be quite good enough—not strong enough, not hard-edged enough, not dominant enough—to be taken seriously.

But after spending a long moment staring at the pile of clothes—two weeks' worth, at least, so how long was he planning on keeping me here?—and watching the weapon shine dully in the overhead light, I realized how foolish I was being. When I heard the shower turn on somewhere down the hall, I realized I might not get another shot, so I wrapped the gun in a T-shirt and hid it under the mattress, tied my borrowed sweatpants a little tighter, slipped my shoes back on, grabbed the multitool, and headed for the window.

Having watched Reed check the lock earlier, it was easy enough to repeat his steps and get it open, and since I was pretty handy with tools—a consequence of occasionally, not often, and never intentionally breaking things was that I'd learned to fix them—it only took a second to jimmy the screen out of the way. I heaved a leg over the sill, grabbed the flamingo-bedecked trellis I'd noticed earlier—John Ruffian would be *so* proud of my situational awareness—and started to climb to freedom.

Unfortunately, it seemed the trellis wanted freedom, too.

The second my entire weight was on the thing, whatever had been attaching it to the house detached without warning, and I tumbled to the lawn in the side yard with pieces of rotting wood and several decorative pink birds on top of me.

"Whoa," a man's voice said appreciatively. "That was freaking *sick*, bro. You looked like Superman. Until the landing."

It took me a moment to remember how breathing worked and two more to confirm my entire body was still operational. Once I did, I adjusted my glasses, levered up on an elbow, and looked around. Next door, a man wearing nothing but underpants, flip-flops, and a blanket cape leaned over his front porch railing to watch me. And in his hand, he held a cell phone.

"Thank the stars," I said under my breath. Then, a little

louder, I croaked, "Sir, I need you to call the police. Immediately."

His eyes widened, and I noticed belatedly that in his other hand, he held a cigarette. I sniffed. A very pungent cigarette.

"No way, Superdude. Whatcha wanna call them for?"

"I—*oof*—" I pushed to my feet, wincing, hitched up my pants, and hurried across the grass between us, dodging around the flamingoes. "The thing is, I think I've been kidnapped."

He blinked. "You *think?*"

"N-no, I know. I know I've been kidnapped. Just... really poorly." I darted a glance back toward the house, but Reed seemed to have missed my escape. "Could I please borrow your phone? I wouldn't ask, but my kidnapper threw mine away, even though it was brand-new and really special to me, and..." *Not the point, Chris.* "Please?"

The man blinked at me with unfocused eyes. "Superdude, I want to help you, but I can't call the cops. This is my grandma's house. Cops come poking around, they're gonna ask questions." He leaned over the railing and dropped his voice to a stage whisper. "Like why Gran's got more plants than the legal limit in her garden out back. You feel me?"

I shook my head, confused. They put limits on gardens in Massachusetts? That was awful, considering the plight of butterflies and other pollinators due to habitat loss and pesticide use, but— *Once again, not the point, Chris.*

"I won't call the cops directly, I promise," I agreed. "I'll call..."

It hit me then, how few people I *could* call to help me take care of this. Nonna was gone, and Uncle Danny was someplace in Alaska, Van was out of town, Nicky wasn't speaking to me, and I didn't know anyone in the Hollow well enough to ask for help except maybe Webb, and—I glanced back at the house again—I couldn't call him for obvious reasons.

The circle of people who loved me had never been huge, but it had shrunk a lot in the past year, and realizing it made my chest ache.

"I'll call Mrs. Rose," I said, with a confidence I didn't feel. "My old neighbor. I think she has a sister in Massachusetts. She'll help me."

A querulous female voice from inside the man's house called, "Kenny? Kenny! Who's out there?"

"No one, Gran," Kenny called back. He took one last drag off the cigarette in his hand and held it for a second before exhaling, then set it on the railing.

"It better not be those Davis boys," she yelled. "I told you not to have them over when I'm watching my programs. Don't make me come out there."

Kenny rolled his bloodshot eyes and lowered his voice. "The woman loses her mind if she misses an episode of *John Ruffian*."

I brightened. "She's watching *John Ruffian*?" I moved toward the steps. "That's so cool! Do you think she'd mind if I came inside and—"

He moved to block me. "Trust me, bro, neither of us wants that," he whispered. He darted a glance over his shoulder and handed me his phone. "Here. Have at it. But no cops."

I made a crossing motion over my heart and quickly dialed Mrs. Rose's number, thankful she'd made me memorize it back when I was fourteen. She answered on the first ring.

"Listen, scammer, I don't care how much you say I owe

the IRS, I am not sending you any more gift cards," she yelled.

I pulled the phone away from my ringing ear and remembered why Mrs. Rose, lovely as she was, was perhaps not the best person to call.

"Mrs. Rose? It's me, Chris. Chris Winowski. I need your help. I've been kidnapped—"

"Chris? Oh, hello, honey!" she yelled even louder. "How are you? I was just talking to Mabel about you—you remember my growly Mabel-baby who tried to eat your sweater that one time? I was telling her you were up in Vermont—"

"Mrs. Rose," I interrupted in a whisper, glancing back at the flamingo house, where all seemed to be quiet... but for how much longer? "I'd love to hear about Mabel the Pomeranian, but right now, I've been kidnapped—"

"Kidnapped?" She laughed lightly. "Oh, sweetheart! I told your uncle, I said, 'Danny, that boy watches far too much television. All he does is fantasize about life instead of living it.' But did he ever listen to me? Noooo—"

I felt my face go red. She was talking so loudly I was sure Kenny could hear every word. "Mrs. Rose, this is no fantasy," I whispered. "Please listen. I'm being held at a house in a town called—" I turned to Kenny expectantly.

"Springfield?" He made it sound like a question, which did not fill me with confidence.

"In Springfield, Massachusetts," I repeated into the phone. "Please write this down. The address is—" I covered the phone. "What's your address?" I whispered.

"612 Maple. Two blocks from the Stop and Shop," he said obediently.

I relayed this information, too.

"Well, sweetheart, what do you want me to do about that?" she wondered. "I could call the police for you—"

"No cops!" Kenny shouted into the phone.

"Doesn't your sister Paula live in Massachusetts?" I asked desperately. "Maybe she could come get me—"

But even as I spoke, Kenny's eyes tracked over my shoulder and widened, and I knew it was too late.

I turned oh-so-slowly and found a very wet, almost naked, seriously irate Reed Sunday running toward me. Despite the small, pink towel clutched around his waist, he jumped over the flamingos like hurdling lawn ornaments was a part of his daily workout, all the while eyeing Kenny with killer intensity.

I sighed. "Never mind, Mrs. Rose," I said, bleak and resigned. "I'll figure something out. In case I don't make it, tell Mabel I forgive her for eating my sweater."

I shoved the phone into Kenny's hand, then turned and held my arms out, shielding him. "Please don't blame Kenny," I cried as Reed approached. "He did nothing wrong. He's only trying to help me, and it's not his fault—"

Reed careened to a stop directly in front of me and cupped my jaw in two large hands. "Jesus Christ," he breathed. I could practically see his pulse pounding in his throat. "Are you okay?" His eyes roamed up and down my body, from my glasses down to my borrowed (and now slightly grass-stained) sweatpants, and then he patted my back and torso like he was checking for invisible injuries. "What happened?" He pulled me closer so my cheek and the edge of my glasses got squashed against the damp, hard, hot wall of his chest as his eyes scanned the neighborhood. "Where are they?"

"Um?" *What was happening here? Oh God, how did he smell so good?* "Who?"

"Superdude fell," Kenny volunteered helpfully, pointing to the remnants of the trellis. He tucked his blanket cape closer around him. "While he was climbing down."

Reed pulled back, leaving me damp and chilly. His confused gaze shifted from me, to the house, and back again. "Wait. You... climbed out? Of your own volition?"

"Escaped," I corrected, lifting my chin, because if I was going to be punished, I at least wanted it known that I'd made it out using my smarts and survival instincts, which were fearsome and finely honed, despite what Uncle Danny thought, and despite the fact that my kidnapper wasn't a particularly competent—

"The whole point of protective custody is to *not* escape!" Reed exploded. "Jesus. You might be the worst protectee I've ever worked with."

I gaped at him. "Protective custody? P-protectee? But I'm not—"

"Yes, you fucking are, at least until your uncle's testified as part of his plea deal. 'Chris is scary,' Ernie said. 'Chris is a weapons expert.' Nobody said, 'Chris is foolish enough to climb out a fucking window and practically beg to be captured by—' *Shit*," he broke off with a shake of his head. "I'm not discussing this out here when I don't have a weapon or a clear sight line or—" Reed hitched up his towel. "—pants! Get in the house." He turned and stabbed a finger at the unmistakably pink building beside us. "Now."

"W-weapons expert? But I'm not... Oh." My stomach clenched. "Oh, no."

"I swear to God, Chris." Reed's towel slipped an inch, and he grabbed it with both hands. "*Now*," he roared, so loud Kenny winced.

"I guess I could call the police," Kenny offered reluctantly. "If you think he's, like, going to kill you, or—"

"Kill him?" Reed snorted. "At this point, I feel like I'm trying to keep him from accidentally killing himself."

"Thank you anyway, Kenny," I said in a low voice, shoulders sinking along with my spirits. "But don't do anything to endanger your grandmother's garden. Besides, I think I know what happened here, and it's all a terrible misunderstanding." I patted his hand. "Thank you for your kindness."

"If you need anything, Superdude, you come right back!" Kenny said as I turned to follow Reed. "And *you*—" He tried and mostly failed to focus his bleary eyes on Reed. "—be nice to him, you hear? Or I'm gonna tell my gran."

"Fucking Christ," Reed muttered under his breath. He gave me a none-too-gentle nudge, so I hiked up my borrowed pants and trudged obediently through the field of flamingoes toward the front door he'd left hanging open.

It was strange and wrong and maybe a little pathetic, I decided as I reluctantly marched up the front steps with Reed on my heels, that I dreaded going inside more now than I had the first time. But, in retrospect, things had been really straightforward, back when I'd thought Reed had kidnapped me.

I realized the truth was far more hecking complicated... and more embarrassing, when I hadn't thought I could *get* more embarrassed.

Reed had taken the wrong Chris.

CHAPTER FOUR

REED

THE MAN HAD no sense of self-preservation. That was the only explanation.

Admittedly, he hadn't killed himself making it down the trellis—a trellis someone should have noticed before approving this safe house, which was going on my long list of complaints to Janissey, along with the doomsday prepper supply of soup (and only soup), the eye-searing paint job, the interior and exterior flocks of birds, and the utter lack of Division-monitored security alarms on the entry points. But the very fact that he'd ventured out on his own and tried to contact someone was enough to have me seeing red.

I forced myself not to stare at his pert little ass swaying in my too-big sweatpants as he slogged dejectedly up the stairs past a faded wallpaper border of ducks marching in bonnets. He didn't seem angry so much as honest-to-God disappointed that his escape to stoner-land next door had been cut short.

Escape, I scoffed to myself, remembering how proud and defiant he'd looked when he said the word, big eyes glinting behind his glasses in the glow of the streetlight. I pushed down an instinctive desire to clarify that if I'd actually been trying to keep him in, the man's ass wouldn't have made it two centimeters out the door, no matter how hard he tried.

Against my will, my eyes slipped to that ass, which was tantalizingly close to my face when he hesitated at the top of the stairs, but I forced myself to blink away. He had me on the knife edge between wanting to hold him down so I could throttle him... and wanting to pin him down for a very different reason.

Not that I was actually going to do either.

I was a freaking professional, I reminded myself as I hitched up my slipping towel.

"To the right again," I prompted once he reached the top.

Chris entered the small bedroom and sat down on the mattress in defeat.

"Look, I'm sorry, Mr. Sunday, but there's been a giant misunderstanding," he began. He stared at his ragged and dirty fingernails, and my eyes jumped to the still-open window and the broken pieces of trellis sticking out from the frame.

I quickly stepped over to shove the window closed and lock it again.

"If you mean *you* misunderstanding that you were supposed to stay here, then yes, I agree," I snapped. "What the hell were you doing?"

"Well." Chris's chin went suspiciously wobbly, but he tried his best to firm it and glare up at me. "I assumed, as anyone would, that you were trying to kidnap me—"

"You..." I opened my mouth. I closed it again. "*What? Why?*"

"Because you were grumpy, and you took my phone, and you wouldn't take me home, and..." His eyes roamed over my naked chest and the spot where my towel was knotted at my waist. His whole face turned the same vibrant pink as this godforsaken safe house, but he lifted his chin stubbornly. "What else could I conclude but that you had nefarious intentions?"

"*Nefarious?*" I repeated, outraged.

"That means bad," he explained politely.

"I know what the fuck it *means*, Chris," I shot back. "I still don't know why you think—"

"I don't think it! N-not anymore. That's what I'm trying to explain. From what you said outside now, you were trying to help someone. Protect them. Which is really admirable. Except, um..." He gave me a look that was both apologetic and pitying. "You got the wrong person."

"That's ridiculous. And could you stop being so..." *Distracting*. His stammering words and pink cheeks were making me think thoughts I had no business thinking, and my thin, damp towel was going to make that clear sooner rather than later. I held up a finger. "Stay here. If you move, I will tie you to that bed."

Within seconds, I'd marched across the hall to grab my discarded jeans and the primary weapon I'd left behind when I ran from the house. I returned to Chris's room before replacing the towel with a clean pair of jeans and a T-shirt from the bag on the bed next to him.

The bag I would have known better than to leave with him, damn it, if I hadn't let myself get distracted in the first place. I would not make that mistake again.

As I yanked on my clothes, Chris's eyes got wider and wider until I felt the heat of his gaze on my skin. If this adorably flustered act was one of his ploys to distract me, I'd be damned if I'd let it.

"Explain," I demanded. "And so help me, do not act innocent this time."

His eyes remained wide, like a puppy with a hurt paw, only now the wide eyes were coupled with an even deeper pink stain on his cheeks. I felt my back teeth grind in frustration.

Unprofessional frustration.

"I already explained as much as I know. What it boils down to is... you've taken the wrong Chris." He let out a huge sigh like the entire scenario was a massive disappointment.

I squinted at him as I threaded my belt into the loops on the jeans and attached the holster at my hip. "I can't believe I'm saying this, but I'm going to need you to use more words. The wrong Chris?"

He shrank into his overly large sweater and picked at one of his sweater cuffs. "See, there are two Chrises who work at the Bugle, and people get us confused all the time. Like, *all* the time. There's Crys, short for Crystal. She's gorgeous and tough and extremely competent. One might even say scary competent. And she knows things. You know?"

I definitely didn't. In fact, the longer I spent with this adorable walking disaster, the less I knew, period.

"And then there's me." He pointed to himself with the stretched-out sweater cuff that had now completely overtaken his slender fingers. "Other Chris. Not tough and competent like Original Crys, b-but an extremely hard worker who rarely—seriously, hardly ever—makes the same mistake twice. Which," he added earnestly, "is more than can be said for a lot of people, if you think about it."

"This is crazy." I rubbed the center of my forehead, where a headache was forming. "You agreed to protective custody earlier this week—"

"Nope. Crys might have." When he tugged at his cuffs this time, it made his sweater slide down his collarbone. "I didn't."

"But Agent Janissey or one of his people called you—"

"Mr. Sunday... *Reed*... I'm telling you, nobody called me. Nobody offered me protection. And why would they? I don't need protecting. Which is why I'm saying for, like, the third time... you've got the wrong person," Chris insisted with utter sincerity.

"And I'm telling you, for the third time—"

He held up a hand to cut me off. "You said something about an uncle who's 'testifying' as part of a 'plea deal,' right? Like he's a criminal? Well, there you go! I have only one living uncle in the whole world, but he's currently on a fishing sabbatical, and he's never done a bad thing in his life, so he has nothing to testify about. After my mom died, he helped my dad raise me, and after Dad died, he helped Nonna raise me, and after *she* died, Danny raised me himself. He's a prize-winning gardener, and he runs—well, *ran*—the Cellar, the premiere wine and cheese shop in central New Jersey. Oh, and one time, I cursed in front of my Nonna, and Danny made me scrub the floors at the shop for weeks. See? I still have a callus." He held out one hand, displaying a small red scar on the webbing between his thumb and first finger like it was the smoking gun in a high-stakes courtroom drama.

"So?" I demanded. "What the fuck does that have to do with... literally anything?"

"Soooo.... those are not the things a criminal would do." He shrugged like he'd made his case.

I didn't get his angle here. Why was Chris lying about his uncle's innocence when Dante had already turned himself in and was *this close* to signing a plea agreement?

But the why didn't matter, just like my strange attraction to Chris didn't matter. I needed him to drop his act and realize that the best way to help his uncle was to stop putting himself in danger.

"That's cute. Really. For future reference, you're protesting a little too much to be believable." I sprawled in the wingback chair, only to realize the chair was way too hard for sprawling, so I sat up. "You can drop the act 'cause I'm not investigating your uncle. In fact, no one's investigating him anymore 'cause he turned himself in, and he's currently negotiating that plea deal I mentioned." I yawned. "What you need to understand now is that you're under my protection—"

"No."

I raised an eyebrow. "No?"

Chris's face worked, flitting from annoyed to nervous to stubborn and back to nervous. "No. You're wrong about my uncle, so it only makes sense that you're wrong about me, therefore I'm not your protectee. But, um, thank you anyway?"

"Jesus," I muttered.

I'd never had to convince a protectee that he was supposed to be my fucking protectee before. The guy was straight-up lying—had to be, since no one could live with Dante Fromadgio and not know exactly how his uncle made a living—and I really loathed the idea of having to play along like I bought his little act.

But I was a trained Division agent, and there wasn't much I wouldn't do to keep my job. Charming my protectee—my fake-adorkable, mobster-Bambi protectee—

and playing along so he wouldn't make another escape attempt was simply another part of the punishment I'd have to endure for deliberately fucking up my last assignment.

Besides, how hard could it be?

I leaned forward and gave Chris a smile I hoped was friendly and disarming. "We got off on the wrong foot, I think. Maybe your uncle didn't tell you that he was taking a plea deal. Maybe that happened after you left town. So maybe you don't get how much danger you're in—"

Chris blinked and visibly softened before shaking his head as if to clear it and squaring his shoulders. "Of course he didn't tell me about a plea deal. He hasn't done anything wrong. So either you've made a mistake, or... or..." He gasped, literally gasped, and gave me an accusing stare. "Maybe you're framing him for a crime he didn't commit! I saw that once in a *John Ruffian* episode—"

Jesus Christ. *Framing him?* Was he serious with this shit?

"I'm definitely not." I forced a smile. "Let's review the facts, okay?"

Chris looked like he wanted to protest some more, but he shifted back on the bed and shrugged. I took this as agreement.

"Great," I said, still smiling. "Now. First things first, your uncle is Dante Fromadgio—"

Chris's lips parted in a startled O.

"—aka Dante the Cheese—"

At this, he jumped to his feet with a little gasp of outrage. "No. Nuh-uh. I... I'm very confused right now, but I was trying to be respectful and kind. But I'm not going to listen to you insulting my family, okay?"

"Whoa! What did I say?" I held up both hands,

genuinely surprised. We hadn't even gotten to the crime part of the "facts." I hadn't expected him to protest yet.

His voice trembled. "I was only seven when my mom died, but I remember her telling me how hard it was growing up with the last name Fromadgio when her family owned a cheese shop. People mocked her all the time. She told me she was so relieved when she got married and got to be Carmelita Winowski she never used her maiden name again. She asked *me* never to mention it. Can you imagine? My mom was beautiful and kind, but she was ashamed of her own name because of the thoughtless, cruel comments of thoughtless, cruel people." *People like you*, his tone implied.

I opened my mouth, then closed it again because it turned out Chris was stunning when he was angry... and because I felt like an asshole for even noticing that when he also appeared to be on the edge of tears.

You're falling for it, Sunday. He's giving an Oscar-worthy performance, and you're about to fuck up your redemption assignment.

"Sit," I commanded. But like Chris's nonna's voice was in my head, I added, "Please." And then, even more grudgingly, "I didn't mean to insult you. I won't use that name again. Okay?"

Chris's fingers clenched and released on the cuffs of his sweater, but eventually, he sat, his gaze fixed on the wall over my head. "Fine."

"Fine," I repeated. I took a deep breath. "Your uncle is Dante Fromadgio, yes?"

He glanced at me, then away. Though he looked troubled, he nodded once.

"Right." I relaxed slightly. "As you probably know, Dante Fromadgio has been under investigation for years for various crimes. Tax evasion, money laundering, et cetera. Last March, he turned himself in. He and his lawyers have been negotiating a plea deal, which will probably require him to testify against his former business associates the Evanoviches to avoid jail time. He's currently in protective custody, but he sent you out of state and must've had someone protecting you who alerted him when—why are you shaking your head?"

"Because I don't know anyone called Evankavich or whatever you said, and I know every supplier and business associate the Cellar has... or *had*. And Danny's fishing. And he didn't send me out of state; he gave me the opportunity to visit his old army buddy because he thought it would be good for me to decide what I wanted to do with my life. And Van—you know Van, right? From the Bugle?"

"Obviously," I huffed. "He coached my hockey team when I was a kid."

"Right. Well, unless he's a secret agent like you, I haven't had 'protection.' And I think I'd know," Chris added, "since 'protection' feels an awful lot like being kidnapped."

Was it possible that Van knew Dante Fromadgio, or was that another lie? It was something to look into, but not now. *Eyes on the prize, Sunday.*

"Can we keep going?" I asked, determined to make this guy admit he knew exactly what was happening here and wasn't the innocent he claimed to be. "This week, the Division was contacted because whoever was keeping an eye on you had credible evidence that you'd been tracked to the Hollow. The Powers that Be decided to put me in charge of picking you up—"

Chris flinched, and his gaze met mine. I'd swear those

shiny brown orbs were fucking weapons. Every time he flashed them at me, I felt like I'd been gut-punched.

I really fucking hated it.

"What?" I demanded. "Something ringing a bell finally?"

"N-no." He wrapped his arms around himself. "Just realizing certain phrases mean different things to different people, that's all. Carry on."

I made myself ignore this nonsensical statement the same way I'd ignored his gut-punch eyes and kept talking. "Someone was supposed to brief you that I was coming. Once I had you with me, we were supposed to stay at this safe house and keep you under the radar until your uncle testified—"

Chris opened his mouth like he was going to protest again, so I talked louder.

"Ah-ah-ah! Still my turn! I was *supposed* to keep you here at this safe house," I repeated. I knew I sounded pissed off, but it was impossible to keep up my friendly act when he was looking at me like that. "Unfortunately, that plan's been blown to hell because *someone* took a fucking swan dive off a trellis and borrowed the neighbor's phone to alert the world where we are, so now I need to find us a new safe house. Which I will, but at this point, it probably won't be until tomorrow." Which was going to make for a hell of a long night. I fixed him with a cool stare. "And you're saying *all* of this is news to you, huh?"

He regarded me for a long, silent moment, adjusted his glasses, then asked politely, "Sorry, is it my turn to talk now?"

Like that stopped you before. I folded my arms over my chest. "Yes. Talk."

"First, that was a very exciting story, Reed." He smiled

kindly. "More exciting than the time in season two when John Ruffian had to infiltrate a cookie-smuggling ring to intercept the government secrets being baked into the Macadamia Chip Delights—"

"Jesus Christ," I muttered.

"—but none of that means I'm the person you're looking for, unfortunately. Or... fortunately, I guess, since if I were that person, this whole situation would be high-key terrifying instead of, you know, bewildering and inconvenient." He pushed up his glasses and leaned toward me confidingly. "I don't know if you can tell, but I'm not an adventurous person in general. Really, aside from one tiny, little Alepocalypse—which was blown all out of proportion—I'm the most boring person ever."

He said this with perfect frankness, like he wasn't a metric fuckton of oversized eyes and words and clothing, all wrapped up in one small and distractingly sexy package. Like he hadn't escaped a safe house, climbed down a trellis, and earned the loyalty of the guy next door, all within fifteen minutes of our arrival. Like he was truly as innocent as he was claiming to be.

"Sure," I agreed blandly. "Totally ordinary."

Chris nodded. "So's my uncle. Look, I don't mean to argue with you about this." His eyes pleaded with me for understanding. "I hate arguing, so I *never* argue, as a rule, but it feels like you're not listening. Uncle Danny is a gardener—you should see his sedum! He can't read the labels on a wine bottle without glasses, but he refuses to wear them. He's been doing amateur theater for years, but he's so self-conscious he's never let me come to one of his shows. He has a heart condition, and he should be following a special diet, but he makes—*made*—pasta carbonara for me every Sunday because he knows it's my favorite. This person you're talking about, who's in trouble with the law, and confessed to crimes, and has enemies, and went into witness protection without me? That's not the man I know. And I could prove it to you right now if I still had my phone. My cousin Nicky would tell you—"

"Nicky?" I straightened, my heart beating faster. "You mean Nicky Knives? Please don't tell me that's who you were calling when you were next door. Fuck me, Chris. That guy is straight-up psychotic."

To my surprise—though, really, I wasn't sure how anything about this guy surprised me anymore—Chris laughed. It sounded strained but genuine. "Oh my gosh. Nicky *Knives*? My cousin wishes someone would call him that!" He leaned forward again and said in a hushed voice, like someone might overhear, "When we were little, his mom called him Snickerdoodle. He *haaaated* it. Later, when he moved in with Danny and me, he'd go around demanding, 'Call me Nicky Steel, Chrissy.' Or 'Call me Nick Fury.' But Uncle Danny always told him you couldn't force a nickname like that, you had to earn it, and—"

Chris glanced up at my unamused face, and his shoulders slumped. "If you must know, I called our old neighbor Mrs. Rose, back in New Jersey, only she's hard of hearing, and I don't think she understood what I was saying. I didn't call Nicky. He and I aren't close, and he's currently not speaking to me." Somehow, Chris sounded almost *disappointed.*

"Thank fuck for that," I said fervently. "The only thing that would make this little situation worse is for Nicky Knives to show up."

Chris's lip trembled. "Please stop saying things like that. You're talking about my family, Reed. The only people I have left. A-and they're not perfect. I know that. But they're *mine*."

Before I could clap back with something heartfelt and probably unwise, I heard a noise outside. Motioning Chris to stay where he was—which earned me an eye roll and a sigh—I moved toward the window.

Next door, a rusted sedan pulled into Kenny's driveway, quickly followed by a pickup truck, and six men piled out. Kenny stepped onto his porch and greeted the newcomers with fist bumps and back thumps before ushering them inside. Which would have been totally normal... except I could see from the glow of the streetlight that one of the men had a shoulder rig, and when Kenny hugged another, there was a visible bulge in the middle of his waistband that suggested he was carrying, too.

Great. Six large unknowns—at least two armed—visiting Reefer Heaven next door. I considered going outside to get a better view of their license plate numbers but quickly rejected the idea. I'd have to contact local law enforcement to ask them to run the plates, which begged the question of whether anyone at the Division had even contacted the locals, per protocol, to let them know Chris and I were here. The person who briefed Chris should have done that, but—I darted a quick glance at my protectee, who'd pulled his knees up on the bed and wrapped his arms around them, like maybe if he shrunk into a small enough ball, I wouldn't be able to see him—given the other serious failures of protocol here, I wouldn't bet money on it.

I let the curtain fall, then compulsively pulled out my Glock, removed the magazine to check that it was loaded, and slid it back into place. From the corner of my eye, I saw Chris tracking my movements before quickly averting his eyes.

This gave me an idea of how to prove he was a liar, once and for all. The guy was supposed to be a weapons expert, right?

"Hey, what'd you do with my, uh... my Colt?" I demanded, gesturing toward the duffel bag on the bed.

"P-pardon?"

"My gun. My backup weapon. The Colt .45 that was in my bag. When I came in here to check on you after my shower, I saw it was gone—"

"Oh, *that*. It's under the mattress." He cocked his head. "But is it a Colt? I thought it was a Hellcat subcompact nine millimeter."

I snorted. He knew a Hellcat subcompact on sight but wanted me to believe his family was a bunch of innocent cheesemongers? *Sure.* I couldn't believe I'd actually started falling for his act.

"My bad," I lied easily, retrieving my weapon from the area where he'd pointed. "I get those two confused."

Chris frowned, as well he might, since a Colt .45 and a Hellcat had about as much in common as Shrek and Tinker Bell. He opened his mouth to say something—probably another rambling story about how his crime lord uncle actually ran a sanctuary for displaced honeybees and donated kidneys to orphans in his spare time—and I immediately held up a hand to cut him off.

I couldn't listen to that bullshit. Not now.

As it was, I knew I'd be spending the night keeping watch in the wingback chair. Not only was the situation next door giving me a bad feeling—the kind I'd learned not to ignore—but I hadn't managed to make my protectee drop his act and admit he needed protection. The second I left the room, Chris would probably start tying his bedsheets together and making another break for it.

"Go to sleep," I told him. I took my seat right next to the bed and set my jaw so he'd know I meant business.

"Now? Here?" He bit his lip. "Okay, but I'd really like—"

"I don't care. I'm done talking for tonight, and neither one of us is going anywhere, so stop fucking arguing and *sleep*."

He blinked at me from behind his glasses. "I'm not arguing," he said softly. "I don't argue. I was going to ask if I could use the bathroom and brush my teeth."

Fucking Christ. How did he always make me feel like *I* was the asshole?

Maybe because you're being an asshole? a voice in my head that sounded suspiciously like my brother Knox suggested.

I ignored it.

"Yeah. Fine. Use the bathroom."

But because, asshole or not, I was also determined not to fuck up this assignment. I stood in the hall outside while he used the bathroom, brushed his teeth with a spare brush, and drank several glasses of water.

Finally, he climbed back onto the bed, and I retook my chair, which hadn't gotten any more comfortable. In an effort to ignore him, I took out my Hellcat and ran through my usual checks. The familiar clicks reassured me everything was in order, so I placed the gun back in the bag and dragged it closer to my chair.

Chris tried a stare-off with me for about three seconds before inhaling a shaky breath and scooting up the bed to slide under the covers. He removed his glasses and set them under his pillow. Then he finally, *finally* closed those pretty eyes—I mean, *duplicitous* eyes—pulled the covers up to his chin, and let out a forlorn little sigh that made my chest clench.

The quilt was a mishmash of garish purple cow-print patches and pastel fabric imprinted with faded peaches. The pattern hurt to look at but was also strangely hard to look away from—or at least that's what I told myself as the minutes passed by and I continued to stare at my protectee.

There was certainly no other reason why I watched his chest rise and fall beneath the blanket. No other reason why I noticed the hank of brown hair falling over his pale forehead and had to clench my fingers against the need to smooth it back. No other reason why my chest felt hot and an unfamiliar, heavy discomfort in my gut made me turn away and glare at the window while imagining him throwing his leg over so he could scramble down the damn trellis.

Thank fuck he hadn't gotten seriously hurt.

"Reed?" he whispered after a minute. "Are you going to bed also? Because if you are, you should probably—"

"Sleep, Chris," I barked. Though his eyes remained closed, I felt like I'd been caught out somehow, and it made me sound more pissed off than I'd intended.

"*Sleep, Chris,*" he muttered. "*Sit, Chris. Stay, Chris. You know nothing, Chris.*" He turned on his side toward me and pounded his pillow. "*I don't believe you, Chris.*" He paused before tightening his lips and inhaling through his nose. "You're... you're not very nice, you know."

"Neither are you," I snapped back while trying to get comfortable in the chair. It was going to be a long night, but I wasn't about to leave him alone again.

He froze. "I am so." Then, he added more uncertainly, "Sometimes people tell me I'm too nice."

I thought back to how quickly he'd agreed to get in a

stranger's car earlier today. Maybe he *was* too nice. "Hey, if no one contacted you to let you know I was coming—"

"They didn't." Chris sighed. "I swear they didn't."

"Then why the hell did you get in my car?"

"Because I thought..." Chris's cheeks went from annoyed pink to mortified red. He swallowed. "Er. Never mind. I-I think you're right. I should go to sleep now."

I frowned. What the hell did that mean?

I opened my mouth to insist that he reply but clamped my teeth together at the last second. It didn't matter what he said when I wasn't sure I could believe him. And, if I was brutally honest with myself, it didn't even matter if I believed him because either way, my job was to protect him.

When his breathing finally evened out in sleep, I grabbed my phone and typed out an update for Janissey because *somebody* around here needed to follow protocol, though I had no idea when he'd receive it. Were there support people still in the office? Was anyone monitoring the Evanoviches? Would I be getting regular updates? In the morning, I'd have to demand some answers... from somebody.

I flipped off the light, settled back into the chair, and used a breathing technique I'd learned during training to finally fall into an uneasy sleep. But it was only an hour or so later that I woke again, this time to the sound of men's voices below the window.

Probably Kenny and his buddies, but I pushed out of my chair and peeked out the curtain again to be sure.

On the lawn below, at least half a dozen men in ski masks spread out between Kenny's house and ours. They moved with the grace of lumbering elephants, heedless of the streetlights, like they didn't expect to be seen or care if they were. And every one of them was heavily, visibly armed.

What the fuck?

Had we been followed? No one could have gotten here this quickly, even if Chris had called someone... could they?

I shook myself quickly. There'd be time for speculation once we were safe.

Scrambling to my bag, I retrieved my backup weapon, even as I bounced the mattress.

"Wake up," I hissed at the quilt-covered body on the bed. When Chris didn't move, I shook him firmly, trying to ignore the warmth from his body and the way he'd curled into a tiny ball during the night like a pill bug. "Chris. We have a situation."

He suddenly lurched up, the whites of his eyes visible in the dark room. "Wha—?"

I leaned down to grab his shoes and shove them on his feet. I'd prefer not to leave the safe house, but if we had to run, he'd never be able to make it without shoes. "Stay low and quiet. Follow me and do exactly as I say."

Half-asleep, he nodded and reached for my shoulder to keep from being pulled off the bed when I yanked his laces tight. I slung my duffel over my shoulder, grabbed his hand, and moved toward the door.

"Wait!" he cried. He fumbled back toward the pillow, found his glasses, and shoved them on his face.

"Take this." I shoved the Hellcat into his hand. "Eleven shots plus one. Slide rack."

He fumbled the damned thing like it was a hissing cobra.

I reached out to steady his hand on the grip. "Deep breath. In and out. You got this."

"Sure. Yeah." But under his breath, he added, "Oh, man, I do *not* got this," almost too softly for me to hear.

For once, Chris didn't argue or attempt to talk my ear off. He did exactly as I said and stayed close to me as we crept out of the bedroom and down the hall. I'd familiarized myself with the layout when we arrived, so I knew there was a secondary staircase off the last bedroom. We made our way there on silent feet.

Halfway down, a loud pop of gunfire split the night, and Chris huddled against me with a muffled scream. I wrapped my arm around him to keep him close.

"We know you're in there, Chris!" a man's voice shouted, showing the operators had given up any attempt at a stealthy entrance. "Come on out."

More gunshots followed.

Fuck. Since when did the Evanoviches open fire on a residential neighborhood? I had no idea what or who we were dealing with, which made escape a more tempting option... assuming it actually *was* an option.

I half carried Chris the rest of the way downstairs. At the bottom of the staircase, I peered around the corner and saw a clear path to the back door. More pops came from the side yard, but there was no movement at the front or back porch. No one was trying to breach the doors, and as far as I could tell, none of the shots had actually hit the house; they were just making a hell of a lot of noise.

"Should we call the police?" Chris whispered.

"I bet someone already has," I said grimly. This wasn't necessarily a good thing. If I had to explain our identities and the circumstances surrounding the incident, that would only bring up more questions, especially if Chris talked about being "kidnapped." They might separate us until they could sort it out, which could take hours if no one at the

Division bothered answering their phone. Hours when Chris would be unprotected.

Chris's hand clutched the back of my T-shirt as we moved across the tacky vinyl floor. Rabid ducks followed our progress from every angle, making an already tense situation that much more creepy.

Outside, glass broke, and more shots were fired. In the distance, sirens wailed. We were almost out of time.

I cracked open the front door and crouched down. My car appeared untouched, and all the activity still seemed to be on the side of the house where—I darted a quick glance out the door—Kenny and an elderly woman in a housecoat stood on the front porch, each clutching a weapon.

"Whoa. Is that Kenny's grandma?" Chris squeaked, peeking around me. "I'm *super* glad I didn't disturb her TV program."

"Come on." I tugged him back to the kitchen door.

The sirens were approaching, and waiting inside was no longer an option. I had to hope that there were no assailants waiting in the bushes for us to be flushed out and that everyone had been too busy with the firefight to disable my car.

Once again, Chris nudged up next to me and peered out. "What if you shot at that, uh... that thing with the water in it? You know, like a distraction? One time in season three of *John Ruffian*—" He broke off with a muffled yelp as another barrage of gunfire rent the night.

It took me a minute to recognize that he'd been pointing at a plastic rain barrel positioned at the back corner of Kenny's house to collect runoff from the gutters. There was no telling whether it had water in it, but from the number of plants in the backyard, it seemed likely.

I pulled Chris to my other side so I could aim. Before

taking the shots, I leaned to whisper, "As soon as I say, run like hell to the passenger side, and get on the floor. Understand?"

He nodded jerkily. "But can you please t-take this back?" He held the gun with two careful fingers, like the cobra might bite.

"Don't you wanna keep it for protection?"

"Good gosh no," he said firmly. "No way."

I had no time to consider why a Fromadgio was so uncomfortable with a weapon. I tucked the gun in my waistband and squeezed his hand before letting go and aiming at the rain barrel.

My first shot didn't give me quite the result I'd wanted, but water did begin hissing as it spit upward from the hole in the lower portion of the barrel. One guy turned toward the sound just as my second shot hit its mark higher up the barrel and sent a hissing stream arcing toward the side of the house. Thankfully, this one managed to hit the metal of a nearby gutter, making a loud, metallic sound.

I gave Chris a shove, and he started running for the car a split second before I did. His door was still halfway open as I threw my bag over the seat, slammed the car into reverse, and sped backward.

"Chris!" someone yelled. "Don't go with him! Jump, for fuck's sake!"

From the corner of my eye, I saw Chris freeze, shock and indecision on his face.

As my car fishtailed out onto the street, I shifted into drive and stomped on the gas pedal, swerving a little to try and help the door close. "Don't even *think* about jumping," I shouted, reaching for Chris's wrist to hold on to him. "They'll kill you."

"I won't." His voice was small and scared. "Was that

Kenny yelling? Do you think he believed me when I told him I'd been kidnapped? Was he trying to save me?"

"No," I said. "A bunch of guys with guns got out of a Toyota not long before the shooting started. Kenny's guys with guns took positions in the windows and returned fire."

"Kenny has guys with guns?" Chris cried. "No way! He..."

"Please," I said, voice dripping with sarcasm. "Tell me how you're positive he's a good person."

I took several turns on our way out of town in case any of the men had been able to get in a vehicle quickly enough to follow us. Thankfully, I didn't see anyone behind us as we finally turned onto I-90, heading west.

At some point, I realized I was still holding Chris's hand. What had started off as my making sure he didn't bail had become... what, exactly? Comfort? Low-tech handcuffs?

I quickly let go and stretched my fingers before curling them around the steering wheel. "You, uh... you okay down there?"

"What? Oh. Yes. Totally. Fine." He seemed to realize he was still crouched on the floor and belatedly hoisted himself into his seat. "You know, the more I think about it, I think it had to be Kenny trying to help me back there. That's why no one was actually shooting directly at us. It was *really* sweet of him even if, you know, violence is never the answer."

I glanced sideways at him. Was he for real?

"Oh, dang!" He froze in the act of buckling his seat belt. "Reed, if the police come, do you think they'll look closely at Kenny's grandmother's garden? He mentioned they have more plants back there than they're supposed to."

"Why am I not surprised?" I snorted. "Yeah, Chris. I

think that's the least of what they'll be looking at Kenny for, but definitely that, too."

He sighed. "This is what's wrong with the world, you know. Why put limits on how many plants a person can grow? Like, what if you wanted zucchini *and* peppers *and* tomatoes, enough for the whole neighborhood? What if you wanted to make sure there were some pretty flowers to attract your pollinators to make sure your vegetables flourish? It doesn't seem fair, does it?"

I opened my mouth, then shut it again. "You're... Is that... Are you joking?" I demanded. "Please tell me you realize that Kenny was talking about *marijuana* plants. As in, he's probably selling whatever he's not smoking? Blink twice if you are an actual inhabitant of this planet."

"Marijuana," Chris breathed, blinking significantly more than twice. His glasses slid down his nose, and he shoved them up impatiently. "Are you sure?"

Despite everything... maybe *because* of everything... I found myself fighting the urge to laugh. "Positive. Maybe you need to rethink your idea of what a criminal looks like, hmm?"

"So, then..." He wrinkled his nose in thought. "Was it the police shooting at him? You know, for *the drugs*?"

I resisted the urge to punch myself in the face. "No, because the police don't wear masks or drive rusted-out Toyota Corollas. Also, they generally don't open fire on private residences in the middle of the night, no matter how much *zucchini* a person might be growing." I glanced at him again. "They called your name, Chris. Twice. I'm guessing they were looking for you, but Kenny somehow intercepted them. Maybe he assumed that if gunmen showed up in his neighborhood, they were looking for him. Maybe he didn't have time to think at all and just started shooting back."

He swallowed hard. "Or. *Or.* They were calling for someone else. A Christina or a Christopher or a... a Chrysanthemum. You have no idea how many Chrises there are in the world, Reed. Billions, probably. Common as dirt."

Any lingering amusement I might have evaporated in the flash-fire heat of the anger that washed over me. Was fear causing his denial? Was he simply so committed to his act that he refused to give it up? Was he truly the sweetest human in the world and incapable of seeing the danger he was in? It didn't fucking matter. Because unless he recognized the danger he was in, he wouldn't let me protect him.

"Haven't you fired a gun before?" I asked suddenly, needing to know how the man could both recognize a nine mil and have no clue how to hold one.

"Yes," he admitted.

"Then why'd you act like you didn't know what to do when I handed you one?"

"Because I've never actually shot at a person. I couldn't. I-I don't even want to hold one."

"You're an ax thrower. You do martial arts. You're a weapons expert—"

"Oh, for heaven's sake. No. I'm *not.*" Chris thunked his head back against the headrest. "Do you have any idea how frustrating it is to be told who and what you are by someone who thinks they know better than you, Reed? Because I've been dealing with that my whole life, from people who know me a whole lot better than you do, and I'm kind of over it. Okay?" He scraped his lip with his teeth before adding, "Sorry."

I could feel the weight of his eyes on me, but I didn't know how to respond, so I didn't.

A moment later, he spoke again. "I really, really want to go home. Can we *please—?*"

"No. It's not safe."

His sigh came from the depths of his soul and made my heart turn over in my chest. Without consciously choosing to, I reached out and pushed a stray curl out of his eyes. "I'm sorry, too," I said softly.

He squeezed his eyes closed and turned his face away, and I clenched my jaw to keep from murmuring more reassurances.

Once he was slumped in a little ball in the passenger seat, snoring softly, I pulled out my phone and called the Division. A sleepy-voiced Margot from Accounts finally got on, sounding about as confused as I felt. She promised she'd pass on my "concerns" and very helpfully suggested that I "hang in there, buddy, and, like, improvise or whatever" until she could get back to me in the morning. She disconnected without saying goodbye.

Fuck.

I clutched my phone until the edge of the case dented my palm. From the first day of training, the Division had taught us to live their motto, "Security Through Trust." In order to succeed in a mission, protectees needed to trust us... and *we* needed to trust our bosses and fellow agents because we were always stronger as part of a team. I used to scoff at the rah-rah bullshit... but a month ago, when I'd almost gotten myself fired, I'd started to realize how much I *had* come to rely on it. If I wasn't a Division agent, if I wasn't part of that team, who the fuck was I?

I hadn't wanted to find out. I still didn't.

But now here I was, twisting in the wind with no support, effectively on my own, and—

"*John.*" Chris's voice was so clear I turned my head, sure

he was awake, but I quickly realized he must be dreaming about that TV character he kept mentioning.

I snorted. Chris Winowski was a fucking terror. An adorable, utterly confusing menace. John Ruffian could have him with my best wishes.

But then Chris frowned in his sleep and sighed, "Reed," and my stomach clenched.

Okay, so I wasn't entirely alone. I had one distractingly adorable, horrifically misinformed, ridiculously talkative protectee with me.

And I'm going to protect him, I vowed. *Whether he likes it or not.*

It turned out he didn't like it one bit.

CHAPTER FIVE

CHRIS

I USED to think living inside a *John Ruffian: Pretender* episode would be fun, but now that it was sort of happening to me, I realized it was only fun if you were John Ruffian.

When I came awake in Reed's car, the first thing I felt was a kink in my neck from sleeping hunched against the passenger door. The second was an overfull bladder. The third was a sudden, bone-deep terror because I realized I was alone, and I couldn't stop hearing the sound of my name being shouted while gunfire blasted through the air.

I glanced around to get my bearings and noticed we were stopped in the parking lot of an old-fashioned motel. Beside me, a flashing neon sign read Bed-Rock Inn... though with the last light burned out, it looked more like Bed-Rockin', which made me burst into anxious giggles that did nothing to help my bladder situation.

Thankfully, Reed exited the lobby before full panic set in and sent me racing into the night. I popped open the car door as he approached.

"Hey. You hungry?" He shoved a big plastic key ring into his back pocket.

"Um. Not really?" I adjusted my glasses. "I suppose the whole going-home thing is still off the table?"

Reed didn't answer, which kind of *was* an answer, but his face softened a bit. He tilted his head, gesturing across the narrow country road where a sprawling wood building was lit up and faint sounds of country music escaped from its cracks. A hand-painted "Trickster's Roadhouse, Pittsfield, MA" sprawled across the front of the building in faded red paint.

"C'mon. Motel lady said they've got good burgers, and they serve all night."

It felt like it had to be five in the morning, but I had no idea what time it actually was. When we'd gotten into the car back at the safe house, the dash clock had only read eleven thirty.

I thought back to all of the soup Reed hadn't offered me, and the granola bar he *had* offered me but I hadn't accepted because I'd believed Reed was a nefarious kidnapper, and realized I was kind of hungry now that he mentioned hamburgers.

It had been an eventful day.

I let him pull me out of the car but almost stumbled because one of my legs was asleep. He released my hand and headed across the abandoned highway. "Let's go."

The painful leg tingling caused me to do a weird hop-shimmy as I hurried to catch up, and I pulled my sweater tighter around me. I wasn't sure where we were, exactly, but it was chilly.

"You think those, um, folks from earlier might be around?" I looked up and down the road for any telltale signs, like headlights or the bright-orange pop of gunshots.

Reed darted a look at me. "We weren't followed if that's what you mean."

"Yeah, no, of course not." I nodded with feigned confidence and tried to will my tension away. "I figured. So, um, about the mistaken identity thing—"

"Can we not do this right now?" Reed interrupted. "I'm tired and hungry, and I really don't have the patience to have this conversation again."

I felt a very uncharacteristic urge to tell him *I* didn't have the patience to be dragged all over creation when I didn't *need* protection... but I was tired, too, so I bit my tongue.

Even though I firmly believed the situation at the safe house had been a coincidence and no one had been coming after me—there was no way in the world my uncle had done any of the stuff Reed said he had, so therefore, there'd be no *reason* to come for me—I was still feeling a little shaky. I guessed maybe that was normal after a person had spent the early part of the evening thinking he was being kidnapped and then the later part of the evening witnessing a low-key gunfight, but it was the opposite of normal for *me*.

When we entered the loud roadhouse, it looked like something out of an old movie. Pool tables took up the far-right side of the cavernous space, red vinyl booths skirted the edges of the room, mismatched tables and chairs filled in the space in the middle, and a giant wooden bar spanned the far-left wall. Neon beer logos shone from various spots on the wall, and random sports collectibles spotted all the bare places where there wasn't a beer sign.

It lacked the Bugle's charm, but the place still felt familiar, right down to the sticky floors. It was packed with a familiar assembly of people, too, from bikers, to preppy college kids, to rode-hard barflies shouting at the Bruins on the flat-screen TV to "get the lead out and learn to skate," though they, themselves, looked like they might have gotten winded on the walk from the parking lot.

Heads turned our way as we stepped inside, but most everyone ignored us again within seconds. I spotted the sign for the restrooms and beat a hasty retreat in that direction with a muttered explanation to Reed.

When I returned, I found Reed taking up one side of a booth shoved between the doors to the kitchen and the pool tables.

"Ordered you a chocolate milk," Reed announced as I sat down. He shoved a sticky menu at me. "Pick something to eat."

I lowered the menu to look at him, surprised and touched. "Oh my gosh, thank you so much. You'd be surprised how many places don't serve chocolate milk. How'd you guess it's my favorite?"

He lowered his own menu to stare at me, a spark of amusement in his green eyes. "I was kidding. I ordered you a beer, babydoll." He frowned. "Did you *want* a chocolate milk?"

Heat flared in my cheeks. "Oh. No. I mean, beer's great, too." I cleared my throat and tried to make it sound gruff and deep. "In fact, beer's way better. H-heck yeah. Good stuff."

I glanced back at the menu but not before seeing Reed's expression soften again.

Gosh, the man was complicated.

On the one hand, Reed Sunday was a total pain in my behind. The whole competent, commanding, grumpy-and-taciturn thing was hot when John Ruffian did it, but it was seriously flipping frustrating when it meant someone was failing to communicate important information (like *"Hey, Chris, you're not actually being kidnapped... in case you were worried about that.*") or failing to listen when you were trying to communicate equally important information (like "*Hey, Reed, my uncle's not a criminal, which means you accidentally 'picked up' the wrong protectee.*").

On the other hand, Reed was kind of great. He was beautiful (which wasn't *new* news but worth repeating, since I was pretty sure on the way here I'd dreamed John Ruffian came to save me and I'd told him "no, thank you" because Reed was already on the case), but more than that, Reed made me feel safe.

There was no logical reason for this to be true. I'd spent most of our time together trying to seduce him (or, okay, be seduced *by* him), escape him, question him, or force him to listen to me, and I hadn't been successful at any of those things.

But considering I'd never had the courage to seduce, escape, question, or talk back to... well, anyone ever in my whole life, the very fact that I'd done all those things with a person I'd only known for a handful of hours felt sort of... momentous.

Also, if I was being honest, the way he'd done that *click-click* thing to check his gun back at the house was the hottest thing I'd ever seen, because it turned out I could hate guns but still appreciate when a brave, muscly person was willing to use one to protect me... which might have made me a giant hypocrite, but here we were.

I startled a bit as an older woman with bright red hair appeared at our table and set down two glasses of draft beer.

"What can I getcha, boys?"

"Oh. Um. Do you have any specials tonight?" I asked politely.

She lifted one eyebrow and sucked a tooth. "The burger's real special. You want special cheese with that?"

"Uh." I glanced back down at the menu. "Sure? But can I get a side salad instead of fries, please?"

Her eyes got squinty. "Burger comes with lettuce already." She turned to Reed. "What about you, handsome?"

"Same, but I'll take the fries. Thanks."

She grabbed the menus and disappeared.

When she was gone, an awkward silence descended—or, at least, a silence that felt awkward to *me*, probably because I'd been thinking about how sexy Reed was.

Reed didn't seem to feel awkward at all. He was focused on the television across the room, though I got the feeling he was very aware of everything else happening around us. He had that same kind of tiger vibe that Crys gave off, but with Reed, the vibe wasn't scary so much as... scary-attractive.

When I found myself tugging at my sweater cuffs while staring at the open collar of his flannel, watching the way his throat bobbed rhythmically as he swallowed his beer and feeling an answering rhythmic throb in my pants, I gripped the edge of the table and looked away in a panic.

Christoforo Winowski, control yourself.

This whole situation was banana-pants-weird—I'd been adjacent to a *gunfight*, for the love of John Ruffian—and the only thing that would make it weirder was me thinking spicy thoughts about the man who thought he was supposed to be protecting me.

"So!" I smiled brightly, determined to overcome my awkwardness. "What's the plan after the burgers? What are you planning to do with me?" I sucked in a horrified breath. "I mean, not *with* me, like... like..." I pressed a hand to my stomach and glanced around the bar, desperate for a conversational life preserver—or perhaps a handy hole to fall into

—and noticed the bikers in the corner groaning about what was happening on the television. "Good gosh, those Bruins need to *get the lead out*, am I right?"

Reed cocked his head. When he really focused those green eyes on me, the effect was hypnotizing. "Hockey fan, are you?"

"Um..." I bit my lip, hesitating, but admitted, "No. More of a figure skating fan, to be honest. I, ah, took lessons when I was a kid for a little while."

He frowned a little. "Why do you sound like you're making a confession? My sister skated for a bit. It's not as easy as they make it look on TV."

"It's really not." I exhaled shakily. Something about big, gruff Reed complimenting the sport hit me hard in the best way. "Pretty cool when you learn how to do something you didn't think you could, though."

"Always." He sipped his beer. "How'd you get into it?"

"Oh. Ha. Funny story." I toyed with my fingers. "When I was about seven, Uncle Danny told me I needed to play a sport. *A man needs a physical outlet to hone his mind, Christoforo.* Even that young, I think he knew I'd never pick anything really aggressive like boxing or football, but I'm pretty sure he was hoping for baseball or soccer. Maybe even golf." I grinned. "But Nonna and I had this little ritual whenever she wasn't feeling well, where we'd sit on her sofa and watch one of the movies in her collection of VHS tapes, and her very favorite was *The Cutting Edge*—"

Reed groaned.

I laughed. "It's a really good movie. The kind of movie where if you like it, I'll probably like *you*, you know? Have you ever seen it?"

"Yes," he admitted. "My uncle Drew shares your grandmother's taste in movies."

"Well, anyway, I loved everything about it. The characters, the romance, the way the big, burly hockey guy learns there's more to life than... you know, pushing people into the walls of the rink—"

"Checking them into the boards," Reed corrected.

"Sure. So I told Uncle Danny I chose figure skating. I wanted to be a butterfly on the ice." I gave Reed a half smile. "Danny, uh... had some concerns—"

"I'll bet he did." Reed's nostrils flared. "Guy like him? Bet he had plenty of old-fashioned bullshit opinions—"

"He did not!" I said, instinctively defending my uncle. "You don't know him, Reed. His concern was that it wasn't practical. It was too many hours away from the family, doing things that wouldn't toughen me up and prepare me for life." I ran my finger down the side of my beer glass. "He used to say that it wasn't safe to be too gentle. If you didn't *show* people how strong you were, they'd take advantage of you."

Reed grunted. "And don't they?"

"Maybe. Sometimes. But I'd rather be too kind than not kind enough, you know? What's wrong with making the world a little softer and a little prettier for other people?" I shrugged. My uncle had never understood that, so I didn't really expect Reed to either.

But Reed didn't dismiss the idea. Instead, he shrugged a little and said, "Nothing wrong with it," which was so thrilling my whole body went hot and shivery.

"So why'd you stop taking lessons?" he went on.

"Oh, that." I waved a hand. "I was pretty good on the ice, and I even took some dance classes to improve my flexibility, so when I was around ten, I told my coach I wanted to be paired up so I could start doing the cool aerial moves.

I'd been working on my salchow, and I wanted to do a *throw* salchow so badly—"

"You really just wanted to do the *Pamchenko* like in the movie, didn't you?" Reed asked dryly. "Admit it."

"Heck, yes." I smiled. "Or, you know, whatever the real-life equivalent was. I knew some other kids had gotten paired as young as nine. But, um... my teacher said it just wasn't feasible for *me* to do that. None of the other kids, even the biggest ones, were strong enough to handle the lift and the throw, and it would be dangerous to try. And I... I guess I just lost my fire for the sport after that. I mean, if you can't fly like a butterfly, why bother?"

"Why bother?" he repeated softly, his green eyes so intense on mine that no amount of firm warnings to my dick would make it deflate.

I reached for my beer with sweating hands and drained the whole nasty thing in one go.

"Wow," Reed said with a blink. "You do like beer, huh?"

I coughed a little as the last dregs of foam went down my throat, then set my empty glass on the table. The taste was questionable—why people enjoyed carbonated bread juice, I'd never know—but it was a great distraction.

So great that I smiled at the server as she passed and leaned over to ask, "Could I please have a refill, miss?"

She snorted a little and glanced at Reed, almost as if asking for permission, then shrugged. "You got it, kiddo."

The second beer went down easier than the first, and Reed's smile became a concerned frown. "I'm, ah, guessing you're still in shock, or maybe your denial's wearing off. Either way, maybe slow your roll."

The world had gotten the tiniest, loveliest bit hazy around the edges, making it easy to forget things like gunfights, and concerning accusations about my uncle, and how badly I wished I'd gotten to kiss Reed, back when I'd thought there was a chance he was interested in me that way.

"You know how Norm Avery sometimes stands up on the rungs of his stool at the Bugle and yells 'In beer there is freedom!'?" I licked my lips. "I think I get it now."

He lifted an eyebrow. "Oh, yeah? Freedom from what?"

From being me, I thought, but I didn't say it out loud. Reed wasn't an overtalking, not-often-but-occasionally distracted, and generally hard-to-take person. When he wanted to accomplish something, he took action, like John Ruffian. When he thought a thing, he said it. He wouldn't understand.

After the server delivered a third beer along with our burgers without me even having to ask—gosh, we really needed to leave her a nice tip—Reed rapped his fist on the wooden table to get my attention. "You asked me before what our next step was."

I blinked at him. "Did I?"

"You did. Two beers ago. And, I want to be clear— everything's going to be alright, Chris. The safe house situation sucked, but it's no big deal in the grand scheme, okay?"

"Sure. No big deal," I agreed, wondering if Reed realized how often he said that.

"I've got you," he continued, "and we're gonna stick to the plan."

Reed was so sweet, and he looked so darn serious, but when he said, "stick to the plan," I couldn't help giggling a little. Until I'd gotten into Reed's car a few hours ago, my *plan* had been to start a side hustle as a charcuterie maker, and I'd considered it a wild, oat-sowing adventure. I'd sure as heck never planned on Reed Sunday.

And there was a good reason for that.

"Do you suppose there's a bus station in this town?" I wondered, chewing one of the french fries I hadn't thought I wanted.

If Reed dropped me at a bus station, I had enough money to cover a ticket... assuming I could figure out where to go. The Hollow was probably the right option, but being around Reed's family would feel weird now. I could go back to New Jersey, but with Danny's house closed up and the Cellar gone, it would be pretty hecking lonely and would worry my uncle if he heard about it. That was how he'd gotten me to go in the first place, even though I really hadn't wanted to. *You'll be lonely, Christoforo, and I'll worry.* And I'd agreed because... well, because I always agreed.

Reed's green eyes narrowed, and he waved a hand in front of my face. "Focus, Chris. I'm going to make some calls and find us a new safe house—"

"Reed." I sighed, pushing up my glasses. "I don't mean to be disrespectful, since I appreciate that you communicated a clear boundary in saying that you didn't want to discuss the whole, um, uncle thing—"

"No, I'm done *arguing* with you about it." He set his jaw. "Our safe house got attacked by people looking for you—"

"*Or* maybe no one was looking for me at all and it's a... a coincidence that someone called my name! And, yes, maybe it seems like a weird and unlikely coincidence, I grant you —" I hurried on when it looked like he was going to interrupt. "—but no weirder than anything else that's happened to me today, getting p-picked up and kidnapped—"

"You were not fucking kidnapped!" Reed exclaimed, eyes dark and cheeks suddenly flushed. He darted a glance to the side to make sure no one overheard and leaned forward before continuing in a harsh whisper, "You were not being held against your will. You got in that car on your own."

My face flamed. "Yes. *Technically*. But I didn't know where we were going, and I didn't know there were going to be guns involved, and I didn't know you were going to tell me my uncle isn't who I thought he was, and my whole life isn't what I thought it was, and now I can't go h-home." My voice cracked. "This isn't me. I'm a very boring person."

He snorted. "Bullshit."

"It's not," I assured him. "I'm a charcuterie specialist. I like recommending wine pairings. I like talking to shoppers. I don't go to wild parties. I don't have adventures. I have never thrown an ax. Heck, Danny didn't let me take over the Cellar when he retired because he thought I was too s-soft. *Too soft to run this business, Christoforo.* That's what he said when he told me he was selling the place. And I..." I pressed my lips together because I was suddenly afraid I might cry. I blamed the beer. And possibly also the gunfight.

I took a deep breath and continued. "I'm not arguing with you, Reed. I'm not, because I hate arguing, so I don't argue... er, generally. I'm simply saying that you can't expect me to stay with you—"

"Then you're going to wind up hurt!" Reed scrubbed both hands over his face. "Fucking *fuck*. How the hell am I supposed to protect a person who insists on *tra-la-laing* around like life is a field of daisies and rainbows?"

Stung, I straightened in my seat. "That's *not* what I'm doing—"

"Yes, it fucking is," he snapped. Fiery green eyes fixed on me, and a pair of big, strong hands reached across the table, grabbing mine and stilling the nervous fluttering I hadn't even been aware of. "You could be hurt in a million ways, Chris. You could be kidnapped for real. Held as insurance so your uncle won't testify. And the things they could do to you..." He inhaled sharply and gripped my hands so tightly I squeaked.

He released me immediately and straightened, his face closed off. "Get your head out of your ass," he said sharply. "Because you might think this whole 'sweet and lovable' act makes me think you're innocent, but it just makes me think you're stupid."

I sucked in a breath as the word ricocheted around the table and lodged itself beneath my heart.

It probably shouldn't have felt like such a blow. Heck, Reed's comment wasn't even the worst or most embarrassing thing that had happened to me that day. But something about hearing it from his lips after I'd tried to be so honest with him, after he'd been so supportive about the other things I'd told him, after I'd thought we were... well, *connecting*... made my eyes burn and my whole chest crumple.

Maybe Uncle Danny was right. Maybe I was too soft.

But in that moment, I didn't *feel* soft. In fact, for the first time I could remember, I didn't feel the need to brush off Reed's comment so things wouldn't get awkward or roll with the punches and hide my hurt with a smile. I *was* hurt, but I was also really angry.

"Fuck," Reed growled, squeezing his eyes shut. "I didn't mean that—"

"It is not stupid to believe the best of people, Reed Sunday," I said, quiet but firm. "And it's *never* stupid to be loyal to your family."

"It is when it's going to get you killed—" Reed reached up and grabbed his hair with both hands, yanking at the dark, wavy strands. "No. You know what? I said we weren't talking about this again, and I meant it. All that matters is that you're my protectee and I'm your protector. Your job is to do what I say." He picked up his burger and jabbed it in my direction. "End of story."

I'd never had a temper. Being angry and letting myself feel it was new to me. I didn't know how to handle the hot, clean fizz that choked my blood. And... it turned out there was kind of a learning curve. Because despite being truly incandescently angry at Reed Sunday, with his handsome face and his strong hands and his quirky smile and his big mouth, when I thought about lashing out at him, my mind continued down the same track it always seemed to take with Reed.

I envisioned myself kissing the heck out of him.

Except, like, *angrily*.

Since I definitely—almost definitely—wasn't going to do that, I climbed out of the booth on shaky legs and stuck out my chin. "I no longer consent to being protected, Mr. Sunday. I... I release you."

He snorted around his burger. "Doesn't work that way, Daenerys. This isn't *Game of Thrones*, and I'm not your servant. Sit down."

"No."

He cast his eyes to the ceiling. "And where are you gonna go, Chris? You have no phone, no car, and no ability to stay out of trouble for more than two minutes—or do I need to remind you *again* that people were shooting at us a couple of hours ago?"

I definitely didn't need to be reminded of that.

I cast my eyes around the room. The college kids had left, and the guys at the bar seemed a bit too interested in the game for conversation, but there was a table of three women sort of close to where the rowdy-looking biker crew was hanging out. They had a spare chair at their table.

Normally, I'd never be so impolite as to interrupt them, but at the moment, it seemed like the lesser evil.

"For now, I'm going over there," I informed Reed, pointing. I picked up my beer... and, on second thought, grabbed the remainder of my meal, too. Reed didn't deserve my extra fries.

"For fuck's sake. Get back here," I heard him say as I marched away, but I didn't listen.

And it felt really dang *good* to not listen. Who knew?

"H-hi, excuse me," I said as I approached the ladies. "Do you mind if I sit here?"

Three sets of eyes swung toward me in surprise, then surveyed me up and down.

The oldest-looking of them leaned to one side and aimed a glare back at Reed. Her eyes narrowed. Then she looked at me. "Y'okay, cutie?"

I nodded. Then shook my head. Her concerned voice made my burning tear ducts threaten to overflow.

"Aw. Sit, honey," a blonde woman said, pushing out the empty chair. "Boyfriend trouble? Join the club."

"N-no. Reed's not my boyfriend. He's..." I broke off with a head shake. The story was too wild to be believed anyway. "I only met him today. And I thought he was into me, but he wasn't really." I sighed. "He wanted something very different than I thought."

"I bet I know exactly what he wanted," the third woman said bitterly. She tucked a strand of auburn hair behind her ear, her eyes red-rimmed but fierce. "Same thing men always want. You're adorable, sweetheart, and men are pigs."

"Uh... thank you. Are *you* alright?" I asked.

The blonde woman leaned over to pat her friend's

hand. "Amber's having trouble with her old man, Knuckles," she confided, aiming a dark look at the bikers' table.

Following her glance, I adjusted my glasses and immediately spotted an older gentleman with long gray hair who wore a black leather vest over his naked chest. His vest had the word "Knuckles" embroidered right on the front like a name tag, which was cool. He also had a very young lady in a very small top practically perched on his lap, which was... not.

"I see." I winced and reached over to grip Amber's other hand. I pushed my plate toward her. "French fry?"

Amber laughed, but it sounded watery. "No, thanks. In fact, I think we might need shots. Cheri, can you—?"

The older woman stood. "On it."

She returned a moment later with a bottle of Fireball and four empty glasses. "It's my night off, but I work here," she said by way of explanation as she set a shot glass in front of each of us.

"Oh. Wow. Thank you. But I've already had two beers..." I gestured toward my half-empty glass. "Or, um, two and a half, if I'm being honest. And I don't drink, as a general rule, so..."

"You do tonight." Cheri filled my little glass to the top.

I resisted the urge to peek over my shoulder at Reed, though I could sense his disapproval and frustration radiating across the room.

"Because we deserve to be appreciated for who we are, not shit on 'cause we're not who they want us to be," the blonde lady proclaimed, raising her glass in a toast.

"Because some men—" Amber lifted her own glass. "—are bossy, mistrusting know-it-alls, and I say fuck 'em."

And if that wasn't the truth, I didn't know what was, so I followed Amber's lead and gulped the whole shot at once.

———

"Six months." Amber brushed away a tear. "I gave that asshole six months of my life. I thought we were committed. I thought it was love."

I shook my head sadly, and the movement almost made me fall out of the chair. I'd started to notice that the chairs were really wobbly two shots ago, but I didn't want to say anything about it in case that was rude.

I also refused to look over my shoulder, though I knew Reed was still there because from time to time, I could feel a pair of green lasers burning a hole in my sweater.

"What did Mr. Knuckles do?" I demanded. I was trying to whisper, too, but by the way Cheri and Gina—the blonde lady—jumped, I wasn't sure I'd succeeded.

Amber's lip quivered. "He saw me chatting with a customer at the salon where I work. I was only trying to sell the guy hair product! I wasn't even flirting!" She sniffled. "Or... okay, maybe I was, a little, but when you act interested, guys buy more, you know? I maybe did that thing where I pulled my top down a tiny bit?"

"That's a thing?" I wondered, worrying at the cuffs of my sweater.

"Sure," Gina said. "Show some skin and men go cross-eyed. But only an asshole thinks that means you're giving free samples."

Cheri and Amber agreed vehemently, so I nodded, too, as though I'd ever attempted to show skin or give anyone a free sample of anything but a nicely aged Gouda.

"I thought... I guess I thought Knuckles might be a *little* jealous," Amber went on. "But jealousy can be a good thing—"

I frowned. "Can it?"

"Oh, hell yeah," Cheri said. "Spices things up. Makes a man confront his feels, too. You should try it."

Huh.

I pointedly didn't glance back at Reed as I filed this information away. Reed was bossy and unkind, and I was definitely not interested in him... much.

The wires in my brain needed to uncross themselves immediately.

"But when Knuckles saw me talking to that guy, he accused me of cheating on him. As if I ever would! I tried to explain tonight, but he totally ignored me. And then that *woman* came over to him, and he... he..." Amber broke off with a sob. "I don't know how to make him understand."

Cheri wrapped an arm around Amber's shoulder. "He's a fool, honey."

"Yeah. I think you're *way* cooler than she is," I agreed loyally. I peeked at the bikers' table to find that while Knuckles still had the other woman draped against his shoulder, he kept glancing over at Amber like he hoped she'd notice.

So rude.

I felt my anger against rude and mistrustful men intensify.

"You think so?" Amber asked me.

"Of course. You're kind and intelligent, and your hair is *beautiful*," I said. "And you did nothing wrong!"

My voice might have been a bit too loud again since people at nearby tables glanced my way and I felt the heat of a certain green-laser glare intensify, but I was speaking truth, gosh dang it, and I would not be silenced. "It's not *fair* when people think they know who you are better than you do—"

"Preach," Gina said.

"And it doesn't matter how nice he seemed to be when you first met him, or how handsome he is—"

"Huh. I dunno if I'd call Knuckles handsome," Cheri muttered.

"Cheri!" Amber chided.

"—or how tall he is—"

Now, Amber frowned. "Well, Knuck's not tall, per se..."

"—or how... how competent he is—"

Gina wrinkled her nose. "Competent's not the first word that comes to mind to describe Knuckles—"

"Or how *tall* he is," I continued.

"Sweetie, you already said tall." Cheri looked at me in concern.

"And..." I pushed up from the table with such violence the whole floor swayed. "He should apologize for not believing you and for saying mean things," I declared. "I'm going to tell him so."

As I marched over to the bikers' table, I heard a panicked female voice say, "Oh, shit," and a panicked male voice say, "Jesus fucking Christ," but I didn't pause or hesitate.

"Excuse me, Mr. Knuckles?" I said loudly.

The gray-haired man—who had to be uncomfortably cold with only that vest on, which maybe explained some of his negative attitude—narrowed his eyes at me. "The fuck're you?"

"My name is..." I hesitated, concerned that I might give Reed an actual heart attack since the man was still wrong-headedly convinced I was being targeted. "Unimportant right now," I concluded. "What's important is that I'm here to avenge Amber."

He slow-blinked at me for a second. "Avenge her."

"That means I'm here to address your wrongs on her behalf," I added in a lower voice since he seemed confused.

"I know what the fuck it *means*," Knuckles said hotly. "If Amber wants to talk to me, she can do it herself."

"But will you listen?" I blurted. "Because... the truth is, Mr. Knuckles, you've been unfair in the extreme."

"Are you kidding me right now?" he demanded. He turned to one of his associates, who wore a matching vest. "Is he kidding me, Grim?"

"He better be kidding," Grim growled, pushing to his feet. "Or he's got fucking brass balls and a death wish."

"That it, kid?" Knuckles asked me curiously. "You got brass balls?"

I shook my head, then had to do a little shuffle-step when the floor tilted. "N-no, sir. I just know what injustice feels like." I pressed a hand to my heart. "I'd bet a powerful person like yourself has never been called a liar. O-or stupid. But words can hurt—"

Knuckles, whose chest had puffed up at being called powerful, scowled ferociously. "Hold up. I ain't ever called Amber stupid. Only an asshole would do that."

I fought the urge to look back at Reed. "I agree."

"Yo, you don't know what you're talking about, Big Brass. Amber's a cheater," another of the bikers spoke up.

"She's not." I kept my gaze on Knuckles. "She would never cheat on you, Mr. Knuckles. She loves you, and she deserves better than to watch you canoodle with another woman. It's cruel." I winced guiltily at the woman draped over his shoulder. "No offense to you, of course. I'm sure you're a lovely person."

She nodded and straightened.

Grim jumped to his feet and gave me a threatening glower. "Don't talk shit about Knuckles." He shoved my shoulder—not particularly violently, but enough to make me glad I was holding the back of the chair in front of me so I didn't topple. "Go siddown, kid."

But I couldn't. My gaze remained locked on Amber's one true love. "You might not *think* you're being cruel, Mr. Knuckles. I understand that sometimes people say things in anger that they really shouldn't say. That doesn't make them a bad person, but they do need to apologize and make amends. For example, my uncle Danny is a very caring person. He sometimes cries at Bruce Springsteen songs. But when my cousin Nicky got suspended from school for fighting, Danny was so angry he said, 'You'd know better if you were a true Fromadgio, Nicolas.' And Nicky was *so* upset he—"

"You're a... you're a Fromadgio?" Spike's eyes went wide. "Wait, shit, when you say *Danny*, do you mean—"

"Grim, you asshole." A biker stood and cuffed Grim on the side of the head. "You assaulted Dante the Cheese's blood."

"Excuse me, that's not a nice way to talk about—" I began.

"I wasn't assaulting him," Grim protested, glancing around at his friends with panicked eyes. "I wasn't! I was protecting Knuck."

"How's he gonna be protected when Dante comes after him?" one of the others shouted, sliding his chair back. "Now we're all fucked!"

"No, that's not—" I protested, but they were too busy shoving and bellowing at each other.

One of the regulars pushed off his barstool and turned. "Can you assholes shut the fuck up? I can't hear the game with you yelling."

A biker faced off against him, shoving him back against the bar. "Who're you calling an asshole, *asshole*?"

I wasn't entirely sure, afterward, who threw the first punch, but I did know it took only half a minute until the whole bar was engulfed in a melee. Fists flew, beer glasses sailed through the air. A man in a golf shirt was thrown across Amber's table, and when his head ended up in Cheri's cleavage, all three women jumped up and unleashed bloodcurdling screams.

I stood frozen in shock as the fight flowed around me, rowdy bikers facing off with enraged sports fans while bartenders hopped around, trying to control the chaos. I didn't know who to help or how to help them or even which way I should turn to get to safety. But then Reed was there, right in front of me, Sunday-green eyes locked on mine, and suddenly, I was able to move again, to *breathe* again.

"Come on," he shouted, propelling me toward the door.

I nodded, but before I could move, someone in a leather vest knocked into Reed, sending his elbow into Reed's jaw and making Reed's head snap back.

Reed's nostrils flared, and in one fluid motion, he delivered a punch that made the man's eyes roll back in his head.

I abhorred violence—honestly, no kidding, hated it—but I couldn't deny that something about the move made my muscles clench with want. *I really am a hypocrite*, I thought with a sigh.

"Move, Chris," Reed insisted. He grabbed me around the waist and pulled me bodily toward the door. "Jesus Christ," he muttered. "Jesus fucking Christ. My protectee started a goddamn bar brawl—" He shoved the door open without a word.

"I did not start a brawl," I protested. "I was righting a wrong! I was doing a good deed. Did you see how Knuckles was protecting Amber and her friends back there? How he had his arms wrapped around her? He loves her, and once I pointed it out to him, he really saw the error of his ways. It was beautiful."

Reed carried me out into the parking lot without slowing down or letting go.

"Besides, would you call what happened a *brawl*, really? I think at most it was a... a minor altercation."

He set me on my feet once we reached the road, but only so he could grab my wrist and tow me through the night to the motel.

"It was a small, contained misunderstanding... with regrettable fisticuffs," I decided as Reed paused to grab his bag from the car before tugging me around the corner past a little alcove of vending machines toward one of the motel's numbered doors. "A low-key—seriously negligible—accidental... tussle."

The world was still spinning a little, and it was really flipping cold, except for the very hot spot on my wrist where Reed's fingers were wrapped around me.

"You're going to be the death of me, Chris Winowski," Reed muttered. "You really might."

Huh. Who knew Reed was so dramatic? I decided not to comment on it since he'd gotten me out of the tussle pretty effectively, and I figured I owed him one. Also, I had to admit that no matter how angry I was with him—and I was for sure still angry—when Reed touched me, I felt good. Grounded. Safe.

Unfortunately, I also felt lots of other things, too. Inappropriate things. Things that made me want to rub my chin against Reed's neck just to feel the bristles, and trace the hard lines of his muscles with my fingertips, and know how his lips tasted. Things that made me ache to know what it was like to have someone's body and hands on mine. Things that made my cock hard and my thoughts flutter like butter-flies in a windstorm.

Things I needed to stop thinking—and totally, absolutely *would* stop thinking—just as soon as I put some distance between myself and Reed, let my logical brain take over again, and got my cock to settle the heck down.

Unfortunately, the moment Reed opened the motel room door, I realized things weren't likely to settle down.

Not hecking likely at all.

CHAPTER SIX

REED

I used to think being an agent for the Division meant I was ready for anything. After today, I was thinking nobody in the universe could be ready for Chris Winowski.

"There's plenty of room if you'd like to sit down on the bed," I told the man standing in the corner by the window for what had to be the seventh time since we'd entered the shabby motel room.

The wood-paneled space was maybe a couple of hundred square feet—too small to hold more than a single queen-sized bed, a tiny dresser, and a huge television that had probably been the height of technology the year I was born—but the sheets were clean, and the lock on the door was sound.

"Oh. N-no, thank you," Chris replied softly, also for the seventh time. "I'm fine here."

I tilted my head back into the pillow and stared up at the textured ceiling. I'd bet that ceiling had witnessed all kinds of ridiculous shit over the years. Quick sexual encounters, arguments, possibly an illegal act or two. But I wasn't sure it had ever witnessed anything quite as ridiculous as a trained Division agent trying to coax his protectee—the same man who hadn't freaked out during a gunfight and had cheerfully provoked a fucking bar brawl—into sitting six inches away from him.

"You can't sleep standing up," I pointed out. I pressed a dripping bag of ice against my face while another sat melting against the bruise on my ribs where one of the bikers had landed a glancing blow. "You're going to have to sit sometime."

"I will," Chris agreed, eyes wide behind his glasses. "Sometime."

I huffed out a breath. "If you're gonna stand there, at least drink some fucking water."

"I d-did. Thank you. I had three glasses—"

"Then drink a fourth," I nearly growled. "Otherwise, you're gonna be hungover, the way you were throwing back shots." *Three* shots of Fireball, to be specific—you'd better believe I'd been counting—which was a lot for anyone, let alone a man who weighed next to nothing. "I'm surprised you're able to stand, period."

"I don't feel drunk anymore." He hovered in the small space between the green-and-gold-patterned curtains and the door and sounded almost regretful when he added, "I'm very much... m-myself."

No, I snorted. He wasn't. The quirky, chocolate-milk-loving, figure skating chatterbox who'd stood up to me at the safe house and again at the bar—*It's not stupid to think the best of people, Reed Sunday*—had fled the scene, leaving behind only a polite, stammering, agreeable shadow. And though I appreciated that shadow-Chris wasn't throwing himself (and therefore me) into danger at the moment, part of me missed the other version.

A lot.

I'd like to think Chris's anxiety was a normal human reaction to being in danger—a shootout and a bar brawl in one night would stress anyone out. Hell, they stressed *me* out—but that wasn't the case here. Chris had been tipsy but cheerful on the walk over from the roadhouse, our earlier angry words seemingly forgotten.

As soon as I'd opened the door and he'd seen the small room with its lone bed, though, he'd gone wide-eyed and flustered. After a quick trip to the bathroom, he'd stood awkwardly, shifting from one foot to the other. And when I'd taken off my shirt and laid down so I could apply the ice I'd retrieved from the vending area to my ribs, he'd retreated to his corner, as far from the bed as it was possible to get in the tiny space. Which meant it wasn't the proximity to actual life-threatening situations that had stressed him out; it was proximity to... me.

And my big *stupid* mouth.

I took a breath and tried to summon a patient smile. "Look, if the bed-sharing thing is freaking you out, I promise I've bunked with all four of my brothers. It's no big deal. We all survived uninjured. Except Porter," I added after a moment of thought, "but that blanket thief deserved what he got."

Chris swallowed hard.

"That was a joke," I said gently.

He nodded, eyes round.

I sighed. "Or why don't you take the bed," I offered. "I'll sleep on the floor."

"What? No. Not when you're injured, Reed." Chris gave my ribs a worried glance, then bit his lip, blushed, and looked away, obviously uncomfortable.

"Is it..." I blew out a breath. "Are you worried I might

hurt you if you get close to me? Because I wouldn't, Chris. I swear. No matter how angry I was."

His gaze swung back to mine in surprise. "No, I believe that," he said softly.

"Good," I grunted. "That's good."

Except I *had* hurt him, back at the bar, and we both knew it.

"I, uh, I wanted to say..." I cracked my neck from side to side. "What I said back at the roadhouse... about you acting..."

"Stupid?" He lifted one fine eyebrow.

I winced at the sound of that word on his lips. "Yes. That. I'm sorry. I didn't mean it, and I shouldn't have said it." I shifted in the bed, which made my ice packs fall to the mattress with a wet *plop, plop*. "I fucking hate that word. I've hated it ever since my fourth-grade teacher said it to me, and I really hate that I said it to you."

I hated that I'd seen it hit him, center mass, and I hadn't apologized immediately. Hated that I'd protected him from bullets and flying punches but hadn't protected him from my own fear and frustration.

"I was upset. And I know that's no excuse, but someone incredibly smart once told me that people sometimes say things in anger, and it doesn't make them a bad person." I gave him a winning smile as I quoted his words back to him. "They just need to apologize and make amends."

"I don't understand why you were so upset in the first place."

"Don't you? For one thing, your safety's at risk, and you're not taking it seriously—" I broke off, realizing that I was getting upset again just thinking about it. In a more conciliatory tone, I added, "I shouldn't have taken my anger out on you, though. I was thinking about that while you were off drinking with your new friends." I shook my head, remembering how quickly the women had adopted him. "The way I acted was unprofessional."

Chris lifted his chin. "And unkind."

"Yeah." My voice was rough. "The thing is, it pissed me off that you keep saying you were kidnapped. I, ah... my last job was..." I scrubbed a hand through my hair. I didn't talk about this stuff. Talking wouldn't change anything, so it was better to move on and *keep* moving. But maybe I owed him an explanation. Maybe that was how I could make amends. So I talked.

"My protectee was going to be the star witness for the prosecution in a business fraud case against her ex-husband. A few weeks before the trial was to start, she told me she'd changed her mind. She didn't want protection. My bosses figured—correctly—that she'd gotten cold feet about testifying. They wanted me to keep her under protection temporarily and give them a chance to talk her around because otherwise, her ex would walk. She argued that she had a right to change her mind, to not spend the rest of her life looking over her shoulder. She said I was holding her against her will. She begged me to let her go before anyone could talk her into anything."

Chris watched me carefully. "What happened?" he whispered.

"To her?" I shrugged. "I don't know. I like to think she crossed the border to Canada and changed her whole life around so no one, including her shitty ex-husband, could find her. That's what I'd do if I wanted to disappear."

"No. I-I mean, what happened to you?"

I snorted. "Nothing good."

"B-but you did the right thing."

Right for her? Maybe. If she stayed safe. But the case *did* crumble. Her ex went free. Justice hadn't been served.

"No, I didn't. I nearly lost my career—a career that should have always been my highest priority—in the aftermath. My priorities are back on track now, and I'll be damned if I let any of that happen again." It came out like a warning because it was. "But none of that is an excuse for what I said. So, I'm sorry. I promise I'm going to be more professional from now on."

Chris nodded slowly. "Okay."

"Okay," I repeated. But the damn man didn't move a centimeter closer or look any less wary than he had when we got here. "So... could you maybe stop trying to blend into the wallpaper or whatever you're doing? I hate to break it to you, but I can still see you."

In fact, I couldn't *stop* seeing him, which was another thing I'd realized back at the bar while Chris was pounding whiskey. Every freaking inch of Chris Winowski radiated "Notice Me, Reed Sunday," from his expressive face to his red-bitten lips to the borrowed sweatpants—*my* sweatpants—which he hitched up periodically. He was like a tiny splinter in my consciousness, a spark in my peripheral vision that kept riling me up and throwing me off my game.

I didn't only *need* to keep him safe because it was my job; I *wanted* to keep him safe because... Christ, who even knew why? Maybe because I was attracted to stubbornly loyal, bafflingly adorable miniature humans with soft, brown eyes and questionable taste in movies and television shows?

Which didn't mean I planned to act on that attraction. I didn't. *Couldn't* if I wanted to keep working for the Division. And as I'd told Chris, I loved this job. Way too much to risk it because I couldn't keep my dick in line. No piece of ass, no matter how sweet or fascinating, was worth that.

I sat up, rubbing a hand over my sore ribs—nothing broken, and they'd be fine by tomorrow—then patted the end of the bed in friendly invitation. "Come. Sit."

Chris stared at me, then stared some more. His throat clicked as he swallowed. And then he honest to God pulled the ugly curtain in front of him. "N-no, thank you. I'm comfortable right here."

"Right. Sure you are." I squeezed my eyes shut. "Look, if you want to stand all night, that's your business. But I need to make a phone call to figure out where we're going next, and then I need to sleep for at least a couple hours, so I need you to promise me you're not going to attempt another daring trellis escape the minute my back is turned."

Chris frowned. "There's no trellis here, Reed. We're on the first floor—"

"Chris," I said, louder now. "Tell me you'll stay here with me. That you'll let me protect you."

"Tonight? Oh. I mean, sure." But his eyes immediately darted to the door, giving him away.

Jesus Christ. Was this how I would finally lose my mind?

"I'm starting to think the Division was right, back in August," I told the ceiling conversationally. "Maybe I *have* taken on one job too many. Maybe I *am* losing focus. I must be if all it took was one doe-eyed, mini mobster to send me over the edge—"

Chris raised his chin. "I'm not a mobster," he said with quiet dignity. "I told you, I'm a charcuterie specialist."

The hell of it was... I believed him. Not that his uncle wasn't Dante the Cheese—pardon me, *Dante Fromadgio*—but that Chris somehow, unbelievably, wasn't aware of it. I'd fought as hard as I could to convince myself he was a liar, but somewhere around the time he'd begun calling the grizzly biker president "Mr. Knuckles"—or maybe back when he'd thought the police were hunting Kenny for his excessive zucchini? It was hard to pinpoint, really—I'd had to wave a white flag and admit defeat.

Chris Winowski was as much a criminal mastermind as I was a Disney princess, and if his uncle had raised him to be the heir to a powerful, dangerous crime dynasty, not a single bit of that training had stuck. In fact, the longer I spent with Chris, the more shocked I was that he'd existed this long without constant supervision. The man was a magnet for trouble, and he was only a danger to himself.

And, it seemed, to my sanity.

I groaned and swung my legs over the side of the bed and hunched over, bracing my elbows on my knees.

"Are you in pain?" Chris asked a moment later.

I touched a hand to my ribs again and shrugged, my gaze on the mottled green carpet. "I've had worse."

He made a *tsk*ing noise. "You really should get some rest. You said you were tired earlier, and you seem a tiny bit... overwrought?"

"Overwrought." I snorted. "Thought you said I was *disgruntled*."

"That too. I-I'm not saying that to make you feel bad," he added quickly. "Even John Ruffian might be over-whelmed after so many completely unpredictable and unavoidable occurrences in one evening. And I'm sure it must be weighing on you, too, that there's a chance I'm right about there being a mix-up with my uncle, especially now that you know I can take care of myself." After a brief pause, he added, "Though obviously it was very sweet of you to try to help, back at the bar, and you did get me out much faster than I would have on my own. I don't mean to sound unappreciative."

I glanced up on the slim chance that he was joking. He didn't appear to be. In fact, the sweet, soft expression on his face suggested he was trying in the worst possible way to... comfort me?

"It'd be a lot for anyone, Reed," he continued earnestly, knitting his fingers together. "A-and when so many tough things happen at once, it can be hard to focus on the positive, no matter how hard you try. But my nonna always said that things will look better in the morning, and that was one of the things she was definitely right about... unlike the, um, money-in-the-shoe thing."

He gave me a lopsided smile that turned his handsome face truly gorgeous and made something small and hot and utterly unwanted blossom in my chest...

Until he killed it dead by adding, "Which is why I've been thinking it's probably for the best that we say our good-byes now and get separate rooms."

"Jesus fucking Christ." I jumped to my feet, all thought of patience evaporated. "You haven't heard a word I've said, have you?" I hadn't intended to move closer to him but suddenly found myself looming over him. "We are not getting separate rooms, damn it! You're staying right where I can see you. You're staying where I can keep you safe."

Chris bit his lip. "Okay, make that a *lot* overwrought," he whispered.

I found myself wanting to laugh out loud and shake the man silly, all at the same time. Maybe I *was* overwrought.

I compromised by gripping his shoulders tightly and crowding him against the wall. "You. Are. In. Danger. Chris. I know you don't want to hear that. I know you keep trying to reframe things in your mind to pretend it's not happening. But I need you to trust me—"

He blinked up at me, his brown eyes huge behind his glasses. "I do, Reed," he insisted with utter earnestness, the kind that was going to get him and therefore me in trouble. "I do trust you. But... what if you're wrong? Even trustworthy people mess up all the time, right? Like maybe your bosses messed up and sent you to find the wrong person—"

"Because there's another Chris in Little Pippin Hollow who has an uncle named Dante Fromadgio, who also looks exactly like the driver's license photo the Division provided me of you?"

He froze for a second, like he was actually considering this, before expelling his breath in a disappointed rush. "Okay, no. Not that, I guess. But what if... what if someone investigating this whole thing gave your bosses the wrong name? What if there's a different Dante, with a different nephew, and everyone's been confused—?"

I ground my molars together. "Someone's confused, alright."

"—and if I explain this to your bosses, they'll understand, and you won't get in trouble again," he babbled, the words coming out in a panicked flow while his hummingbird hands flapped a mile a minute in the inches between us. "The last thing I want is for you to lose your job, I swear. But, but... you think I'm this criminal-adjacent person who can handle a gun and a high-speed chase. You think I'm someone brave and fierce, like you—"

"Stop," I said. "Stop talking."

"But you're going to realize that I'm not actually that guy. That I'm not *qualified* to be that guy. That I'm really a... a soft person who likes butterflies and charcuterie boards and can quote entire episodes of *John Ruffian*. And you'll be *so* upset that you wasted your time protecting me—"

"I said *stop talking*," I repeated around the gravel in my throat.

He was killing me. Fucking *killing* me. I had built defenses—sturdy ones—over the years that made me immune to threats and manipulation, but damn if they were any match for Chris's sweetness. He was so small. So warm. So infuriatingly stubborn, and stubbornly cheerful, and cheerfully infuriating.

When I leaned closer—*wait, why was I leaning closer?* —I found that he smelled like a combination of fresh air and beer and grass, which seemed to be the missing key to a lock in my brain. From this angle, the freckles across his nose looked like a map to a hidden treasure.

"Y-you know," Chris said, wheezing like he'd been doing wind sprints. "Bossiness isn't attractive. Amber said so."

"Amber?" I repeated. I watched as my hand stroked his hair, my calloused fingers catching on the silky strands.

"M-my new friend. Mrs., ah... Mrs. Knuckles?" He frowned at my lips and licked his own. "She says it's not —*oh, merciful heavens.*" His breath hitched as my fingers traced a path to his jaw. "Not at all, um..."

"Chris," I said softly. "I'm going to kiss you now."

"Oh." He swallowed and let out a puff of air. "Thank goodness."

When I lowered my head the final few inches and our lips brushed, Chris let out a stifled squeak, but before I could pull back to question him, he pushed up on his toes, wrapped his arms around my neck, plastered himself to my bare chest, and sighed longingly into my mouth.

After that, it literally didn't occur to me that I should

pull back any more than it occurred to me that I *shouldn't* run my hands over the curves of his ass and haul him up so he was braced between me and the door. I never considered the possibility of *not* running my tongue against the seam of his lips and drinking down the happy, surprised little sounds he was making and sucking on his tongue until I could no longer remember the danger he—*we*—had been in. The only thought I was capable of was "*More.*"

And holy fuck, holding Chris was like holding a live wire. He was all awkward eagerness, which was more of a turn-on than I'd ever dreamed it could be. His hands sank into my hair, and his ankles locked firmly against my ass. When I finally broke away for air, he rutted against me restlessly while his mouth explored the side of my neck.

"Oh, Reed," he panted. "Good *guh*... That is *ungh*... Oh, *uh. Wuh.* I think... I might... *Hnohnooooo!*"

He pressed his face into my shoulder as his whole body seized, then shivered, then froze, then let out an unsteady breath.

Had he just...?

"I-I... I..." Chris stammered. His feet loosened from around my back, though his hands still clung to me. "Oh, man. I can't believe I... I mean, I *can* believe it, because you're you and I'm me—" His face was beet red, and a distinct wet spot bloomed on the front of his borrowed pants. "But also, really, shouldn't the universe have limits on the number of times a person can mortify himself in one day?"

I was not the person to ask about that.

My fucking protectee had come in his pants—in *my* goddamn borrowed pants—after less than five minutes of frotting... and it had been the hottest thing I'd ever seen.

Worse than that, I wasn't far from doing the same. My

cock was hard as steel in my jeans, Dante Fromadgio's enemies could have been breaking in through the window for all I'd been paying attention, and the man whose trust I'd been trying to earn back stared at me, trembling and wide-eyed.

That was an erection-killer, right there.

"Adrenaline," I said firmly.

Chris looked up at me, eyes shining and glasses askew. "Huh?"

"Adrenaline." I made sure he was steady on his feet, then took a giant step away from him. "That's what this was. An adrenaline rush is a normal reaction in the aftermath of a life-threatening situation, and adrenaline causes arousal."

He blinked. "Does it?"

"Definitely." I reached out and adjusted his glasses because I couldn't help myself. "It's life-affirming... or tension relieving. Something. No big deal."

"Oh." He wrinkled his nose. "But you didn't—" He motioned toward my pants, and his cheeks went even redder. "If you want, I can..."

Fucking God, I wanted, but...

"No!" I said, taking another step back. "Nope. I'm... all set. You should shower so you can get to sleep." I gently grabbed his shoulders and steered him toward the bathroom with a gentle shove. "And I need to call a man about a safe house."

"N-now?" Chris demanded. He glanced at the clock on the nightstand, which read 3:47.

"No time like the present." I grabbed my T-shirt and flannel from the end of the bed where I'd thrown them and hauled them on, heedless of my bruises. "I'm gonna step outside, but I'll keep an eye on the door the entire time, so don't get any ideas." I opened the door, then paused. "I'll keep you safe, Chris. I promise."

"Right. Safe." His shoulders slumped. "Sure."

Outside, I locked the door and leaned back against it, taking a deep breath of cold air and willing my cock to deflate. The parking lot was nearly empty of cars and dark except for the neon motel sign. Across the road, though, Trickster's Roadhouse seemed back to business as usual, as though the bar fight really had been nothing more than an "accidental tussle."

I snorted, then quickly sobered.

Christ. What had I done?

So much for professionalism. So much for doing whatever it took to keep my job. I kicked a rock and watched it ping off a tree on the opposite side of the lot.

And what the fuck was I supposed to do now?

I should take myself off the job immediately. But then what? There was literally no qualified Division agent to hand this job off to. Which meant Chris would... what? Get passed on to Margot from Accounts? Get transferred to a different agency altogether? Would *they* keep him safe?

No. Not like I would.

I thunked my head back against the motel room door and made a phone call.

Seconds later, a deep, perpetually amused, and perpetually wide-awake voice answered. "Reed Sunday, as I live and breathe! You never call, you never write..."

Despite everything, I found myself giving a reasonable facsimile of a chuckle.

Oak Bartlett was a security expert and former colleague who now did private protection work, but he was also a friend... and I didn't have many of those.

"Oak," I said roughly. "I need your help."

He was instantly all business. "Talk to me, boo. What do you need?"

"My ass kicked, to start with," I muttered. "Look, I've got a situation..."

Leaning against a tree a few feet away, staring at the motel room door, I gave Oak a rundown of Chris's case, from my first contact with Janissey—God, was it really only yesterday?—through the mistaken pickup, the not-so-safe house, and the minor, low-key bar altercation.

By the end, I could tell Oak was trying—mostly unsuccessfully—not to laugh.

This was *not* the reaction I'd expected.

"Can it, Oak. There's nothing funny here," I growled.

"No? Hypervigilant, ultra-dedicated, always professional Division agent Reed Sunday, fleeing a flamingo house, only to insult his protectee, who then flounced off and started a fight with a biker gang?" Oak laughed so hard I worried he might sprain something. "Bet they won't be inviting you to do the new recruit trainings anymore."

Actually, fuck that, I *hoped* he sprained something.

"I didn't call to provide you with comedic relief," I said testily. Before thinking better of it, I added, "And I apologized to my protectee, I'll have you know."

"Oh, well, as long as you apologized." He laughed harder. "And did he accept?"

"He did, I think. At least until I, ah... kissed him," I mumbled.

Oak stopped laughing. "You... Wait, sorry, this connection is shitty. It sounded like you said you kissed him."

I said nothing.

He whistled. "Well, *shit*, Sunday."

"Yes, thank you, I know. I'm an ass. An unprofessional ass—"

"Is he cute?" Oak asked slyly.

I sputtered for a moment before finally deflecting. "Also not the reason for my call. I need a safe house. Someplace I can take this guy for a little while, where trouble can't find him and he can't find trouble. I know that's not your gig, and I know it's a lot to ask on short notice, but I don't have any way to pay for a house that's untraceable, and—"

"Chill, Sunday, I've got this. Gimme two minutes to check something."

I exhaled and stretched my neck from side to side. "Thank you."

"Of course. I owe you about twenty favors by now. Not to mention, we're *friends*," he added pointedly. "Not that you keep in touch."

"I keep in touch!" I protested. "Sort of."

"Yeah? 'Cause I heard a rumor that you had some trouble at the Division last month. That the witness just up and fled your custody, and the Powers that Be weren't pleased. Why the fuck didn't you call me?"

I huffed. "And say what? That I screwed up?"

"See, that's not how I heard the story—"

"But that's how the Powers that Be saw it." I rested my shoulder against a tall tree. "Security Through Trust, remember? If they can't trust me to obey orders, what good am I?"

"As an agent?" he asked. "Or as Reed Sunday?"

"It's the same damn thing," I said, almost sure it was true. "Now, can we change the subject, please?"

"Sure," Oak agreed easily. He paused for a beat. "So... is he cute?"

At that moment, a shadow flitted past the curtain as Chris moved around the motel room. The light turned off, and I sighed.

"Yeah, he's cute," I admitted helplessly. "He's... interesting. Funny—sometimes intentionally and sometimes not. He's sweet. And I mean genuinely kind." I realized I sounded besotted and made myself add, "He also doesn't stop talking, which is annoying as fuck, and he couldn't walk across an open field without triggering a groundhog rebellion and compelling the bumblebees to fight for him to the death. A total trouble magnet." Over the sound of Oak's cackling, I added, "But none of that matters. I shouldn't have kissed him. The Division has rules against that for a reason."

"They do," Oak agreed. "All kinds of reasons why it's a bad idea to get involved with your protectee. What interests me, though, is that you did it anyway. That you wanted to."

"I didn't *want* to," I lied. "It just... happened. It won't happen again. And before you ask, this doesn't mean I've lost my edge."

"Because that's the only reason anyone would ever leave the Division, right?" He snorted. "You don't have to mess up in order to move on, Sunday. Maybe part of you's starting to think about what happens when the job is over."

The idea was so ridiculous I laughed. "When this job's over, I'll be on to the next. That's how it goes."

"No, Reed, what happens when the *job* is over? When you realize Security Through Trust is a one-way street and you're ready for something better?"

"I won't. I said the guy's cute and we kissed, Oak. I'm not upending my entire life for *cute*. I'm not marrying the guy."

"Right, right. You're not the marrying kind."

"Jesus, no." I shuddered at the thought.

"I'll keep that in mind." He chuckled to himself. "Okay, safe house is all set. I'm sending a text to my cousin, letting him know you'll be arriving tomorrow morning. I'm giving him your real name and telling him you're my friend. He'll probably show you around the place personally. I'll text you his address."

"Hold up. Your cousin?"

"My cousin Watt. I'm sure I've mentioned him once or twice. He lives on an orchard in Copper County, New York."

"An orchard," I repeated. "Like... with apples?"

"Uh, yeah, dude. Obvi. Hey, didn't you grow up in apple country?"

"I did." I shut my eyes and bit back a groan. "I definitely did."

"Perfect! See, when I was there over Labor Day, Watt was telling me about his elderly next-door neighbor who owns a campground with a bunch of RV hookups and some cute little cabins. Used to be kind of a vacation destination, back in the day, but the owners got too old to take care of it, and the lady's husband died, and then she ended up in a nursing home or something herself. Watt's been taking care of the place, but it's a lot to keep up with when he's busy running his orchard. So he posted an ad online in some agro-tourism group to see if someone wanted to come do the clearing and renovation work in exchange for room and board and a small stipend." He snickered. "Shockingly, there've been no takers."

I was pretty sure I knew where he was going with this. "Until now?"

"Yuuuup. You'll love it, I promise. The property's really private—like, backwoods private—and the only nearby town is tiny, too."

"A small town," I said in a strangled voice. "Wow. *Perfect.*"

"O'Leary is really pretty. When I was there, Watt took me to this bar that serves the best chicken wings I've ever eaten. And I think there's a bakery—"

"Isn't there always?" I groaned.

"Oh, God, and don't get me started on the festivals. I mean, what kind of unrepentant shithead doesn't love a small-town festival?"

I almost whimpered. *Me. I was the unrepentant shithead.*

I'd just managed to shake off the dust of the Hollow, so of-fucking-course Oak was sending me to another freaking small town.

"What exactly do I have to do to fix up this campground?"

"Dunno exactly. Watt will tell you. Mow lawns, I guess? Fix cabins. Paint some stuff. Nail some stuff. Screw some stuff." Oak snorted. "Not your protectee, though, 'cause you're not gonna make *that* mistake again. No, sir. Not even if he's cute and funny and kind. Not even if he is the first protectee whose tonsils you've ever examined *orally*."

"You're hilarious," I said blandly. "Thank you so much."

But when I thought about it, being a campground caretaker wouldn't be so bad. It was private, Oak had said, which meant no chance for Chris to find himself a weed-dealing bestie or a posse of bikers' old ladies who needed a drinking buddy. Chris could relax and do… whatever charcuterie experts did on vacation while I did some light physical labor. Orchard and small town aside, it really was pretty ideal.

"Seriously, Oak, thank you so much," I repeated, this time meaning it.

"I'm always looking out for you, Sunday," he said gleefully. "You remember that, okay? Always. Looking. Out. For. You."

"Sure," I agreed, wondering why he sounded so damn happy. "I'll be in touch."

"Do that. And when you're ready to ditch the Division and come work with me in the private security business, you just let me know."

"Never gonna happen," I shot back, but Oak had already disconnected. A moment later, a text came through with Watt Bartlett's address and contact info. Just that easy.

But when I went back inside the shabby motel room, my eyes immediately traced Chris's sleeping form, curled in a ball under the covers right on the edge of the bed. He'd cleared away my ice packs and rifled through my bag, probably for another pair of pants.

Remembering why he'd needed them made my gut clench.

Silently, I crossed to him and slid his glasses off his face before setting them gently on the nightstand.

What's your story, Chris Winowski? I wondered, tightening my hands into fists to keep my fingers from running through his hair. *And what the hell are you doing to me?*

Whatever it was, I decided as I laid down carefully on top of the covers beside him, it wasn't going to be nearly as easy and straightforward as I'd imagined my redemption job would be.

It wasn't until the next day that I realized exactly how complicated things were going to get.

CHAPTER SEVEN

CHRIS

THE FOLLOWING MORNING, I was not feeling my best.

It turned out there was a price to pay for freedom, especially beer-based freedom, and that price was steep.

"Just a little further now!" Watt Bartlett called cheerfully over his shoulder. "The Wrigleys' land starts at that gate—" He lifted one big paw and pointed toward a fence that seemed to be miles away. "—and the campground itself is just through those trees—" The paw lifted toward the forest all the way on the horizon. "—so not too far."

"Not far at all," I echoed. I pushed sweat-damp hair out of my face, ignored my rolling stomach, and dredged up a weak smile for the man—a cousin of a friend of his, Reed had said, though Watt was tall and broad, bearded and flanneled enough to have been a missing Sunday brother. "I just love walking. I can walk for miles and miles."

Reed, who walked beside me—looking fresh as a daisy and disgustingly handsome despite being bruised and unshaven and loaded down with all our baggage, including a soft cooler we'd bought at the grocery store in town and some me-sized clothes I'd purchased at a nearby thrift store —shot me a look that called me a liar.

It wasn't a lie, though. Not exactly. I *did* love walking.

I just maybe loved it a little less when I was wearing my big sweater and another pair of borrowed too-big pants, and the autumn day was summer hot, and I was scrambling to keep up with two men forged in the same giant mold, which meant taking two running steps for every one of their long strides, while my stomach begged me to leave it behind and carry on without it. I knew my cheeks were bright red, and the little rivulets of sweat rolling down my back beneath the sweater were *not* my favorite-ever sensation.

I wasn't going to complain, though. Uncle Danny always said nobody liked a complainer.

And I was definitely not going to complain where Reed could hear me and think I needed him to, I don't know, pick me up and carry me or whatever.

I lifted my chin stubbornly and shot him a look right back, but Reed merely grunted and said nothing.

Nothing, I was quickly learning, often accompanied by a grumpy grunt, was one of Reed's very favorite things *to* say, along with "It's no big deal, Chris," and "I'll keep you safe, Chris," and "Listen, Chris..." the latter of which actually translated to "Do as I say."

But the strange, disobedient compulsion that had come over me in the bar last night was still in effect—The leftover effects of the alcohol? The silver lining of a hangover? I wasn't sure—and the more Reed Sunday told me to do something, the less I wanted to do it.

"You know, we really should talk at some point," I murmured low enough so only Reed could hear.

Reed ignored me just as he'd been doing all morning.

"About the kiss," I went on. "*Our* kiss. Last night."

Another grunt.

"I think we should discuss—" My toe caught on a piece of gravel covering the path around Watt's raised garden beds, but I managed to catch myself before I stumbled.

Reed looked at me in concern, but when it was clear I was steady, he looked away again. "We discussed it when it happened. I told you it was no big deal."

I clenched my hand into a fist. "You did say that. You did. But that's not a discussion. Discussions are supposed to involve you sharing your thoughts and feelings about a thing and then asking me my thoughts and feelings about a thing. And, um, not to argue with you—since I hate arguing—but it *was* kind of a big deal. You kissed me," I reminded him unnecessarily. "And you... I mean, we... I mean, *I*..." I cleared my throat. What was it called when someone held you in his big, strong arms and moved his cock against yours so perfectly that the whole world went silent, and your brain exploded into fractals of light, and you felt more aware of yourself—more awake—than you ever had before? I didn't know, so I fell back on what Mrs. Rose's romance novels always called it. "I... *released.*"

Reed heaved a sigh heavy enough to make the trees in Watt's orchard bend. "I know," he said in a low voice. "But I shared my thoughts and feelings. I *think* it was caused by an adrenaline rush." He side-eyed me, jaw set like concrete. "I *feel* like it will not be repeated."

"Oh." This... was disappointing.

When I'd gotten in Reed's car yesterday, I'd been prepared for a hookup... or, at least, as prepared as a person with zero practical experience could be. I'd expected I'd sort of follow Reed's lead and go along with whatever he wanted. Any way the man wanted to touch me or kiss me would have been fine.

Now, though... now I had *opinions*. I wanted Reed Sunday to give me more of those drugging kisses. I wanted his hands on me again. I wanted him sprawled nearly on top of me in bed, his hard cock against my thigh, like he'd been when I'd woken up in the motel this morning... though, ideally, without Reed's eyes flying open in sleepy horror, or him muttering oaths and apologies as he fled to the bathroom before I'd woken up enough to enjoy the moment. Next time, I wanted to make *Reed* lose control.

But all of that only worked if Reed wanted a next time.

"Not to be repeated," I agreed, trying not to sound as sad as I felt. "Good to know."

"Did *you* have thoughts or feelings you wanted to discuss about this?" Reed sounded about as enthusiastic as I would if invited to go free climbing. Naked. In a blizzard.

"N-no. Nope." I waved a hand airily. "No feelings whatsoever."

Now, see, *this* was a lie.

I glanced sideways again. A breeze caressed Reed's thick brown hair and plastered his T-shirt to his thick chest. Just the sight of him made my mouth go dry.

I couldn't help asking, "You're *sure* it won't be repeated?"

This earned me a full head-turn. Reed surveyed me from head to toe, and his eyes went soft, but when he spoke, his voice was firm. "Positive. I'm a professional, Chris, and I won't kiss you again under any circumstances. That's not something you have to worry about. Okay?"

I'm more worried about you not *kissing me, but okay.*

Reed's words were an important reminder, though, that he wasn't with me because he wanted to be; he was with me because he thought I couldn't take care of myself. In fact, if it hadn't been for him thinking he had to protect me, our lives would never have intersected in the first place. Which meant I should probably be thinking about how to, you know, *dissect* us rather than fantasizing about us, erm, intersecting further.

I knew Reed's feelings about us going our separate ways since on *this* particular topic, he had plenty to say. He was convinced I was the person he'd been sent to guard, that my uncle was in witness protection, and that Danny was a criminal who was working out a plea deal to testify against his "enemies," who were now out to get me.

I... I believed that he believed that. I truly did.

Reed was kind, and smart, and trustworthy, and he made some compelling arguments. It was pretty clear I was the guy he'd been sent to protect—I blamed being flustered yesterday for my silly suggestion that I might not be. And there were many facts to support his story, like the wacky coincidence that my uncle was on a never-ending vacation cut off from all communication at the same time Reed claimed he was in witness protection, and the way those bikers last night had known my uncle's name and feared it, which I couldn't explain away.

But unlike Reed, I knew Danny. I *knew* he was a good person. It showed in the way he loved me—in the way his eyes got misty when he looked at me and said I looked "just like Carmelita" and how he'd sometimes run a hand over my head, back when I was younger, and say, "Ah, Christoforo, you're heart of my heart." I knew it in the way he'd let me cheat at poker when I was a kid but had put a stop to that when I turned thirteen because "A true Fromadgio is honorable." I knew it from the way he worried about me when I was bullied for being stammer-y and shy and in the way he'd taught me that if a person has good character, is responsible and considerate, keeps his head down and thinks before he speaks—which I remembered to do almost always, except where Reed Sunday was concerned—that other people's opinions didn't matter.

So no matter how much I instinctively trusted Reed, I had to believe he was acting on bad information. Danny was not a criminal.

It was possible that Danny was in protective custody, though. Someone might have threatened or lied to get him involved in something shady or blamed him for something he hadn't done. Maybe Danny was testifying to set things right. In all of those scenarios, it was all too believable that Danny wouldn't have told me because he knew I'd worry.

So until I figured out what was actually happening, I'd agreed to go along with Reed's plan and come to the safe house—erm, safe campground?—at least until I figured out what the heck was going on with my uncle and how I could help fix it.

The fact that this also gave me more time with Reed was—seriously, no kidding—neither here nor there. I wasn't even thinking about that.

Much.

And if it just so happened that I was determined to be cheerful and display a John-Ruffian-like competence, to not complain or seem needy even if it killed me, and to show that I was totally capable of taking care of myself... well, that had nothing to do with Reed or me wanting him to stop seeing me as a professional responsibility so he'd kiss me again either.

Definitely not.

To prove this point, I swiped a hand over my sweaty face and spoke my next words firmly. "So, um, about the whole thing where you think my uncle is a felon—"

"Oh sweet Jesus, not again," Reed groaned. "I am not

going through this again. I'd rather talk about the fucking kiss."

I turned to stare at him. Wait, was that an option?

No, Chris. For heaven's sake. Think of Danny.

"Because I am truly sorry for taking advantage of you," Reed went on. "And I will not, not ever, under pain of death, kiss you again—"

"Yes, I got that," I said, a little edge in my voice. "You've made your position quite clear. And for what it's worth, you didn't take advantage of me, so I don't want your apologies." I waited a beat and added, "What I want is... *proof.*"

"Proof?"

"Yes. Like, evidence about what Danny's been involved in. I guess some of the evidence is maybe, um... classified or whatever. At least, it is on TV. So I'm not asking for that. Just... I don't know, a list of the things he's been accused of. The people you think are involved. Because you asked me to stay with you based on your word alone, and I agreed... but I don't think it's unreasonable for me to want to see that stuff, do you?" I peered up at him.

Reed didn't dismiss the idea right away. "I don't have anything like that right now," he said slowly, "but... yes. That's reasonable. I'll get it for you."

"Okay." The intensity in his eyes made my stomach flutter. "Thanks."

"Thanks?" Reed repeated. He narrowed his eyes suspiciously. "That's it?"

"Well, yes." I blinked up at him. "Unless you wanted to discuss the kiss more?"

"Fuck, no," he said fervently, which, honestly, was kind of hurtful.

Fine, then.

I lifted my chin and hurried to catch up with Watt, ignoring Reed's impatient huffing.

"You've got some beautiful sedum growing here, Watt," I called, pleased that I only sounded a little bit breathless. I pointed at the nodding purple heads of the plants in the bed next to us. "*Autumn Joy*, right? It's one of my favorite annuals."

Watt turned so he was walking backward—which was pretty impressive since I was having trouble covering the acres facing forward—and beamed at me from beneath a bright blue cap that said *Organic Farmers are Out Standing in Their Fields*. "It is! You a gardener, Chris?"

"Oh, um, no… I wouldn't say that. My uncle is, though, and I've helped him out."

From behind me, Reed gave a throaty growl like he disagreed, or disapproved of something, or possibly had spotted a bear in the woods. Since he didn't speak actual words, I decided it wasn't my problem, and I continued ignoring him.

"Ah. Well, the sedum was actually my sister Iris's choice. She was pregnant a couple years ago and begged me to grow cantaloupes." He stopped walking—mercifully—and gave a good-natured eye roll at the mostly empty bed behind the sedum's tall, nodding heads of pink flowers. "Do you know how difficult it is to grow cantaloupe in this part of New York?"

"Um… pretty darn difficult, I'd guess?"

His lips twitched behind his beard. "Pretty darn difficult," he agreed. "After a few years of experimentation, a friend of mine suggested the melons weren't self-pollinating properly, so—"

"So you needed to plant some flowers nearby to attract bees and butterflies!" I finished as understanding dawned.

"And your sister picked sedum? What a great idea. My uncle used to plant marigolds near his tomatoes for the same reason."

"This year, we had a bumper crop of cantaloupe, just in time for Iris's second pregnancy." He grinned. "Only took four years to make it happen."

"Worth it," I said happily. "Cantaloupe's really an underappreciated fruit. *Great* on a charcuterie board."

Watt smiled so hard his eyes crinkled, which was really kind of sweet. "You'll enjoy the little gift basket Iris left for you guys at the campground." He considered me for a moment. "You know, I do some gardening classes—kind of a community outreach thing—and that friend I mentioned tricked me into running a booth at the local farmer's market where I diagnose people's plant maladies. Since you're going to be in town a while, I'd love it if you'd—"

Reed cleared his throat and pointedly shifted his gear from one shoulder to the other. "Sorry to interrupt," he said, not sounding sorry at all, "but could you show us to the campground before you chitchat?"

"Ah, shit. Sorry, Sunday. I'm sure you two want to, ah... relax." Watt gave us a little smirk that had Reed and I exchanging a befuddled glance after he resumed walking. "You sure you don't want me to take one of those bags?"

Reed grunted a negative. "Just eager to get settled in. We spent a lot longer in town than I'd planned."

I flushed. "I couldn't help it," I explained to Watt. "O'Leary was so pretty, and everyone was *so* nice. We met this incredibly tall man outside the bakery who had the biggest dog I've ever seen, and I couldn't *not* pet him and chat with him for a while—er, chat with the man, not the dog."

Watt nodded. "That'll be Ash walking Cupcake. Silly

name for a mastiff, but he and Cal insisted. They own the bakery."

"Oh, and I had the best conversation about imported cheeses with this really adorable man at Lyon's Imperial Market, and he appreciated my advice so much, he said to stop by his shop and he'd give me free flowers—"

"Best guess, that was Micah." Watt shook his head. "Poor guy's been trying to fancy up our football-watching parties for a couple years, but it's not working so far."

"And the sweetest, friendliest guy gave me a flyer about a bulb-planting demonstration he's doing at the Pumpkin Festival the Saturday after next. Were you aware that there's going to be an actual *festival of pumpkins?*" I demanded excitedly.

"I was." Watt outright grinned, making his kind face even kinder. "And the man you're talking about was probably Constantine—the friend I mentioned earlier. He's also Micah's husband."

"Husband!" I said, delighted. "Are there a lot of LGBTQ people around here?"

"Oh yeah. Loads in O'Leary and plenty in Copper County, too. It's a really accepting place. Some of my best friends are gay and bi. In fact, my buddy Parker set up a social group, if you're interested—"

Reed gave another loud grunt, this one accompanied by a narrow-eyed glare at Watt, who, inexplicably, chuckled.

I shot Reed a look over my shoulder. He seemed to be getting progressively grumpier as the day went on, and I didn't understand it. He'd been borderline rude to every one of the guys who'd struck up a conversation with me that day.

I would have teased him about still being a bit overwrought, but he probably would've only grunted at me some more.

"Ha. Sorry, man." Watt held up his hands. "I understand, believe me. I was in your shoes once, sort of, though it's been a while." He gave us an indulgent smile. "Nearly there now."

I wasn't sure what Watt understood, exactly. The complex grunty language of grumpy people, perhaps? Maybe it was only taught to folks who were bearded, and buff, and neither talkative nor vertically challenged. If so, I wished someone would clue me in because I did not—seriously, no kidding, did *not*—understand Reed Sunday's shifting moods.

In my hurry to keep pace with Watt, I didn't notice a large boulder in my path, and this time, I wasn't fast enough to catch myself. But before I even had time to contemplate hitting the ground, Reed's arm shot out from behind, and *he* caught me. "Careful," he murmured, pulling me against him for a steadying moment. "Do you need us to slow down?"

My heart beat so hard I could feel it in my throat, and my stomach swooped like I was still in mid-fall, but I didn't think any of that was related to me tripping.

"N-no, I'm fine." I tried not to breathe in the scent of Reed's woodsy cologne, in case it made me spout nonsense like it had yesterday. "I'm a very good walker. I've been walking for years."

Okay, maybe the cologne wasn't entirely to blame for my nonsense-spouting.

Reed pressed his lips together like he was fighting a laugh, but as quickly as he'd caught me, he released me, and his grumpy frown returned. "Let's go," he said, all business.

See? Seriously, *so* confusing.

My fingers twitched to touch him some more, but his

whole demeanor said "back off," so I hurried to catch up to Watt again, paying attention to my feet this time... which meant I nearly plowed into Watt when he stopped suddenly and spread his arms wide.

"Here we are! Welcome to your new home away from home."

We stood in the middle of an overgrown field of rye and bluestem crisscrossed with dirt paths. A semicircle of trees bordered half the field—cottonwood and birch, pine and maple—with a few small, gray-shingled sheds peeking out at intervals. To the right was a low building—a slightly larger version of the sheds—with weathered Adirondack chairs arranged in the waist-high grass out front. Beyond that was an unpaved road that led uphill past a comfortable, Craftsman-style house before disappearing into yet more trees.

"That's the driveway," Watt said, following my gaze. "Follow that up the hill and you'll come to the main road, a little further down from the turnoff to my place. And that's the Wrigleys' house over there." He pointed at the Craftsman. "Oak set up a security system in case anyone decides to pinch their antique kaleidoscope collection, so the house itself is off-limits, but the rest of this place is all yours for as long as you want to stay."

"All ours?" I said, turning in a wide-eyed circle. Bees buzzed through the grasses, and crickets chirped like it was still summer, but the thick stands of trees promised cool shade and hidden treasures to discover. "Wow!"

"All ours," Reed repeated, shifting the cooler on his shoulder and dragging the toe of his boot through the overgrown grass. "Wow."

"It needs a little work," Watt allowed. "I've kept up with it as much as I could since old Abe died and Mrs. Wrigley had a stroke a couple years ago, but it's a lot for one person to do part-time, especially during apple season. I mowed a couple times this summer, and my son Derry and his friends cleared some brush back in June. He *says* it's because the lake access on our property's too stony, but I know it's because—"

"Wait," I interrupted. "Pardon, did you say there's a *lake*?"

Watt's smile warmed. "Copper Lake. Prettiest spot around. Even the O'Learians agree..." He quirked an eyebrow. "At least the smart ones do."

"Copper," Reed said thoughtfully. "Is there a copper mine nearby? Or was there, at some point?"

"Nah." Watt adjusted his ball cap. "Some of the first European settlers to this area were big into butterflies, and they found the area around the lake is inundated with them every summer. So the name comes from the—"

"Copper butterfly!" I exclaimed. "Like the American copper and the scarce copper and the bronze copper. Not the metal!"

"Exactly." Watt beamed like I'd just passed some kind of test, and I grinned back.

Reed grunted impatiently.

Once again, I ignored him. He was the one who'd asked about the name in the first place, for gosh's sake.

"I think it's cool to have a whole county named after butterflies," I said to make up for Reed's lack of enthusiasm over this cool fact.

"Actually, Copper County's not a county," Watt explained. "It's a town and a tiny one at that. Even smaller than O'Leary, population-wise."

"Not just small but *tiny*?" Reed said. "How... great."

"It is," Watt agreed. "See, we used to be part of Piermonte, back when Piermonte was a huge sprawling town.

But then Titan Security bought up some land to build their headquarters, and a buncha people moved in, and they built a Costco and a Mega-Wegs and a Massage Envy, and folks started calling that part of town Piermonte Village, and this area around Copper Lake became known as 'Copper County,' and there was a municipal split, which is kinda like a town divorce, and..." He waved one huge hand. "Anyway. We didn't end up with much. Our kids go to the regional schools, and we do most of our business in O'Leary, which is closer to us than the Village anyhow, but we got the lake and all the houses and families around it, which was the important part."

"And now you have a *town* named after a lake that's named after a butterfly," I pointed out.

Watt smiled. "Exactly." He pointed past the little sheds to a gap in the trees. "About a hundred feet back on that path through the woods, you'll find the campground's dock and a little beach. Some of the local retirees go fishing there in the mornings, but I'm not sure they catch much. They mostly sit there and enjoy the view. For my money, though, the best view of the water on the whole property is from right about..." He ambled over to the driveway, walked uphill a few paces, and squinted at the trees like he was assessing. "*Here*. Come see."

I hurried toward him, and Reed followed, dropping the gear he was carrying on the grass. Both of us peered obediently at the trees like Watt had.

After a second, Reed's face creased in a reluctant but genuine smile. "Huh. It *is* pretty."

Even standing on my tiptoes, though, and moving this way and that, I couldn't see anything but branches. It reminded me of staring at those Magic Eye puzzle books when I was a kid, when everyone else would *ooh* and *aahh*, and I'd wonder what the fuss was all about.

"Hmm," I said doubtfully. "Maybe I'll just go down and check out the view from the dock later—"

Reed nudged my hip. "Come on. I'll give you a boost."

I hesitated. I could think of nothing less John-Ruffian-competent than a man standing in an open field needing a boost.

But Reed didn't seem put off. He squatted slightly and patted one thigh like he boosted vertically challenged folks all the time. "Put your foot here and lean your hand on my shoulder," he commanded.

Oh, man. *Stay down*, I warned my dick firmly. *Don't get ideas.*

"So bossy," I sighed as I complied. "Like this?"

"Yup. Now, lift." He wrapped his arm tightly around my waist and straightened, lifting me easily, until I was plastered to his side with my feet dangling a crucial foot or two off the ground. "Can you see?"

I nodded, but I couldn't actually answer out loud. The sight was too glorious for words.

The cottonwoods on this side of the lake had just started to change color, framing the sliver of shining water in green and gold like a painting in a book, while the trees on the opposite side were already a half-turned riot of russet and scarlet and neon yellow. A warm breeze made the trees whisper like they were having a cozy chat and set the lake sparkling. And when I sucked in a deep breath, the air smelled like...

"Honey," I said in satisfaction, closing my eyes and digging my fingers into the meat of Reed's shoulder. "Smell that? That's sweet alyssum. There must be some growing around here. It's good for your lungs, Nonna used to say."

"Your nonna said a lot of shit," Reed said softly. "Not sure I'd take her medical advice."

I laughed. "She did make herbal remedies sometimes, but I think with the alyssum, the cure comes mostly from breathing it in. It's relaxing." I opened my eyes and looked down at him. "Don't you feel it?"

Reed looked up at me, which was a novel sensation, and his fingers tightened at my waist. "Yeah," he said roughly. "I think I—"

Watt snickered, and I whirled to face him, almost falling out of Reed's arms. Somehow, I'd forgotten we weren't alone.

Reed straightened and set me down gently, then stepped two paces away, scowling at the ground like it had hurt his feelings.

"Oh, don't mind me." Watt rocked back and forth on his heels. "I remember those days fondly. Just a couple more things before I get out of your hair. First... did Oak happen to mention that the campground has become a teen hangout?"

Reed frowned sharply. "No. In fact, he specifically said this place was private. Remote."

"It is, which is why the kids like it." Watt shrugged. "Don't tell me you and your friends didn't have a secret place where you'd drink beer and fuck around when you were a kid."

Reed grunted and shrugged, conceding the point. I nodded sagely, too, though if the kids back in New Jersey had a secret place, I hadn't known it.

"Most of 'em are good kids," Watt went on. "They'll leave if you remind them they're trespassing. And aside from swimming and drinking, they don't cause any trouble... although someone did tag a couple of the cabins with graffiti last spring." He pointed toward the little sheds, which I now saw had miniature windows and chimneys, like tiny houses. "Derry won't tell me who it was, though. The little shit's all, 'Dad, I'm nearly seventeen. I have it under control.'" Watt's tone was wry but affectionate. "Anyway, if things ever do get out of hand, you can call the cops, and someone will do a drive-by."

"No worries. We can totally handle it," I assured him.

Reed shot me a look. "*I* can handle it," he corrected.

I tried not to roll my eyes.

"Apologies it's not in better shape and that I don't have more to offer besides the small stipend. Unfortunately, the next of kin is a selfish jackass out in California who can't be bothered to show up." He exhaled and pressed his lips together. "But the less said about Jasper Wrigley, the better."

"Aw. That's too bad." My mouth twisted in sympathy. "I mean, too bad for her, obviously. My uncle Danny says family is the most important thing in the world. But don't worry, Watt. You can take our stipend and put it toward renovation costs. I'm happy to do it for free."

"You are?" Watt said.

"You are?" Reed lifted an eyebrow.

"Yes, of course," I said. "Fixing this place up will be its own reward."

Reed glanced around the majestic clearing, but I got the feeling he wasn't seeing all the potential I saw. The next words out of his mouth confirmed this. "I appreciate you hooking us up with a place to stay, Watt, but this is a bit more work than I imagined. We'll need supplies and tools and whatnot."

Watt nodded. "I'll tell Hen Lattimer at the hardware store you can charge stuff to my account."

"We can do it," I assured Watt, laying a comforting hand on his forearm. "I'm *very* handy."

"You are?" Watt asked, pleased.

"You are?" Reed repeated. His eyes narrowed warningly on the spot where my hand touched Watt... which, honestly, was ridiculous. Did he think Watt posed a danger? Because, if so, he was not only bossy but delusional.

"I am." I lifted my chin. "I am a very competent individual, Reed."

Watt rubbed his lips together like he was fighting a grin. "Do what you can," he repeated. "I'm sure you there'll be plenty *inside* the caretaker cabin to keep you occupied. We've done as much as we can to make it comfortable, including bringing in a new mattress." He gave us another one of those winks I didn't understand. "I was newly married once, too."

"I'm sure the cabin's adorable," I agreed, "but I won't want to be inside much when I could be exploring the lake and the woods and the..." I stopped and stared at Watt. "P-pardon, did you say... *married*?"

I glanced at Reed, but his body had frozen unnaturally still, and his expression gave nothing away.

"Yeah, I was married." Watt ran a calloused hand over his beard. "Don't look so surprised. I'm a lot like the campground, okay? I need a little work, but I used to be pretty."

"What? N-no, you're very handsome, Watt," I assured him. "Very." He really was, especially with his hands tucked in his pockets like they were then, which showed off the corded forearms peeking out from the sleeves of his rolled-up Henley. I shook my head. *Not the point, Chris.* "But you said *married* like you thought... as though Reed and I were..."

Watt looked back and forth between us, a pucker

between his eyebrows. "Oak's message said, 'The Sundays are newlyweds looking for a place to spend their honeymoon.' Did he get it wrong?"

"Oh. Ha. Yes. That's not, um—" I broke off with an *eep* as Reed wrapped his big arm around my waist and hauled me against him with a little jiggle that clearly meant *be quiet*.

"Sweetie. There's no need to keep it to ourselves," he said. "Since Oak's clearly told Watt the whole story."

Sweetie?

Wait... what whole story?

"Uh." I glanced up at Reed. "When you say *the whole story*, you mean..."

"I mean..." He narrowed his eyes in warning. "Watt knows we're married."

Married?

Me?

To... Reed?

What in the...?

Reed jiggled me again, this time to make me start talking.

"Oh. Ha! Right." I chuckled faintly. "*That* story! Yup. That's us. Married, married, married. So married! *Super* married."

"It's a big change, and it's taking my babydoll a little while to get used to it," Reed told Watt apologetically. "We haven't known each other long. It was kind of a whirlwind romance from the moment we met. Isn't that right?" The man gave me another jiggle... which, honestly, was excessive.

I was a terrible liar, and I knew it, but I was trying my best to process what was happening here with no information, and jiggling me wasn't like flipping a hecking on-off switch.

"Very much like a whirlwind." I glared up at Reed, daring him to jiggle me again. "Actually, pookie bear, it's reminded me quite a bit of season five, episode six of *John Ruffian: Pretender*, where John wakes up in a—"

"Mirror universe!" Watt crowed. He clapped a hand to his hat. "Oh, shit yeah. Where the sky is green and the coffee is blue, and suddenly, he's a notorious criminal who needs to stay one step ahead of the law by stealing cars until he can figure out how to get back to his own world?"

I smiled, delighted. "Oh my gosh! You're a *John Ruffian* fan, too?"

"Pfft. Who isn't? Awesome fucking show," Watt enthused. "My favorite was season one, though, where he was—"

Reed let out a protracted grunt, and his scowl was hotter than the sun. "If we could get back to reality for *just* a second—" he prompted.

"For a certain definition of reality," I muttered, low enough for only Reed to hear.

"—what my honeybear and I really need is some privacy, Watt," Reed went on. He forced a smile. "A break from work and stress so we can, you know, focus on our relationship and, ah... discuss shit." He scratched his beard. "Chris is all about discussions. Aren't you, love muffin?"

Somebody grunted angrily.

I was shocked to realize this time, the grunter was *me*.

"Discussions are a good thing." Watt gave me an approving look. "Communication's vital, or your little issues will snowball into bigger ones, and then you'll find yourselves snapping at each other over the slightest provocation. Believe me, I know."

I was pretty sure Watt had no idea. No one in my life had ever made me feel the way Reed did. Angry and argumentative, but *seen*. Protected and safe, but frustrated. Wanted—maybe? At least a little?—but also literally *aching* with want.

I clenched my fists. "It's funny you should say that, Watt," I said sweetly. "I knew a man once who ended up married to the first person he'd ever kissed, even though that person later claimed the kiss was a regrettable, no-big-deal mistake and never wanted to discuss it again."

Reed frowned. "The first person—?"

Watt frowned, too. "Wow. That's... concerning."

"It *is*," I agreed. "It is concerning. And also, this man's husband *grunted*."

"Grunted?" Watt glanced between Reed and me again, this time suspiciously. "About what?"

"About nothing. About everything. He grunted when his husband wanted to discuss things with him but also grunted when his husband discussed things with other people. Just *grunt, grunt, grunt*, all day long. Can you imagine?"

"Yes, definitely." Watt lifted his cap and scratched his head. "Wait. I mean... no?"

"Angel cake," Reed bit out. "Maybe we should—"

"Like, can you imagine if you were *married* to a person who frowned incomprehensibly every time you mentioned your favorite television show, or expressed enthusiasm for pumpkins, or had a polite conversation about love and trust with the head of a motorcycle organization? Serious lack of communication right there, huh?"

"Lover, Watt has work to get back to, I'm sure." Reed tried to do the warning jiggle again, but I was ready this time and refused to be moved.

"Or what if your *husband* cut you off every time you tried to talk about your beloved uncle who raised you to be a hardworking person who never—or, like, hardly ever, except for a few select, forgettable incidents—caused trouble? Wouldn't that warrant a discussion?" I demanded.

"Wow." Watt looked a bit nonplussed, but he nodded. "Yeah. I guess I'd, ah, have a lot of communication work to do in that case."

"You would," I agreed. "And what if—*mmmpfh*." A pair of soft, warm lips crashed into mine, and a pair of strong arms wrapped around me tightly, stealing my words, stealing my breath, stealing my thoughts.

The kiss was desperate. Bruising. Freeing. It made my knees weak and the world around me fade into blurry colors. He tasted like frustration and helpless amusement and longing all at once, and man oh man, it was a heady combination. I wrapped my arms around his neck and clung to him as it went on and on, softening and slowing until I couldn't help but seek just a little bit more.

When he eased back a few moments later, I pressed my fingers to my lips and realized that I might not understand his grunts, but there was one way in which Reed and I seemed to communicate just fine.

This time when he released me, he tucked me back against his side like he was proving a point, and I took a deep, gulping breath of his woodsy cologne, very much enjoying whatever point he was proving.

When I looked up, Watt was busy squinting at the sky like the clouds had become very interesting.

"Sorry about that," Reed said, though he didn't sound sorry. "My *husband* is hard to resist, especially when he's passionate about something."

Watt's mouth tilted up in a lopsided grin. "And that

makes you a lucky man, doesn't it?" He punched Reed lightly in the shoulder. "Congratulations, Reed, and welcome to Copper County."

He turned to me. "And congratulations to you, too, Chris Sunday. I have a feeling you're going to like it around here." He winked again, but this time, it wasn't knowing, just... friendly. "And I think Copper County's definitely going to like you."

Unfortunately for Reed's peace of mind, it turned out Watt was right.

—————

CHAPTER EIGHT

REED

It had happened again.

I woke in the tiny wood-paneled bedroom of the caretaker cabin with a warm, comfortable vanilla-scented weight against me, soft snores floating over my bare chest, and my cock hard enough to drill for water.

I groaned silently.

How. The. Fuck?

The first time I'd woken up in this situation—or the first time *in this cabin*, at least, I mentally corrected—I'd been honestly shocked. The night we arrived, I'd gone to sleep on the little pink-and-green-striped love seat in the living area after a protracted argument about sleeping arrangements with my protectee, who had a fuckton of opinions for a man who claimed he hated arguing.

Chris had pointed out that the love seat was less than half the length of my body and seemed to be upholstered in burlap, that I was still bruised up from the fight at the roadhouse, that he'd fit there better than I would if I insisted on sleeping separately. He'd also claimed that he had no problem with us sharing the bed—"You told me you'd bunked with all your brothers, Reed! You said it was no big deal!"—which was a hell of a change from his wide-eyed, stammering reluctance to get within two feet of me back at the motel *and* from the way he'd snarkily called me on my shit when Watt had showed us around the place.

I'd stood firm, though, even when he'd given me the pursed-lipped, roll-eyed glare that I was coming to think of as Chris's "Bossiness is Unattractive, Reed" look. I was the protector, I'd reminded him. I'd sleep closer to the door, end of discussion.

What I hadn't admitted was that given my predilection for kissing him—twice now, for fuck's sake, and the second time had been purposeful and premeditated and achingly arousing because, apparently, I *liked* Chris snarky and angry every bit as much as I liked him sweet and cheerful— sleeping next to him would be a *very* big deal...

And a really bad idea.

Which was why it had come as such a shock when I'd woken up the next morning in Chris's bed with the quilt I'd been using on the sofa neatly spread across the two of us, almost like I'd laid it over us intentionally.

I'd managed to sneak back to the living room with Chris none the wiser, but the slip had troubled me. *A lot.* Had I taken to sleepwalking? That was not only a huge lapse of control but a massive liability in my line of work.

So the next night, after we'd spent the day exploring the property and its ten ruined cabins and eaten a "quick little charcuterie dinner" Chris had thrown together that involved salami rosettes and thinly sliced fans of Watt's homegrown cantaloupe like something out of a magazine, I'd taken precautions.

"Make sure you close your bedroom door tonight," I'd told Chris fake-casually. "It might be chilly in the morning, and you'll be better insulated that way. If it stays cold, I'll need to chop some kindling and figure out how to get this little woodstove working."

Chris had been surprisingly agreeable, calling it a "great plan" and even gifting me a sweet smile and a "Sleep well, Reed!" before going to bed. I'd watched him close the door, for heaven's sake.

And yesterday morning when I'd woken, the door had remained closed...

But somehow, I'd been on the other side of it, with Chris's face buried in my neck and one small hand tangled in my hair.

That time, I hadn't been quite as lucky when I'd tried to slither out from under the quilt—my freaking sofa quilt, *again*—because Chris had woken up. To my relief, he hadn't seemed freaked-out to find me there, though. Hadn't been angry. Hadn't even made a snarky comment. He'd just given me a little kiss on the cheek and a teasing "Good morning, husband!" before heading for the kitchen, chatting cheerfully about how "You probably won't need to worry about the stove since Henry at the hardware store says it's supposed to be sunny and summer-hot this weekend!" and "Oh, hey, can we drive back to town again today and get more fruit?" like me being in his bed was totally normal.

But then, Chris seemed to be taking *everything* about this situation in stride. Living in a drafty cabin so tiny you could reach over and turn on the kitchen faucet without leaving the love seat? "So cozy!" Renovating little shacks in the woods? "These are going to be so pretty! Let's make a supply list!" Meeting a dozen inquisitive strangers during our quick (read: long as fuck) supply trip to town because fucking Watt had either failed to get my message about "privacy" or chosen to ignore it, and now everyone wanted to meet the "honeymooners of Copper County"? "Hi! I'm Chris Sunday"—one small but strong arm around my waist —"and this is my, um, h-husband, Reed."

Hell, Chris was even taking the situation with his uncle well.

He steadfastly refused to believe Dante was guilty of anything until he saw the proof, of course, but that didn't seem unreasonable to me. In his shoes, I'd have wanted the same. And Chris had been patient about getting it, too. Though he reminded me daily—at a minimum—that I hadn't yet fulfilled my promise, he hadn't given me any ultimatums... yet.

And in the meantime, he talked about Dante constantly when we were alone, telling me stories from his childhood. Some were normal stories, like Dante teaching Chris the cheese business and the intricacies of wine pairings. Others were silly stories, like his uncle's commitment to composting but his squeamishness about worms. The rest were seriously WTF stories Chris somehow thought were cute, like when he'd informed Dante he was gay, only for Dante to nod, stroke his mustache, and suggest an arranged marriage with a nice boy.

I figured Chris was hoping to convince me that Dante was way too good an uncle to possibly be guilty of any crimes, like the two things were mutually exclusive, but I didn't have the heart to tell him it wasn't working.

And the stories were definitely helping me understand Chris better.

So when he said things like, "I trust you, Reed, I do... I just can't make it make sense, you know?" with an anxious little frown on his forehead, like he wanted to make sure *I* wasn't upset or taking his mistrust personally... I believed him. And though it shouldn't have meant a damn to me, it did.

All in all, it felt like Chris had accepted the reality of our situation over the past two days and was trying to make the best of it, adapting and settling in to our cover story like he was the professional of the two of us.

I... wasn't doing as well.

I still hadn't heard a single word from the Division—not a callback, not an answer to my request to send me something I could show Chris proving his uncle's involvement, not even a "Hey, we got your message about the safe house fuckery, and we sure are glad you and your protectee are okay, Sunday." The situation was unprecedented in my entire career at the Division, and ordinarily, I'd have lost my shit at everyone from Margot right on up to the Oval Office... but I hadn't.

I was also struggling with our location. Under any other circumstances, the newlywed story—while not my first or even twelfth choice of cover, thank you so much, Oak Bartlett—would have granted us a little privacy, but nothing trumped a small town's need to ferret out a story. And while Chris seemed happy enough here, and his big brown eyes went all soft and gooey every time a handsome local man (and Jesus fuck, there were a statistically unlikely number of them) invited us to a barbecue, or to join the Pumpkin Brigade, or to have a *John Ruffian: Pretender* marathon next Tuesday (this from Watt Bartlett, who was determined to be Chris's new BFF, and his "oh, and you can come too, Reed... if you want" did not fool me for one second), with every invitation, I felt my muscles tense and my blood pressure rise.

I should have put a stop to it. But I didn't do that either.

And why, one might ask, was I putting aside everything

I'd learned through years of training, experience, and common sense?

I blamed my husband.

Fake husband.

Protectee.

Whatever.

Because there were still many things I didn't understand about Chris, no matter how many stories he told. Like, why was he so chill that he'd gotten into my car without question yet he was willing to throw down when I'd informed him that he would *not* be getting on a twenty-foot ladder to fix a cabin roof?

Why did he have zero fucks to give when a biker gang was throwing chairs past his head but zero tolerance for my "grumpiness" and "lack of communication" when I'd tried to put some much-needed distance between us the morning after our motel room kiss?

Why was he savvy enough to recognize the make and model of a gun, and the species of some big-ass flowers in Watt's garden, and whether a shopper at Lyon's Imperial was about to spend way too much on cheese ("It's not *aged* Parmesan, you see? I'm afraid this price is highway robbery, sir."), but not enough to recognize that his family were a bunch of criminals who'd put him in the path of yet more criminals and hadn't even bothered to warn him?

How had he grown up so damn innocent in a cesspool of corruption... and become the hottest person I'd ever met? Why did the idea of him wandering into danger make me insane? Why did I want to make him happy more than I wanted to keep my professional distance? And how was I supposed to do my job when every time I closed my eyes, I imagined him under me in the bed I wasn't supposed to be sleeping in and replayed those sweet, stammery sounds he made when he came?

Last night, I'd waited until after Chris showered in the tiny bathroom off the living room, refilled his water bottle and, with one bare toe peeking out of yet another pair of my borrowed pants to trace across the wood floor, wished me good night and closed the bedroom door. Then I'd gotten up and stacked the empty cooler on top of the industrial-sized package of seltzer cans Chris had picked out at the market yesterday, forming a tidy wall in front of the door to protect myself from bad choices.

No doubt when I opened the door, the wall would be right where I'd left it before I'd somehow, against my will and in defiance of all common sense and professionalism, spirited myself into his bed last night.

And the worst part of all was that with Chris's scent in my nose and his mouth inches from mine, I couldn't even regret it.

I needed to stop this nonsense immediately. As in *now*. Right this second.

My arms tightened around him without my permission, and Chris let out a little moan that made my cock twitch. Eyes closed, he sighed and rolled more fully against me, dragging his slim fingers down my naked chest and bringing his own very excited cock—*ah fuck*—to rest against my hip.

This made it exponentially more difficult for me to sneak out without waking him... but that was the least of my problems.

I sucked in a breath and reminded myself I had been trained to resist torture. I could be questioned at length without giving up information. I'd been placed in high-stress simulations precisely so I could develop resistance and be strong under pressure.

But when his hand snuck down to the edge of the quilt where it sat at my waist, and *lower*, my breath left me in a shudder. This was worse than anything I'd ever trained for. I was consumed by want, and the way Chris was biting his lip and holding his breath even in his sleep meant he wanted it just as much—

Wait a minute. Who held their breath in their sleep?

I slapped a hand down over his when it was still a few precious, crucial inches above my cock. "Getting a little *real* there, fake husband."

Chris made a big production of yawning and fluttering his eyes open. "Reed? Goodness, I must've been sleeping hard!"

Something was definitely hard.

The man was a terrible liar. Yet another thing that shouldn't have been a turn-on, yet there I was, fighting the urge to laugh... and fighting the urge to let his hand continue its quest.

I gave his flank a teasing slap, and when he yelped out a laugh, I took the opportunity to slide out from underneath him. "Come on. Weren't you the one saying how warm it was going to be today? Let's get an early start. Dibs on first bathroom."

Resigned but cheerful, Chris climbed out of bed and put on his glasses. By the time I'd finished brushing my teeth and changing my sleep pants for shorts and a T-shirt, Chris already had coffee brewing in the kitchenette, which someone—probably Watt, I grudgingly admitted—had outfitted with a minifridge, a cooktop, a microscopic microwave/oven combo, a toaster, a coffee maker, and even some coffee. While Chris took his turn in the bathroom, I toasted a bagel and handed it to him when he emerged, damp and pink-cheeked, a little while later.

"Oh my gosh! Thank you so much, Reed." Chris's eyes shone like the slightly burnt bread product on a paper plate was a priceless diamond.

I might have been all twisted up over the situation, but my dick knew exactly how it felt about those big brown eyes... and the soft, clingy fabric of his thrifted black athletic shorts, and the olive-green T-shirt that set off his freckles.

I mumbled something and forced myself to focus on my coffee.

"So... still working on the roof of Cabin 7?" Chris wondered. He curled up in one corner of the love seat, plate on his bent knees, and picked off small sections of his bagel.

I made a sound of agreement. "Turned out to be a bigger project than I thought—" Chris inhaled as if about to speak, and because I knew exactly what he was going to say, I fixed him with a glare. "—and no, I still don't need your help."

He pursed his lips. "But I know what I'm doing," he said with a sigh. "I'm really good at fixing roofs. Practically an expert."

"Yeah, you said," I agreed. "Then I asked you how that was possible for a charcuterie specialist, and you said, '*I contain multitudes, Reed Sunday.*'" I sipped my coffee. "Which certainly put me in my place but, believe it or not, does not reassure me that you have practical experience."

"Well, I do." Rolling his eyes, Chris pulled his knees to his chest and balanced his plate on top—a daytime version of the protective position he sometimes adopted when he was sleeping. It was really, unbearably, annoyingly adorable.

I slouched against the counter, coffee in hand, and watched him steadily.

"Ugh, fine." His cheeks went pink—probably more with pique than embarrassment. "If you must know, I learned to fix a roof because I broke one, okay? One time I... I pulled a telescope out onto the little porch roof outside my bedroom window so I could watch a meteor shower. And it's possible that it was a very expensive telescope, and also that Uncle Danny might have..." He coughed. "...casually indicated that I was definitely not allowed to take it out on the roof."

My lips twitched. "You? Mr. Straight and Narrow? Disobeyed on purpose?"

"I have never claimed to be s-straight." Chris gave me a look that made my blood sizzle. "And yes, I suppose technically I disobeyed. But it was a tiny, trivial, inconsequential disobedience. And if Danny had understood the extenuating circumstances, he might have understood." He adjusted his glasses. "Nonna always said that if you make a wish on a falling star, it's guaranteed to come true. It was a once-in-a-lifetime cosmic event, Reed."

I ran a hand over my mouth to hide my smile. "Not quite seeing how this led to your roof repair expertise. Did you smash the telescope through the roof?"

"Gosh, no! Nothing that dramatic." He waved a hand. "I just, you know, put my foot through it."

"Your *foot*?" I straightened out of my slouch. "Through the *roof*? What the fuck?"

"There was a spongy spot I didn't notice until I was just about to make my wish, and my foot sort of... broke right through it, and I lost my balance. But I didn't fall off, and I saved the telescope," he added proudly. "Which wasn't what I was going to wish for, exactly, but was good luck anyway, don't you think?"

Who gave a single shit about the fucking telescope?

"Were you hurt?" I demanded. "You could have broken your ankle." Though he was sitting in front of me with two perfectly functional feet, I was ready to carry him off for an X-ray... eight years after the fact.

Ridiculous.

"I was fine. A little sore and a little scared, but mostly, I felt awful that I'd damaged Danny's house," he said earnestly. "So I watched some YouTube videos, and the next day, I drove to the hardware store and used my savings to buy supplies so I could fix everything myself." He ripped off another piece of bagel and chewed it thoughtfully. "In the end, it all worked out because whoever did the roof initially hadn't done the waterproofing right, and it might have been a much bigger issue later if I hadn't taken care of it. Plus, now I have this amazing roofing experience, so... all's well that ends well, right?" He smiled brightly.

"Jesus," I muttered. "Your uncle just let you fix his roof?"

"Well..." His cheeks went red. "Not exactly. It was only one small section, and I was able to finish it while he was at work. But what's important here is that I got it done—"

"You repaired the roof in secret."

"No! I mean... well, yes. Technically. But you make it sound like I'm some kind of criminal." He laughed lightly. Then he froze with a piece of bagel halfway to his lips, and his eyes went impossibly wide. "Oh my gosh, *am* I a criminal?"

I snorted, simultaneously charmed and turned on. At this point, I wasn't sure Chris could do anything I didn't find attractive.

The thought was enough to make my laughter die. "Not a criminal, a typical teenager," I said shortly. "Now, eat up and let's go."

Chris chewed his bagel obediently, and for a second, I allowed myself to think that the conversation was done and I could escape without further distracting thoughts about my protectee.

Silly me.

"Did you have a teen hangout spot when you were growing up?" Chris asked abruptly.

Confused by the topic shift, I shrugged. "Sure. There's a little clearing in the woods behind the Apple of My Eye— you know, the inn right off the main road in the Hollow? We called it the Grove because it was in the trees, and we had no imagination whatsoever. Why?"

"Just curious. I've never been to a place like that. I kinda missed out on that part of being a teenager." Chris leaned toward me, doe eyes gleaming. "What sorts of things did you do there? Secret rituals? Gambling? Lovemaking? *Duels?*"

If he'd been one whit less sincere, I might have laughed. "No secret rituals, unless you count standing around drinking stale beer in the freezing cold. But I guess occasionally we..."

A hazy memory floated through my brain of Jonas Pilkey's cousin Seth—pretty, shy, inexperienced Seth— who'd been visiting the Hollow the summer I turned sixteen, giving me my first blowjob. Jonas had punched me in the mouth afterward—for his cousin's honor, maybe? Who remembered?—but I'd still thought it was worth it because I'd finally understood what my dick was for.

"Occasionally?" Chris prompted.

I looked over at him, easily as shy and inexperienced as Seth but a billion times prettier.

The last thing I needed was to discuss blowjobs with him. As annoyed as I was at having to fix up these cabins, I recognized we needed something to keep us busy and away from other... activities.

"Nothing," I mumbled. "We're burning daylight. You gonna eat that bagel or shred it for compost?"

His face fell a bit, but he nodded and pushed his plate onto the counter. "I'm not hungry. Let's get started."

We walked outside, past the fire pit and across the path that cut through the grassy field at the center of the property. Chris trailed his hand over the tall stalks of grass that bordered the path, which came up to his thighs in some spots.

I bumped my arm into his. "You're still working on Cabin 3, right?"

"Huh? Oh. Yeah." Chris perked up. "I should finish scraping and sanding the trim around the windows this morning. Later, I'm going to work on the section of the ceiling that needs to be replaced. And when I'm done with that, maybe I'll go down to the lake for a bit. I bet it's gorgeous in the sunshine."

I hated the idea of him having to do this work. The poor guy had been yanked out of his life, sent on the run, and now he was scraping rotten wood for no pay. But I had to remind myself this cover story was for his protection, and this work was critical to the cover story.

"Don't work too hard, okay? The renovations are only our cover story, not an actual job." I'd had to remind *myself* of that several times this week. It was unexpectedly satisfying to see the cabins shaping up and tempting to want to take on larger jobs. Jobs I might not be here long enough to finish.

"Oh, and don't go in the water," I added. "It's cold. Like, hypothermia cold. I waded in just a few feet yesterday, but the lake bed drops away very quickly, which means it doesn't get warm, even close to the shore—"

He sighed. "You told me already. I wasn't planning to swim."

"Good," I said gruffly. "Hey, call me when you're ready to do the ceiling. I'll give you a hand."

His eyes flicked up to me. "Why? I can do it. I'm pretty good at repairing and repainting ceilings, too."

My lips twitched. "Do I even want to know how you obtained *that* skill?"

"I suppose you could ask Van about the Ale-pocalypse..." He hesitated. "Actually, on second thought, please don't."

Once again, I found myself fighting not to laugh. Had I ever been this amused this close to sunrise? If so, I couldn't remember.

"Come get me when you're ready," I reminded him as the paths to the cabins split.

Chris set his jaw, looking distinctly unhappy. "If you need *my* help with the roof, just yell." Without another word, he turned right toward the lake and Cabin 3.

For half a minute, I imagined Chris putting his foot through a roof again, only this time getting truly hurt. The idea made me shiver despite the warm sunshine.

"Not gonna happen," I muttered as I turned left and headed deeper into the woods near Cabin 7, where I'd left Watt's ladder and a bunch of borrowed tools.

The day before, I'd set out to replace a few shingles on the east-facing side of the cabin. Only once I'd gotten up there and started removing the damaged spots I'd noticed just how much rot was hiding beneath the surface. I'd ended up stripping everything so I could replace the plywood underlay, and today, I needed to finish the job.

Unlike certain people, I was *not* skilled in roof repair, so I'd have to concentrate—which was a good thing because for once I'd be too distracted to think about Chris at all.

Or so I thought.

But after I'd crawled off the ladder and begun laying the shingles, soaking in the hot sunshine, the wail of the loons, and the faint, rhythmic sound of Chris's sander in the distance, I remembered the look on Chris's face earlier. It wasn't quite sad, but definitely not happy. Thoughtful, kind of. Wistful, maybe?

Jesus Christ.

Wistful, Reed? Really? I'd be spouting poetry next.

The last time I'd been so consumed with someone that I'd spent actual minutes of my life thinking about their expressions and wondering at their moods was... never. Literally never. I was living in upside-down land. But I couldn't think of a way to get things back on track short of... well, simply giving in and fucking him.

If I did give in—if the next time I woke up with his body in my arms, his clean vanilla scent in my nose, and his sleepy brown eyes blinking up at me, I simply rolled *into* him instead of away, pressed my lips to his, kissed my way down his body, took him in my mouth, fingered him until he made those hot little whimpers he'd made the other night, and then sank inside him—then his spell over me would be broken. One hundred percent definitely. No matter how great the sex was, new experiences were my catnip—one reason why my career at the Division was so fulfilling—and once this thing with Chris wasn't new anymore, it wouldn't feel so tempting. So necessary.

So fucking inevitable.

Afterward, Chris would go back to being my protectee, and I'd be able to focus on something besides my needy dick for a change. I'd quit allowing the Division to blow off my many requests for status updates and copies of Dante's file because I wouldn't be dreading the moment Chris realized the truth and his gut-punch eyes filled with tears. I'd stop growling like a jealous caveman—a ridiculously embarrassing turn of events I'd never experienced before and hoped to never experience again—whenever Chris struck up a conversation with yet another buff, friendly dude in town. I'd stop being so annoyed that Oak's reply to my "WTF? Why'd you tell Watt we were MARRIED?" text had been a string of laugh-cry emojis and a very misguided "I have a feeling you'll thank me later, bro." I'd stop being so agitated all the damn time, and maybe Chris would stop being so unhappy. In a way, I'd actually be able to protect Chris better if we—

I sat back on my heels. Holy shit. Was I really considering this? Was I high? Was I dehydrated? What the *hell* was in those shingle fumes that was making this seem like a plausible idea?

You will not have sex with your protectee, I reminded myself firmly. Because the potential damage to my career wasn't the only risk.

Chris had said something the other day about our kiss at the motel being his first. If that was true... Well, for one thing, it meant the man was a kissing prodigy because that had been a hell of a kiss. For another, though, it meant he probably wasn't looking to me for a quick, enjoyable fuck. More than likely, he'd deluded himself into thinking this whole situation was romantic or something—a common and normal reaction when you were in danger and dependent on someone to protect you, and one of the reasons the Division forbade agents from these sorts of entanglements.

Chris really didn't want *me*, Reed Sunday—how could

he when he didn't know me? He wanted someone to cling to because the rest of his life was in upheaval.

But I was not that person.

I lifted the hem of my T-shirt to wipe the sweat from my eyes and decided I needed a cold drink. Dehydration still wasn't off the table, and if I was feeling it, Chris could be, too.

Crawling over to the ladder, I realized I couldn't hear the sound of Chris's sander. I couldn't say how long it had been since I'd heard it either, which wasn't good. If I couldn't keep my eyes on him at all times, I at least needed to keep my ears on him. Odds were, he'd started replacing the drywall on the ceiling and hadn't bothered to come and get me.

I scowled as I stowed my tools in the five-gallon bucket Watt had provided and mopped my sticky hands with a rag. I had never met anyone who hated accepting help as much as Chris did. He was too used to working alone. Too driven to prove how capable he was.

And he *was* capable. I could admit that. The other morning, he'd riffled around Watt's tool shed and found everything we needed. At the hardware store, he'd known precisely what sorts of fasteners to get for every job. And fuck knew the man could assemble a meal fit for a party from just a few slices of cheese and a melon. But knowing how to do things didn't mean he should be climbing tall ladders and using circular saws and lifting heavy drywall over his head alone.

He was small. Breakable. Important. Precious.

Fuck.

Maybe Chris wasn't the only deluded one.

I stalked through the trees toward Cabin 3, my boots sinking into the thick carpet of pine needles and releasing a spicy scent that made me think of Vermont and my siblings. For the first time in a long time, I wished I could call one of them, or maybe *all* of them, and get their advice on this crazy fucking situation. I imagined Porter would make a ridiculous joke at my expense, and Emma would make me a to-do list. Knox would make a sarcastic comment that turned out to be surprisingly insightful. Webb would be calm and no-nonsense, dispensing advice like trick-or-treat candy, and Hawk would make drama out of the smallest details and probably be able to tell precisely what Chris was thinking.

But what would I even say if I called them? How could I get their help without coming clean about everything else?

Maybe, like Chris, I was just used to working alone.

When I got closer to Cabin 3, I noticed immediately that the place was too quiet. Chris had a tendency to hum when he was working, but there wasn't a single off-key note of Taylor Swift to be heard. The peeling trim around the windows and doors was neatly scraped and sanded smooth, just waiting for a fresh coat of paint after our next trip to the hardware store, and Chris's tools had been tidied away, but he hadn't touched the ceiling or anything else inside the cabin.

This should have been a relief. Instead, I thought about Chris's earlier wistful expression, and my stomach twisted guiltily. I didn't want him to feel bad or incompetent, I just wanted him to be safe. He had to understand—

Chris's panicked cry rent the air, followed by a loud *splash,* and I took off down the path to the lake at a run. Had he fallen in? Had someone found us?

"Oh my goodness! That was amazing!" Chris shouted a second later. "Ten out of ten."

"Eight out of ten!" a young female voice called. "You need to point your toes, Derry."

"Three out of ten," a bored male voice corrected. "I could *fall* in and look cooler."

What the hell? I stopped short, just out of sight of the dock, and crept forward cautiously, staying behind the tree line. Scanning the scene, I found my protectee, still wearing his green T-shirt and athletic shorts—though both were now damp with perspiration and clinging to him in all sorts of pleasant ways—leaning against the railing of the Wrigley Campground dock in the sunshine, watching as a teenaged boy with long limbs and a smile like Watt Bartlett's hauled himself out of the water.

On the dock near Chris's feet, two teenage girls in bikinis and a smaller, dark-haired boy in shorts were seated cross-legged on beach towels, helping themselves to seltzers out of our soft cooler and snacking on something that looked suspiciously like one of Chris's charcuterie boards.

Where the fuck did he keep coming up with the damn things? Was he magic?

"Three out of ten? Please," Mini-Watt scoffed, rolling his eyes at the other boy. "I'd like to see you do better, Zach."

Zach yawned and leaned back on his hands, tilting his face up to the sun. "No way I'm getting in there. It's practically October. The water's too fucking cold."

"You shouldn't say *fuck* in front of an adult, Zach," the blonder of the two girls scolded. "For fuck's sake."

It seemed to take Chris a second to realize he was the adult in question. When he did, he shook his head so hard his glasses slid down his nose. "Oh, no, don't mind me," he insisted, pushing them back up. "I don't mind fresh language at all. I'm used to it. You should hear Reed. He's all eff this and eff that. He effs *everything*." He paused and added darkly, "Well. *Almost* everything."

"Reed's your husband, right, Chris?" the darker-haired girl asked eagerly. "I overheard Theo—my uncle's boyfriend—telling Uncle Bennett that you guys were here on your honeymoon."

"Oh, um, yes," Chris agreed. "Reed is my h-husband. Who I'm married to. No doubt about that." His fingers fluttered in an anxious, half-assed impression of jazz hands, and I snickered.

Such a shit liar, but why is it so cute?

"Don't mind her. Vega is a sucker for romance," the blonde girl explained.

"And Mary-Kate thinks romance is for suckers," Vega returned, giving her friend a good-natured shove. She turned back to Chris. "Theo said your husband was *handsome*. Nearly as handsome as Bennett himself."

Chris smiled. "Oh, yes. Reed's gorgeous."

"And Mr. Lattimer said he was tall," she continued.

"Yeah." Chris's smile grew.

"And Liam Mason said he was grumpy," Mary-Kate chimed in.

"Yea— Wait, what?" Chris frowned. "That's not very nice."

"I think he meant it as a compliment," Vega explained. "Luke's husband is super grumpy, so I think he enjoys grumpy guys."

"Oh." Chris shrugged and smiled, soft and relaxed. "Well, Reed *is* grumpy. Sometimes." A pause. "Or... okay, maybe *often*. But he's also very brave. A-and trustworthy. And smart. And funny. And loyal. And thoughtful. He makes me a bagel every morning, even though he doesn't make one for himself, and he insists on me wearing his pajama pants, even though I have my own, and sometimes when I do things for him—just tiny, small things like throwing together dinner—he'll give me a sweet, lopsided smile, like he's really pleased and doesn't know how to show it, and it *melts* me. Oh, and don't get me started on his forearms because... um..." Chris paused again and cleared his throat. "Anyway."

I gripped the tree in front of me so hard the rough bark dug into my fingers.

Was this part of his husband act? But no, it couldn't be. I knew when he was lying. Anyone with eyes knew it. And this... this was truth.

"You're so lucky," Vega sighed. "He sounds *perfect*."

"Perfectly lame," Zach said.

Chris shot him a disappointed look that had Zach closing his mouth quickly, looking a little shamefaced.

"I didn't say Reed was perfect," Chris told Vega. "But if you go into a relationship thinking your partner will be John Ruffian, you're likely to be disappointed. Reed's a wonderful man, but he has his flaws."

Did I?

"Does he?" Vega echoed.

"Heck yeah. He's stubborn—once he gets an idea in his head, it's cemented there. He's overprotective in a way that veers perilously close to bossiness. He's a really terrible singer who makes up his own lyrics," Chris said, but he smiled that soft smile again when he said it, like he didn't really mind it all that much. "And he's *loud*. He wakes me up every night when he gets into bed because he has to fix the blankets just so."

I stared at him without blinking while some nearby woodland creature inhaled and exhaled in a noisy wheeze.

It took me a second to realize it was me.

Chris woke up every *night? He'd known I was there all along?*

"And Reed doesn't like to talk about himself much," Chris went on. His shoulders hunched slightly, and he toyed with the hem of his shirt. "What he enjoys, or what he wants, or who he is. It's like... it's like he doesn't want anyone to know him, which is kinda funny because my whole life, all I've wanted was for someone to know me. And, you know, that might make it sound like *why do you like this guy?*" He laughed lightly. "But I do. Gosh, I really do. I like being with him. I like who I am when I'm with him. I feel excited. And safe. And *seen*... mostly. With him, I don't always have to be cheerful even when I'm not, which is..." He glanced up, realized he had the rapt attention of four teenagers, and turned bright red. "...nice?" he concluded weakly.

Chris didn't realize it, but he had my rapt attention, too. How the hell did he know me so well? How did he know me *at all?*

Then again, that shouldn't have been a surprise any more than Chris's adaptability was because if I'd learned one thing about my protectee, it was that Chris didn't just see the best in people; he saw people, *period*. And he treated them as if they were worthy of his kindness and his time, whether they were weed-smoking gardeners in blanket capes, or angry biker-girlfriends, or an orchard owner in love with his land, or... or a grumpy, bossy Division agent who absolutely did not butcher song lyrics, no matter what Chris said.

Listening to him talk, I wondered when I'd gotten so jaded about things. When had I started expecting people to lie and situations to get fucked up? Maybe it was after fifteen years at the Division, or maybe it had started way earlier, when my stepmother left my dad—

Or maybe it doesn't fucking matter when it started because it's kept you and your protectees alive, hmm?

I blew out a breath.

See? Upside. Down. Land.

It was fucking intolerable.

"I think it's *amazing*," Vega breathed. "Wow."

"It's pretty cool," Mary-Kate grudgingly allowed.

"So how'd you two meet?" Mini-Watt demanded. He leaned against the railing close to Chris because, apparently, he didn't understand personal boundaries any better than his dad did.

"Oh. Well. That's a... a funny story, actually." Chris's fingers fluttered, clenching and unclenching so fast I could practically hear them hum. He rubbed the column of his neck. He shifted his weight. "We, uh... we met when I was a... a hardworking charcuterie specialist and Reed was a... a... down-on-his-luck cheese enthusiast," he began before launching into an utterly unbelievable tale involving arsenic baked into cheese straws that I was pretty sure drew heavily from the plot of that television show he liked so much.

I shook my head, torn between horror and amusement.

"So you see, Reed basically saved my life. And now, here we are," Chris croaked. "Honeymooning."

Both girls sighed. Even Mini-Watt looked impressed.

"That's stupid," Zach pronounced, and despite my own concerns about Chris's story, I briefly debated the ethical implications of smacking the shit out of a teenage boy for insulting my husband.

Fake husband.

Fucking *protectee.*

Whatever.

Fortunately for him, Zach quickly continued. "Who decides to come *here* for a honeymoon?" He waved a hand to indicate the placid, sunlit lake, the perfectly blue sky, the wild calls of the loons. "It's boring as fuck."

"You think?" Chris smiled, clearly not offended. "I think Copper County's awesome. O'Leary, too. You might take it for granted, living here and all, but it's pretty special to find people this friendly in a place this beautiful. Then again, I'm a pretty boring person."

I couldn't help snorting loudly at that. Luckily, no one heard me.

"You're exactly right about this place," Vega agreed. "I only ever came here for a week or two in the summers growing up, but my uncle and I moved here permanently last fall. I thought I was going to seriously, seriously hate it 'cause it's so small. But honestly, it's been kind of awesome for both of us. Uncle Bennett found Theo earlier this summer, and I got a job and made friends." She slung an arm over Mary-Kate's shoulder. "I kinda wish I'd lived here always."

I turned and leaned my back against the tree, letting the cool lake breeze wash over me as I settled in to listen. It turned out small-town drama was a lot more fun when I wasn't involved in it.

"How nice for you." Zach sounded simultaneously cranky and superior, the way only a teenager could. "*I'm* leaving the millisecond I graduate. I can't wait."

"Sure," Chris agreed. "If you're not happy, that makes sense."

"See? *He* gets it," Zach said.

"Assuming you *do* graduate," Mini-Watt taunted. "And don't wind up arrested for reckless driving or tagging Copper County with your shitty graffiti."

"Zach," Chris said sadly, like he was the kid's long-suffering parent and not someone who'd known him for... what, an hour? "Are you the one who spray-painted that stuff on one of the cabins here?"

Zach's boredom evaporated, and his voice shook with anger. "Fuck off, Derry. Keep your mouth shut."

"Don't get pissy with me," Mini-Watt said. "Just stating facts."

"Well, nobody asked you to share *my* facts, asshole," Zach shouted.

"Calm down," Chris said. "Hey, no pushing!"

This time when I heard the splash, I grinned. I wasn't sure which of the boys had ended up in the water, and I didn't care. I hoped it was both of them.

"Oh, for fuck's sake," one of the girls—possibly Mary-Kate—yelled.

"I... I didn't do anything." Zach's anger fled as quickly as his boredom had, and he sounded young and unsure. "I pushed Derry."

"Except you missed, dumbass," Mini-Watt said. "Shit. Where'd he go?"

Frowning, I peered around the tree. Counted heads. And realized that one adorable charcuterie specialist was missing.

Literally the damn minute my back was turned.

My vision narrowed, and my chest clenched tight.

"It wasn't my fault," Zach said, even as he toed off his shoes and tore off his shirt. "Mr. Sunday? Chris?"

I was halfway down the dock before Zach jumped, and after leaping over the girls and their towels, I hit the water the instant after he did.

The shock of brutal cold made my muscles seize and my lungs burn. I forced my eyes open, but the water that had looked so clear from above was murky down below. I'd known it was deep, but now I saw that it was *unnaturally* so, almost like someone had purposely dug it out to make the area safe for diving... which also made it seriously fucking *un*safe for someone who might at this very moment be drowning.

Christ, where was he?

Through the thin light filtering down from above, I made out vague, blurry shapes on the lake bed, none of which looked remotely like the man who'd turned my life on its head in the span of five short days.

A tire. A sunken rowboat. A small something that glinted like a pair of glasses—

Narrowing my eyes on the place where I'd seen the glint, I kicked hard, pushing myself through the water. I quickly saw that the glasses were still attached to one gorgeous and very frightened man. I reached for him, pulled him close, and propelled us upward.

As we broke the surface, I sucked in a huge, coughing breath and heard Chris do the same.

"Mr. Sunday? Is h-he okay?" Zach demanded. He was still bobbing in the water, though his teeth chattered.

"He will be," I said grimly.

I swam us to the shore, bypassing the dock entirely, and laid Chris on his side on the stony beach. "Talk to me," I commanded. "Tell me you're okay. Baby, please."

"S-so b-b-bossy," Chris complained softly, and I nearly sobbed from the relief of it. "I'm f-fine. Just a b-bit... c-cold?" A head-to-toe shiver racked his body. "H-how am I th-this cold, Reed?"

"Mr. Sunday?" Derry called. "You want me to call an ambulance? Or go get my dad?"

"No," I snapped. But because I knew Chris would

complain at me about it later, I added in a kinder tone, "Chris will be okay. I'll make sure of it. But thanks for asking. And thanks for going in after him," I told Zach, who'd managed to haul himself onto the dock and was being aggressively wrapped in beach towels by three sets of hands.

I locked eyes with Mini-Watt. "Get him someplace warm and make sure he's okay."

Then I hauled Chris's shivering body into my arms and took the path back to the caretaker cottage at a dead run. Later, I wouldn't recall how I managed to get the door open without setting Chris down or how I managed to extricate him from his clothes while he clung to me, shivering, but somehow I did. I turned on the shower one-handed and, still fully dressed, hauled him with me under the spray.

Chris moaned when the warm water hit him and uncurled like a plant blossoming in the sun.

I pressed my forehead against his. "Thank fuck," I breathed. "Thank fuck."

Chris managed a shaky laugh. "D-don't say that word in front of an adult, Reed."

But I wasn't in any mood yet for laughter. "Did that Zach kid push you in?" I demanded.

I set him gently on his feet, but his knees wobbled, so I wrapped my arms around him and let him rest against me.

Chris pressed his nose to my T-shirt and shook his head. "N-no! Not exactly."

"Then what did happen, exactly?"

"Well. It turns out I still don't know how to swim. And I'm starting to wonder if the 'swimming instinct' my nonna assured me would kick in when I really needed it might be a myth."

I tugged gently on the back of his hair to make him look at me. Water ran off his glasses in rivulets, streaming down his cheek to his lips. "Are you telling me that you were standing near the edge of the dock when you don't know how to swim?" I shook his shoulders slightly. "What the *hell*, Chris?" Another thought occurred to me. "And if he didn't push you in, how'd you wind up in the water?"

"Zach and Derry were going to fight. I didn't want either of them to get hurt, so I distracted them. I jumped," he said, for all the world as though this were a reasonable fucking answer.

"You *jumped*." Emotion clawed up my chest, clogged my throat. My fingers clamped his shoulders like twin vises. "Please tell me you're kidding."

"Well... no? I didn't think it would be quite that deep, and anyway, my nonna always said—"

"No." I shook my head forcefully. "No."

I let go of his shoulders, but only so I could run my hands up and down his arms, his chest, his neck and face. His skin was getting warmer, finally. Turning rosy pink all over. And soft... so damn soft. His breathing got heavier with every brush of my fingertips.

"First, shootouts, then bar fights, and now..." My throat clicked as I swallowed. "I don't give a shit what your nonna says, Chris Winowksi. You don't take chances like that—"

One small hand lifted to my mouth, silencing me. "Chris Winowski *doesn't* take chances," he whispered, voice barely audible under the thunder of the water. "Not ever. But... I'm thinking maybe Chris Sunday does. Sometimes. When it's important."

I shook my head again, dislodging his fingers. My hands continued tracing the lines of his body, the lean muscles, the fine bones and perfect symmetry. "What the fuck am I going to do with you?" I demanded. It wasn't an angry statement but an honest question. A *plea*. "I'm losing my mind here. I can't think. I can't focus. I can't stop wanting— Tell me, Chris. Tell me. What am I going to do with you?"

Chris's teeth sank into his lower lip. His big eyes stared up at me like it was Christmas morning and I was his very best present. Then he lifted on his tiptoes and pressed his lips to mine.

CHAPTER NINE

CHRIS

I just wanted to make Reed stop talking.

There were some things I wouldn't mind hearing him say again, like the way I was almost positive he'd called me *baby* back at the dock. But the way he was talking now, the fear in his voice, made everything feel too real.

That near-drowning had been scary as heck. I hadn't really thought about jumping before I did it—which, in retrospect, probably had not been the sort of jumping-without-thinking Van had advised me to try—and the second I'd hit the water, I hadn't been able to think at all. I'd been so cold, cold all the way to my bones, and I'd tried to be brave and claw my way to the surface, but I hadn't known which way was up. The harder I fought, the deeper I'd seemed to fall. And maybe—I mean, probably, almost definitely—I would have gotten out on my own somehow, but in that terrifying instant when I'd thought perhaps I *couldn't*, with my lungs burning so badly I thought they might burst, the one thought my panicked brain had latched onto was that I refused to die before Reed Sunday kissed me again.

Now, with his hands on me and his lips warm on mine...

I was done waiting for him to kiss me. I was going to take matters into my own hands.

He was so much bigger than I was in every way. My toes slipped on the shower floor, and if it hadn't been for his strong arms around me, I probably would have tumbled to the ground in a sodden, shivering heap.

But Reed hadn't taken his hands off me since he'd pulled me out of the lake, and at this point, I kind of hoped he never did. Or... or at least didn't for as long as I could keep him kissing me.

His mouth was firm on mine. Just like last time, he took control immediately and dominated my mouth in the very best way.

"Don't stop," I begged when he gave me just enough space to draw breath. "Please."

I was terrified he'd suddenly realize what he was doing and go back to the regretful hecking grump he was after our first kiss in the hotel room.

My brain spun with ideas... well, mostly fantasies... things I'd only dreamed about doing with a guy. But I knew with complete certainty I wanted to do them with *this* guy.

And I wanted to do them now before he changed his mind and got all... bossy protector... on me again.

"Suck you," I said. The words were muffled against his lips and may have accidentally sounded like the eff-word. I winced.

"Suck," I clarified. "Suck. Like with my mouth. Er... my tongue. My lips? I'm not sure how *mpfh—*"

Reed's tongue entered my mouth again, and his hand crept up to gently hold the front of my throat. An embarrassing sound came from my nose as I gasped in pleasure at his grip.

When he finally finished vacuuming all rational

thought from my brain, he pulled back and pinned me with his eyes. "As long as it's not teeth, sweetheart, it'll be good. You sure this is—"

Now, it was my turn to take charge. Before he could finish his question, I slipped out of his grip and dropped to my knees, accidentally falling sideways a little bit and scrambling to catch hold of something.

That something ended up being a shampoo bottle and a scrunchie poof. The two items shot off the shelf, slipped through my fingers, and clattered around the shower floor.

"It's fine!" I called up to him in hopes he wouldn't interpret the teeny-tiny incident as an indicator that his current sexual partner wasn't actually graceful or suave enough to participate in adult activities. "I'm fine. Everything's fine!"

The small trickle of blood from a new scrape on my knee washed easily down the drain without anyone the wiser.

I straightened up and faced Reed's... impressive manhood. Well, it was an impressive bulge. In his shorts. Because he was still fully dressed. Still. It was... I swallowed around a lump in my throat. Large.

Large and probably in charge.

I inhaled a shaky breath. I could do this. I would do this. And if it was terrible for him, at least he was kind enough not to say anything about it later. Probably. And then I'd have a wild oat fully sown. Which would be something.

Before I could lean forward and begin sowing, Reed leaned down and grabbed me under the arms. "For fuck's sake," he muttered before hauling me out of the shower and standing me on a bathmat.

I stared at him and tried not to register my disappointment. It was too good to be true. Of course it was. And I couldn't blame him for being disappointed.

"Yeah, sure. No, I get it. Super fine."

He turned back to me with a fluffy towel and wrapped it around my shoulders before reaching for my glasses and removing them. He placed them carefully on the vanity before reaching for a second towel to dry my hair. I risked a glance at his face and saw a soft, affectionate expression that surprised me.

"I don't know what you're thinking," he said in a low voice. "But I can tell it's not good."

I forced a smile. "No, it's good. It's really good. I was thinking how lucky I am to have such a good friend who was brave enough to pull me out of the lake after my…" I thought of the words my cousin Nicky had used when I was twelve and the handlebar brakes on my bike had locked, and I'd nearly crashed my bike into a car in the Cellar parking lot. "Stupid stunt."

Reed's eyes darkened. "It might have been ill-advised. I might have recommended a different way of diffusing the situation. But it wasn't stupid, and it wasn't a stunt."

He moved the towel down and began drying every part of me while he stood there fully dressed, dripping on the floor.

"That feels good," I admitted.

"Go get in bed." His voice held a familiar, commanding tone that did things to me. I started to nod when he added, "I'll join you as soon as I dry off."

I wondered if that was when he'd give me the lecture about water safety. After wrapping the towel around my waist, I headed into the bedroom to look for dry clothes.

His voice called after me. "Don't even think about putting clothes on, Chris Winowski."

I nearly ran into the doorframe. "W-what?"

"If you want to finish what you started in the shower,

you'll get into that bed naked. If you put clothes on, I'll understand."

My jaw dropped comically before I tossed off the towel, took one giant leap from the doorway onto the bed, and scrambled under the covers.

I tried to control my breathing, but I was still panting heavily when he arrived.

Reed Sunday was miles of hairy-chested lumberjack fantasy come to life. As he entered the bedroom with nothing but a small towel around his waist, I wondered just how desperate he'd have to be to accept a tumble with a guy like me.

But then I remembered Amber's words at the roadhouse.

You're adorable, sweetheart.

I sucked in a breath and remembered the looks of appreciation I'd gotten from some of the men in O'Leary. Maybe I wasn't half-bad. Maybe... maybe after getting some experience with Reed, I would be less awkward and more attractive to other men.

I don't want other men.

I shook my head to rid myself of the thought, but Reed must have misinterpreted it. Because he stopped approaching me and frowned.

"No, yes!" I barked. "Yes! I want this. That was... that was a, um, head shake about something else."

He grinned. "What were you head shaking about?"

I scraped my lip with my teeth and decided to be honest. "I know I'm not a great catch. But I appreciate you—"

Reed's face turned stormy. "Stop talking. Stop talking right now." He stalked closer and pulled back the covers until I was completely exposed. My manhood was noticeably unmanly, and my legs looked like spaghetti noodles.

"You are fucking gorgeous, and I'm going to prove it to you."

He ripped off the towel from around his waist and dropped it on the floor before stroking his obviously *very manly*... manhood. "Oh," I squeaked.

Instead of climbing onto the bed so I could give him a blowjob... or attempt one, rather... he knelt at the bottom of the bed and leaned over to press a soft kiss to the inside of one of my ankles.

"Oh," I breathed.

He took his time about it, pressing hot, open-mouthed kisses into my skin as he made his way up the inside of my leg to my most private places.

And then he pressed open-mouthed kisses *there*. Over and over again until I was thrusting into his mouth in mindless desperation, clutching his hair with greedy fingers and babbling incoherent commentary.

My body convulsed as my release hit, and my brain went completely offline the way John Ruffian's communication devices all died in episode... episode...

"Baby?"

I snapped my eyes open and saw Reed's smug face above mine. "You okay?" he asked with a teasing grin.

"Please tell me I didn't call you John Ruffian just now," I blurted. It had always been one of my biggest fears, and considering I'd just thought of the man...

Thankfully, Reed let out a laugh. "No. But you did call me the greatest lover of all time, which I think I'm going to have printed on a T-shirt and noted on my Grindr profile."

I sighed happily. "Do with it what you will. Ten out of ten. Excellent service. Will come again." As soon as my unintended pun hit my ears, my face ignited. "I d-didn't mean—"

Reed's laughter filled the room and immediately put me at ease. His eyes danced as he gazed at me. "You're beautiful when you come," he said, reaching out a hand to caress the side of my face.

My chest hitched. "Can I... it's only... I'd really like to see what you look like, too. When you c-... release, I mean."

He leaned in and kissed me slowly. The salty edge to his kisses seemed debauched and forbidden. Knowing it was my taste in his mouth made me feel worldly and experienced and... happy. Just really, really happy. Happier than I could remember in forever.

"You can do whatever you want with me," he said, shifting to lie on his back next to me. "I'm at your mercy."

He was big and muscular. His chest and belly were covered in dark hair. I tentatively reached out my fingers to feel the crinkly texture. As soon as I touched him, he sucked in a breath. His nipples tightened, and his stomach clenched.

I watched his cock as I leaned in and pressed a kiss to one of his nipples.

It jumped off his belly.

I tugged his nipple between my teeth and flicked it with my tongue.

His cock jumped again.

I was fascinated by his reactions. I kissed and touched and tasted him, all the while alternating between watching his cock and watching his face. Reed's eyes darkened, and his cheeks flushed, but he didn't say a word.

His chest raised and lowered with rapid breaths, and his cock seemed painfully hard.

He still didn't say a word.

I finally moved down between his spread legs and ran my tongue up his shaft while watching his face. He squeezed his eyes closed, threw his head back, and made a low, guttural sound.

So I did it again. And again. I finally lifted it up and sucked the tip into my mouth, reveling in the salty tang of him and the warm press of his length on my tongue.

I sucked and licked him, learning what he liked and what made that sound come out of his throat. When Reed's hand cupped the back of my head and guided me gently, I purred in satisfaction.

"Just like that, baby. So good. Fuck. Just like that. Your mouth... fuck, baby..."

Once his mouth opened, words began spilling out. They warmed something inside of me and only made me want to please him more. It was exciting and satisfying to bring him pleasure the way he'd done for me.

I reached up and cupped his balls in my hand. He made a choking sound and warned me to pull off. When I didn't, he pulled me off and yanked me up his body to crash his mouth onto mine as the hot wetness of his relief landed on my hip.

He kissed me for several more minutes as his body periodically shuddered until finally, he pulled back and moved to get off the bed.

"Please, Reed," I whispered, trying not to sound desperate and awkward. "Don't... don't leave? I... will you stay with me?"

He brushed the hair back from my forehead and gave me a small smile. "I'm just going to get a cloth to clean you up first."

I let out a breath and lay back against the soft bedding.

When he returned from the bathroom, he laid my

glasses carefully on the nightstand next to me before cleaning me up with a wet cloth and climbing into bed again.

Later, after our nap, we kissed some more. I made a quick dinner, and we kissed again. And this time, when it was time for bed, Reed didn't bother pretending he'd be sleeping on the tiny sofa. He climbed right in beside me, took me in his arms, and kissed me one last time.

As I drifted off to sleep, I felt different, somehow. Freer, maybe.

And I was sure everything had changed for the better.

———

EVERYTHING HAD *NOT* CHANGED for the better. The next morning when I woke up and leaned over to give Reed a good-morning kiss, my entire head throbbed like the bass drum in a marching band, and my throat was on fire.

"I'b fide!"

"You're definitely not fine. You're staying here and resting today," Reed pronounced. He pulled the quilt up and tucked it more firmly around me... which was really unnecessary since he was perched on the bed near my hip wearing nothing but a pair of cargo shorts, and the sight of his bare chest already had me uncomfortably warm. "I'll get you some cold medicine while I'm in town."

I sniffed, hoping I sounded offended rather than miserably congested. "But... but I wanded to come wid you."

I'd had big plans for the trip, too. Plans that involved letting Reed go to the hardware store while I dropped by the library to chat with Ms. Dorian and maybe, sort of... use one of the library's computers.

I knew Reed would lose his mind if I suggested getting

within ten feet of the internet... but I'd also learned that Reed was overly cautious about everything when it came to me. He didn't think I was capable of climbing ladders, or using a circular saw, or even talking to friendly O'Learians without winding up in grave danger, let alone googling unsupervised.

I wasn't stupid—I wasn't going to make a Facebook post with my location and Reed's identifying information, for gosh's sake. I simply wanted to search my uncle's name to see if there was any public information on his supposed criminal activities.

Reed's Division contacts still hadn't gotten me any of the proof I'd requested, even after five days of me pestering him and him pestering them, and I was antsy. It felt wrong to enjoy myself even a little (and yesterday, I'd enjoyed myself a whole lot more than *a little*) while Danny was maybe (okay, probably) in protective custody, all alone, and I hadn't done a single thing to help.

"Mebbe if I had some hod coffee, I'd feel bedder—" I began, not ready to let go of my plans, but Reed shook his head like the conversation was over.

I sighed. I'd also low-key hoped the library might have a book or periodical called *Twenty Ways to Convince Your Lover that You're Actually A Competent Person*, but apparently, that would have to wait until Reed thought it was safe for me to leave my bed. There was some irony there.

"Or mebbe you could stay here wid me," I suggested hopefully. "We could both, umb... rest?"

Reed lifted one eyebrow. "Both of us in that bed, huh? And you think you'd actually rest?"

I bit my lip at his flirtatious tone. That *was* flirting... wasn't it? In light of new information, Reed's "pickup" back in Little Pippin Hollow had not actually been a pickup in the flirty sense, so maybe Van had been right when he said I had no clue what flirtation really looked like. But the implication of Reed's words and the way the look in his eyes made my heart pound suggested this might be it.

I wanted to ask Reed if last night had changed things between us or if it was just a onetime thing, but I'd sort of figured he'd grunt a lot about adrenaline and professionalism. If he was flirting, though, maybe that meant he'd enjoy a repeat as much as I would.

"Sure I would," I said. I tried for a flirty wink in return. "U-unless dere was someding else you wanted to do in dis bed, because if you wanded, we could..." I broke off on an utterly unsexy cough and managed to strangle out, "...do udder dings instead?"

"Udder dings. Tempting, but no." Reed stood and shoved his feet into his boots. "You're sick, Chris."

"But I can'd be sick," I insisted, though the words came out more like a croak. "Nonna used to say I was healdy as a horse. I haven'd missed a day of school or work since I was ten. I don'd *ged* sick."

"Sure. Just like you don't argue and you don't take risks and you're actually a very boring person." He pawed through the T-shirts he'd stacked on a shelf in the closet and chose a light gray one.

"Exacdly." I sat up. "You understand."

Reed reached out one large hand and gently pushed me back down. "I *understand* that you took a polar plunge yesterday—"

"Bud everyone knows you don'd catch colds from being in cold wader, Reed." I sound whiny. I was never whiny. "My nonna used to say—"

He covered my mouth with his hand. "Unless you're going to tell me that your nonna used to say a severe chill can weaken your immune system, making it more difficult for your body to fight off a virus it might already have contracted, I really don't think I want to know." He frowned and moved his hand to my forehead. "Damn. I think you have a fever."

Come to think of it, that might also explain my uncomfortable warmth, especially since I was still feeling it despite Reed's chest being covered.

"Your choices are these." Reed sat down again. He combed his fingers through my hair, and the gentle tug on my scalp felt so good my eyes shut and my whole brain went numb in an instant. "You listening?"

"*Hnnn*," I agreed.

His voice lowered to a rumble. "You can stay here and rest up while I make a quick trip to town for supplies—and I mean *genuinely* quick, not Chris-level quick, which isn't quick at all—"

"Uh-huh. I mean, nuh-uh. I mean…" I frowned. "Do the ding wid your hand again?"

Chuckling, he repeated his movement. "Or your other option is that I take you to an urgent care place and get you checked over. You can tell *them* about your superhuman immune system. I'm sure they'll be impressed."

I sighed. "Bud Ash at the bakery said dey'd have maple bacon cupcakes today. I've never had a maple bacon cupcake."

"Mmm." Reed dragged his fingers over my scalp again. "That's tough."

"And Micah at the flower shop wanded to talk to me about a unicorn-themed charcuderie for his niece's birdday party. I had so many ideas…"

"Uh-huh. They'll keep for a couple days," he soothed.

"And Watt's friend's never seen *John Ruffian*, so Watt

told him we could rewadch the whole series starting tonight. Poor Oliver just broke up with his boyfriend, so he's feeling kind of low—"

"Jesus Christ," Reed muttered. "Is there a single gay man in this town or the next that you don't know?"

My eyes flew open. "Huh?"

"Nothing. *Nothing*. I'll let everyone know you're sorry you missed them, okay? And I'll tell Watt you're very contagious," he added darkly.

I sniffed, which made me cough and my head pound until I closed my eyes again and rubbed the spot between my eyebrows. "I guess so. But I'm nod sick, so I won'd sleep, and I'm going to be really bored."

"I'm sure you're right." Reed stood. "I'm going to lock the door behind me, and I'll be home soon. My backup gun is up on the shelf—"

"Doesn'd matter," I reminded him. I let out a yawn so wide my jaw cracked. "I won'd use it."

"I figured, but I wanted you to know just in case." He leaned toward me and inhaled deeply, almost like he was... sniffing me? Maybe I was sicker than I thought.

He pressed a gentle kiss to my forehead, and before I could wrestle my eyes open to kiss him further, he was gone.

To my surprise, I *did* fall asleep and only woke up again when I heard Reed's key in the lock, followed by a muffled *thud* like he'd been carrying something heavy.

"Reed?" I mumbled. I sat up and rubbed my eyes. I sniffed cautiously and found that my congestion had cleared up a lot. "What time is it?" The sky outside the small bedroom window was twilight dark.

"Early afternoon." He appeared in the bedroom doorway, dark hair curling and T-shirt splattered with raindrops. "Pretty sure Hen Lattimer at the hardware store is some kind of witch. My weather app said clear skies all day, but the man predicted it was going to storm." A loud boom of thunder shook the small building, and Reed scowled. "And he was right."

He was so adorable when he was grumpy. Unfortunately for me, that was pretty much all the time.

"Did everything go alright? You, um, left quite a while ago," I ventured. I drew my knees up under the covers.

"I did." He leaned a shoulder against the doorframe and scowled. "Four hours ago. Four fucking hours for a trip to the hardware store and the pharmacy."

"Did something happen?"

"Yeah. *You* happened."

"M-me?" I glanced around the room, searching for a clue about what I'd done this time. "I've been here. Sleeping."

"I know." Reed kicked off his shoes, flopped sideways across the foot of the bed, and blew out a breath. Then he turned, propping himself up on one elbow, and pressed a hand to my forehead. "How are you feeling? Seems like your fever broke, and you sound better."

"I'm fine," I assured him. "Totally cured." My voice cracked on the last word. "Or nearly cured, anyway."

"Good." He flopped back down. "I'm sure your fan club will be glad to hear it."

"Fan club?" I leaned forward to peer down at him. "I don't get it."

"When I got to town, I started out at the hardware store." His green eyes fixed on the ceiling. "That was my first mistake."

I frowned. "But Hen's so friendly."

"He is," Reed agreed. "He asked me where my better half was, and I told him you'd caught a cold. He and all the old guys who hang out there already knew what happened at the lake yesterday. I guess Mary-Kate Jefferson is Hen's niece."

"Is she? I didn't know that."

"I *wish* I didn't know that." Reed sounded aggrieved. "Once Hen heard you were sick, he was so concerned he was ready to drive out here and give you last rites until I convinced him you were okay."

"Aww." I'd only met Hen twice, but I'd gotten the impression that he was a very kind man.

"No, Chris. Not *aww*." Reed shifted his eyes to look at me. "Because once I'd finally finished there—after spending forty minutes on a five-minute errand—I went to Hardison's Drug Store and got accosted by Doug Hardison and a couple of other people. Someone from the hardware store must've fucking run down the street to share the news because everyone *there* believed my husband had pneumonia after his heroic plunge into deep water—"

"Heroic plunge?" I wrinkled my nose. "Me?"

"Exactly what I said. But I guess Vega got a splinter on the dock, so her uncle came by the pharmacy for ointment and told Doug Hardison about the incident at the lake, and then he told all his customers."

"Oh."

"Yeah, *oh*. One lady complained that Abe Wrigley should never have dug out the bottom of the lake because it was a drowning hazard. Another said she could tell from looking at you that you were delicate, and was I *sure* you shouldn't be in the hospital? Like I don't know how to take care of my own husband, for fuck's sake." He pursed his lips and shook his head. "Doug Hardison sent you a box of chocolates, and his wife sent along some magazines for you. She wanted me to tell you there's a whole article on charcuterie boards in one of them, which she thought you'd enjoy since she heard you're a charcuterie specialist, and the other has ideas for turning your garden shed into a rustic retreat, which she thought would help with your renovation plans for the cabins." He raised an eyebrow. "Which was news to me since I thought we had no renovation budget and were just making them habitable."

"Well, yessss," I allowed. "But Watt said they can't rent them as they are, right? And they won't have money to renovate until they're rented? So I was thinking... what if we made a little effort to get a couple of them really pretty and maybe also get a couple of the RV parking sites cleaned up? We could attract people *now*, and then everyone would be..." I coughed. "Better off."

"Sure. Because what we need is more people around. Because it wasn't enough that when I finally managed to get away from the drugstore and headed back to the car, that huge guy you met the other day stuck his head out of the bakery, all 'Mr. Sunday? We heard Chris got a *severe lung infection* from his *catastrophic plummet* into the lake. Is he gonna be okay? Should we send flowers? Should we start a *meal train* for him?'" Reed shot me another dark look. "If only you'd been there to assure everyone you never, ever get sick."

I pressed my lips together but couldn't help the snicker that escaped.

"Yeah, yeah. Laugh it up. While I was talking to him and assuring him that my husband's titanium immune system was handling the infection, *his* husband brought out a big box of cupcakes for you—"

"Maple bacon?" I breathed.

Reed's eyes softened. "Yeah, baby. Maple bacon."

I manfully restrained a squeal that was half about the cupcake and half about the endearment. "*Yay*."

He snorted. "And *then* while I was standing there trying to juggle the cupcakes and the shit from the drugstore, the guy at the flower store came out and gave me a giant-ass purple plant for you—which, let me tell you right now, is staying on the porch, because there isn't room in this cabin for all three of us."

My breath caught. "Oh my gosh! Micah is so sweet. I am making him the *best* unicorn charcuterie board."

"And *then* while I was trying to wrestle the plant into the car, the lady at the grocery store brought out some soup for you—"

"No way! Oh." I pressed both hands to my chest. "Reed, this sickness is the loveliest thing that's ever happened to me. *Ever*."

"You are insane," Reed pronounced. "Insane. It's not lovely, Chris. I get that everyone means well, but we're supposed to be laying low and hiding out here. Now every single person in Copper County and most of the folks in O'Leary know you. They know *me*. Small towns are the worst hiding spots ever—"

I shook my head. "They don't know you."

Reed rolled back to his side so he could glare at me more effectively. "I beg to differ."

"I mean, they know your name, but they don't know *you*. They don't really know me either... yet. They don't know that you're a Division agent, and they don't know what brought you here."

He pursed his lips. "I guess."

"They don't know if you like football or what your favorite movie is. They don't know that you're bossy and grumpy—

well, maybe they've figured *that* out—but they don't know *why*. They don't know where you went to school or what your hobbies are. They don't know why you're ridiculously overprotective, or how you got your job, or whether you like white or wheat toast, or what your favorite smell is—mine is jasmine —or why you're so overprotective." I laughed a little. "I mean, *I* don't even know those things, and I'm your husband!"

"Chris," he began. His voice was gentle, so gentle, and cautious. A tone that meant he was about to let me down gently by reminding me about his job and my uncle and danger and possibly—very likely—adrenaline.

I forced myself to laugh again. "Fake husband, obviously. Fake and temporary husband." I swallowed hard but kept my voice light. "I-I'm just saying, don't knock small towns entirely just because you didn't fit in *one* of them." I shrugged. "People in the Hollow think they know you because they used to know you, and they don't anymore— not the real you, anyway. So I bet being there feels like... like putting on a sweater from when you were a kid. It's too big in some places, because someone knit it for you to grow into and you never did, and too tight in other places no matter how much you stretch it out. Being *here*, though..." I leaned forward and put a hand on the rain-damp sleeve of his shirt. "That's a whole other thing. In Copper County, nobody has any preconceived notions about you. You can let people get to know the real Reed Sunday. Knit your *own* identity so you *know* it'll fit."

Reed's green eyes fixed on me so intently it felt he was trying to read my mind. I really, really hoped that wasn't one of the skills the Division had taught him because if it was... well, he'd be able to see all kinds of things. Things that would freak him out.

And I wasn't just talking about my plan to google my uncle.

I squirmed slightly. "So, um, now that I'm feeling better, maybe we could—" I cleared my throat, which made me cough, which made me sniff loudly.

Reed huffed out a laugh. "Yeah, you're totally better... from that sickness you absolutely didn't have." He did an ab roll and got to his feet in a movement so smooth I could never copy it, even if I practiced for years. "We are not messing around again—"

Before I could even process the disappointment of that, Reed continued. "—tonight."

That was *way* less disappointing.

"Stay here," Reed instructed before striding out into the main room of the cabin. I scooted to the edge of the bed and swung my legs over, but then he was back, carrying...

"Is that a... a TV?" I demanded.

"Yup. Did I not get to the part of my day where Watt— your new super-bestie—accosted me on my way out of the grocery store and insisted that I follow him back to his house so he could give you an ancient fucking television/DVD player for you to use during your recovery?" Reed rolled his eyes. With one hand, he opened a folding tray table, then set the small TV on top and knelt to plug it in. "He also gave me this."

He tossed a reusable grocery bag on the end of the bed, and a bunch of DVD cases spilled out.

I gasped. "Is that..."

"Seasons one through three of *John Ruffian: Pretender?* Yes." Reed pursed his lips like he was tasting something sour. "Watt may have mentioned bringing the other seasons over at some point so you could watch them together." He set his hands on his hips and gave me a narrow-eyed glare. "But I told him you needed to rest because you had a near-fatal lung infection, and that's nothing to mess around with."

I opened my mouth, then closed it and nodded. If I didn't know better, I'd almost think Reed sounded... jealous? But that couldn't be right.

Reed glanced at the floor. At the door. Out the window. Then at the empty side of the bed where he'd slept last night... and all the nights since we'd gotten here nearly a week ago.

"I suppose..." he began slowly. "*I've* already been exposed to you." His eyes met mine. "If I was going to get sick, it probably already would have happened."

Though I was almost positive that wasn't true, I nodded again eagerly. "Absolutely. Yes."

"So maybe I could heat you up some soup and then sit with you while you eat it."

"While we, um, watch *John Ruffian?*" I felt light-headed in a decidedly non-head-cold sort of way. All my favorite things at once? If I was still asleep, I had no interest in waking up.

"Sure." Reed rocked up and down on the balls of his feet. "I mean, it would probably be good for our cover story if I at least knew what the show was about. If we were really married, I'd have seen the series three times. That's what people in love *do*, from what I've seen."

"Yeah." Overwhelmed, I could only nod once more. "G-good point."

He nodded once and headed toward the kitchen, but he stopped in the doorway and turned back.

"Cars," he announced.

"Um. What?"

"My hobby. I like cars. My dad was pretty handy with them—with all kinds of machinery, really—and he helped me fix up my first car. It was a 1999 Toyota Camry, but we swapped in a 3.5 liter V6 engine, added headers and a high-flow catalytic converter, and a cat-back exhaust. That thing *roared*. When I got my Challenger—" He tilted his head toward the car parked outside. "—I always planned to trick it out. Customize it. I haven't made time to do that yet, but I will."

For the first time, I understood why Reed sometimes stared at me uncomprehendingly when I was speaking plain English. "Car" was not a dialect I spoke.

I didn't mind, though. The fact that he was sharing something about himself—anything at all—made me grin at him dopily.

"That's cool! So cool. Thank you for telling me."

"And my government name is... is Ernest Reed Sunday."

"Ernest," I whispered, delighted. "Really?"

"It's not the kind of thing a person would make up, Chris. No one who doesn't share my DNA knows that name," he warned, eyes narrowed. "And I swear to God, you'd better not use it. Five siblings, remember? I've heard it all. I do not respond to Ernie, Ern, or Nessy. I will not find it amusing if you ask me where Bert is. I will not laugh if you say *Earnestly, Reed*—"

Pressing my lips together, I attempted to look solemn and chastened.

"But I figure that's a... a thing a husband should know," he concluded.

There was no way this subject would come up even if we stayed undercover for the rest of our lives. No reason I needed to know this information, except that Reed wanted me to know. No reason to give it to me, except that he wanted me to have it.

To know him, at least a little.

And I would treasure it like the gift it was.

"It is," I croaked. "Super husband-y info. You can trust me, Reed."

He nodded and turned toward the kitchen, only to stop and turn back once more. "Oh, and Chris?"

"Yes?"

"I'm starting to think my favorite scent might be vanilla." His gaze softened, and he winked. "Sometimes, but not always, mixed with lime soda."

I blinked, not really understanding what he meant, but before I could ask, Reed grinned—a full-on devastating grin that made my heart pound and my brain hum happily—and I decided I could ask him about it later.

Maybe after an episode of *John Ruffian*...

Or ten.

CHAPTER TEN

REED

"IF YOU DON'T COME with me to the hardware store, you know they're all going to assume you've died of lake plague or something." I cast a glance at the gorgeous man in my passenger's seat as we drove down the winding two-lane road that led from Wrigley Campground to O'Leary.

Fall had come on for real now. The trees were a riot of color, and the distinct chill in the air made last weekend's warmth a distant memory. Chris was back in the hand-knit sweater he'd worn the first time he'd ridden beside me, but this time, his sunlight-dappled hair was a little damp from the shower we'd shared, and his cheeks were pink beneath his glasses... probably because that shower had involved blowjobs, and he'd been replaying it in his mind, if I knew my husband.

Fake husband.

Protect—

Never mind.

I couldn't get too up in arms about what I called him since my dick had been in his mouth half an hour ago, and I could still taste him on my lips. Especially when just the sight of him made me more than a little tempted to pull over and repeat the experience.

It turned out the need to have Chris in my bed—and shower, and sofa, and once yesterday up against a tree in the woods—hadn't gone away immediately after I'd given in to the temptation of him. The way Chris pulled at me was like gravity. You could fight it—and I'd tried—but it was a losing battle when your body knew exactly where it needed to be.

I mean, *for now*.

In a few weeks, when things with Dante were settled and I was off on my next assignment, when Chris and I weren't spending every waking moment just a few feet apart, when I didn't need to be close to him all night to make sure he wasn't feverish or thirsty or being hunted by his uncle's former associates, things would be different. Normal. The pull of him would fade until it died off entirely.

"Died. *Pfft*. As if." Chris waved a hand. "I'm fine. Super, entirely fine. Totally recovered... assuming I was ever actually sick in the first place, which I still don't think I was. I was, at most, ever so slightly under the weather. But that was three whole days ago—"

I made a noncommittal noise.

"—and Watt saw me just yesterday when he and Oliver stopped by with more DVDs—"

"Because the man doesn't understand what *contagious* means," I muttered.

"And I'm sure he's told everyone how, you know, fine and cured I am." Chris waved his hand again.

Chris had been fluttering quite a bit, come to think of it, ever since he'd given me my teasing "good morning, husband" kiss this morning and talking at increasing speed ever since we'd pulled out of the campground. *Hmm.*

"So tell me again why you don't want to come to the hardware store and see your fan club," I said, narrowing my eyes. "The whole time you were recovering, you were all, 'I wonder if Hen's leg has been acting up since it's been rainy.' And 'Hen said he'd take me to the diner where his wife works because they have amazing pancakes.'"

"O-of course I want to see them!" he argued. He toyed with the edge of his glasses. "Any other time, the hardware store is the first place I'd go. But I promised Ms. Dorian I'd swing by the library to get a library card, and that was nearly a week ago, so..."

"So all the library cards might be gone if you don't go today." I nodded. "That makes sense."

"N-no." His face reddened. "Today is the last day of the library card *drive* that she's running. She's giving out free laminated card sleeves. I appreciate good lamination."

"Uh-huh." I ran my tongue over the inside of my teeth. He was lying. Almost definitely. But about what?

"A-and I want to support her," Chris went on. "For some reason, people don't like Ms. Dorian very much. I think it might be because they just don't know her. I think she needs a friend."

And of course, he thought that friend should be him.

I sighed. "You know they're going to want to check your ID before they give you a library card. You can't—"

"Give her my license with my real name and address on it?" he snapped. "Yes, Reed. I know. I didn't even bring my wallet, so if she asks, I can tell her honestly that I left it at home." He softened his tone. "It's not about the card. It's about trying to do something nice for someone."

I stretched my neck to one side and then the other. I was being ridiculous, and my bad attitude was probably responsible for Chris's nerves. "I'm sorry," I said finally.

"It's hard for me to let you out of my sight. It feels like whenever I'm not with you, something dangerous happens."

Chris's big eyes went shiny with sympathy. "Oh, gosh, I should have known."

"Known what?" I scowled. "There's nothing to know. I'm supposed to protect you. That doesn't mean—"

"We watched season two, episode two last night, and it freaked you out when John Ruffian got trapped in the antique doll workshop," he said knowingly. "Nothing to be ashamed about. That one freaks me out, too."

"Uh, no. No way. I didn't freak out. I'm not *freaked-out*. I had a moment of concern because the workshop was on fire, and he had that dog with him, and I wasn't sure the dog made it out safely." I slowed as we approached the center of town, past quaint shops adorned with pumpkins and plants I now recognized as sedums. "And because those dolls had those fucking *eyes*."

"Yuuup."

"And because the show has zero relation to reality! None. It's a show about a man who goes around pretending to be a new person practically every episode, for goodness' sake. That's not sustainable."

"Right."

"And the villains *monologue* to their captives. No villain monologues in real life! *Jesus*. It'd be like saying, 'Hey, I'm gonna be over here mentally jerking off, so now would be a great time for you to escape.'"

"Mmhmm."

"Also? No professional in the universe would think, 'Oh, the building is on fire, let me construct a bomb out of doll-making equipment so I can blow the door open, and never mind that all the creepy doll hands and creepy doll feet will become creepy doll *shrapnel* that could fucking *decapitate* someone.'"

"Uh-huh."

I shot Chris a glare. "And I really don't understand why he needed to take his shirt off and oil his chest before he did the bomb making."

Chris pulled his lips in, trying unsuccessfully to hide his smile. "Yes, I remember you said the same thing last night—"

I nodded.

"—right before you asked me to turn on the next episode," he concluded, smug as fuck.

"Only because I wanted to see about the dog!" I insisted, pulling into a diagonal parking spot half a block down from the library. "Not because I like the show or anything."

"No, I would never think that, Reed," he said sweetly. "Not when you've made it so clear that you were only watching for my benefit last night. And every night. For the past three nights."

Reluctantly, I laughed. "Fine, maybe I don't *hate* it."

"I know that, too," he said saucily.

But when he reached for the door handle, my laughter fled, and I grabbed his sleeve. "Just... promise me you'll keep your guard up, okay?" I glanced up and down the street, where cheerful moms in knee boots and sweaters pushed baby carriages, two older gentlemen, both on walkers, chatted as fall leaves swirled around them, and a hand-chalked sign outside Nickerson's Books n' More announced it was *Mystery Monday, All Mysteries Half Off!* "I feel like there's something going on. Something I'm missing."

To my surprise, though, Chris's good humor fled as quickly as mine had. He let go of the door handle, but only so he could turn toward me, arms folded over his chest. "Do you honestly think something's going to happen to me, Reed? *Here?*" He waved a hand toward the sidewalk.

Someone walking by mistook his wave for a greeting and waved back enthusiastically.

Chris tilted his head as if to say, *See?* And I did see. But also...

"Look, O'Leary and Copper County seem safe enough, I grant you. But I thought that about the flamingo house, too, and there was a fucking gun battle on the side lawn—"

"And we still don't know if that had anything to do with us. We don't," he insisted when I opened my mouth to argue. "No one followed us, and no one knew we were there. You *suspect* it was related because you look for the danger in everything. And I understand it, sort of—that's your job, right? But you have no proof." He tilted his head. "Just like I haven't seen a single shred of proof about my uncle, even though we've been in Copper County for a whole *week*. I'm trusting you completely, Reed, and you promised—"

"I know." I clenched the steering wheel with both hands. "You're right. I need to message Janissey again and—"

"And *really push the issue this time?*" He cast his eyes to the roof of the car. "Because that's what you said two days ago, but then you got busy and forgot—"

"Because I really *was* busy! I cut down all the trees and grass that were choking the RV parking areas, I got the electric and water hookups working, I helped you paint the interior of Cabin 7 that Peace Yellow color you like, which took two coats, and I... I ran to town for supplies so you could make the butter board from the magazine— which was delicious, by the way." *And I am trying to protect you because when you see the proof, it's going to hurt you.*

My excuses sounded pitiful to my own ears, though, and clearly, Chris agreed.

"What happened to this work being only a cover?" he said, and though his voice was quiet, I knew an accusation when I heard one.

"I already agreed you're right," I said grudgingly, watching the older gentlemen inch down the sidewalk. I blew out a breath. "I'm sorry. Really. You've been more than patient. You deserve to see the proof you asked for. I'll get someone to handle it today. I swear."

"Okay," Chris said stiffly. "Thank you." He hesitated a moment, then blurted, "Look, I don't want to argue with you—"

I turned my head toward him and lifted an eyebrow. "Because you hate arguing?"

His lips twitched, and his shoulders loosened a little. "Yes. That. Although, with you, I don't actually hate it. It's even sometimes kind of fun because you don't get angry about anything except my safety. But I also don't want to argue because I know you're still worried about John Ruffian's dog. Spoiler: Lola lives."

I snorted. "Thanks a lot, husband. You've just ruined the whole series."

"The thing is," Chris continued in a more serious tone, "I'm an adult, Reed. I can take care of myself."

I lifted the other eyebrow.

He blushed a bit. "In any situation that doesn't involve guns," he conceded.

I lifted both eyebrows.

"Or... sudden, completely unpredictable outbreaks of beer-fueled aggression," he added.

I curled my lip.

Chris huffed. "Fine, *or* unexpectedly deep bodies of water. But I'm not very likely to encounter any of those things in the library, am I? And the thing is..." He ran a hand through his hair, disordering the damp strands, then bent his knee up on the seat so he could lean toward me. "Reed, you know how much I love my uncle, right? How grateful I am for everything he did for me?"

"Yeah, I know." I closed my eyes briefly. "You need to think the best of him. I get it—"

"That's not what I was going to say." He laid one small hand over my mouth. "Of course I think the best of him. He's not a criminal, whatever he might have gotten mixed up in. But the last few days, being with—I mean, being in Copper County, I've started thinking Danny kept me a little *too* protected."

I narrowed my eyes. Was that even possible?

"See, I didn't have a lot of friends when I was growing up." Chris rubbed his thumb over my lip and spoke abstractedly, his eyes watching his fingers. "And I always figured it was my own fault. I'm shy and I get nervous around people, which means I babble a *lot*. I get distracted sometimes, which can be annoying. My interests are kinda specific and unusual. I'm just not the easiest person to be around—"

"Bullshit," I said. The sound came out muffled by his fingers, so I grabbed his hand and held it so I could repeat myself. "Bull. Shit. Every person in this town decided after thirty seconds of knowing you that they wanted to be your friend. And *I*—"

I had thrown professionalism out the window because I craved him so badly—not just his hot body and his enthusiastic kisses, but his sweet smiles, his stammering, and even, sometimes, the arguing he claimed he was definitely *not* doing.

"Yeah," Chris sighed happily. He pushed up his glasses with his free hand. "It's been kind of amazing. But like I said, it's made me think. If I can fit this well in Copper County, why not back in New Jersey? Why not in a beautiful place like Little Pippin Hollow? Was it that people didn't like me? Or did I hold myself back so much I didn't give them a *chance* to like me?" He turned his hand in mine so our fingers slotted together. "Danny used to tell me all the time not to trust too easily because people had ulterior motives. He told me the world was dangerous, so I needed to be smart and tough and protect myself. When I was sad about some kid at school not wanting to be my friend, he'd flare his nostrils—that's a thing he does—and say, 'Don't you waste another minute trying to make people like you, Christoforo. You don't need friends when you have family.' And when I wanted to take the money Nonna left me and go to Italy on a cheese tour, he said it was risky to go alone and impractical to go at *all*. And when I wanted to take over the Cellar…" He sat back in his seat and twisted his fingers together. "Well, I already told you about that."

"Yeah." Chris, *too soft?* Please. I wished, not for the first time, that Dante Fromadgio wasn't under protective custody so that he and I could have a little chat.

"I know Danny only said those things because he cares for me. He wants me safe. He doesn't want me bullied, or to lose the business, or to accidentally take a train to Romania instead of Rome because I got distracted, daydreaming about a *John Ruffian* episode." He blushed. "Not that I would ever do that, obviously."

I huffed out a laugh. "Obviously."

"But when I came here, everything in my life was

already so... so mixed up—I was worried about Danny and keyed up from the business at the safe house and the low-key altercation at the roadhouse—"

"The bar brawl," I corrected.

"The *low-key altercation*," he repeated. "And, well, I might also have been trying not to, um, let a certain bossy person see that I was really quite attracted to him—"

I felt a slow smile spread across my face, and I squeezed his fingers. "Is that right?"

Chris's blush was one of the unrecognized natural wonders of the world. "I didn't say *you*. I said a *certain person*. I could have been talking about Watt."

I scowled, pulling him closer. "Not funny," I said darkly.

"The point is, I didn't have the energy to pretend to be anyone else, or to hold myself back. I just acted like my own, weird self. And... people liked me anyway." His voice held a kind of wonder and disbelief that made my stomach plummet in sympathy while my fingers itched to find every person who'd ever hurt him and show them the error of their ways. *Slowly.*

"So, now I'm thinking all that protection Danny gave me wasn't as helpful as he thought it was. Because maybe if I hadn't expected people to hurt me everywhere I turned, I might have put myself out there sooner." Chris bit his lip. "You can't cut a plant off from sunlight and expect it to thrive, you know? You have to expose it to the elements a little bit. You have to let it do its plant thing. You have to trust that it knows how to bloom."

I sighed. "You're saying that I'm making you feel stifled."

"No!" He hesitated. "Not... exactly. I know this is a different situation. I know you think I'm actually in physical danger. I know you're a Division agent, first and foremost, and you're doing your job. And I *like* how protective you are. I *like* that I feel safe with you and know you're looking out for me. A *lot*. I just... I don't want to be kept in a little pot anymore. I don't want to go through life scared. What good is being safe if it means you're not happy?"

I'd wondered a lot about how Chris had ended up so innocent with an uncle like Dante, but I hadn't considered what it had taken to *keep* him that innocent. How much effort Dante must have put into it, how many big and little lies he'd told... or what kind of toll that had taken on Chris.

I ground my teeth together. I shouldn't give a shit about any of this. My job was to keep him physically safe and whole, not to encourage him to "bloom" or whatever. Chris was right; I *was* a Division agent first and foremost. Or at least I should be.

The trouble was, I liked Chris. Very much. And I respected him, too. He was thoughtful, and intelligent and, yes, capable. I trusted his judgment. I trusted *him*, even now, when I was pretty sure he was lying about something, because I knew his intentions were good.

Keeping him safe at the expense of his happiness didn't seem right. It made me feel a little too much like the figure skating coach who'd told him he couldn't fly because nobody was strong enough to lift him.

A tall, dark-haired, solidly built man in a police uniform strolled down the sidewalk in front of us. When he spotted Chris, they both waved.

"You 'blooming' might not bother me so much if every man in this town didn't seem so interested in pollination," I muttered.

Chris turned to me with a frown. "Pardon?"

I shook my head. "Nothing."

"That was Silas." Chris jerked a thumb at the cop, who'd pulled open the door to the diner a block down the street. "His fiancé, Everett, is Hen's grandson."

I had no idea how Chris knew all this since he'd actually spent less time in town than I had this week, but I wasn't surprised. Not anymore. People, like charcuterie boards and horrifyingly unrealistic action shows, were Chris's thing.

I ran my free hand over Chris's smooth cheek and cupped his jaw. "Go on," I told him, nodding toward the library. I squeezed his fingers one last time, then released them. "Get your embroidered card holder or whatever the fuck. Just please try to avoid *all* bodies of water, even the small and placid ones, until I can teach you how to swim. I'll meet you back here in an hour and a half. Okay?"

Chris's answering smile was warmer than sunshine. But instead of reaching for the car door, he bit his lip again... this time with intent. "You know, the husbandly thing to do would be to kiss me goodbye. It would probably be good for our, um, cover story."

My stomach clenched with want, even as I pretended to consider this. "Good thinking," I finally agreed. My fingers slid around to cup the back of his neck, tangling in his soft hair as I drew him closer.

I'd meant it to be a short kiss. A tease. But as so often happened, the moment Chris sighed against my lips and I tasted his sweetness, my intentions went out the window. My hand slid down his back, pulling him closer until he was on his knees in his seat, fully leaning over the center console with his hands clasped behind my neck and his chest against mine.

He still wasn't close enough. I yanked at the hem of his sweater, needing to feel his soft skin against my palms—

Someone knocked on the passenger-side window.

"Chris? Chris Sunday, is that you? Are you feeling better? Have you finally come for your library card?"

Startled, we jumped apart. A woman I vaguely recognized as the librarian we'd met last week waited impatiently on the sidewalk like *I* was the one interrupting *her* morning.

"Fucking *fuck*," I muttered. "You will never convince me that I like small towns."

"Liar. This town's growing on you already." Chris laughed as he sat back, but it came out a little breathy, and when I turned to look at him, I noticed his glasses were askew. I fixed them so they sat perfectly straight on his face, resisting the urge to pull him against me again.

"Later?" he asked.

"Definitely," I agreed.

As he scrambled out of the car and greeted the woman, I fought the urge to follow. But Chris wasn't the only one affected by our kiss. I adjusted my pants before reaching for my own door handle. By the time I got to the sidewalk, he'd disappeared into the library.

My errands at the hardware store took considerably less time this morning since Hen Lattimer wasn't manning the cash register, and his replacement, a blue-eyed, young charmer named Theo, was quick and helpful without being nosy.

Is that the Theo whose boyfriend is Vega's uncle Bennett? I wondered as I loaded my supplies into the trunk. *Because if Bennett's old enough to have a teenage niece, there must be quite the age gap. Bet there's a story there...*

I froze in horror. Was Chris right? Had the town been growing on me? I slammed the trunk lid closed, silently vowing to gouge out my own brain with a paint stirrer if it ever produced such a gossipy, small-town notion again.

With an hour to kill and no desire to wander into any

other shops and face an inquisition about my husband, I knew I couldn't put off my call to Janissey any longer. I looked up and down the main road, searching for a relatively private place to make a call—a call that might ultimately involve a lot of yelling if anyone tried to stonewall me from getting the answers I needed—and decided the open lot under the "O'Leary Farmer's Market" sign on the far side of the street was good enough.

I walked purposefully down the sidewalk but couldn't help inhaling the crisp autumn air that carried the faint hint of woodsmoke, or grinning when I saw a mint-condition sunshine-yellow Chevy Corvette from the 1960s that could have been my dad's dream car, or shaking my head as the world's largest and ugliest camper gave a little warning honk as it putt-putted down the center of the street.

The town had its charms, I could admit that. It felt comfortable. Familiar.

Maybe it *was* growing on me...

Like a zombie virus.

I passed under the sign, parked myself on a nearby bench, and placed my call. To my shock, Janissey answered on the first ring.

"Sunday! I was just about to call you. You must have a sixth sense—" he joked.

But I was not in the mood. "A sixth sense? I've been trying to get in touch with you for over a week, and you've been putting me off. I haven't gotten an update on Dante or the Evanoviches, I still don't know what the fuck happened at the safe house you arranged, and it seems like nobody over there gives a good goddamn where I am or whether my protectee is still alive. He *is*," I added. "No thanks to you assholes."

"I get it. I'd be pissed, too. But you know what I'm

dealing with here. I just got back in the office yesterday, myself. And of course we know where you are. I got all your messages. I just trusted you'd be doing your job, just like I was doing mine—"

"If I don't have the information I need, how am I supposed to do my job effectively? How am I supposed to keep my protectee safe? What happened to 'Security Through Trust'?" There was a distinct note of bitterness in my tone that I didn't bother trying to hide.

"If you'd shut up a second, I'd give you information."

I shut my eyes and took a deep breath, trying to calm my temper. The sun filtering through the trees made brightly colored lights wheel across the back of my eyelids. It felt a little like kissing Chris. My voice was noticeably calmer when I said, "Tell me."

"Dante Fromadgio's agreed to the terms of a plea deal. Fucking *finally*. The attorneys say he's signing tomorrow morning. He's not happy about it, but he's going to testify against Robert Evanovich."

I opened my eyes. "Which means the Evanoviches are going to come after him harder." Come after *Chris* harder.

"Actually, no. Our sources now claim the Evanoviches aren't moving against Dante at all."

"Not moving against...?" I frowned. "Your sources are wrong. Someone was looking for Chris back in Vermont. That's what prompted this assignment in the first place. And they attacked our safe house—"

"Nope. We still don't know what happened in Vermont that got Dante spooked. And what we're hearing now is that the Evanoviches have turned their backs on Robert. He's not popular in the organization—a little too crime-y and violent even for them. Old Man Evanovich washed his hands of Junior and passed leadership of the family business down to a grandson, passing over Robert entirely. Now, the old man's gone to ground to ensure a peaceful transfer of power, and the grandson's trying to clean up the family's act and take their businesses legitimate." He snorted. "We'll see how that goes. In the meantime, everyone seems happy to have Robert in jail for a good long time, and everything's tied up in a bow. If there's a threat, Sunday, it's not coming from them."

If there was a threat?

"Well… shit." I stood and paced the area around the bench, trying to think. Did this mean Chris had been right all along? Was the shootout at the safe house related to Kenny's business, not ours? Had Chris's presence been nothing but a coincidence? Was I really just so determined to look for danger that I saw it even when it wasn't there?

"So what happens now?" I demanded. "If there's no danger, what does that mean for Ch—for my protectee?"

"Once again, asking the good questions, Sunday," he approved. "We maintain the status quo for a bit, but the end is in sight. I'll probably need to loop you in on a preliminary call about your next assignment in the next day or two, but we can circle back to that."

"Sure." I rolled my eyes. "Loop me in and circle back. Leverage those assets."

I tried to ignore a twinge of unease at the thought of my next assignment. Usually, I was more than ready to move on to the next assignment as soon as the first one was finished…

But nothing felt finished here.

"In the meantime, I don't suppose your protectee's heard from his family?"

"Oh, sure. The Marshals brought Dante over for a tea party just last night. Super fun. Sorry we didn't invite you."

"Smart-ass. I meant the cousin. Nicky. He's been trying

to find Chris… at least according to our FBI friends who've been keeping tabs on him—"

"Keeping tabs on him for what?"

"Usual shit." A squeak in the background suggested Janissey was leaning back in his chair. "They call him Nicky Knives for a reason, you know."

"And he's looking for Chris?" I demanded. "Is he making threats?"

"Chill, Sunday." He snorted. "Jesus. Yes, Nicky's looking for Chris. He's also looking for Dante. Which is what people do when their family members fall off the face of the planet. No threats. More likely, he's looking to contact his cousin for business reasons."

"They don't have business together."

"Not yet. But Nicky's lost a lot of clout since Dante took himself off the chessboard. And since he fancies himself next in line, that shit's gonna sting. He probably wants to get his cousin in line to consolidate power. Fromadgio 2.0 or whatever the fuck."

The very idea that Chris would agree to co-rule a criminal empire was laughable… at least to *me*. Janissey wasn't laughing.

"There's never been any indication that Chris had a role in Dante's illegal activities," I reminded him. "When I took this assignment, you told me he had no arrests, no investigations, not so much as a parking ticket. You said he was squeaky-clean. And that's definitely been my impression, as well."

"I told you he *looked* clean. But when you're dealing with a family like that…"

He trailed off, expecting me to finish his sentence, to agree as I usually did that there was no such thing as innocent. This time, I refused.

"Anyway," Janissey went on. "We'll have to see how things shake out now that Uncle Cheese is out of the way. But I don't think—"

"Could you not call him that?" I said without thinking. "It's a stupid nickname. Dante might be a criminal, but he's a person."

Janissey was silent just long enough for me to play back what I'd said and mutter a curse under my breath.

"Sunday," he began, "you better not be going soft for your protectee." The *not again* was unspoken but strongly implied.

I kicked at a rock. "This is nothing like last time," I said truthfully. "*I* provided us with a safe house, Janissey. *I* have been doing twenty-four-seven protection with zero support and no updates from you, which is like having one hand tied behind my back. I'm doing my job."

"Uh-huh. And the information on Danny's crimes you asked for? What's that about?" he asked, suspicious.

I hesitated. I'd already explained to Janissey, in my many unreturned messages, that Chris had no idea he'd been signed up for protective custody but was cooperating fully. I hadn't explained just how ignorant Chris was regarding his uncle's activities, though, because I knew Janissey wouldn't believe it any more than I had at first. You *couldn't* believe it unless you'd met Chris and experienced his kind, open nature firsthand.

Worse, I was afraid that if I tried to explain it, Janissey would realize that I wasn't soft for my protectee; I was... well, *hard* for him. Janissey would have me off the case so fast I'd leave a cartoon dust cloud behind, even if it meant he had to leave his precious office and come and take over this assignment himself.

A week ago, I might have agreed that was a good idea.

Now... I didn't trust anyone to protect Chris the way I would.

"It's about me having all the information I can get on the situation," I said, injecting a little righteous anger into my tone. "It's about me not getting a callback for ten goddamn days while the Division left me twisting in the wind. It's about no one thinking to share this info about the Evanoviches *or* Nicky Knives until now so that I don't know where the fucking threats against my protectee are coming from or if I'm wasting my time over here. Are you really questioning me, Janissey, after I prevented this assignment from turning into a massive clusterfuck *you* would've had to answer for?"

Janissey sighed. "No. You're right. You're a good agent, Sunday, and I owe you one. I'll talk to the Marshals and get you a copy of Dante's agreement today. My word on it."

"Good. And keep me updated on *anything* regarding this case. If Dante so much as twitches, I want to know about it."

"Fair enough. Look, I know this assignment has been a shitshow," he offered. "I take full responsibility for that. We should never have gotten so short-staffed. We shouldn't have been forced to let untrained people take support roles—"

I blew out a breath. "Not entirely on you," I protested. "That shit's above your pay grade."

"Yeah, well. This isn't the first time the Powers that Be have gotten their priorities fucked, and it won't be the last. Next time you call, Sunday, I'll answer. Security Through Trust, right?"

This, *this*, was why I'd spent so much of my life with this organization. Not because of the higher-ups and their questionable priorities but because of the incredible men and women I'd worked with over the years. Because I'd felt like I was a part of something. Something big. Something *good*.

"Right." I stretched my shoulders, trying to dislodge the nagging tension there. "Thanks, Janissey."

"Sure. Oh, hey, before I forget, I got a message for you from your family. They called the emergency 'think tank' number a few days ago, but the message got routed to *my* inbox somehow, and I didn't see it until—"

"My family?" I interrupted, tension returning. "What was the emergency?"

Was it Uncle Drew? He was getting older, but he'd seemed fine when I'd left just over a week ago. Had something happened to Emma? Was Hawk in trouble? Was little Aiden okay?

"I dunno, man. Message just says Knox Sunday—"

"Why did they call you and not me?"

But I already knew the answer. They'd called the Division because I didn't carry my personal cell phone while I was on assignment. They couldn't get hold of me because I was busy working.

The idea that they'd needed me *days* ago and I hadn't known was an acidic burn in my gut, and it was tempting to vent my frustration at Janissey, but it wasn't really his fault any more than the other fuckups this week had been.

Besides, I was the one who'd chosen this career and then chosen to hide the truth of it from my family. I'd been the one who'd not only put distance between myself and the people I loved but erected a wall of lies between us.

This was entirely my fault.

"Gotta go, Janissey."

I jabbed the End button and quickly dialed my brother.

CHAPTER ELEVEN

CHRIS

"So, the thing is, Ms. Dorian, I'm not really sure I qualify for a library card," I said as she held open the library's thick walnut door. "I don't actually live here. We're just staying at the campground temporarily. So..."

"Learning is a lifelong endeavor, Mr. Sunday," she said firmly. She peered at me over the top of her glasses. "And there's no better way to learn than to read, is there?"

"Uh... well, no, that's true," I agreed. "It's just... I don't have ID or an address."

"You leave that to me," she whispered to me as she led me past a sitting area with comfortable couches and chairs to the circulation desk. The building was hushed and quiet this early in the day, but the silence held all kinds of happy potential. Dust motes floated in the sunlight streaming through the window, making the polished wood shelves that ringed the room positively gleam. "The upside of being known around O'Leary as *Dragon* Dorian is that no one in town will question me." She shot me a wink.

I laughed out loud before clapping a hand to my mouth to muffle it, and she smiled her approval.

"Now," she said, turning on her computer. "Name... Chris Sunday."

I nodded.

"Address... we'll use the campground for now," Ms. Dorian went on. "And date of birth?"

I mumbled out the date.

"Hmm." She tilted her head to look at me. "You know, I'd never have picked you for a Virgo. You have real Libra energy."

"Right?" I pressed a hand to my chest. "That's what I've always thought, too. Not that there's anything wrong with being a Virgo, but it makes people think I'm a certain way, and I'm really not."

"Mmhmm. It'll take me just a second to print your card and get your holder ready. Feel free to explore on your own if you'd like. Or if you'd like me to show you around, I could—"

"Actually." I licked my lips. "You mentioned the other day that you had a... um... computer lab?" I said the last words in a guilty whisper, half expecting a SWAT team led by Reed Sunday to come bursting through the doors and stop me.

Instead, when the door opened, a tall, grumpy-looking man came in, towed by a pair of exuberant toddlers.

"Gideon," Ms. Dorian said calmly. She assessed the children, who quieted and straightened under her watchful stare. "Harrison. Harper. Good morning."

"G'mornin'," the little ones singsonged.

The man glanced around the space, looking a bit overwhelmed. "The kids wanted to pick out some stories. Er... bedtime stories. About firefighters? Liam's usually the library dad in our family, but he's out of town."

"Certainly." She folded her hands on her desk. "And I

trust we won't have a repeat of the unfortunate magic marker incident that occurred last time you were here... will we, Harrison?"

"N-no?" The little boy glanced up at his father, who lifted an eyebrow. "No," he repeated.

"And Harper, will we tear pages?"

"No," the girl said firmly.

"Excellent." Ms. Dorian smiled warmly and stood. "Let's head up to the children's section, and I'll help you find some books." She held out a hand to each child. To me, she called over her shoulder, "Computer lab is down in the basement, Chris. Let me know if you need help."

I stared at her for a long moment. I thought I understood why some people called her The Dragon... but I also low-key thought I'd just gotten a glimpse of what Reed Sunday might have become if he'd gone to librarian school instead of the secret agent academy.

I didn't think he or Ms. Dorian would appreciate the comparison, though.

I made my way downstairs, flipping on the lights as I went. Down here, the air was a little musty, but the place was neat as a pin. One half of the space was subdivided into a couple of private meeting rooms, each of which was outfitted with a large table and a stack of folding chairs. This half of the space held a tiny kitchenette with a water dispenser and minifridge and a dozen small cubicles set in two rows of six. Each cubicle contained a desktop computer that had seen at least a decade of life, along with a rickety rolling chair.

I walked all the way to the back of the room and pulled out the chair.

Did I feel a bit guilty that I hadn't been entirely up-front with Reed about what I wanted to do at the library? Maybe. A little.

But I needed to know things. Things about my family. Things that affected me. And despite how understanding Reed had been this morning, despite how much I honestly liked his protectiveness—good gosh, it was the hottest thing in the world—I wouldn't ask permission for things I, a competent adult human, knew weren't dangerous. I didn't want to live that way anymore.

Reed could trust me to make good choices. I would trust him to respect them.

All of which sounded pretty hecking dramatic, especially since the results that came up when I googled my uncle's name were... well, boring.

There was an old Yelp review of the Cellar—*4.6 stars, Best Gouda in Central New Jersey.*

There were several write-ups from our local newspaper over the years about Danny's gardening and the awards he'd won.

There was Nonna's obituary, listing Danny and me as "survived by."

There was a mention of him sponsoring the community theater's production of *Carrie: The Musical*... which was kind of a crime but not the type to get you in serious trouble.

I sat back in my chair, studying the screen, and bit my lip.

On the one hand, this was a huge relief. I hated to admit it, even to myself, but the more Reed talked about Danny being a criminal like it was a given, the more I'd... well, started to wonder, even though I knew better. I *did*.

But on the other hand, nothing in these search results proved Danny was innocent. Nothing told me where he was or how to help him.

If this were a *John Ruffian* episode, there'd be some sort of clue—a combination to a bus station locker or a convenient coded message that fell out of a book. But as Reed had pointed out, that show was just the teeniest bit... fictional. In real life, Danny hadn't left me any way to trace him or even a reliable way to contact him in an emergency. The only way I even knew he was still alive was...

The postcards.

Without giving myself time to question *What Would John Ruffian Do?* let alone *What Would Reed Sunday Most Definitely* Not *Want Chris Sunday To Do?* I sat forward, opened another browser tab, and pulled up my Instagram.

I'd started keeping an Instagram when I moved to the Hollow so I could share it with Danny when he got home, kind of like a modern-day slideshow of my time away. Since I hadn't gotten close to any Hollowans—hadn't tried to, as I'd told Reed—I hadn't done anything very exciting, and my Instagram reflected this. There were three dozen pictures of charcuterie boards. There was a picture of a photograph—specifically, the photograph of me, Danny, and Nicky at Nicky's high school graduation that used to hang on Danny's fridge—which I'd taken and posted the day I left New Jersey, already feeling homesick. There were a few pictures of cows doing cute things. And there was a picture of the first postcard I'd received from Danny so he could see how long it had taken for it to reach me via supply plane from his remote Alaskan fishing village.

Come to think of it, this might be why I had zero followers.

I quickly scrolled back to May and located the snap of the postcard Danny had sent—a vista of a magnificent Alaskan fjord that I'd hung over my bed at Van's house. The date on the postcard, in Danny's distinctive handwriting, was April 13th, and according to the date of the post, I hadn't received the card until May 7th.

I leaned in closer, examining the familiar slashes and curls of Danny's writing.

Dear C—

Caught a twenty-pound salmon today! Biggest you've ever seen. I miss you and I miss my garden, but I'm having the time of my life. And don't worry for a moment—I'm protecting my heart.

Love, Uncle D.

My eyes stung a little. Gosh, I missed him.

But there were no secret messages on the card that I could discern, and I doubted Danny had expected me to randomly dip the postcard in lemon juice to reveal his hidden plea for help—or, wait, was he supposed to write the message in lemon juice? I never remembered how the trick worked, which was probably why he hadn't gone that route —so I'd arrived at another dead end.

I moved the mouse to close the image, but just as I clicked the X, I noticed the postmark on the bottom of the card—a faint and barely legible P-something, New York— for the first time.

My breath left my body in a deflating rush.

No matter how much I'd suspected (okay, fine, pretty much *known*) that Danny wasn't in Alaska, it still hit me funny to see the proof in black and white and brought on a surge of emotions I hadn't expected.

I was hurt. No doubt Danny had invented the Alaska trip to hide the truth so I wouldn't worry. I was sure he had the best intentions. But still, this was a *lie*. A big, huge lie, from a person I thought I could trust.

I was also angry. What happened to "true Fromadgio honor"? What happened to family pulling together? Had he thought I wouldn't be able to handle the truth? Had he thought I'd be too weak to help him?

But above all, I was really hecking worried. Even more worried than I had been. Because now I *knew*-knew that my uncle was out there somewhere, possibly right here in the state of New York, caught up in something he might not be able to get out of. Was he safe? Was he lonely? Was he taking his heart medication? Was he anxious about what might happen to him? Was he missing me and Nicky?

I knew the answer to that last one, at least. Of course he was worried. He loved Nicky and me—that was one thing I'd never doubt.

I scrolled forward a bit to the family picture throwback I'd posted in July. The picture was ten years old, but I remembered that day like it was yesterday. Nicky, long-haired and slender in his cap and gown, me with my glasses glinting in the sun, Danny standing between us with one arm slung around Nicky's waist and the other over my shoulders since I hadn't made even a modest attempt at a growth spurt until I was seventeen. All of us were cheesing at the camera.

Three very different people, but a family. A unit, I'd thought.

Danny had raised Nicky and me as brothers after Nicky's mom—Danny's wife's sister—and her husband were killed in a car accident. Danny and Nicky had been close because they both liked guns and girls and football. Danny and I had been close because we'd both loved Nonna and the Cellar. And Nicky and I... well, losing our parents was about the only thing we had in common, and he was impatient and sometimes rude to me because I was a hard person to like, but I'd tried extra hard to keep the peace between us, and it had all worked out.

At least until Danny had gotten sick last winter and decided to close the Cellar. Because while I'd been seriously hecking disappointed, Nicky had been *angry*. He'd yelled all kinds of things about how the family business was the only job he'd ever wanted, and how the only reason Danny hadn't given the business to Nicky was because of *my* feelings, and how I'd always thought I was better than him because I was a "true Fromadgio" by blood... which wasn't true, and also not what Danny meant when he said a "true Fromadgio."

But instead of talking things out, Danny had let Nicky storm off and made me promise not to contact him while Danny was gone. "I know you want to heal things, but promise me you'll let him cool down first, Christoforo. Give him time and space. When I get home, we'll all talk, and things will be back to normal. You'll see."

Now, though, I wondered if I'd be happy if things went back to *exactly* the way they'd been before.

Because after being around a whole town full of people who really liked me—who appreciated me for who I was, like Gina back at Trickster's Roadhouse had said—I was starting to think my issue with Nicky wasn't about me being unlikeable but about something deeper. Something he and I would both need to work on.

And after spending over a week with a man who protected people *as his job* but had been willing to listen this morning and accept that I needed respect and autonomy as much as I needed safety, I really wanted my uncle to give me the same respect. No more secrets. No more lies.

But before I could get to work on either of those relationships, I needed to figure out what was going on with Danny and get him home safely... I just didn't know how.

Requesting information from the Division hadn't worked yet, and I couldn't exactly call Danny up when the people protecting him would have confiscated his cell phone for his protection. But maybe... *maybe*... wherever Danny was, he had access to a library with a computer, too.

I gnawed at my lip for a moment, then opened another browser tab and brought up my email account.

Dear Uncle Danny,

I'm not in Vermont anymore, but you might already know that. I can't tell you where I am or else the person protecting me would lose his mind—and not in the cute way he loses his mind when John Ruffian does something I think is heroic and he thinks is "utterly unbelievable, by which I mean I literally cannot believe it Chris, because no portion of this man's actions is based in reality"—but in a very serious, shouty way. But I want you to know I'm okay. In fact... I'm doing great. So please don't worry, okay?

I don't know what's going on, and I really wish you'd told me the truth before you left. I wouldn't have been angry, no matter what it was. I would have tried to understand because that's what family does. I would have helped you.

I still want to help you.

If you get this message, please write back and let me know how you are and what I can do to help, okay?

I love you,

Chris

I sent the email, then closed the browser, making sure to delete my search history because I'd seen enough John Ruffian—and heard enough Reed Sunday—to know how important that was. Then, I made my way upstairs.

I felt surprisingly *good*. Lighter, kind of. Stronger, too.

I still didn't know what was going on with Danny, obviously, but it felt good to do *something* because I'd hated doing *nothing*.

Upstairs, an envelope was propped on Ms. Dorian's desk with "Chris" written on the outside in pink highlighter, and when I opened the envelope and saw my new library card emblazoned with CHRIS SUNDAY in bold, black letters, I felt even better.

Gosh, I liked that name. And I really liked the person I'd become now that I had it. Chris Sunday felt like a person who took risks. Who made things happen and didn't ask for permission. Who told people who he was and what he wanted—well, sometimes. Who was never confused with Christine Pritchard, the high school teacher, or Chris Marin, the mechanic. Who made out with the hottest man in the universe right in the middle of O'Leary on a random Tuesday morning and only blushed the littlest—seriously, just the tiniest—bit.

John Ruffian could learn a lot from Chris Sunday, just saying.

I traced my fingertips over my name and smiled. I knew on some level that the sooner I got this mess with my uncle straightened out—which I wanted to happen ASAP, obviously—the sooner I wouldn't need protective custody, and the sooner my name, and this town, and *Reed* would be nothing but an amazing memory, but I refused to dwell on that... much. Everything had worked out so far, right? So I'd deal with all that when it happened, too.

I left the library and strolled down the street. The big clock in the window of the Books n' More said I had another half hour before I needed to meet Reed, and I didn't see him near his car, so I decided to stop into the bakery to thank Ash for my cupcakes... except I didn't get quite that far.

Out on the sidewalk in front of Micah's Blooms, the

biggest RV I'd ever seen—the kind that looked like a huge tour bus, with a satellite dish on top and a car hauler hitched up behind—was double-parked. And on the sidewalk beside it, a man and a woman were having a spectacular argument.

"Well, I don't know where the heck to park it, do I, Bob?" A middle-aged woman sporting vibrant red hair and a pink sun visor scowled at a thin, potbellied, older-looking man wearing very short shorts and very tall black socks. "*I* have never claimed to be an expert in these matters. *I* wanted to take a cruise, like Raquel and Jerry. Let's celebrate your retirement by taking a cruise, I said. It's been twenty-two years of you focusing on business, business, business, I said, and now I want to have some fun. Didn't I say that?"

"You said it," the man agreed. The unbuttoned plaid shirt over his white T-shirt fluttered in the breeze.

"But did you agree, Bob? For once in twenty-two years, did you say, 'Yes, Dolores, let's do what you want?' No you did not. Let's cruise *on land*, you said. It'll be *fun*, Dolores, you said. I'll take care of *everything*, you said." She set her hands on her hips.

The man swiped a hand over his thinning gray hair and sighed a long-suffering sigh. "Alright, Dolores, alright—"

"*Alright*, he says! *Alright*. Is it alright, Bob? Is it *really*? Because the next thing I know, you're spending a big whack of our retirement savings on a camper because it's an *investment, Dolores*. And *think of the freedom, Dolores*. And *pick anywhere you wanna go, Dolores*. And what did I say, Bob?"

The man shook his head and rolled his eyes to the sky like the cloud patterns were particularly fascinating.

"I said I want to visit Fanaille. I said—and I remember this specifically because you were watching your bang,

bang, shoot-'em-up program at the time, and I said, 'Bob, are you listening?' and you assured me you were—I said, 'Bob, my angel, my beloved, my delight, what I'd truly like is to go to the bakery that did Marissa Corcoran's wedding cake. It's called Fanaille. It's out in O'Leary. And I want to stay there a week and eat every kind of cake on the menu.' And you said, 'Mhnnmh, sounds good.' And then I said—do you remember me saying this, Bob? Because I certainly do—I said, 'Okay, then you'd better book us a campground close by because I bet those places fill up fast in the autumn when the leaves are turning.' And you said, 'Yeah, yeah. I'm on it, Dolores.' But were you on it, Bob? *Were you?*"

I bit my lip to stifle a laugh because Bob's guilty expression suggested he had not been on it. Not even close.

"And now here we are." Dolores threw up her hands and gestured around the picturesque center of O'Leary. "We have arrived in Mecca. The cake is *right there*, Bob. And do we have a place to park the camper?"

"No," he muttered.

"No," she repeated triumphantly. "No, we do not. The Pickett campground is completely full, just as I predicted. And the bed-and-breakfast is full. And the hotel in Baxter is full also. And we cannot keep that beast of yours parked here for very long. So I don't know what *you* are going to do, Bob. I really don't. But if we'd followed *my* plan, we'd be in Aruba right now, sipping coconut-flavored alcoholic beverages while I worked on my tan and you pretended not to be watching ESPN on your phone. Instead, we are here." She lifted her chin imperiously. "And *I* am going to eat cake."

With that, she marched toward the bakery and flung the door open, setting its string of bells ringing.

And I... well, I did something Reed Sunday might never forgive me for.

CHAPTER TWELVE

REED

After dialing Knox, I managed to pace a path up and down in front of the bench, waiting for him to answer. I was only distantly aware of where I was—of the sunlight shimmering through the trees and the cool fall breeze making the bare skin of my forearms tingle.

"Hey there, stranger!" Knox answered. His cheerful tone had me bracing my hand against the back of the bench in relief. "Good to hear from you."

"I just got the message you left with the... with my company. Is everyone okay?" I demanded. "Did something happen?"

"No, Reed. Everyone's *fine*," he said firmly. "And that was the first thing I told the person who took the message, but I guess they didn't relay that part, huh?"

"No," I said, my heart rate slowing to its normal rhythm. "They didn't."

"Ah, well. Those are the breaks when you have a fancy-pants secretary who takes messages for you, eh?" Knox teased.

A muffled voice cut in. "They're not called *secretaries*

anymore, Knox. God." Gage Goodman, my brother's boyfriend, sounded like he was pressed against Knox's side... which tracked since the two of them were generally inseparable. "They're administrative assistants. Saying *secretary* makes you sound really fucking old."

"Thank you so much, Goodman," Knox said dryly. "What would I do without your advice and support?"

"Lucky for you, you'll never have to find out," he said happily. "Now, ask Reed about the thing and stop stalling."

"I wasn't stalling. I was reassuring him that we were all fine and then easing him into a conversation. In fact, I'd already be asking him if it weren't for *you* interrupting—"

"By all means, continue stalling by claiming how you're not stalling," Gage said eagerly. "This is fascinating, baby. Next-level stall tactics right here. I learn so much from you."

Knox heaved a sigh. "Never fall in love, Reed," he grumbled. "It starts out all hearts and flowers, then when it's too late to pull back, you realize you've signed on to spend forever with someone who won't hesitate to call you on your shit."

"It's hell," Gage agreed. "Now, *ask him.*"

I shook my head, amused. "Ask me what?"

"What my beloved means," Knox said, "is that there was an incident here in town last week—"

"Incident?" Gage squawked. "An incident could mean *anything.* An incident could be a... a traffic jam. Or Mrs. Hendelmann's cat sneaking into Jack's diner to give birth again. Or the cows in the orchard pasture finally staging the coup I know they've been planning for months, even though no one believes me. This was no incident, Knox—this was a potential *felony.* Right here in our beloved Little Pippin Hollow." He gave an aggrieved sniff.

"You know, Goodman," Knox said. "Some guys might

not think it's sexy that you sound like my third-grade teacher when you clutch your pearls like that, but not me. No, sir. Your little squawks and gasps of outrage really do it for me."

Gage squawked again, and I heard a muffled *thump*, followed by Knox's laughter.

"You are so fucking lucky I have a thing for lumber-jacks," Gage said hotly.

I snorted. "I miss you guys," I blurted. "I mean, I know I just saw you a week ago, but... you know I love you, right?"

Both men went quiet for a minute, and I rolled my eyes as I imagined them exchanging one of those silent, speaking glances that people in relationships seemed to master.

"I'm not dying," I put in. "I just had a... a *moment*, after I got your message. I thought someone was hurt or what-ever, and I realized I really need to make an effort to call more. Tell you about my life. I want you guys to, ah... know me better, I guess."

I wasn't sure where all of this was coming from. Chris would probably say I was *overwrought*. Possibly *freaked-out*. The idea made me smile reluctantly.

"You could move back to the Hollow, you know," Knox said. "I did. It's not Boston, but..." He paused, and when he spoke again, the smile in his voice told me he was looking at Gage. "...it has certain attractions."

"See, now, I don't think he needs to move home just because he misses you guys," Gage countered. "I appreciate my family way more since I left Florida. I still get all the Whispering Key weirdness on the group chat, but now I've also found a place where I really fit. Not to say that the Hollow's not weird, too, in its own way, but it's *my* kind of weird." He added sagely, "Life's all about embracing your own personal weird, Knox."

"So true," Knox agreed. "And I *do* embrace you, Goodman. Regularly. But Reed—"

"*Reed*," I interrupted, "is going to jump through the phone and strangle you both if one of you fuckers doesn't explain the felonious non-emergency you called me about. Immediately."

There was the sound of a brief struggle like they were fighting over the phone. Apparently, Gage won, because he put the cell phone on speaker and spoke next.

"See, Reed, the thing is, Norm Avery claims he saw you kidnap someone outside the Bugle last week. One of the servers left town about a week ago—"

"Chris," Knox put in.

"Not Crys," Gage said impatiently. "I just saw her yesterday."

"I mean Other-Chris," Knox said. "The one who helped Webb at the orchard. The guy who does those cheese board things... what do you call 'em?"

"Charcuteries," I mumbled.

"Charcuteries," Knox confirmed. "Thank you. That's the word."

"Ohhhh," Gage said. "Right, right! The quiet one. Keeps to himself a lot. Sweet, but kinda... I don't know if *boring* is the right word, exactly, but... well, boring. Except for the Ale-pocalypse." He snickered. "That was a hoot. Anyway, I guess that's the guy. He hasn't been around, and the last time anyone saw him was—"

"Are you serious right now?" I exclaimed, standing up again. One of the most gorgeous, quirky, sweet, intelligent, and genuinely funny men on the planet had lived in the Hollow for half a year, and *that* was what they remembered about him? How the hell had they gotten the idea that he was *quiet*?

When Chris said he hadn't fit in the Hollow, I'd thought he was being modest. I couldn't imagine anyone not liking him—hell, even when I'd *tried* not to like him, I couldn't help it, and God knew every woman, child, and *man* in Copper County had adored Chris at first glance. But from what Gage was saying, he truly hadn't fit there any better than I did.

Boring? *Chris?* Good Christ. If the man were any more exciting, my heart couldn't handle it.

"Calm down, Reed," Knox said, misunderstanding the reason for my outburst. "The fact is, Chris might have left of his own free will—nobody in town knows him well enough to say for sure except Van, and Van's gone camping. Norm claims he saw someone get in your car and that you peeled off... but since Norm was about four pints deep at the time and had already done his 'in beer, there's freedom' schtick, nobody's paying attention. And nobody has tossed around the word *felony*," he added, "except Goodman, here. You know how some people in town love drama—"

"I do not love drama!" Gage insisted. After a second, he admitted, "I might *like* drama. Drama and I are *dating*. But we're not in a committed relationship or anything. Nobody's using the L-word."

"Thank you for clarifying, baby," Knox said. "Anyway, Reed, I—*we*—figured there'd be no harm in contacting you to see if you had any information that could clear this up. I don't suppose you happened to give him a ride somewhere or if he mentioned where he might be heading—?"

"Or kidnapped him and stuffed him in your trunk because you suspected him of crimes?" Gage teased.

"For fuck's sake, Goodman," Knox said witheringly.

"What? It happened in season five of *John Ruffian: Pretender*. There were these vigilantes, and... Okay, okay.

Yeesh. Stop with the look. Reed knows I'm kidding," he protested. "You know I'm kidding, Reed, right?"

I couldn't respond right away. What the hell was I supposed to tell them? More lies, obviously. My Great Wall of Lies was already big enough to be seen from outer space. What were a few more?

I gritted my teeth and started with a truth. "I didn't kidnap anyone."

"Of course you didn't," Knox said.

"What happened was..." I began slowly, hoping for inspiration or, ideally, an interruption.

But when my deliverance came, it was in the worst possible form.

"Mr. Sunday!" a familiar voice called from way too close by. "Hey, Mr. Sunday! How's your husband doing?"

I turned and saw Derry Bartlett, aka Mini-Watt, bearing down on me, wearing a huge, goofy smile and a Camden-O'Leary High School Hockey sweatshirt.

Shit. Had my brother heard?

"Knox?" Gage whisper-shouted. "Knox, did he just say *husband*? As in *Reed*'s husband?"

"I think he did," Knox said grimly, removing all doubt.

"I swear to God, if *two* of your brothers get married before we do, Knox—"

Summoning a smile for Derry, I tried to tune the others out. "Uh. He's good. Much better. Thanks for asking. Hey, now's not a great time—" I gestured with my cell.

"Oh, sure," Derry agreed easily. "I get it. Just please tell Chris we're thinking about him, okay?"

"Chris!" Gage hissed. "*Chris*, as in—"

"Yeah," Knox said. "I know."

I closed my eyes briefly. "Yeah, I'll, ah... let him know.

Thanks again," I said, trying to subtly convey *Go away* without actually hurting the kid's feelings.

But Derry was as impervious to subtlety as his father. He rocked up and down on the balls of his feet, still grinning. "So, my dad said you're doing an awesome job renovating the cabins. Let me know if you need any help with the construction, okay?"

"Will do," I said. "But I think we're good."

"Construction!" Gage whispered again, so loud I had to pull the phone away. "Knox, he said construction."

"Shhh," Knox insisted.

"That's cool!" Derry said, happily unaware that he was the wrecking ball single-handedly dismantling a wall fifteen years in the making. "Oh, hey, Thursday night, a bunch of us are going out to Bennett Graham's house to watch the Draconid meteor shower. He's got an observatory at his house—or, like, *in* his house, actually—and it's kind of a Copper Country tradition for some of the families who live around the lake to head over there. Maybe you and Chris want to come, if you're not too busy doing, ah... honeymoon stuff."

"Honeymoon! Knox, did you hear—?"

"Baby, despite my advanced age, my ears do still work," Knox hissed. "I don't know what any of it *means*, but I hear."

"Derry," I said desperately, gesturing with my phone again. "I'm a little busy."

"Right! *Right.* Sorry." With another cheerful smile, he stepped away, and I turned my mind toward damage control.

"Except before I go..." Derry turned back around. "I just gotta say, it kicked ass the way you jumped in the lake to save your husband the other day. Like, seriously *so* impressive, man. Like you were his bodyguard or Navy SEAL or something."

"I'm, uh, definitely not a SEAL. I just... you know..."

"Love him?" Derry smirked. "I can tell."

"I..." I opened my mouth to deny it, then closed it again. "He's special," I said in a whisper.

"Sure. Anyway, see you!" This time, Derry finally did lope off... about a minute too late.

"Hooooly shit, Knox," Gage whispered. "Holy shit."

"That about sums it up," Knox agreed. "Reed, when you said you had things to tell us..."

"Yeah." I tilted my head back and glanced up at the sky. White, puffy clouds shifted by, heedless of the destruction below. "But I can't tell you anything right now, Knox."

"You *can't?*" he repeated slowly. "Or you don't want to?"

I swallowed hard. "Can't," I said, though I knew this admission, coming on the heels of Norm's accusations and Derry's revelations—*"like you were his bodyguard"*— would pretty much kill any idea of me being a mild-mannered think-tank accountant.

There was no Division requirement that my family couldn't know what I did for a living, as long as I didn't share details. It had been *my* choice to keep my two lives separate. But I couldn't discuss the details of an ongoing assignment, so I couldn't open the door any further than I already had right now.

Nervously, I awaited Knox's judgment and anger over my lies.

But when he spoke again, all he said was, "Jesus fucking Christ. Porter was right, wasn't he? That fucker bet me a hundred bucks you were some kind of secret agent back when he was fourteen, and now I'm gonna owe him, with interest. I can't believe I didn't see it."

I didn't know what to say, so I remained silent.

"Right," Knox went on, all no-nonsense now. "Look, we won't tell a soul about this conversation—"

"Agreed," Gage said readily.

"—and I don't expect you'll ever be able to tell us anything, but you'd better tell us what you can *when* you can... and soon. Otherwise, I'll hunt you down, Reed. Don't think I won't. I'm still your big brother."

"I know you are." My voice came out scratchy and weak, so I cleared my throat and tried again. "I'll call."

"Good. You better fucking take care of yourself, too," he demanded.

"And take care of *your husband*," Gage said gleefully. "Maybe include him on the call, also, hmm?"

After we said goodbye, I hung up and blew out a breath I'd been holding for fifteen years. I slid my phone into my pocket unsteadily.

The trouble with letting people believe you're someone you're not is that eventually, it feels impossible to correct them... to even know how to begin. I'd started out keeping my job a secret, compartmentalized and tucked away, but I'd told myself it was no big deal because I was protecting my real life—my family—from my work. Gradually, though, my work had taken larger and larger chunks of my time and focus. Had become my life. I'd been so deeply committed to being *Agent* Sunday that I'd forgotten who *Reed* Sunday was.

Until now.

Because over the past week, I'd found myself remembering. Remembering the hobbies and interests I hadn't made time for. Remembering my friends and family, the ones whose safety I'd prioritized so much, I'd cut them out of my life. Remembering the decisions I'd always said I'd make sometime in the nebulous future about whether I wanted a partner, or children, or a permanent home. Remembering... well, *me*.

And it had felt fucking strange at first, let me tell you. Like the pins-and-needles feeling of blood rushing into a constricted limb. But Chris's words at the dock the other day kept coming back to me—*it's like he doesn't want anyone to know him*—and that wasn't the way I wanted to live...

I just hadn't realized it until this sweet, sweet man had crashed "entirely unpredictably but low-key unavoidably," as Chris himself might say, into my path.

And so... I'd talked to him. I'd shared with him. More than I had in years because Chris was so easygoing and open, it was hard not to reciprocate.

So, in between episodes of *John Ruffian* the past few nights, I'd opened up. I'd told Chris stories about growing up in the Hollow.

I'd told him what it was like having a big family—how there was always someone around or underfoot, and I'd have killed for quiet and privacy—and then felt a little shitty about how much I took my siblings for granted when Chris explained how quiet his own childhood had been.

I'd told him what it had been like when my dad remarried and then, later, when my stepmother, the only mom I really remembered, left town.

I'd even told him about Seth and my first blowjob in the Grove back home, describing the awkwardness in detail because Chris was strangely fascinated by my teenage antics, and hearing him laugh out loud made me feel lighter.

Talking to my family today, just taking that first step toward telling the truth, made me feel lighter still.

Because it turned out Chris was right. There was something pretty fucking amazing about having people know you. See you. Accept you. Care about you. It was worth the risk to let yourself be seen.

As I walked back to the car to wait for Chris, I knew I should have been thinking about my job like the professional I claimed to be—checking my email to make sure Janissey had come through with the proof I'd asked for, anticipating ways that Dante and Nicky and the Evanoviches might still pose a threat, wondering what the new assignment Janissey mentioned might involve.

Instead, all I could think about was taking Chris back to the campground, laying him out on our bed in the cabin, and showing him that I saw *him*, every awkward, adorable, magnificent inch of him.

And then maybe Thursday night, I'd take Chris to Vega's uncle Bennett's house so the man could watch a meteor shower without having to steal a telescope to do it. Because Chris made things pretty and soft for other people and deserved to have people make things pretty and soft for him.

So lost was I in thoughts of Chris that when I heard the man himself calling my name excitedly from down the block, I turned to greet him with an unrestrained smile on my face...

A smile that died when I saw him leaning out the passenger-side window of the world's largest and ugliest RV, grinning from ear to ear.

"Guess what, Reed?" he shouted. "I found us *campers*!"

CHAPTER THIRTEEN

CHRIS

"She was so happy when I said we had room for her," I told Reed later, hurrying after him to the caretaker cabin, which was kind of tricky since his stride was a million times longer than mine, and I'd had to stop to get my groceries from the back seat. "And her husband was so relieved. I think I—well, Wrigley Campground, really—just saved their marriage."

He paused in the act of unlocking the door to give me an eyebrow lift.

"Seriously! Dolores is actually *very* kind when she's not annoyed at Bob. And she likes charcuterie! She helped me pick out all of this stuff—" I hefted the two enormous shopping bags from Lyon's Imperial. "—which are really *premium* meats and cheeses, so I could make them a board tonight. She's *very* well-versed with cheese and told me all about her favorite cheese shop in the city. I kinda wondered if she'd ever been to the Cellar. But obviously, I didn't ask her," I added quickly when he glanced at me again. "I didn't even mention the place."

Reed threw open the door and stalked directly to the

bedroom. I followed after tossing my bags into the little fridge in the kitchenette.

"And I thought it was kind of perfect timing since you just finished cleaning up the RV parking spots down by the lake. And she didn't bat an eyelash when I gave her the price. And Watt was thrilled when I told him—how lucky was it that he was right there in the bakery at the time?"

Reed grunted noncommittally as he crouched to take off his boots and throw them in the closet. His thin T-shirt clung to his back and arms distractingly as he hunched over.

"Look, I know you're probably annoyed that I brought home campers, and I'm sure it has something to do with my safety, but we *talked* about this, Reed, and if you're upset, I really wish you'd say so instead of—*mmmph.*"

In one lightning-fast move, Reed stood, stripped my sweater over my head, grabbed me around the waist, and crowded me face-first against the bedroom door. A second later, his warm chest plastered to my naked back.

He dipped his head so his nose grazed my neck right behind my ear and inhaled deeply. I wasn't sure why that was so, so very hot, but it was. *Oh, man, it was.*

"Chris?"

"Y-yes?" I asked breathlessly.

"I'm not upset."

"N-no?" I licked my lips and tilted my head to allow him better access. "That's... good?"

"Mmm. I'm a bit disappointed, but only because I had some ideas about what we might do tonight, now that you're feeling better. Ideas that didn't involve *John Ruffian.* Ideas that definitely don't involve premium meats and cheeses."

"Oh?" I asked curiously.

Reed nipped at my neck with intention.

"Ohhhhh." *Spicy* plans. Yes, please. Except...

"Oh," I said a third time, disappointed to remember Dolores and the hecking charcuterie board.

"Uh-huh." He chuckled and pulled me back against him with a hand on each hip. He was hard. Hard *everywhere*. And it felt so, so good. "You know what else I think?"

"Yes! I mean, n-no? I mean..." He rubbed his cock against me again and again through our jeans until my hole clenched and my own cock swelled so rapidly I was surprised there was any blood left in the rest of my body. But my mouth didn't stop talking. Nope. Didn't even slow down, even though I didn't know what the heck I was saying anymore. "It's hard to concentrate when you're doing that... *nghhhh*... but please don't stop 'cause this is the best feeling ever."

And it *was*. Nothing could feel better.

But when Reed opened his mouth, he proved me wrong.

"I think you're pretty fucking amazing," he whispered.

The words branded themselves into my skin, a sweet, hot pain.

"Really?" I couldn't help whispering.

He didn't reply but moved his hand to stroke my cock through my jeans, and even though it was not the first time —or even the tenth time, at this point—that he'd touched me like that, the blatant ownership of the gesture was so freaking hot my head swam. I arched into the touch, leaning my head back against his chest.

His hands moved to the button of my pants, and my breath shivered out of me.

Unfortunately, it took a whole bunch of words with it.

"I... I think you're pretty amazing, too, Reed. Like, so amazing. From the first minute. And I'm so glad I got in your car that day, even if it meant I thought my first date was kind of a low-key, slow-motion abduction—oh, *gosh,* oh my *hecking gosh*—" I cried as he oh-so-slowly lowered my zipper, and my dick sprung free with enough force to win an eager beaver award. "*Yesssss.*"

I waited for Reed to wrap his hand around my cock—every tiny cell of my body was legit screaming for it, like I wouldn't be whole until we were connected that way—but the touch didn't come because Reed had frozen behind me.

"You... what?" he whispered.

"Uh..." I replayed my chatter and realized what I'd revealed.

I squeezed my eyes shut as embarrassment filled me. I'd been hoping Reed would never, ever know how silly I'd been that first day. I'd been determined never to tell him and prayed he'd never ask.

One bout of sex-induced babbling later, that ship had sailed, never to return.

"Nothing!" I squeaked. "Honestly, nothing. You know I just... say things. Pay me no mind! Carry on. Do the... the thing. With your hand. Now, please?"

"Baby." He spun me around, green eyes tracking every millimeter of my face. "You thought I was asking you on a date?"

"Um, yes?" Substantial portions of blood were now flowing to my cheeks, and I knew it because my whole face felt like it was on fire and my manhood was un-manning at an alarming rate. "You said you were there to pick me up, remember? And you had the... the beard, and the flannel, and that smile. And I thought... I thought..." I swallowed hard, and my shoulders slumped as I admitted, "You were so handsome, I honestly didn't think. Van had told me to get out and live a little. Sow wild oats. Jump at opportunities. And then you were there, so I jumped. And it was a mistake. Obviously. Because you didn't want... I mean... Can we please forget this?" I pleaded. "I was really into the other thing."

I attempted to turn around and face the door again, partly so I wouldn't have to see the stunned realization on Reed's face and partly because I hoped that it would prompt him to resume what he'd been doing and get my blood flowing in the proper direction.

But Reed put his hands on my shoulders and stopped me.

"I would have," he said. His gaze shifted from one of my eyes to the other.

"W-what?"

"I would have picked you up. If you hadn't been my assignment. If you hadn't been my protectee. If I'd walked into the Bugle some night when I was home and spotted you working behind the bar, and you'd looked at me with those big brown eyes... I'd have picked you up. I'd have tried my luck, anyway. And if you'd agreed, I'd have taken you somewhere." He smiled. "Maybe to the Grove since you're so fascinated by it."

I smiled, too. "Okay." I wasn't sure if Reed was being honest or just really sweet, but gosh, I wanted it to be true. "Now, can we—"

"Chris." He shook my shoulders lightly. "Do you believe me?"

I sucked in a breath. His expression was more serious than I'd ever seen it... at least, when I wasn't actively in danger.

"I wanted you from the minute you got in my car, smelling like vanilla and lime." He pressed his forehead to mine, and his hands traced down my arms so he could link our fingers together. "I couldn't keep my eyes off you. I could barely keep my hands off you. I *see* you, Chris. Right now, you're all I see."

Reed sounded a little desperate. A little lost and a tiny bit uncertain. It was very un-Reed-like, but it made my stomach flip and warmth spread through my middle. Because seeing him like this, thinking maybe he was having... you know, *feelings*, even temporary ones... was so much more than I'd ever expected.

I liked it. I maybe even—my heart beat so loud I couldn't hear my own thoughts—maybe even *loved* it.

Loved... *Reed*.

It was hard to be embarrassed or ashamed about that when every time I shared some new weakness of mine with the man, he listened to me and supported me and made me feel strong. It was hard to hold back my feelings, or even *want* to, when every day Reed shared more of himself, making me feel like I wasn't just an assignment or a person he protected out of duty but someone he actually cared about.

So it was okay if he was a little lost right now. Because this time, he could follow *my* lead.

"If I'm all you see," I whispered. "Keep your eyes on me."

Then, I sank to my knees.

As I slowly and deliberately peeled Reed's clothes off, touched him and licked him in all his—and my—favorite places, he never stopped looking.

His eyes followed my every move. He saw me when I ran my tongue slowly around the head of his cock, when I lapped up the stickiness from the tip. He saw me when I reached down and stroked myself after he started making those deep noises in his throat that told me he was about to lose control.

And he never took his eyes off me as I took him deeply enough to choke and sputter.

His eyes were dark and knowing. All seeing. They touched parts of me no one had ever even considered looking at before, and they saw parts of me I'd buried so deep, even I barely knew they existed anymore.

His eyes on me were like an intimate caress that turned every nerve ending into a live wire.

As my release hit and my eyes started to roll back, I heard his rough voice break.

"Never want to *stop* seeing you."

CHAPTER FOURTEEN

REED

EVEN KNOWING that people were Chris's *thing* didn't make it easier to accept when the man threw an impromptu welcome party in the clearing outside the caretaker cabin where we were supposed to be hiding out.

To be fair, the party hadn't entirely been his doing.

He'd created an epic charcuterie spread for Dolores, Bob, and the two of us, as promised, but when Watt Bartlett and his friend Oliver had wandered over from next door just as we'd started to eat—probably to fanboy over *John Ruffian* with my husband—I knew Chris would *never* have been rude enough to send them away. And when Hen Lattimer had pulled up in a car driven by his grandson and grandson-in-law and had hobbled over on his cane to "see for himself" that Chris was okay after hearing he'd been spotted in town earlier, I knew it just made sense—in Chris's mind, at least—for him to offer them chairs, on account of Hen's leg, and then offer to light the fire pit so Hen wouldn't get a chill when the sun set.

And who in the world could *evvvver* have predicted, living in one of the most close-knit, gossip-loving towns in the known universe—having spent my formative years in the Hollow, I could say this with accuracy—that once you had three Coppertians and a few O'Learians in your yard, they'd proliferate like rabbits?

I mean, *I* could have predicted it.

In fact, I *had* when Hen had gotten out his phone—one of the ones with extra-large buttons so you couldn't misdial—and started making calls. Because when Hen had tried to call Micah, the florist, to come see some of the paint colors Chris had chosen for the cabin renovations and get inspiration for fixing up his husband's office, Hen had called Jamie from the Bar and Grill by accident. An easy mistake anyone could have made since those two names were so very, very similar. And naturally, Hen had felt the need to tell Jamie where he was and what he was doing, and Jamie and his boyfriend, Parker, who claimed they lived in a state of "perpetual renovation" at their own house, had wanted to swing by.

After that, it hadn't really been much of a surprise to anyone—except my sweet protectee—when Jamie had told one of the bakers, and Parker had texted his pal Gideon, and *they* had told their spouses, friends, dentists, weird cousins, and preschool playmates about the "party."

Literally thirty minutes later, four dozen people had packed up their pets and children, pillaged a couple of grocery stores, stolen every cupcake in Fanaille, and possibly hijacked a couple of DoorDashers before congregating on our lawn.

By which I meant—and this bore repeating—the lawn of the cabin where we were supposed to be *hiding out*.

Still, watching Chris swan around the yard, eyeglasses glinting in the firelight as he refilled his guests' drinks, cheeks blushing as they praised the food he'd prepared, smile glowing with newfound confidence as he explained his renovation plans, it was hard to be too upset.

Especially since I knew his happiness wouldn't last.

Janissey had finally come through a couple of hours ago. I had the proof Chris had asked for and more. Dante's unsigned plea agreement, detailing his many crimes, was waiting on my phone, weighing down my pocket. And I knew Chris deserved to know the truth, deserved better than for me to protect him at the expense of letting him live. But I also knew it was going to hurt him, badly. And at some point in the past ten days, that had become completely unacceptable to me.

As I stood against the caretaker cabin, keeping a watch over the clearing, Watt caught my eye and broke away from the people he'd been chatting with. He strolled toward me, pausing only to grab a couple of beers from one of the coolers someone had brought.

"Sunday." He handed me a drink, then took up a spot beside me, propping his back against the cabin wall to look over the assembly just as I did. "Nice of you to have us over."

Without moving my head, I side-eyed him up and down. He wore an insulated vest over a thick Henley and work-worn jeans, his booted feet braced slightly apart. In some ways, he gave off the same steady, tree vibes that my older brother Webb had—as though Watt, too, had grown out of the land he tended and would stay planted here until he died. But Watt didn't feel quite as settled as my brother. His eyes traveled around the group over and over again like he was searching for something or someone. Possibly for my husband.

My fake husband.

My...

My *Chris*.

"I had nothing to do with this gathering," I told Watt honestly, confirming what he had to have already guessed. "I just set up the folding tables and stayed out of the way."

Watt grinned and brought his beer to his lips. "Still. I doubt this was what you expected your honeymoon to look like." His eyes slid toward me. "Strange choice you two made, coming here."

"Oh my *God*, Gideon, try this fig compote!" Parker cried, drawing our attention. He grabbed a muscular guy by the arm and stabbed a finger toward one of the dishes Chris had set out. "It's the best thing I've ever had in my mouth!"

"You wanna tell Jamie that, or should I?" the other man —Gideon—said wryly.

Around the fire pit, laughter broke out as an O'Learian wrapped up a story I figured everyone had heard a dozen times, and folks sat back in their folding chairs—chairs they'd brought *themselves*, mind you, since people around here were apparently prepared to crash a charcuterie spread at a moment's notice—with contented smiles.

Further away from the fire, a gaggle of children ranging in age from toddlers to maybe twelve-year-olds sat in a circle, laughed and shouted as they played keep-away with Cupcake the dog, while Vega, Derry, and Zach—who seemed to have undergone some kind of personality transplant in the last few days and had actually dragged himself over here yesterday to help Chris clean up the cabin he'd graffitied—watched over them.

Dolores, Chris's new camper, chatted animatedly with Parker's boyfriend, Jamie, and Cal, the other baker, probably comparing notes about what it was like to be a redhead in a world that both loved and feared them. Meanwhile, her henpecked husband, who'd barely said a word all evening, sat in an Adirondack chair and watched his wife with a little smile on his face, like he hadn't a care in the world now that he'd parked his RV and his wife was enjoying herself.

I understood that feeling acutely.

"I suppose it *was* a strange choice," I said in answer to Watt's earlier question. "But Chris is happy."

"Seems like it." Watt picked at the gold label on his bottle. "You know, Oak never said how long you and Chris had been married."

He sounded faintly suspicious, and I fought not to show any reaction as I shrugged. "A while now. Sometimes, it feels like forever." Other times, it felt like the nine craziest days and nights of my life.

"Uh-huh. He also didn't mention where you guys are from. Or how you came to be on a honeymoon of indefinite length. Or what either of you do for work. Why do you suppose that is?"

I turned to face him, eyes narrowed. "I *guess* it's because I told Oak we wanted privacy.... not to share our business with a whole nosy town."

Watt didn't take exception to my cranky tone. In fact, he nodded like this was exactly the sort of reply he'd expected. "You know, I had my doubts about you and Chris, at first."

"Doubts? What doubts?"

"About who you really were." His eyes met mine. "I love my cousin, but the man doesn't have a normal friend. They're all famous rock stars, or Hollywood actresses, or foreign royals, or private bodyguards, or government agents."

I locked down my expression. "Is that so?"

"Yep. So when he messaged to say his friend was dying to renovate my neighbor's campground and he was bringing his new husband, I sort of wondered which kind of friend you were." He regarded me thoughtfully. "You and Chris definitely didn't seem married that first day—"

"Pfft. Not married? That's ridiculous." I scowled. "Sounds like wishful thinking to me."

"But then I saw the two of you together more over the last few days," Watt went on, unbothered and unhurried. "I saw the way you look at each other. I saw the way you take care of each other. Like, when you ran around doing errands for him the day after his accident at the lake. Or when he refused my invite for the two of you to come over and watch *John Ruffian* yesterday. Dead giveaway that he was trying to protect your dignity—"

"Protect my— No. No way. Chris declined because he's still recovering from his virulent and highly contagious lung pestilence."

"He seems to have made a miraculous recovery," he noted, watching Chris now. "And by my calculations, you two were probably ready to watch the creepy doll factory episode." Watt's voice held equal parts pity and amusement. "So I'm thinking Chris gave up the comfort of a big-screen TV and a living room that's more than six feet wide just so Ollie and I wouldn't see you scream."

"I didn't *scream*. Jesus Christ. I had a small but very justifiable fear for the dog's safety, okay?"

"It's the eyes," he said knowingly. "Gets me every time."

"Did you have a reason for coming over here? Or was it entirely to piss me off?" I demanded.

Watt's lips twitched. "I just wanted to tell you I'm happy for you two. That man's head over heels for you—" He tilted the neck of his bottle toward Chris.

Chris looked up from a conversation with Dolores at

precisely that moment and gave me a delighted grin that said, *Can you believe this turn of events?*

And I couldn't. I really couldn't.

"And you..." Watt snorted. "You're fucking gone for the guy. Big-time in love. It's kind of disgusting, frankly."

"I... I'm..." I opened and shut my mouth like a fish, not sure where I'd been going with that statement.

Instinctively, I wanted to deny it.

I didn't *love* Chris. I was attracted to him. Very. And I liked him. Liked him a lot. An aggressive amount.

And, yes, because I liked him so aggressively, I wanted to spend every waking moment kissing him, watching him cook, listening to him babble, sucking him off, snuggling him while he enjoyed low-quality television, working beside him, letting him remind me of who I really was, protecting him from every real and imagined threat up to and including paper cuts, and fantasizing about sinking into his delectable ass.

But that wasn't *love.*

I wasn't *in love* with my protectee.

Jesus. I couldn't even imagine what a clusterfuck that would be.

Because if I was in love, how would that even work? I might have been starting to cautiously consider my life outside of the Division, but that didn't mean I was ready to make a move. Not now. Not yet. And I'd seen what happened to people who fell in love and then decided they weren't happy, which was why I'd never wanted it for myself.

So Watt was wrong. Very wrong.

I wasn't in love.

I was just... really fond of charcuterie.

I couldn't say any of that out loud, though, obviously.

Not to Watt. Not when he'd believed our well-acted cover story.

So I cleared my throat and managed to croak out, "I... am." Then, I let out a long breath because it felt good to say it even if it wasn't—couldn't be—accurate. "Yup. I definitely am."

"Good." He knocked his shoulder into mine. "Chris is a sweetheart. The breath of fresh air we needed around here. I appreciate his friendship. Yours too."

I took another sip of my beer. "Wasn't aware you and I were friends."

"Well, that's only because we don't know each other yet," he said reasonably. "Do you like fantasy football?"

I snorted. "Not really."

"Same! Do you like... car restoration?"

"Yeah, I... Wait." I turned to look at him. "Did Chris tell you I was into cars?"

"Nope. Are you? 'Cause I have a couple I'm working on right now. I've got this sweet sunshine-yellow—"

"Chevy Corvette!" we finished together.

"Holy shit. I saw that car in town. That was yours?" I demanded.

"Yep. I'll bring it by sometime so you can see what I'm doing with the interior." He smirked. "See how much we have in common? Tell me you like hockey and I'll make us friendship bracelets right now."

Against my will, I laughed. "I grew up in Vermont. Yes, I like hockey." I ran my tongue over my teeth. "How do you feel about *The Cutting Edge*?"

He stared at me blankly. "The... the old skating movie? I don't think I've ever seen it. Should I?"

I remembered Chris's words from a few days ago. *It's a*

really good movie. The kind of movie where if you like it, I'll probably like you, you know?

I relaxed back against the wall, watching Chris float around the party like the world's prettiest, sexiest, most confident butterfly. Some new and rare kind of Copper that could only be found right here in this tiny town.

I wasn't in love with him. No. But I couldn't deny that watching him emerge from his chrysalis this week was a rare gift.

One I was damn sure going to miss.

One I wanted to hold on to and keep for myself as long as I could.

"Definitely not," I told Watt.

———

THE NEXT MORNING, Chris was still buzzing, despite the party not breaking up until after midnight and me keeping him awake until after two. When he woke up, it was with a grin on his face, and his good-morning kiss was fucking effervescent.

"I'm so tired, but yesterday was such a good day, and last night was so much fun." He nestled back against my chest as rays of golden morning sunlight filtered through the window. "And I'm very happy you and Watt are best friends now."

"We're *not* best friends." My hands tightened on Chris's waist. "We might have been friends, one day. We were heading toward a civil relationship. Until..."

"Until he made you recite the friendship pledge in front of everyone and pretended it was a Copper County tradition? Because I thought it was adorable. *I solemnly swear that I will be friends with Watt Bartlett—*"

"It was not adorable." I dug my fingertips into Chris's ribs in punishment, which had the added benefit of making him laugh and squirm against me.

"Did I say adorable? I meant... *hot!*" he protested. "Adorably *hot*. And sexy!"

I bit his earlobe as he chuckled, and his chuckle turned into a sigh. "I don't know why you pretend to dislike him, Reed."

"No?" I grumbled. "Maybe because he's always making moony eyes at my man—I mean, the man he thinks is my man," I corrected.

"He does not make moony eyes! He's friendly and respectful. If I didn't know better, I'd—" Chris snapped his mouth shut.

"What?" I demanded, propping up on an elbow so I could see his face better.

"N-nothing." He shifted onto his back. "Just... if I didn't know better, I'd think you were... jealous." He laughed lightly. "Which obviously you're not, but I'm just saying—"

"Uh. Obviously, I *am*. Because, once again, since you seem to have missed it, he thinks you're my husband." I scowled. "So he needs to keep his moony eyes to himself."

Chris blinked up at me, an expression of slow-dawning wonder on his face. "You're jealous? Really?"

"That's not the point," I muttered. I squinted at him. "What's that expression on your face about? What's going on in your head, Chris Sunday?"

"I was just thinking of something Amber said once about jealousy making a man... uh. Never mind." His expression turned thoughtful. "Do you think she and Knuckles are okay?"

"The biker dude? Yes." I threw myself flat on the bed

beside him. "I doubt that was Knuckles's first... what did you call it? Low-key tussle?"

"No, I mean *relationship-wise*, do you think they're okay?" Chris sat up and scooted back against the pillows. "I hope they mended fences and he realized the error of his ways. I hope she forgave him. I mean, he did rush to protect her when the chairs were flying. And nothing says *I want to be committed to you* like getting hit in the face with a chair for the person you love, right?"

I shook my head. "You're terrifying."

"Am I? I've never been called terrifying before. I kinda like it." He grinned brightly as he threw back the covers, grabbed his glasses, and slid out of bed. "Let's get up! I have big plans for us to work on Cabin 13 today. Some people say it's an unlucky number, but not me." He pulled on his underwear. "I had to tear out huge sections of drywall Monday so I could replace the wiring, and by the time I got the old wires all un-stapled from the studs, I'd run out of steam. Today, it's finally time for that old ceiling fan to come down—"

I sat up and grabbed his hand before he could move out of the room. "Actually, why don't you sit down with me for a minute first?"

"Why?" When I tugged his hand, Chris crawled back onto the bed obediently and sat facing me. His brown hair was messy above his worried face. "What's going on?"

I rubbed my thumb over his knuckles once, twice, three times. "Janissey sent me an email yesterday, just as Hen arrived. I couldn't show you last night while everyone was here, but I promised you—"

His eyes widened. "Oh. You got... you got proof?" He swallowed. "About Danny?"

"Yes. I'm sorry it took so long. If I hadn't been trying to

protect you, I would have forced things along sooner. I just..." I brushed his hair back, combing my fingers through the silky strands, unable to stop touching him. "I need you to know it's not because I thought you couldn't handle it. Jesus, look at how much you've handled this week alone. I just hate seeing you hurt." I set a hand on his thigh and rubbed my thumb under the hem of his boxers. "Not your weakness. Mine. Okay?"

Chris bit his lip and nodded. "Yes. Very okay."

I grabbed my phone off the nightstand and blew out a breath. I was tempted to keep touching him. To kiss him. To make him forget all about his uncle for a little while. I knew I could do it. I knew he'd let me.

But I wouldn't.

I unlocked my phone, opened the email, and handed the phone to him.

"I'd like to sit here while you read it." I adjusted his glasses. "Answer any questions you might have."

"Yeah," Chris agreed. He scooted closer so we were hip-to-hip on the bed and both staring down at the screen. I wrapped my arm around his shoulder...

And I felt the shudder move through him as he began to read.

"United States of America v. Dante Mario Andrea Fromadgio," he whispered. "So... official, you know? Double middle-named him and everything. And it makes it sound like he's got the whole c-country against him."

I nodded but said nothing.

"Parties and Charges..." Chris skimmed the first section of the plea. "Illegal imports. Bribery. Money laundering. Tax evasion—" He looked up at me. "See, that's just crazy talk. He filed his taxes every year! His accountant is Mrs. Rose's nephew—"

"But did he file them on what he actually earned," I corrected gently. "Including any income from illegal business dealings. That's probably what they're talking about there."

"Oh." His eyes clouded. "I... I don't..."

"I know, baby. Keep reading," I urged.

Both of us sat perfectly still except for Chris's scrolling thumb. I wasn't sure if he was even breathing.

"This says..." His voice cracked, and he cleared his throat. "The Defendant admits to knowingly conducting financial transactions designed to conceal the proceeds of... of illegal activity. When they say admits, they mean he... he confessed? He agreed that he—?" He broke off, shaking his head. "I know that's what *admits* means, I just don't understand..."

"I know," I agreed. "It's a lot."

He leaned into me further and continued swiping. A moment later, he uttered a broken noise and glanced up at me, eyes shiny. "This... this says Defendant agrees to forfeit assets obtained through illegal activities, including the Cellar. He didn't sell the business because he retired; he's going to have to give it to the government?"

"That's what it says." I squeezed his shoulder tightly. Eleven days ago, when I'd been frustrated as fuck at Chris's escape attempt, I'd have given a metric shit-ton of money to be able to shove this document in his face and show him who his uncle really was.

Now, I'd pay that same amount of money to have Dante Fromadgio actually be in the remote Alaskan village where Chris had expected him to be. "I'm so sorry, Chris."

"It says he's waiving the right to a trial and he can't appeal. He's going to testify against someone named..." He consulted the phone again.

"Robert Evanovich," I supplied. "Yeah."

"That's the danger?" he whispered. "Like maybe this guy—o-or his people, I guess—would want to prevent Danny from testifying?"

"Maybe. Actually…" I ran my hand down his arm. "Yesterday, Janissey told me the Evanovich organization has no feud with your uncle. They've washed their hands of this Robert—" I nodded at the screen. "—and they supposedly don't care if Dante testifies and puts him in jail. On the surface, it doesn't look like they have any reason to move against you."

Chris huffed out a laugh that was a little high-pitched and a little wrong. "So… so I was right? There's never been a threat? We… we came to Copper County for nothing?"

"No," I said firmly. "I'm telling you that the Evanovich family isn't officially taking action, but for all we know, Robert might still have loyal lieutenants out there. And Dante named names and pointed the finger at plenty of other people. Any one of them could be more angry than we realize. My instincts have been telling me there's a threat since the very beginning, and that's not overprotection," I added quickly. "That's real talk. And we can't forget what happened in Springfield at the flamingo house. Something's not adding up, but I can't put my finger on it."

Chris jumped up and began pacing the three feet of empty space between the bed and the door. When he passed the hand-knit sweater lying exactly where it had landed when I'd stripped it off him yesterday—just before laying him down, kissing the smile off his face, and sucking him down my throat until he screamed my name—he gave the garment a vicious kick. Then he stopped, picked it up, shook it out, and put it on, pulling the sleeves down his hands.

It felt like watching someone put on armor.

"Chris." I jumped out of bed and grabbed him by the shoulders. "Talk to me. Please."

"I just keep thinking there's been a mistake. I... I thought when I saw that list—" He nodded at my phone on the bed. "—I would be able to say, 'Aha, Reed! This is where you went wrong.' But..." He shook his head, and a tear tracked down his cheek.

"Baby." I brushed my thumb over his cheek, catching the wetness and rubbing it away.

"I already knew he... he wasn't telling the truth about Alaska," Chris said in a whisper. "I'm not sure why this is hitting me so hard. I mean... I mean... it's still possible there's a mistake, right? Or that Danny's covering for... someone?" He caught his breath with a little sob.

I opened my mouth to agree with him. To say, "Yeah, baby, that's totally possible," even though it wasn't, just to see him smile again. But wouldn't that just be another kind of false protection? If I could burn the world to fix this for him, I would. Since that wasn't an option, I'd give him truth.

"Chris." I pulled him into a hug. "You remember me telling you before what I knew about Dante, right? This investigation has been going on for a long time. Your uncle knew they had evidence on him, and that's why he turned himself in. He made this plea deal to avoid prison time. I wish, I *wish*, there was another explanation that made sense. But I won't lie to you, I can't think of one."

He rubbed his cheek into my chest, leaving tearstains over my heart. "I know," he whispered.

"You didn't read the whole document, so you might not have gotten to the part where it says he's not going to prison," I offered. "Once he testifies and forfeits the property as agreed, he'll have paid his debt to society."

"That's good." Chris sniffed. "But you said there are other people angry at him. He's going to be in witness protection after he testifies, isn't he?"

"That's usually how it goes, yeah." I ran a hand up and down his spine.

"So, um…" He glanced up. "What will happen to me?" he asked in a small voice.

"You…" My hands tensed involuntarily on his skin. "You have options. Danny could request that you go into protection with him. He's going to be looking over his shoulder for a while, so that might not be the smartest option, but it exists." I brushed his hair back from his face so I could see his eyes. The bleakness there killed me. "The other option is… you don't go into protection. The threat against you was so you could be used as leverage against Danny testifying. Once he testifies, you should be safe."

"Right." He closed his eyes. "Safe."

"You can do anything you want. Go anywhere you want. Back to New Jersey or… or to the Hollow. I'll take you myself."

"A round-trip abduction." Chris forced a smile that was only half as bright as it usually was. "And you'll, um… you'll be on to the next person who needs protecting, right?"

I felt like I was choking. "Yeah. Janissey's already talking about my next assignment, but I…"

But what, Reed? What are you gonna offer?

I wanted to tell him he didn't need to be alone. That I wanted to be with him.

But all the things I'd thought about when talking to Watt still held true. My job was incompatible with a relationship, which was why I'd chosen not to have one. Chris deserved someone to listen to his stories every day, to hold him while he fell asleep each night, to wake with his sweet kisses every morning.

I didn't know how to be that person.

"...but I'm here with you until the trial," I finished. "Four weeks, at least."

Chris nodded, then bit his lip, seeming to come to a decision. This time when his smile came, it was nearly bright enough I could pretend not to see the shadows haunting his eyes. "Then I think we need to use our time wisely while we're here," he said firmly. "Do the things we... we really want to do."

I tried to ignore the sinking in my stomach, the feeling that we'd engaged a timer that was slowly ticking down the seconds we had left together. "Cabin 13?"

"No." He closed the short distance between us, pressing himself against me fully, arms wrapped around my neck. "I want you, Reed."

"Chris." I shook my head, trying to clear it. "But..."

"I want to know what it feels like to have you inside me so, *so* badly."

My head was a mass of confusion, but his proximity made my heart beat frantically in my chest, and my cock, which was always primed when Chris was in the room, had zero hesitation.

Just imagining being inside of him made my head empty until it was nothing but a bobbing vessel filled with scattered images of what it would be like to feel the hot clench of Chris's body around me.

I leaned down and closed my mouth over his, reveling in the familiarity of his kiss. No matter how many times I kissed him, it was exciting and new. I had a vague thought about work—about the meeting Janissey had scheduled for tomorrow to go over my next assignment—but it didn't stand a chance of remaining in my head when my thoughts and senses were so full of Chris.

"Lie down, sweetheart," I murmured, guiding him onto the bed.

Chris's eyes followed me as I carefully stripped off his clothes and leaned over periodically to press a kiss to a particularly tempting spot as it was revealed. There was no hesitation or fear on his face. His tear-bright eyes warmed under the attention, and by the time he was fully naked, every trace of his earlier upset seemed to be gone.

This was something I could do. I could not fix things for him, but I could distract him from the horrible discoveries about his uncle, from the revelation that his life would no longer be the one he'd imagined, that within weeks, he might be more alone in this world than ever before.

A deep, growling sound came out of me at the thought. It was unacceptable for this effervescent soul, this beautiful, sweet, generous human to ever be alone.

I yanked off my clothes as quickly as possible so I could lie with him, press my body against every inch of him, and show him exactly how *not* alone he was.

"Reed?" His big brown eyes blinked up at me.

"Yes, baby?"

His hand reached out to caress the side of my face, his fingertips light as a hummingbird wing on my cheek and chin.

"Thank you."

His words were like a spear gun straight to the chest. They were spoken with a tone that made it seem like he didn't feel worthy, like I was doing charity work by having sex with him. The very idea pissed me off. "What the hell are you thanking me for?"

My response came out gruffer than I'd intended. Thankfully, he didn't seem to notice.

"Thank you for making me feel love—l-love*ly*." Pink blotches colored his cheeks and began to streak down his neck.

I lurched forward and kissed every inch of those revealing blushes until Chris began babbling incoherent nonsense and I lost myself in his tight, welcoming body.

If anyone was going to make Chris Winowski feel love*ly*, it was going to be me.

If I couldn't stay with him forever, I was for damn sure going to do my best to set the bar too high for any other man to reach.

Because this man deserved all of it. And more.

CHAPTER FIFTEEN

CHRIS

Sometimes I was able to catch glimpses of the real Reed, and it was never more likely than when we were in bed together, when the world was miles away and it was just the two of us together.

The affection in his eyes while he proceeded to kiss my cheeks and neck was undeniable, and it made me slip easily into the fantasy.

To believe he was my husband for real and the tender attention he gave my body came from genuine adoration.

It was easy to believe it when, like now, his hands seemed to shake as they skated over my skin. His voice caught periodically when he told me how beautiful I was. And his cock arched stiffly toward me as if I was hot and alluring.

So tonight, I chose to believe the fantasy. I let myself feel *everything* with him as he moved over me, gently prepped me, and murmured reassurances into my ear.

"Just like that, sweetheart," he soothed as his finger circled my entrance for the thousandth time.

"I'm ready," I slurred. He'd teased me into brainless oblivion. The truth was I was past ready. Ready had left the building absolute eons ago. Ready was a distant ancestor who was nearly forgotten to history.

Ready could kiss my hecking behind.

"Is that what you want?" Reed's amused voice got my attention. I blinked my eyes open and caught him grinning at me. "Knees up, baby."

I obeyed immediately. Reed might have been bossy, but there'd never been a single moment where that bossiness in the bedroom hadn't resulted in very good things for me.

"That's it," he cooed. I felt the warmth of his exhale on the very sensitive skin of my—

"Wh-whoop?" I blurted stupidly. *Whoop? What the heck did that even mean?*

The hot press of his tongue on my hole was accompanied by his deep laughter. The vibrations gave the incredible sensation an extra kick.

"*Mrpfh,*" I added. My head lolled to the side as the sensations overwhelmed me. His mouth was magical, that was no surprise. But this was... this was more than that. This was extra.

"You like that, huh?"

I reached down and threaded my fingers through his hair to keep his head there. His laughter rumbled as he teased and tormented me with his tongue.

I'd never even known this kind of feeling was possible. Never known I could feel so close to another human. As he continued to pay every attention to prepping me, his hands roamed over my stomach, my thighs, my chest, and he even took one of my hands in his and held it tightly.

My heart thundered. Errant thoughts of a future with

Reed tried to sneak their way into my head and heart, but I forced them out. There was no room for reality in this fantasy.

"Please," I begged. "Want to feel you. Please."

Reed finished what he was doing, wiped his mouth on the T-shirt he'd discarded earlier, and moved up to kiss me under my ear. It was his favorite spot, the one he'd discovered early on made me whimper like a begging puppy.

He murmured soft instructions as he moved me into the position he wanted. When he was finally ready to push inside me, he paused until I met his eyes.

"You will tell me to stop if you need me to stop."

"Yes," I breathed, even though my brain was saying, *Like heck.*

"Take a breath. That's it." He continued to encourage me to relax, his deep voice slithering into my ears and turning my entire body to goo.

By the time his big cock began to stretch me out, I felt the sting of tears in my eyes, not from discomfort but from just how overwhelming it was to be this close to him.

Reed treated me like something precious, and at that moment, I suddenly realized just how much he'd opened himself up to me. He'd told me more about himself, shared bits and pieces of his life with me, and allowed me to see behind his big, thick walls.

"Reed," I breathed into his chest as he moved above me.

"You feel so good," he said on a groan. "Baby, fuck."

I tilted my head back to watch him as he thrust in and out of me. His face was flushed and his eyes glassy, his lips red and full from all the attention they'd paid to me earlier.

"*Reed,*" I said again.

"I have you."

Reed's cock struck something indescribable inside of

me, and I let out a feral noise. His eyes sharpened and darkened—intent on my pleasure, intent on *me*—as his cock struck me again and again in the same spot.

When my release finally came, I felt like I was flying. Like the butterfly I'd once wanted to be.

But at the same time, some part of me felt solidly anchored, too. Truly understood and really, truly safe... for the first time I could remember.

———

AFTER MAKING LOVE WITH REED, my emotions were a total whirlwind, and I spent the rest of the day on autopilot.

That afternoon, Reed had cautiously tried to bring up the topic of my uncle and suggest things I could do with my future—he even mentioned Little Pippin Hollow more than once, which was kind of funny since I knew how he felt about the place. He was trying to be supportive and helpful, which was so, so nice, and I appreciated it.

But for the first time in... well, ever... I didn't want to talk. I didn't want to discuss Danny or how confused and heartsick I felt after seeing the document Reed had shown me. Didn't want to consider whether Danny was actually guilty of the crimes he'd admitted to. Didn't want to plan for a time when I'd say goodbye to Copper County. And definitely didn't want to think about saying goodbye to Reed.

I wanted to linger in my afterglow and live in the fantasy a little longer.

So I lost myself in my work and allowed my mind to drift. I painted cabin interiors and sanded trim boards until my back hurt and my arms shook with fatigue. I barely spoke to Zach when he came by to help, and when Dolores sought me out to discuss custom charcuterie boards over cupcakes, I put her off, even though that would have been an irresistible temptation any other day.

There were some problems even charcuterie couldn't fix.

That night, I practically attacked Reed the minute he finished clearing up from dinner and led him back to the bedroom. I didn't want to discuss the party at the Observatory House he'd told me about, though I'd been fascinated by the house across the lake since the first time I'd seen it. I didn't even want to watch *John Ruffian*.

All I wanted was for me and Reed to crawl into a bubble together and shut the world out. I wanted his hands on me. His mouth. His hard cock. I wanted to memorize the exact placement of every tiny scar and freckle on his body and to learn exactly where to kiss him to make him groan, and curse, and melt.

Unlike the other times we'd been together this week, this time, there was no laughter or teasing banter between us. Reed kissed every inch of my body with slow deliberation, the intense heat in his green eyes not cooling for a second. And every kiss, every touch, had spoken volumes about how much he'd come to mean to me.

Before exhaustion claimed me, I reminded myself firmly that this wasn't the end. Reed and I had a month left together—which was weeks and *weeks* longer than I'd ever thought I'd have with him. That would have to be enough. I'd make it enough.

When I woke up the next morning, I was filled with a new determination. If I'd learned one thing over the years, it was that the only thing I could control was my reaction to a situation. So I could be sad—and I was—but I would also be hopeful. I could be uncertain, but I would also believe that things would work out, somehow. Because they usually did, in all kinds of ways I could never have imagined or believed.

Just a couple of weeks ago, I'd been a lonely, never-been-kissed virgin who didn't know beans about adventures. Now, I was a man who'd gotten kidnapped (but not), been in a gunfight (without firing a shot, thank goodness), witnessed a low-key (high-key) bar tussle, survived an acci-dental-on-purpose plunge into excruciatingly brisk water, gotten surprise-fake-married, made a whole bunch of friends, kissed Reed Sunday so many times I'd lost count (two hundred and seventy-three, give or take), had *sex* (of multiple varieties in way more locations than I'd dreamed sex could be possible!) with Reed Sunday, and fallen madly in love (in an unwise and doomed-to-be-unrequited way, yes, but still!) with Reed Sunday.

What were the hecking chances, right?

So I'd figure out a way to fix this, too. Fix things for Danny, fix things for me. Somehow. And in the meantime, I would enjoy the next few weeks here with Reed, soak up every kiss and touch like a squirrel preparing for a long winter, and leave this campground way, *way* better than I'd found it.

The first thing I did was roll over and kiss the heck out of Reed. "Good morning, husband."

"Wow," Reed breathed when I finally let him up for air and hopped out of bed. "You seem... happy." He pressed his head back into the pillows and licked his lips like he was still tasting my kiss.

"I am. I have lots to do." I pulled on underwear and jeans and only blushed a little when I noticed Reed watching me avidly. "Dolores wants to talk charcuterie, and I promised her I'd tell her about these Etsy shops where you can get custom boards. And I still haven't fixed the wiring in Cabin 13, but today is the day."

"Well, okay then." Reed sounded impressed. "Maybe wait until this afternoon to do the wiring, though, if you think it might go better with an extra set of hands." He got out of bed, too, stretching his arms up to the low ceiling in a way that put his gorgeous body on display. "I'll be out for a couple hours this morning, remember?"

I was so busy staring at the way his muscles all cooperated so nicely, turning a simple stretch into a full-on symphony of muscly perfection, that it took me a minute to process what he'd said.

Once I did, the realization almost—almost—took the edge off my newly restored optimism.

"Oh, right. That meeting with your boss you mentioned." I nodded and reached for a shirt from the closet. "About your next assignment."

"It's only a preliminary meeting," he reminded me. He cupped the back of my neck and drew me in for a soft kiss that spiraled into something hotter, the way our kisses usually did.

He pulled away reluctantly a moment later. "I need to get ready. The meeting's not until ten, but I'm gonna leave around nine. I need to find someplace that has a good signal or Wi-Fi *and* is private enough to have a Zoom. Something tells me that kind of privacy will be hard to come by in O'Leary." He took a T-shirt from the closet and shook it out. "It'd be my luck Lisa Dorian from the library would come knocking on my window just as Janissey started talking about sensitive information. *Yoo hoo! Reed! How's Chris's malevolent respiratory pestilence today?*"

"Actually, the library's not a bad idea." I sat on the edge of the bed to pull on socks. "They have good Wi-Fi, and if you asked her, I bet she'd let you use one of the meeting rooms in the basement."

Reed froze with his T-shirt around his neck. "How would you know they have good Wi-Fi?"

"I... Oh." I felt my cheeks go hot. "I emailed Danny when I was there the other day. The Division still hadn't gotten us any proof," I hurried to explain, "and I needed to feel like I was doing something, you know? Even if it was just reaching out to tell Danny I knew he wasn't in Alaska and that I loved him and wanted to help. I... I didn't tell him where I was, though. And I didn't mention your name—"

Reed leaned down and captured my lips in a quick kiss. "Okay."

"Okay?" I frowned. "That's it?"

He finished pushing his arms into his sleeves. "Yeah. If you felt like you needed to contact him, then you did. I heard what you said the other day, and I respect your right to make your own choices. I trust you, Chris."

"Oh. That's..." It was hard to express how amazing it felt to hear Reed say he trusted me, but it made me sit up straighter. "Yes. Right. Good."

He grinned. "And I understand. You love your uncle. You're always going to feel protective of him... just like I always feel protective of a certain person, even though I know he's perfectly capable of taking care of himself... in situations not involving guns, bar fights, and deep bodies of water."

I laughed, which seemed to be Reed's intention. "You always feel protective of me, huh?"

"I said a *certain person*." He winked and finished pulling on his flannel shirt, then stepped between my legs to run his fingers through my hair. "I could have meant Watt Bartlett."

I laughed again, harder this time, and leaned into him, my forehead resting against his hip. There was no better feeling.

"My point is, I know you believe the best of people, but *especially* when it comes to him." Reed carded his fingers through my hair again. "Deep down, you still don't believe Danny's guilty, do you?"

I blinked up at him and considered this seriously. "I... I don't know. There were a lot of details in that document you showed me. Like, a *lot*. Maybe too many to make up. And I... I trust you, too. Your judgment matters to me. And *you* believe he's guilty—"

"I wish I didn't," he said.

I captured Reed's hand and pressed a kiss to his knuckles. "Thank you. I'm also really hurt and... and *angry*. Because whatever else he did or didn't do, he lied to me. But... yes, even with all that, it's still hard for me to reconcile the man I know, the man who raised me to be honorable, with the person who did all of those things. I wish I could talk to him. I have a lot of questions." I paused. "And I might want to yell at him. Just a little bit."

Laughing, Reed tweaked my glasses into place. "Have I told you today how amazing you are?"

"You should feel free to tell me that as often as you like," I informed him. "Nonna always said if it's important enough to say, it's important enough to repeat." I wrinkled my nose. "Though, to be totally honest, I'm not sure if that's an actual saying or just something she made up after she started losing her hearing."

Reed snorted and moved away to put his belt on.

"Do you think I'm silly or naive?" I asked. "For still hoping Danny's innocent, even now?"

"Not even a little." Reed buckled his belt. "Believe it or

not, your faith in people is one of the things I lo—" He broke off in a choking cough and stared at the wall, eyes wide.

I looked at the wall too, but there was nothing there except faded floral wallpaper. "Reed? Hello?" I waved a hand. "Are you okay? Do you think you're catching my cold?"

"Huh? No. Yeah. I'm..." He stood. "I've gotta go." He stalked out of the room.

"Wait, what about your shoes?" I called.

"Fuck." He turned around and grabbed his boots, stuffing his bare feet into them. He pressed a hard kiss to my lips and headed for the door once more.

"Don't you want coffee?" I frowned at him from the bedroom. "It's only eight."

"Yeah. I mean, no. I have things to... to figure out." Reed ran a hand through his hair, grabbed his keys, and pulled open the door. "I'll see you later, okay?"

"Yeah. See you—" The door to the caretaker cabin slammed shut. "—later."

What the heck was that? I shook my head as I finished getting dressed. Then after making the bed, toasting myself a bagel, and tidying up the kitchen, I put together a charcuterie plate using the last of the ingredients I'd bought the other day and headed through the sun-dappled autumn woods to Dolores's camper.

She opened the door on the first knock, dressed in a bright orange velour tracksuit appliquéd with sequined autumn leaves. "Honey! I was just thinking about you. I said to Bob, 'Bob, I'm gonna look in on Chris today.' I said, 'That boy is off his stride. I wonder if he's been fighting with that handsome hubby of his.' And he said, 'Mind your business, Dolores.' Can you imagine? As if I haven't been minding Bob's business *for* him for over twenty years, which is a hell of a lot more than his first wife ever did, let me tell you. So I told him, I said, 'Never you mind *my* business, Bob. If Chris is still glum, I'm going to give that tall drink of water he's hitched to a piece of my mind 'cause no way should a ray of sunshine look that sad.' That's what I said. And now here you are." She narrowed her eyes and looked me up and down. "And you seem better, so I suppose your husband is safe from me."

"Reed?" I shook my head. "No, Reed's great. Reed's... he's the best. And I'm fine, I promise." I held up my mini charcuterie plate. "I'm here to talk boards, if you're still interested."

"Hell yes." She stepped back, ushering me inside and onto one of the padded benches by her banquette table. "You picked the perfect time. Bob's gone down to the dock so he can sit around gossiping with the locals and pretend to be fishing. If he were here, he'd have *opinions*. 'Dolores, what are you gonna do with a custom charcuterie board when we live in an RV, please tell me?' As though it was *my* fault *he* retired and wanted to sell the house. Four thousand square feet in New Jersey, and now I'm reduced to this." She waved a hand in the air like a game show hostess. "But I *will* have my charcuterie board, damn it."

"You're from New Jersey? That's so cool! I—" I cut myself off at the last moment. I still wasn't supposed to be telling people who I was, was I? Reed hadn't said, but it was probably better to be safe than sorry. "I've always loved New Jersey!"

She rolled her eyes. "Well, if we ever get back, I'll invite you over and give you an excuse to visit. You can make a charcuterie on my new board." She opened an overhead cabinet, took out a laptop, set it on the table, and gestured to me. "Now, show me the goods."

I pulled up my Etsy account, and the two of us fell down a rabbit hole.

"See, this is the kind of personalization I think is so cute." I pointed at the screen. "It's acacia wood with a custom inlay, which is why it's so expensive. But it would be cool to have it say, 'The...' uh." I frowned. "What's your last name?"

Dolores's phone rang, and she glanced down at it before dismissing the call. "Smith."

"Oh." I blinked. "Okay, well, that's easy enough. The Smiths. It's... it's nice, right?"

"Not bad," she agreed, nodding slowly. "But tell me about this one."

"Ah, *that*. That's for the serious charcuterie enthusiast," I said. "It's got multiple tiers and little bowls for olives and dips—"

Her phone rang again, and this time, she picked it up to look at the screen.

"Who the hell is Paul Fine, O'Leary, New York?"

I shook my head. "No clue."

She sighed. "If this is another spam caller, I'm gonna lose my shit," she promised. She swiped the screen. "Hello? Oh, Bob, it's you! What in the world? Why are you calling from—oh." She glanced around the living area of the camper. "Yes, I see it. It's right on the coffee table. Well, come back for it, then. Oh? How big a fish?" She listened for a long moment. "Good for you, sweetheart. Yes, I'm sure it's very disappointing that you don't have your phone to take a picture. Oh! Well, why didn't you say so? Good grief. Yes, I'll bring it down."

She hung up and shook her head. "That man. I tell you. Just terrible at communicating."

I opened my mouth, then shut it again. "Uh-huh. Sounds awful," I agreed.

"I'm just saying." She shoved her feet into a pair of bedazzled Crocs. "How am I supposed to know what's going on if you don't tell me, am I right? Help *me* help *you*, Bob. Show a little follow-through." She sighed. "Now, you wait here, sweetie. I'll just pop down to the dock and then be back. Find me the perfect board while I'm gone."

I nodded again. But after she clomped down the steps and hurried away, I found myself thinking about communication, along with everything Reed and I had discussed. I clicked on a new browser tab and opened my email to send Danny another message.

But when I logged in, I found a new email waiting for me.

An email from my cousin.

Seeing Nicky's name on my screen unleashed a flood of emotions that made my stomach flip around like the giant fish Bob had just caught, anxious and hopeful and guilty because I hadn't considered reaching out to him even once, despite everything that was going on.

Because he hasn't been a very good cousin, the new, more confident part of me thought. *Because I don't know if I can trust him.*

But you can't fix your relationship if you don't try, the kinder part of me prodded.

I forced myself to take a deep breath, and then I opened it.

Chris—

Hey. I know I'm probably the last person you want to hear from, but I don't know who else to turn to. Some guys came around my place today wanting to know where Danny is. They didn't believe me when I said I didn't know. They beat me up pretty badly and told me to "tell my uncle Robert Evanovich sends his best."

I know we left things in a really shitty place, and I really regret that. I'm so scared Chrissy. I really need your help. We're still family, right?

Love,

Nicky.

My heart squeezed hard, and I stood up from the table in a panic. The Evanoviches had gone after Nicky.

Poor, poor Nicky.

Why hadn't I considered that this could happen? Sure, Nicky never struck me as a person who needed protection before, but that didn't mean he was prepared to handle something like this. I should have contacted him before. Warned him or something.

I *needed* to contact him now.

I grabbed a napkin from the stack on the table and a pen from the little holder on Dolores's counter, scrawled down Nicky's phone number, and slammed the laptop shut. I was halfway back to the cabin in search of Reed before I remembered.

Reed was gone. In town at his meeting. I'd have to handle this myself.

Even as I thought this, a car pulled up the driveway. A bright yellow car, driven by a familiar figure who waved when he spotted me.

"Watt!" I cried in relief, running up to the driver's door. "Hey. Um. Could I use your phone, please? *Now?*"

"Well, sure, but..." Watt stepped out of the car, then pulled his phone from his pocket. "Is everything okay?"

"Yeah. Sort of. It's just a..." A thing I couldn't talk about at all unless I wanted to put Watt in danger, too. "A family thing. One of those times when I really regret not bringing a phone on my, um, honeymoon. You know?"

"Hmm." His gaze narrowed, but he unlocked the phone and handed it over. "Reed around? I wanted to show him my car."

I shook my head. "He had a work meeting, so he went to town for privacy and better internet." I hesitated. "Uh. I'm just going to go make my call—" I pointed at the caretaker cabin.

"Stay here if you want privacy." Watt shrugged. "I wanted to check out the paint job you did in Cabin 5 anyway. I'm thinking the color might work for my downstairs bathroom."

"Sure." I turned away and dialed Nicky's number with shaking hands. A second later, my cousin's cocky voice came over the line.

"Fromadgio."

Fromadgio? I frowned. Nicky's last name was Costello. "Nicky? It's me. Are you okay?"

"Chrissy? Fuck, it's so good to hear your voice." His confident demeanor fled, and he sounded like the kid he'd once been... and happier to hear from me than he'd been in years. "Shit. I've been calling you every day, and you didn't answer, and I figured you were still angry that I was such an asshole before you left. But thank God you called, man. Is this your new number?"

"No. No, no. I'm borrowing a friend's phone. I lost my own, and... and things have been a little weird. I'm sorry I haven't called you. I wanted to give you time to calm down, but I... I should have checked in with you before now." I sat on the steps of the caretaker cabin and massaged my forehead. "Are you okay? Are you safe?"

"I think so. For now, at least. But where are you? Danny

didn't tell me *you* were leaving town, too. Then I found out you were in Vermont—"

"I *was*. But, um..." I licked my lips. "You might already know some of this, maybe, but Uncle Danny's not on an Alaskan fishing trip."

"No?" Nicky sounded as shocked as I'd been. "Are you sure?"

"I'm afraid so. He got involved in some wild stuff, Nicky. Money laundering, tax evasion... And the government caught him. He's pretty much admitted to all of it. He's supposed to be signing a plea deal this week."

"He hasn't signed it yet, though, right?" Nicky demanded.

"Huh? Oh. Um. N-no." I frowned at the tree line in the distance. "At least, I don't think so. But did you hear what I said? Uncle Danny admitted to being a criminal, Nick. Did you... did you know about any of this? Did he tell you?"

"Tell me? Gosh, no. That's so weird, Chris! I just... I can't help thinking there's no way."

I shut my eyes. "I know. That's what I thought, too. But then I saw the list of stuff they're saying he did, and now... I don't know what to think. Except that guy you mentioned in your email, Robert Evanovich? Reed said he's bad news. If people are asking you about him, you need to be careful. Maybe, I dunno, leave town, or call the police, or *both*—"

"Reed? Who's Reed?"

"Reed? Oh." I bit my lip. "He's..." *Shoot.* Nicky was my cousin, and I felt awful for him, but I couldn't betray Reed that way. "He's been helping me out. He's a friend."

"Yeah, right." Nicky snorted. "You don't have friends."

I blinked. "P-pardon?" That casual rudeness was a record scratch, reminding me of the Nicky I used to know.

"I mean... I mean... I don't *know* any of your friends," he explained quickly. "And I'm... I'm so scared, Chris. I don't know what to do."

Nicky's fear overrode my caution. He sounded terrified. How could I blame him for being impolite?

I blew out a breath. "Listen, if those people who mentioned him come around again, call the police, okay? Don't let them hurt you."

"But what if the police are in on it? Who knows how high this conspiracy goes?" Nicky's voice was high-pitched and thready. "You're the only one I can trust, and I... I really don't want to be alone right now. Tell me where you are. I'll come to you. We can figure out how to handle this together. As a *family*."

I opened my mouth, then shut it again. "I can't, Nicky. I'm so sorry. But I'll try to figure something out for you, okay? Find someone to help you."

"Those guys had guns, Chris! What if... what if next time they don't just beat me up? What if they kill me? You'll be all alone once Danny's in prison."

Prison? "But he's not going to—"

"Please, Chris? Please? I know you're not in Springfield anymore."

"Springfield," I whispered. "How did you know—?"

"Mrs. Rose mentioned it. She calls me from time to time just to check in," he said. "And she told me you'd called her with a weird story about a kidnapping." He chuckled, and the sound brought back a lot of childhood memories... none of them pleasant. "But by the time I got there, you were gone."

My skin prickled hot and cold.

"You're calling from a New York number, I see," Nicky went on. He didn't sound terrified anymore. He sounded controlled and... well, *terrifying*. "Unknown Name, Copper

County, New York? Where is that, buddy? Upstate some-where? I can be there in a couple hours. Remember how Danny said family was the most important thing? So why not let your friend protect us both? Just give me your address, and I'll put it in my GPS."

The Caller ID.

Why hadn't I even *thought* about the Caller ID on Webb's phone before I called?

What the heck had I done? Oh, *fricking frickballs*, what had I done?

"Nicky? What's going on right now?" I whispered.

"You screwed me over, cousin," Nicky said. "That's what's going on. But that's okay. It's alright. I forgive you. And I'm going to let you make it up to me." He laughed again. "Talk soon, Chrissy."

After Nicky disconnected, I stared at the darkened phone screen as my entire body went cold and my head swam. It felt an awful lot like I had when Reed pulled me out of the lake.

How freaking naive could a person be? How foolishly trusting? How *stupid*?

I knew better than to trust Nicky, but the second he'd mentioned family and needing my help, my brain had short-circuited, and I hadn't thought at all.

Nicky knew Danny's nickname, knew Danny wasn't in Alaska, probably knew all along about the plea deal—"*He hasn't signed it yet, though, right?*"—but if he knew all that, he had to know I wasn't involved in Danny's business—well, *that* business, anyway—so what could he want with me? Why would he be looking for me at all?

"Chris?" Watt asked.

I lifted my head, and his curious expression transformed instantly to concern.

"Whoa, hey now." Watt crouched down and patted my knee. "What happened? Shit, Chris. Did someone die?"

My eyes filled with tears. I couldn't tell Watt the truth, and I wasn't sure I'd be able to form sentences anyway.

"Shit. *Shit.* Why did I ask that?" he muttered under his breath. "Can I... What can I do, Chris? Do you need tea? Or chocolate? When my wife was upset, she used to like chocolate—"

I shook my head. "Nobody died, Watt. I just... I need Reed."

I had to tell Reed—warn him—Nicky was coming here.

"Fuck, of course. Yeah." Watt stood. "And you said he's in town, right? Want me to take you? Or..." He gave my face another more critical look. "Or maybe I'll just go find him for you and send him back."

"Please? I'll stay here in case he comes home." I ran my hands over my face. Reed would want me to stay here, I thought. Probably. If Nicky was on his way, whatever his intention was, he'd be less likely to find me out here at the campground, surely.

And then once Reed was back... once he was back, I'd tell him I'd done the one thing he'd warned against from the very beginning and let someone know where we were.

I'd tell him that even though he'd trusted me and believed I was capable, even though he'd helped me to feel more confident and empowered than I ever had in my whole life... I'd let him down.

What if he got in trouble with his bosses again because he'd trusted me when he shouldn't have? What if he lost the job he loved more than anything? I'd never forgive myself. *He'd* never forgive me.

"He's going to be so angry," I whispered.

"Angry?" Watt looked mystified. "You mean Reed? I

don't know what's happening here, so I guess it's possible, but if he's pissed, he'll get over it. He's in love with you. A man'll forgive a whole lot for the person he loves."

I gave Watt a sad smile. He was so sweet, but he had no idea that Reed and I weren't the newlyweds we'd claimed to be.

Reed cared about me, I believed that. But love? The kind of love I felt for him? I didn't think so. Especially not after this...

And only now that the possibility was gone for good did I realize how much I'd hoped that at some point, he might.

I tried to smile. "Thank you, Watt. You're a really good friend."

My smile must not have been convincing because it seemed to make Watt more panicked. "Uh, you too? Look, I'll be back in half an hour. Tops. The best thing about a small town is there aren't many places he could be, right? So just... hang tight."

He grabbed his phone from my hand and nearly sprinted for his car.

But after he left, I couldn't make myself settle. I kept replaying my conversation with Nicky, alternately terrifying myself and telling myself I was overreacting. After an hour passed, I began pacing the small cabin. At noon, when the sky began to darken like a storm was coming, I began jumping with every gust of wind. And when the rain began, an hour after that, I was truly panicked.

Where the heck was Reed?

Even if he was angry, I knew he'd come when I needed him. And as much as I dreaded confessing what I'd done, I wanted him with me. Wanted his overprotectiveness and his smile, his snark and his scowls, his steadfast presence and those grunts he used in place of full sentences. I wanted *him*, period.

For as long as I could, in any way I could have him.

It was almost a relief when Dolores, dressed in a sky-blue raincoat with cherries printed on it, knocked on the door a little before two.

"Where'd you disappear to earlier, kiddo?" she demanded, stepping inside. She looked me up and down, much like Watt had. "Everything okay?"

"Yeah. Sorry about earlier. I... I had to do something. But I'm okay. Just a little nervous 'cause Reed's not home from town yet," I explained, which wasn't a lie.

Dolores nodded sympathetically. "It's really blowing around out there. Just got home from town myself. I needed some veggies for dinner—well, more like Bob needs veggies, and I need Fanaille cupcakes." She winked.

I laughed, but it came out sounding strained.

She tilted her head and studied me. "Tell you what we'll do. I'm gonna go put on the teakettle. You can come over, and we'll finish our charcuterie board shopping. Okay? And Bob can stay in the bedroom watching his television."

I shook my head. "I should really stay here. When Reed comes back—"

A gust of wind blew a tree branch against the wall of the cabin, and I yelped.

"When Reed comes back, he'll find you eating tequila lime cupcakes with me and Bob," she said firmly. "Not splattered on the ceiling 'cause you're so jumpy. Trust me."

I smiled. "You're a very motherly sort of person, you know that?"

She hooted. "Tell that to my stepson." Her expression soured. "On second thought, don't. Come on, kiddo."

She was right. I wasn't doing anyone any good here. Being around other people would help.

Reluctantly, I nodded. "I'll be there in ten minutes. Just let me grab a jacket and leave Reed a note."

After Dolores left, I found a pen in the silverware drawer and scrawled a note on a paper towel telling Reed exactly where I'd be. Then I grabbed his thickest jacket from the closet and pulled it on, rolling up the sleeves. I closed the cabin door and locked it behind me, then set off down the path through the woods.

Which was exactly where Nicky found me.

CHAPTER 16
REED

GIVEN how often I'd been in dangerous situations over the years, I was pretty nonchalant about things that scared most people. When a fight was imminent, when guns were drawn, when my protectee's safety was at risk, I didn't panic. I still got a heart-racing, gut-churning, vision-narrowing surge of adrenaline, of course, but through training and experience, I'd learned how to channel it to make me a lethal fighter, a fast thinker, an impenetrable shield.

Put three tiny words on the tip of my tongue, though, and apparently I flailed like a fucking Muppet.

I'd been trying to make Chris smile this morning—my new obsession, since learning the truth about his uncle had understandably brought him low—and when the words "... *one of the things I love about you*" had nearly slipped out, I'd choked. Almost literally.

But it wasn't the fact that I'd nearly *told* Chris I loved him that sent me fleeing from the peaceful little caretaker cabin. It was that, when I'd caught myself in the act and given myself a hard mental shake for nearly saying something off-the-cuff that Chris might have thought was sincerely meant... I found that I *did* mean it. Sincerely as fuck.

I wasn't almost falling for him, I'd fallen. I fell.

I wasn't pretending to be in a relationship, I was in one.

And that... *that* was fucking terrifying.

"Sunday? Sunday!" Janissey's sharp voice through my phone brought me back to reality—to the unoccupied, scarcely-furnished apartment above the O'Leary Bar and Grill, which Parker had graciously let me use after finding me scowling at the locked door of the library earlier, and to this Zoom meeting from hell, now entering its fourth fucking hour, which I should've been paying attention to. "Thoughts on the assessment Neiman just gave us of your upcoming assignment?" my boss demanded.

I cracked my neck from side to side, eyes on the phone I'd propped on an old Formica kitchen table.

I'd barely heard a word Agent Neiman had said, and I was pretty sure Janissey suspected it.

The upcoming assignment, protecting a prominent scientist named Elena Perez who'd be appearing at an international tribunal in January to testify about a toxic waste dump she'd uncovered. The protectee herself, a 53-year old environmentalist who refused to leave her wife, her dog, or her parakeet behind, sounded like a genuinely good person—which wasn't necessary for me to do my job, but didn't hurt. It was exactly the sort of plum assignment that career agents like me lived for.

And it would require me to relocate to Antwerp for three months. Possibly longer.

"I think Agent Neiman's done a thorough job and given us a lot to think about," I said. "Thank you." The agent in question nodded, clearly pleased by the praise but too professional to show it. "I'll review the notes once we're off the call—it's a little tricky managing this all from my phone —and I'll let you know if I have any questions."

Janissey nodded impatiently, face stony beneath his graying dark hair. "Neiman, Burley, thanks for your time. We'll be in touch."

The two agents nodded and their windows blinked out so that only Janissey and I were left on the call. He immediately sighed. "What the fuck, Sunday? Where was your head during that meeting?"

At home. With Chris. Wondering which cabin he's working on, and what song he's humming to himself. Wanting to watch the gap of exposed skin at his waistband grow as his borrowed sweatpants sink down his hips, and then trace every fresh millimeter with my fingertips and tongue. Missing his stories about his old next door neighbor's brush with a Russian mystic—who "honest to gosh, Reed, predicted the future, 'cause she said I'd 'stumble into misfortune' and how else could she have known I'd get distracted trying to sniff snapdragons and trip into that hornet's nest?" —nearly as much as I missed his genuinely insightful views on politics and social issues. Needing to be near him make sure that no one—not Dante's enemies, not vengeful hornets, not Chris's own sweet and impetuous nature—hurt a single hair on his head.

"Do you need respite?" Janissey peered at me through the screen. "Be honest with me. You've been there for nearly two weeks now, and mental fatigue can be—"

"I don't need respite," I assured him. "I'm fine. Better than ever, actually."

"Yeah?" He lifted an eyebrow. "I hope that's true because I'm moving up the timeline. Dante's signed his plea deal by now, so we don't need to placate him anymore, and since there have been no credible threats against your protectee, I want you on Perez full-time starting next week."

"No." The word was out of my mouth before I had time to think twice, but just like earlier this morning, when I thought about it, I realized I meant it. *Huh.*

"Excuse me?" He laughed in disbelief. "*No?*"

"No." I blew out a breath. "I can't put my finger on it, but I'm not convinced Chris is safe yet. There's something we're missing. Overlooking. Someone called his name that night at the safe house—"

Janissey shook his head. "Not your decision to make, Sunday. Things might have calmed down a bit this week, but we've still got a staffing issue—"

"Yeah," I agreed without hesitation and without regret. "If you pull me off this assignment, you sure will. Because I'm staying here for as long as Chris needs me."

His eyes flared wide as he realized what I was saying. "Sunday," he groaned. "Jesus Christ. You did it again, you bastard. Just like last time."

"Nope." This was nothing like my last assignment. *Then,* I'd made a choice in the heat of the moment without fully understanding the consequences. Now, I knew exactly what I was doing.

"You're telling me you haven't gone soft?" Janissey rolled his eyes. "I don't believe—*what, Eloise? Can't you see I'm in the middle of—? Hang on, Sunday. Well, tell them I'll call them back when I'm—What do you mean 'gone'? Jesus, Eloise, they called three hours ago? Why didn't you tell me? Yes, it's an emergency! It's a fucking clusterfuck, is what it is. Sunday!*"

I snorted, amused. "Still here. Clearly."

His brow creased. "And where the fuck is your protectee?"

Immediately, my heart rate picked up. "Back at the campground, as I told you when I joined the call. What's going on?"

"Dante's missing. He didn't sign his plea deal." His computer vibrated as he typed something into his keyboard. "He's in the wind."

"What do you mean *missing*? The Marshals were supposed to—"

"But they didn't. He disappeared yesterday, those fuckers only informed us this morning, and I'm just hearing about it now." His fingers didn't slow down. "Not my shit show, fortunately. But the Marshals are probably gonna want to send someone there to keep an eye on things, in case Dante comes your way—"

"An eye on what? My protectee hasn't told his uncle where we are." Chris had said that and I believed him, one hundred percent. "And five minutes ago, you were happy to pull me off this assignment to fix your personnel issues, so is he even really my protectee anymore—?"

"Don't be naive," he scoffed. "The Marshals have reason to believe Dante will contact your guy, so obviously they'll want to watch him. No better way to do that than by keeping him in protective custody. We'll coordinate—"

Suddenly Janissey's earlier words seemed prophetic, because this *was* feeling an awful lot like my assignment back in August. The Powers That Be wanted to use my protectee for their own purposes under the guise of protection.

It had felt wrong then. Now it made me incandescently angry.

I stood and grabbed my phone, already moving toward the door.

No way would I let the Marshals anywhere near Chris,

at least until he'd heard about the situation from *me* and we'd decided together how to handle it.

"Like hell they will," I told Janissey as I jogged down the hall. "You tell the Marshals to keep their asses away from Copper County. They'll only attract attention and blow our cover."

"Your protectee is connected to a crime family, and—"

"My protectee is not a criminal, and you *will* talk about him with respect," I growled. "Someone else fucked up here. Go bitch at the Marshals. Understand?"

Janissey blinked up at me in shock. "What the fuck?"

"Gotta go." I pulled open the door to the street and realized it had started raining at some point. Water sheeted off the overhang and ran down the street in small rivers.

"Go? Go where?"

"To protect Chris." I jabbed the End Call button and dragged my keys from my pocket before ducking my head and facing the storm.

I'd parked two blocks down, which hadn't seemed like a big deal this morning but now felt a million steps too far. I should never have left Chris alone—

"Sunday! Reed!" Watt Bartlett tore open the door to the flower shop and raced out to the sidewalk as I passed. "Where the fuck have you been? I've been looking all over for you."

I shook my head, not slowing down. "I can't talk now—"

Watt kept pace beside me, long legs eating up the wet pavement. "Well, your husband needed you *hours* ago, asshole. He's all upset, convinced you're not going to love him anymore—"

I stopped and turned to stare at him. "Not love him? What?" I glanced around, trying to spot him through the pounding rain. "Where is he?"

"Back at the campground. He borrowed my phone so he could call someone about a family emergency or something. He wouldn't tell me. And I wondered maybe if it was something to do with... well, you being one of *Oak's friends.*" Watt lifted an eyebrow. "But after Chris's call, he looked like he'd seen a ghost. He cried—"

"*Cried?*" Heart racing, I grabbed the front of Watt's shirt, which was already soaked through and cold to the touch. "Did he say who he talked to?"

Watt, to his credit, didn't seem upset by my manhandling. He shook his head. "He didn't, but when he first made the call, I... I might have overheard him say *Nicky?*"

My numb fingers slipped off Watt's shirt and I sucked in a breath.

Nicky. There it was. The missing piece. The "something" I'd told Janissey we'd overlooked. The cousin who, in Janissey's own words, was "called Nicky Knives for a reason." The cousin who'd been looking for Chris and, considering he'd managed to get him on the phone, had apparently found him.

"Fucking Christ." I spun around, darting across the street to my car, splashing through puddles.

I heard him mutter under his breath, "He must really love the guy."

"Yes," I snarled over my shoulder as I yanked the door open. "More than you know."

The ride back to the campground took far longer than it should have. The rain poured down in torrents so hard the wipers could barely keep up and slicked the fallen leaves strewn along the twisty road. When I finally pulled into the campground driveway, I didn't slow down, even when the deep ruts made the car bottom out. I skidded to a stop beside the caretaker cabin and dove out into the rain once more.

"Chris?" I screamed as I ran, fear and love making it come out more like a howl. "Chris!"

"Reed!" Dolores ran from the woods, waving her arm. "Hey, Reed."

I ignored her, throwing open the door to the caretaker cabin, but there was no happy smile and big doe eyes to greet me. The kitchen area was tidy, but empty, the bathroom open and dark, and in the bedroom—

I rushed through the door, grabbed Chris's hand knit sweater from the foot of the bed, and brought it to my nose to inhale. Vanilla and *Chris*, the most potent fragrance in the universe. I closed my eyes for one second to steady myself, then turned toward the door to question Dolores...

Which was when I saw the gun.

———

"Where the hell is my nephew?"

Dante Fromadgio looked a lot less intimidating in real life. He was thin and short, with eyes a few shades darker than Chris's, salt-and-pepper hair, and a little mustache. With his khaki pants, plaid button-down, and honest-to-god sweater vest (a twin to Chris's sweater) he might've looked like a retired banker...

You know, if not for the fact that he was holding my backup weapon on me.

I held up both hands. While my gun was in its holster against the small of my back, I didn't dare pull it on Chris's uncle. "Dante?" I said. "I'm Reed. Agent Reed Sunday. From the Division."

Dante's eyes narrowed. "That doesn't answer my question, son."

I swallowed. "I don't know where Chris is. I'm looking for him, too. I just got word that you'd escaped from the Marshals and came back here to tell him. But a friend said he overheard Chris talking to Nicky—"

"*Christ.*" Dante's nostrils flared and his shoulders slumped. "If Nicolas already found him—"

I lunged forward, grabbed his wrist, and applied pressure. Dante released the weapon with a sigh.

"I wasn't going to shoot you unless you'd hurt my nephew."

"Good to know." I checked my gun before jamming it in the back of my jeans next to my own. "Now what the hell does Nicky want with Chris?"

Dante shook his head tiredly. "Exactly what I tried to prevent, I assume. Nicolas got the idea in his head that I'd have let him take over my business when I retired, if not for Chris. I told Nicolas over and over that my choice had nothing to do with his cousin, that I didn't want that life for either of my boys anymore, that it was time to fix the mistake my father made decades ago." He sighed. "Nicolas didn't believe me. He said he'd prove to me that he was the 'true Fromadgio' heir. He never understood that being a true Fromadgio had nothing to do with blood and everything to do with honor... or at least it used to." Dante spread his hands helplessly. "I don't know where I went wrong."

"Tell me about it," a male voice said. "I'm in the same boat."

Dante and I turned to see a small, shadowed figure by the open door to the cabin. When he stepped forward into the light from the window above the kitchen sink, I frowned.

"Bob? You should go back to your camper." I moved to put myself between him and Dante. "This isn't a good—"

But to my shock, Bob looked over my shoulder and lifted his chin at Danny. "Dante."

"Bobby?" Dante's eyes narrowed. "What are you doing here?"

"I'm retired." Bob shrugged, smoothing a hand over his thinning hair. "Sort of a forced retirement, since the whole thing with Robert Jr., so we bought a camper and ended up here. Kinda weird coincidence, I guess—"

"Can you two catch up later?" I demanded impatiently. "I'm a *little* busy trying to figure out where the fuck Chris is—"

"I can help with that." Dolores appeared in the door, pulling off the hood of her raincoat to fluff her red curls.

"Dolores," Dante said. "You're looking well."

"Dante." She nodded with a slight softening of her face. "I saw your nephew earlier. Actually, *both* of them."

"You saw Chris and Nicky?" I demanded. "Where?" I was not used to being the person with no information and I didn't like it one bit, especially when the safety of the man I loved—and hadn't told yet—was on the line. "And how the hell do you know our campers?"

"This is Robert Evanovich—" Dante nodded at the man.

"Evanovich?" I repeated, feeling my head begin to spin. "*You're* Robert Evanovich?"

"Senior," Bob corrected. "Important to clarify that, since my son got himself arrested for dealing and bookmaking, amongst other unsavory things." He shook his head in disgust. "No honor in this next generation."

"Where's Chris?" I repeated, trying my hardest not to pull both guns and start shooting.

Dolores's expression was a mix of sympathy and hard-eyed determination. "Chris came over to the RV this morning for online shopping, but when I got interrupted, he skedaddled. I came to check on him a couple hours ago and he seemed kinda nervous-like—on account of the storm, I figured. I invited him back over, but he never showed. His email was open on my laptop—a message from Nicky begging Chris to call. I can only assume he did—"

"He did." I scrubbed both hands through my hair. "Fuck."

"Yeah. Once I saw Nicky's name, I put two and three together real fast. I came back to warn Chris... and that's when I saw Nicky holding a gun on him in the woods." She shook her head. "Didn't like Nicky before, but now...?" She shook her head angrily.

"Nicolas and I are going to have words," Dante promised.

I stared at him in disbelief. No, Nicky was going to end up behind bars for a very long time, if I had anything to say about it... assuming he hadn't hurt Chris. If he had, all bets were off.

"Do you know where they went, Dolores?" I prompted. "Did you see Nicky's car? Or which direction they headed."

"I was getting to that part." She lifted one red eyebrow. "Cabin 13."

"Cabin—? Holy shit! He's *here*? He's at the campground? You saw them?" I demanded. When she nodded, I headed for the door.

Bob blocked my path. "Hold up, kiddo. We need weapons and we need a plan—"

"Kiddo?" I snorted. "No. *You* don't need shit. *I* am a trained Division agent, and *I* need to go—"

"Bobby's right," Dante interrupted. "Three... well,

four," he corrected with a nod at Dolores, "against one is a lot better odds. And I'm sure as hell not going to sit around waiting, Mr. Trained Division Agent, since Chris got kidnapped on your watch. So either take us with you, or we'll go ourselves."

I shook my head as I pulled out my weapon to check it. What the fuck had my life come to that I would be leading an extraction team of two old men and one very opinionated lady?

"We care about him, too," Dolores said firmly.

Because of course they did. Because Chris was... Chris. Gorgeous and warm and so fucking *good*, he attracted good feelings to him like a magnet.

Too bad he attracted trouble, too.

"Fine," I agreed because I didn't have time to argue. "But you three will follow *my* lead."

Dante looked like he would protest, but Bob laid a hand on his arm. "Do as he says, Danny. He's the man's husband, for fuck's sake."

"Husband?" Dante's eyes widened, then narrowed. "The hell he is."

Because Chris eventually *would* be my husband, if I had anything to say about it—and, yeah, that was a mind-fuck revelation I did not have time for at the moment—I leaned toward Dante and bit out, "Get used to it."

Then I headed for the woods.

Cabin 13 was nestled in the center of a grove of fir trees not far from the edge of Watt Bartlett's orchard. Our run through the forest was mostly silent, thanks to a thick carpet of pine needles, and the trees grew so thickly, the ground was barely damp, which helped us move faster... but "faster" was a relative term when you were traveling with The Centrum Silver Squad.

I drew my gun as we reached the clearing in front of the cabin, but Dante grabbed my wrist to stop me.

"What the fuck?" I hissed, yanking it away from him.

"No guns," he said firmly. "Those are my nephews in there."

"*Chris* is your nephew. Nicky is the asshole who's got a gun on him," I corrected.

But Dante shook his head insistently. "Nicolas is..." He sighed. "There's no denying he's gone down a bad path. And maybe that's my fault. But he's still my boy. And I don't want him hurt."

I'd wondered how Chris had become the person he was, growing up with Dante as an uncle. Now I could sort of see the resemblance... though it seemed Dante's belief in the goodness of humanity only extended as far as his family.

"Stay back and stay out of my way," I told him.

Staying behind the tree line, I crept around to the south side of the cabin, where there were no windows, and darted across the small lawn. The grass was spongy and slippery but I managed to keep my footing... barely.

I moved around the corner to the western side of the cabin and, with the worn cedar shingles biting my palms, I flattened myself to the wall. I stepped cautiously toward the single window.

I heard the voices before I got close enough to peer in.

"—all your fault, Chrissy." Nicky's voice was shrill and fast. "I don't want to do this, okay? But they're going to arrest me. *Me!* This shit never would have happened if Uncle Danny had left the business to me as he should've."

"You keep saying that. And I keep telling you, he could have left it to you. I wouldn't have cared." Chris sounded a little scared and a whole lot angry, but unhurt. A bolt of relief nearly brought me to my knees. "I didn't even know this side of his business existed. All I wanted was the Cellar."

"You can't have one without the other. Jesus, Chris, you're so fucking stupid. All those years..."

As Nicky went on, I crept closer to the window. The bottom sill was level with my shoulder and I wished like hell I had a mirror so I could look inside without letting Nicky know I was there. But because luck was on my side—and Nicky was kind of an idiot—he'd turned on the camping lantern Chris had brought out here after he'd disconnected the electricity. I was able to see in far better than they could see out.

Unfortunately, what I saw was not good.

Chris was huddled into one corner of a dilapidated wooden bench built into the wall of the cabin, his hands tied behind his back and his glasses askew on his nose. Chris had taken out most of the wood paneling on the walls and ceilings earlier this week so he could update the wiring and replace the ceiling fan, which meant he was propped against rough timbers, sharp nails, and a bunch of electrical wires that were no longer stapled to the studs.

Watching him track movement on the other side of the room, the side I couldn't see, it seemed that Nicky was pacing back and forth across the small space, probably agitated and definitely dangerous, while Chris was a sitting duck.

"...and once you're out of the way, Uncle Danny will stop caring about trying to 'restore honor to the family' before he dies. In fact, he'll have every reason to stay in the game." Nicky laughed. "For revenge."

"I d-don't know what you're talking about." Chris fluttered his lashes the way he did when he was lying. If his hands had been free, I was sure they'd have been fluttering a mile a minute. "Please, Nicky, tell me the whole plan. In detail."

I closed my eyes. Chris wanted Nicky's villain monologue, and I knew why. Because when we'd talked about John Ruffian, I'd told him *if a villain monologues it gives his captive a chance to get free.*

Jesus fuck, I loved that man. I loved that he was planning his own escape. And I wasn't going to let him out of my sight for a solid month after this.

Make that two months.

Make that *forever.*

I just needed Nicky to walk past the window so I could get a clear shot...

"My *plan?* My plan is to fucking get rid of you. You have any idea how hard it's been to watch Danny go weak because of you? You got in his head." Nicky's voice hardened as he tapped his temple with one blunt finger. "You and your sweet-and-innocent bullshit."

"Ah, Nicolas," a voice at my shoulder whispered sadly. I didn't bother turning since I knew who it was. "So misguided."

"Danny's not weak," Chris said firmly. "He's a good person."

"*He's a good person,*" Nicky sing-songed. "Do you have any idea the things he's done? No. Because he never trusted you enough to tell you the truth. And now he's trying to get out of the game and leave me with *nothing.* But guess what? That's not happening. I'm calling the shots now, the way I should have been all along."

Chris's jaw clenched, but he didn't reply, and I'd never been happier that the man disliked arguing (except with me) because it meant he wasn't provoking Nicky further.

Nicky continued his rant. "Evanovich doesn't wanna be

in prison any more than I want to go, so I tipped off his lieutenants about your location. They're still loyal to him. In fact, Yuri's on his way. He's gonna get rid of you and make it real clear who's responsible for your disappearance. And as soon as Danny hears the Evanoviches got you, *boom!*"

His bark made Chris jump and I growled under my breath.

Bob bit out a muttered curse. "Yuri better hope he's not involved in this. Dolores and I are gonna go find out." He hesitated. "You guys okay without us?"

Okay with losing two members of the Centrum Silver Squad in the middle of a hostage situation?

I grunted an affirmative.

Bob pulled Dolores back toward the path through the trees.

"N-Nicky," Chris said. "Uncle Danny's going to be really angry—"

Nicky snorted. "No shit. He'll be fucking furious. That's what I'm counting on. See, if he's angry enough, he'll give up this plea deal bullshit so he can get revenge on the Evanoviches. No plea deal, no testifying, and Evanovich will almost definitely walk. It's a win-win-win for everyone... except you, I guess."

I could see about five dozen holes in Nicky's logic. For example, at this point, if Danny backed out of his plea deal, he'd end up in prison for the crimes he admitted to, not back in Jersey re-taking the reins of the family business. And if Danny was hell bent on revenge against the Evanoviches, wouldn't that make him *more* motivated to testify?

I could see Chris recognized these flaws, as well, but he pressed his lips together and managed to look suitably scared.

"D-Danny's smart," Chris said, injecting a wobble into

his voice that I was almost sure was fake, but still made my stomach plummet. "He'll remember how you were upset at me before he left. He'll know you were involved."

"Nah. Danny thinks you and I are chill. He told me that as long as I left you alone, he wouldn't rat me out to the Feds and he'd even take the hit for some of the shit I did. All those bribery charges he copped to? That's *me*," he said proudly. "But after he left, I got to thinking and I've decided that deal isn't gonna work for me. Took me months to track you to Vermont, but I did it. And my guy was *this close* to grabbing you, too. Did you really think anyone wanted to buy one of your stupid charcuterie platters?" He laughed... but then his laughter died. "But then you took off again. I managed to find you in Springfield—"

"You didn't find me, Nicky. I told Mrs. Rose who told you," Chris said, sounding disappointed. "It was my mistake."

"Fuck you, Chris. *You didn't find me, Nicky?* Uh, *yes*, I fucking did. I just didn't realize your neighbor would be armed and have a whole fucking crew who was equally strapped—"

"You didn't hurt him, did you? Is Kenny okay?" Chris demanded.

"When the cops came, the grandmother claimed my guys were invading her home." Nicky sounded disgusted. "Like the old bitch didn't have a gun under her housecoat. Four of my guys got arrested that night. That's on you, too."

"I think it's on *you*," Chris whispered.

"So fucking smug. Even soaking wet and tied up, you think you're better than everyone—"

Nicky, his dark water-slicked hair and his skinny form encased in a green tracksuit he'd borrowed from an old episode of *The Sopranos,* stepped toward the bed with his gun arm raised like he was going to pistol-whip Chris.

Absolutely fucking not.

I drew my gun, got him in my sights, and—

Dante knocked into me, throwing me off balance.

"No," he whispered fiercely. "I told you, no guns. He... he won't actually hurt Chris. He's just trying to scare him. See? You heard him yourself, he's waiting for Yuri."

"I swear to fucking God, if you try that again, I'll shoot you too," I hissed back, pushing him aside to reclaim my spot by the window.

Dante was right—Nicky had apparently just wanted to see Chris flinch—but I didn't care. I'd have happily shot him to eliminate the risk. By now, though, Nicky had moved to the far side of the bed. From this angle, my aim would have to be perfect to hit him without hitting Chris. I couldn't risk it. *Fuck.*

"N-no, Nicky, I don't think that," Chris whispered, ducking his head. This time, the fear in his voice was real. "I really don't. I always wanted to be your friend. I wanted you to like me. I gave you chance after chance because you're family. And that was my mistake too. You know, Reed is probably on his way to save me right now—"

I was. I was right here. And his belief in me meant everything. I raised my weapon again. If Nicky moved just a fraction of an inch...

"Reed?" Nicky laughed, lowering his arm and shaking his head as he walked away. "You mean your bodyguard? Oh, shit, you're hilarious. No way he'll find you before Yuri arrives."

"Reed is *probably* on his way to save me," Chris repeated calmly. "But it doesn't matter. Because I am *not* weak. Reed helped me see that. And I can save my own d-damn self."

After that, two things happened simultaneously.

First, Nicky froze in shock in the center of the room—probably as stunned as I was that Chris had actually used fresh language—and I took aim.

Second, and more importantly, Chris propelled himself off the bench, yanking one of the exposed wires with him. Since the wire was no longer attached to the studs—or to *anything*, except the ancient ceiling fan suspended from a single joist in the center of the room—when he pulled, the wire lifted the fan a couple of crucial inches, and when he let the wire go, the force was strong enough to snap the rusted bolts attaching the fan to the joist.

The fan came crashing down on Nicky's head and his gun went flying...

Like something out of one of those motherfucking inconceivably unrealistic episodes of John Ruffian.

"I am *never* going to diss that show again," I muttered. Then I ran around the cabin, took the two steps to the front door in a single leap, and finally, *finally*, got my arms around Chris.

I was not letting him go again.

CHAPTER 17
CHRIS

When Reed came crashing through the door, I jumped to my feet, thinking it was the Yuri guy Nicky had mentioned. It wasn't until my face was buried in a familiar flannel shirt, a pair of strong arms wrapped around me tightly, and a warm, woodsy scent filled my nose that I realized it was over.

Reed was here, which meant I was safe.

"Baby," Reed murmured into my hair. "You okay?"

"Yeah, I think..." I croaked, nestling into him further. "Now I am."

The first instant that Nicky had stepped out of the woods in front of me earlier like some kind of demon in a horror movie, I'd been terrified, but by the time he'd forced me down on the pine needles so he could bind my wrists, marched me here at gunpoint, and started his ridiculous speech, my fear had turned to anger.

How flipping *dare he* blame me for everything? How flipping *dare he* try to intimidate me? How *dare he* manipulate me and ruin everything for Reed?

The anger had cleared my head a lot. It helped me

remember that Reed *would* find me—he'd raze the forest to the ground to protect me if he had to, I knew that for sure—so the most helpful thing I could do would be to stay calm and keep Nicky distracted.

I wasn't sure what had come over me when I'd noticed the ceiling fan hanging right above Nicky and recalled how wobbly it was, but I was pretty sure it had been Nonna's voice in my head saying *You can't fight gravity, sweetheart* that had given me the idea.

I couldn't wait to tell Reed about that. To hear his laughter.

But not yet.

Because the moment I knew I was safe, all the fear and longing and guilt I'd been holding at bay came crashing back like a tidal wave, and I found myself sobbing.

"Stay still, baby," Reed said as I tried to squirm myself further into his embrace. "I need to free your hands."

He pulled something from his pocket and, without stepping away, he managed to cut the zip tie. The second they were free, my arms flew around Reed's waist and I fumbled to hold him with hands that had gone numb.

"Hold me," I begged through my tears, though he already was. "Don't let go."

"Not on your life," he muttered. "Not ever again." And as if to prove it, his arms tightened, squeezing the breath out of me.

I didn't mind.

"Nicky? Nicky!" I turned my head in surprise and found Uncle Danny on his knees beside my cousin, tapping him gently on his face. Nicky lay on the floor on his back, the weight of the ceiling fan pinning him down. He looked dead, but thankfully, I could still see his chest rise and fall. "Christoforo, come help me."

It was a measure of how overwhelmed I was that I hadn't even noticed Danny was here until he spoke.

It was a measure of how much things had changed that I didn't feel the slightest urge to step away from Reed to go to him... not that Reed wanted me to.

"No fucking way. Chris doesn't need to go anywhere near Nicky," he told Danny.

Danny's eyes narrowed as he glanced between us. "Christoforo, I said come here."

"You're not calling the shots right now, Dante," Reed reminded him.

"And you think you are?" Danny pushed to his feet with some effort and I wondered if his arthritic knees were acting up.

"No," Reed said. "I think Chris is."

I glanced up at him in surprise but he was looking steadily at my uncle.

"Chris is my nephew," Danny said. "My family. He knows he's safe with me."

Reed's body went stiff with anger, his voice arctic cold. "Yeah, I saw how you protected him when you wouldn't let me take the shot out there." He nodded at the cabin window. "Nicky could have killed him."

"He wouldn't." Danny set his jaw, a stubborn look I knew well. "Nicky—"

"Was going to let someone else kill me," I said, quiet but firm. My hands fisted in the back of Reed's shirt, locking his big body to mine. "Which is basically the same thing, isn't it?"

Danny's mouth snapped shut. "Christoforo, I'm sorry. This is my fault—" He spread his hands pleadingly and took a step in our direction. "Let me explain."

Reed spun us, positioning himself between me and

Danny. "That's plenty close enough. Say what you need to say, and then I'm calling the police and an ambulance."

"I don't need interference from Chris's *bodyguard*." Suddenly Nicky's gun was in Danny's hand, aimed right at Reed, with a speed that suggested it wasn't the first time Danny had held a gun on someone. "And you're not calling anyone. You'll leave my nephew with me—"

"The hell I will." Reed let go of me, but only so he could tug me behind his back and pull out his own gun. "Put your weapon down. The only reason I haven't already shot you is because your *nephew* is the man I love, and he wouldn't like it. Unless he tells me to go, there's no way I'm leaving him here with you and that murderous asshole you call a—"

"This is none of your—" Danny began.

"Stop!" I yelled, stepping around Reed. "Both of you stop it. Put your guns away right flipping..." I froze, blinking. I turned to Reed, staring in absolute shock. "Wait. Did you... did you say you love me?"

Reed's gaze flicked from me to Danny for a beat, like he was gauging the danger. Then he tucked his gun away, swallowed hard, and focused on me as though Danny and his gun no longer existed. His green eyes heated, and his cheeks went red. He swallowed again, showing an un-Reed-like uncertainty that was almost funny, considering he'd been seconds away from a gunslinger showdown with my uncle and hadn't shown a hint of fear.

He looked incredibly, wonderfully awkward. The kind of awkward that told me he'd meant every word he'd said.

"Yeah," he said softly. He reached out one big hand and adjusted my glasses. "I really do, Chris."

"I see." I nodded. "That's... great. But, um..." I was hyperventilating a little, but I couldn't help it. "Is there any chance this might be, you know, an adrenaline thing?

Because I've heard adrenaline can make people do all kinds of—"

"No." Reed smiled and cupped my jaw with both hands. "Not adrenaline. Not protectiveness, either. And definitely not professional responsibility. I wish I'd told you at a better time. Like this morning, when it finally hit me exactly what I'd been feeling for you. Or a week ago, when you jumped in a lake and I knew nothing in the world, no career or assignment, was more important than having you in my arms. Or... fuck, the first day I met you, when I already knew you were more than a job to me. I *love* you, Chris."

I was not going to do anything embarrassing like cry. Not when Reed was saying everything I'd ever wanted to hear from him.

"But... how?" I choked out instead, which was arguably more embarrassing.

"How did I fall in love with you?" He frowned. "How could I not? You're the most gorgeous, most selfless, most genuinely good man I've ever met. I don't know how anyone could resist you. Just look at how Watt Bartlett can't keep his moony eyes to himself."

I didn't dignify his teasing about Watt by acknowledging it. Especially since Watt didn't even date men, as far as I knew.

"What about your job?" I demanded. "Reed, I know how much you love it, and I know that's one of the reasons you don't want a relationship—"

"Fuck the job," he growled. "Because I already *have* a relationship, and I'm not giving it up. I don't know exactly how it'll work, but I told Janissey today what my top priority is from now on." He pressed a soft kiss to my lips and then pulled back. "It's you, just to be clear.

This is definitely me *picking you up* right now. Permanently."

"Yeah?" My cheeks went hot. "Well, that's pretty convenient because I—"

"Christoforo, he's lying to you." Uncle Danny's voice was like jumping in the deep lake water again, an icy shock that stole my breath and very nearly stole my joy.

"What?" I demanded, looking away from Reed.

Danny had managed to pull the fan away from Nicky, but Nicky was still out cold.

I was pretty sure I should have felt worse about that, but there was no part of me that did. I didn't want any kind of relationship with Nicky ever again.

What bothered me now was the gun Danny still held, pointed directly at Reed. I noticed Reed keeping a keen eye on Nicky's still form and the gun in Danny's hand.

"You heard me. The things he's saying? Lies." Danny's face was mottled red. "You say you're in love with my nephew?" he demanded of Reed, waving the gun in an arc. "*Ridiculous.* You've known him for two weeks. That's what these government people do, Christoforo," he said, turning back to me. "They lie. That's how they got me to turn myself in. *Make a deal, Dante. Bah.*" He spat. "Then once they had me in their clutches, they refused to let me go. Refused to even let me serve my time, when I heard that Robert Evanovich might go after you if I testified. Sign the paper and testify, they told me, and we'll protect Chris. Refuse to sign, we'll tell Robert Evanovich you're testifying anyway, and let him come after your nephew." He shook his head. "Lying, cheating snakes, that's what they are. Don't trust a word this man says."

My fists tightened until my nails dug into my palms and I moved out of Reed's embrace. Reed clutched at me briefly, but I gave him a look—a look that said *trust me*—and he let me go, though his eyes remained fixed on me with that same laser focus I'd felt back at the roadhouse.

I liked it a hundred times more now.

"Uncle Danny." My voice vibrated with anger and I made no attempt to conceal it. "'This man' is Reed Sunday, and he has never lied to me. *You* have."

Danny's face looked almost comically surprised, maybe stunned that I'd disagreed. That I'd *argued*. But he recovered quickly. "I... yes. I know I have," he admitted. He dropped the hand holding the gun to his side and had the grace to look ashamed. "All sorts of lies, from the time you were small. My father started the Cellar and took the business down a certain path. He raised me to take it over. I was already in it before I ever realized I had the option to say no. But Carmelita wanted a different life for herself. For you. If your Nonna or I wanted to spend time with you, she said, we had to promise not to tell you anything about the business—the real family business—until you were old enough to make the choice for yourself." He sighed. "She never expected to die so young. To have your father follow her so quickly. But we honored her wishes. And then..." He broke off.

"And then?" I prompted.

Danny's mouth opened and closed, his dark eyes beseeching me for understanding. "Then I saw how you were. My sweet boy. Heart of my heart. A person who always did right, even when it cost him. Who never wanted to hurt another living thing. I'd already told Nicolas the truth about the business. Given him the choice to join me. Witnessed how that choice... changed him." When he looked down at Nicky, Danny's face was drawn with shame and pain. "I couldn't tell you the truth, Chris. Not after that. I lied to protect you. Protect *one* of my boys, at least—"

I stared at him wordlessly. If he'd told me this months ago, even weeks ago, I would have been incredibly moved. I would have forgiven him anything. But the man holding a gun on Reed wasn't the uncle I recognized.

Reed's arms wrapped around me from behind, supportive without restraining, and I leaned against him, taking the comfort and strength he offered.

Watching this, Danny shook his head again. "You see? You're so trusting, Christoforo. This is why you needed my protection—"

Behind me, Reed straightened. "You know what? No." He gave me a reassuring squeeze, then stepped forward so we were side by side. "You do not get to say that to him. Not while I'm around. Yes, Chris *is* trusting. He believes the best in people. But that doesn't make him an idiot, Dante. It doesn't make him less than. It doesn't make him a child who needs *you* to strip his choices away and decide what he should know. It makes him a goddamn miracle. A fucking angel on earth."

"I never said he—" Danny began, but he shut up quickly when Reed talked over him.

"Chris treats every person he meets—every single one, no matter their circumstances—like they are good and decent and worthy of respect. So you know what it means when someone takes advantage of him? When someone lies to him and he believes them anyway, *especially* when the people doing the lying are his family? It means *they* are assholes. So if you were ashamed of who you were and what you'd done with your life? I get it. You *should* be fucking ashamed. You didn't want Chris to know the truth? I don't blame you. But don't you make it sound like you kept this secret *for* him. Don't pretend that decision was about protection when it's mostly about your own fear of how he'd look at you if you told the truth."

My eyes were wide and I was pretty sure Danny's would be too, if I were able to look away from Reed long enough to check. Reed was magnificent. A broad-shouldered, glowering, avenging angel I wanted by my side *always*.

"You know how I know that, Dante?" Reed went on. "For fifteen years, I lied to my family about what I did for a living because it was easier to keep lying than to admit I'd lied in the first place. But this week, I started being honest... because of this man right here. Because when Chris sees the best in me, it makes me want to *be* better. To be seen. To tell the truth. To stop pretending. To be worthy of him. And if you love him, *Dante*, then own your choices. And do not insinuate that he needs to change one fucking *molecule* of his personality in order to earn your respect. You hear me?"

The things Reed was saying, the emotion on his face, the light in his eyes was better than any declaration of love—

Or, okay, no, but it was at least *as* good.

Because Reed had told me days ago that he saw me. That he couldn't help but see me. And at the time, I hadn't entirely believed him. Now I knew without a doubt that it was true.

I wrapped both arms around his waist. "Thank you," I whispered, low enough that only he could hear.

He dropped a kiss to the top of my head. "No need to thank me, baby," Reed said, making those words sound better than John Ruffian ever had, even in my wildest fantasies. "Never stop being exactly the way you are. I want you to fly like a butterfly. And I promise I'm strong enough to handle the lifts and throws."

A rush of warmth filled my chest and expanded outward, further and further, until every part of me tingled with a sense of security and belonging stronger than anything I'd ever felt before.

Making the worst day of my life into the best one.

"I'm sorry," Danny said softly, drawing our attention. "I'm sorry, Chris. He's right. I knew what I was doing was wrong. That's why I never told you. I was willing to lose the house, my cars, my money, my business. But I didn't want to lose your respect." He looked down at Nicky worriedly. "I've failed both of my boys. I don't know what to do."

"I'll tell you what you're going to do about Nicky," Reed said, his tone daring my uncle to disagree. "He's going to jail, Dante. He abducted Chris. He would have killed him, or had him killed, and if you let him go, he'll try again. You know that. Besides," he went on when it looked like Danny would interrupt. "It's only a matter of time until the FBI gathers enough information on his crimes to make charges stick. Nicky knows that. That's why he was desperate enough to try this." He waved a hand to indicate the cabin.

Danny hung his head and nodded, his face more drawn than I'd ever seen it. He rubbed a hand absently over his chest. "I suppose that's for the best."

"Have you been taking your heart medication?" I blurted. Maybe it meant I was still naive, but I loved my uncle too much to stop caring about his welfare. Even if he'd lied. Even if I was seriously hecking mad at him.

Reed pulled me against his side and squeezed my shoulder affectionately, as if he'd expected nothing less.

Danny's eyes softened. "I am, Christoforo. I promise. It's been a strain, these past few months, trying to do the right thing and keep everyone safe... despite not doing a very good job of it." He ran a hand over his thinning hair and sat down heavily on the bench, staring at the gun held loosely in his hands. "I got your email, you know. I thought... I thought you were safe and everything would be alright. But then I overheard one of the Marshals saying Nicky had managed to slip away from the FBI agents who'd been monitoring him. They said he'd been looking for you, but he'd never find you in Copper County. I knew better. I didn't think he'd hurt you, but I knew he'd try to... to manipulate you. Maybe even use you against me somehow." He glanced at Nicky again and let out a shuddering breath. "He'd probably even think that was the Fromadgio way."

"He did manipulate me," I admitted. I pushed up my glasses with one finger. "He emailed me and claimed to be in a panic because the Evanoviches were after him. I... I borrowed a phone to check on him and forgot about Caller ID." I looked down at my feet. "I'm sorry, Reed. It was my fault he knew what town we were in, and since pretty much everyone around here knows the honeymooners of Copper County and where we're staying—"

"Everyone knows *Chris Sunday*," Reed corrected. He cupped my chin and forced me to look up at him. "And likes you exactly as you are. So please don't beat yourself up over this. I hate that he manipulated you, but it's not your fault. You heard what I said a minute ago, right? This was on Nicky, not you. You did nothing wrong."

"See, that, Bob? They didn't need our help after all." Dolores, still wearing her raincoat, strolled into the cabin with Bob at her heels, and gave a single comprehensive glance at Reed and me, at Danny still sitting on the bed, and at Nicky prone on the floor. She nodded approvingly at me. "Nice work, sweetheart."

"Dolores!" Wide-eyed, I pulled away from Reed and

stepped in front of her, trying to block her view of my cousin. "This, um, isn't what it looks like—"

She held up a hand. "Oh, I think it's exactly what it looks like. On the way back over just now I told Bob, 'That Chris is stronger than anyone gives him credit for. Mark my words, he'll have saved himself.' Isn't that what I said, Bob?"

"That's what you said, Dolores," he agreed. He headed straight for Nicky and kneeled beside him to check his pulse, then patted Nicky's pockets and produced some of the zip ties Nicky had used to bind me. He rolled Nicky over and secured his wrists behind his back with a kind of casual ease that left me blinking.

How had he...?

"Bob and I just took care of a little family business ourselves. Yuri is *not* going to be a problem anymore," she said grimly. When she saw me staring at her, wide-eyed, she smiled softly. "Let me back up. Dolores Evanovich, honey." She pressed a hand to her chest. "Smith's my maiden name. And I promise, we only ended up in Copper County 'cause I wanted maple bacon cupcakes. Just a... a happy coincidence you might say." She glanced at her husband and added in an undertone. "I could explain more, but Bob gets tetchy when anyone starts talking about Robert, Junior."

"Can you blame me?" Bob muttered.

I glanced at Reed, stunned, and he nodded grimly. "Dolores saw your email from Nicky and recognized him in the woods later. She's the one who knew where he'd taken you."

"What are the hecking chances?" I whispered.

"Did someone call an ambulance?" Dolores wondered. "Looks like he might have a concussion." She tilted her head and studied Nicky, who was muttering and cursing as he finally came awake. "If you ask me, he got off easy."

"I haven't called it in yet. It's been kind of a busy ten minutes," Reed said. He took his phone out of his pocket, but hesitated. "Danny, when I call this in, you know what's going to happen."

Uncle Danny nodded once. "Back into custody. Possibly jail, since I left, ah... *abruptly* and without signing the plea deal. I knew the risk. But I couldn't not come when Chris needed me." He smiled at me, and this time, it was the smile I knew and loved. The same smile he'd given me when I did something he was particularly proud of. "Though it looks like Chris didn't need me quite as much as I thought."

My stomach flipped and my lip quivered. I took a step toward him, then another, then Uncle Danny was on his feet and I was hugging him nearly as tightly as Reed had hugged me a few minutes ago.

"I need you," I whispered. "I'll always need you. Not to protect me, but to love me. Thank you for coming. Thank you for... for everything. I love you. And I'll write to you. And visit. And... I'll miss you."

"I love you too, Christoforo." He patted my back gently. "For all that I've done wrong, never forget that, okay?"

"There *is* another option," Dolores said slowly. "Isn't there, Bob?" She arched one bright red eyebrow at Bob, and Bob nodded. "We—that is to say, Bob and I—have made a last minute change of plans. We're going to be leaving Copper County tonight."

"You are?" I said, disappointed. "But you said you wanted to stay for the pumpkin festival. And there's your charcuterie board—"

"I'll leave you my email, honey. We'll stay in touch, and I'll come back for a visit soon. But I was saying to Bob earlier, 'Bob, my sweetheart, my darling, my precious pearl, there is another bakery I'm dying to try in...' Was it Biloxi, Bob? Or Buffalo? Or possibly Billings?"

Bob nodded. "One of them."

"Who knows, we might even cross into Canada at some point." She shrugged and her raincoat made a little squeaking noise. "Bob loves Canadian baked goods."

"Can't get enough," he agreed.

"So maybe, Reed, we should say our goodbyes to you now..." She gave Reed a long look. "And then *you* can run back to your cabin and get Chris a... a fresh shirt." She ran a hand down my arm. "Since his sweatshirt is very damp, and as a *trained Division agent*, you'll want to make sure he stays warm and dry. Meanwhile, the rest of us will say our goodbyes. And then when you come back in... oh, let's say twenty minutes? Bob and I—just Bob and I, obviously—will have skedaddled, and you can... finish up your assignment. So to speak."

When Dolores finished speaking, she, Bob, Uncle Danny, and Reed shared a series of long, intense looks I didn't understand at *all*.

"Hey, um. Sorry to interrupt." I raised a hand. "But I... I think I'm maybe missing something here?" I looked from Reed to Dolores and back again. "Also, what kind of special baked goods do Canadians have? I'm curious."

Danny pressed his lips together like he was fighting a smile.

Bob ducked his chin and kept his eyes on his toes.

Reed huffed out a laugh, shook his head, grabbed my hand, and pulled me toward him for a kiss. "I love you, Chris. I really do," he said, which was always nice to hear but not exactly an answer to my question. Then he added in a voice so low I almost missed it, "And to think I told Oak I wouldn't upend my life for *cute*."

Dolores was the one who finally answered me. "I'm suggesting that Reed could pretend he hadn't seen Dante today, honey, and that your uncle could leave with me and Bob before Reed makes his phone call."

"You... what?" I whispered.

"Oh, and flapper pie is my personal favorite Canadian baked good." She patted my arm. "I'll send you the recipe."

"But..." I looked at Reed, jaw slack. "But your job, Reed. You can't..." I caught the look in his eye that said maybe, possibly, for me, he *could*, and a surge of hope filled my chest. I sucked in a breath. "Can you?"

"I think you should step outside the cabin with me now that the rain's stopped," Reed said, wrapping an arm around my shoulders. "There's supposed to be a meteor shower later tonight, and I have it on the very best and most fact-based authority that if you make a wish on a falling star, it's guaranteed to come true."

"My mother used to say that," Danny said with a frown.

"I know." Reed grinned.

Danny's eyes were suspiciously shiny. He said gruffly, "Take care of him."

I wrapped my arm around Reed's waist and smiled. "I think we'll take care of each other."

As the frogs around Copper Lake croaked their twilight song, Reed and I stood in the clearing by the dilapidated cabin in the woods with our arms around each other and tried very hard not to notice the sounds of two—possibly three, given Dolores's knack for minding Bob's business— retired criminals hustling their way to their oversized green getaway vehicle, while the other criminal still inside the cabin protested loudly the way he'd been securely tied to a bed frame.

It was absolutely not a romantic scenario—seriously, not

kidding, the least romantic situation a person had ever been in, in the whole history of romance—but my love for the man in my arms bubbled up inside me anyway, sweet and pure and impossible to ignore. And since I didn't have to hide it—didn't have to hide anything anymore—I didn't try.

"I love you," I said. "I love you so much, Reed Sunday."

He grinned. "Thank fuck. I wondered if you'd remember you hadn't said it yet."

"In my defense," I argued, because I'd decided I liked arguing, especially with Reed and especially when it was important, "I've had a really eventful day. I was kidnapped... for the second time, which was way less enjoyable than the first—"

"Don't joke about it," Reed growled, nipping at my lip. "It's too soon. It will *always* be too soon."

"—and subduing my cousin—"

"If there's ever a next time," he noted as Nicky's demands for freedom grew louder. "Subdue him harder."

"—and confronting my uncle about decades' worth of lies—"

"Like a fucking badass," he whispered. "I'm so proud of you, baby."

"—and that's a lot," I concluded. "Since I'm actually an extremely boring person."

Reed laughed so hard he startled the owls from their perches in the trees and seemed to frighten Nicky into silence.

"Chris Sunday," he said when he could finally speak again, "there is not a single part of being with you that doesn't *thrill* me. So if you want to live in New Jersey, we will. Or if you'd rather make a home in the Hollow, let's do that. Or if you want to stay here in this tiny town you have, against my will, made me actually sort of like—"

"Yes, please," I whispered.

"Then we'll be Coppertians," he said firmly. "Whatever you want, wherever you want, I will be very happy to live this *extremely boring* life with you for as long as you'll have me."

"It's going to be a very long time," I warned. "Quite possibly forever."

But Reed didn't seem put off by that at all. He fixed my glasses for me so they sat just right on my face, and then he kissed me long and slow and deep, until our every gasp became a promise, our every sigh an affirmation that we were seen and known and loved. That we were *home*.

And later that night, when we crawled into bed and I nestled in Reed's embrace, I thought I might actually feel a teensy bit bad for poor John Ruffian. The man was always going around pretending to be things—doctors and oil magnates and undercover vigilantes—which might be exciting, for a little while.

But I couldn't think of any pretend life more exciting than my own—being Christoforo Winowski (sometimes Sunday), a man who got to build his future in beautiful, tiny Copper County with the love of his life.

EPILOGUE
REED

One year later

SOME DAYS, I couldn't believe how lucky I was to be Reed
Sunday.

"More pasta, Watt?" Chris asked, topping up Derry's
cherry soda. He trailed a hand over my shoulder as he
moved around the picnic table—a teak A-frame table that he
and I had built with our own four hands in front of the caretaker cabin last November—before taking his seat next
to me.

It turned out Chris and I really liked building things
together, so much so that after we'd finished renovating the
cabins last autumn, we'd decided we wanted more projects
to work on together in our spare time. The picnic table had
been the first. The new chairs arranged around the nearby
fire pit had been our second. Fixing up the kitchen and the
bathroom in the caretaker cabin had been the third.

We'd put a temporary pause on all renovation work around
Memorial Day when the campers began arriving, and even

though the last campers of the season had left three weeks ago, we hadn't started anything else yet. Life had simply gotten too busy. Too full of good things. And more were on the horizon.

"I think three helpings is probably enough." Watt pushed his plate away with a groan. "You're a damn good cook, Chris Sun—er, Winowski." He rolled his eyes. "That's *never* gonna sound right."

Chris's cheeks went pink. We'd come clean about the truth of our relationship—a certain version of the truth, anyway—last year, a few days after Danny had left town. We'd omitted the part about Chris's uncle, naturally, but after the O'Leary police had come to take Nicky away, other details about the incident had leaked out, and folks in Copper County had wasted no time embellishing the tale, so we'd felt compelled to get our own version of events out there. "Before they start saying you know where Jimmy Hoffa is buried," I'd told Chris wryly.

The one part of the truth that people refused to believe —or, at least, to remember—was that Chris and I weren't married. Watching Chris's adorable blush under the cafe lights he'd hung over the table, though, I decided I didn't mind that one bit.

"Thank you, Watt," Chris said. "It's my uncle Danny's recipe. He's an excellent cook."

"Sure is," Derry mumbled around a bite of his own *fourth* pasta helping. "This is good shit, Chris."

Watt cuffed his son gently on the back of the head. "Don't use fresh language. Especially in front of Chris."

"Sorry," Derry mumbled. He gave Chris a hopeful smile. "But I might have another helping if you're still offering?"

Laughing, Chris leaped up to refill his plate. "I love

cooking for you, Derry. You have a real appreciation for food."

"It's been nice, having these pasta-and-charcuterie nights," Watt said. He gave his empty pasta bowl a forlorn look. "We're gonna miss this after you move."

This time next month, Chris and I would be knee-deep in renovations again, this time on our own place. A rustic, three-bedroom Adirondack—with a fieldstone fireplace that had brought tears to Chris's eyes and a three-car garage perfect for doing restorations that may or may not have brought tears to mine—had come up for sale a few weeks ago. This was a pretty rare event since we'd learned that most people who lived on Copper Lake stayed from cradle to grave, so Chris and I hadn't hesitated to put in an offer.

In a little over three weeks, I'd be an official Coppertian, a permanent resident of the tiniest town on God's green earth. And I couldn't be happier about it.

As my beloved would say, what were the hecking chances?

I rolled my eyes across the table at Watt. "You do remember we're only moving to the house on the other side of yours and not to the dark side of the moon, don't you? Take a *left* when you go out your back door instead of a *right*. We'll be the ones covered in orange shag carpet dust, picking popcorn ceiling bits out of our hair. You can't miss us."

Watt laughed. "True enough. And it'll be fun to help you out once the autumn rush at the orchard dies down, won't it, Der?"

Derry muttered something around another enormous bite of pasta, and Watt shook his head. "Christ alive, where do you put it?" he demanded. "There's a teenage appetite, and then there's... that."

Derry scraped the tines of his fork against his plate, which was empty once again, and shrugged. "Hockey practice, Dad. I'm training like crazy." He wrinkled his nose. "Really hoping we actually get to play."

"Why wouldn't you?" I asked, automatically lifting my arm as Chris sat back down, then wrapping it around him when he leaned into me.

"Our coach is out for the whole season. They're trying to find a replacement but haven't had any luck yet." Derry ran one big hand through a crop of messy curls that were dark, like his father's. "Worst news ever. Whole team's bummed. Jesse Wise nearly cried."

"Oh, no," Chris said. "Is the coach sick? Is it serious?"

Derry shook his head. "Worse," he said solemnly. "She's pregnant."

Watt huffed out a laugh. "What Derry *means* to say is that Tamsen Monroe and her husband are having a daughter in November, and she's starting her maternity leave next week. None of the other teachers have volunteered to take over coaching yet. But her replacement might," he told his son.

"That'll be better than nothing," Derry agreed. "But they won't be like Coach Monroe. She played for Northeastern. That's a Division I school. And she has brothers who also play. You know Wells Monroe, the right wing for the—"

"Bruins," I finished right along with him. "Wow."

"Yeah," Derry agreed. "It's senior year, and I was really hoping for a scholarship."

"I'm sorry, Derry," Chris said. "I'd volunteer, but I'm better skilled at skating that... you know..."

"Involves a toe pick?" I asked innocently.

Chris's eyes danced. "You could coach the team, Reed."

I shook my head. There were many, many things I would do for my husband...

Former fake husband and protectee...

Boyfriend...

Love.

Coaching a bunch of sweaty teenagers was not one of them.

"I'm guessing they need the coach to be a teacher, baby, otherwise Watt would do it himself," I pointed out, and Watt nodded. "And don't forget I'm an *entrepreneur* now." I wiggled my eyebrows, then added dryly, "And I don't want Oak to fire me immediately after making me a partner in Bartlett Security when I have a mortgage to pay."

"True." Chris grinned. "Not to mention a half stake in a new but promising charcuterie business."

"Exactly. Once Cheese and Charm takes off, I'll quit and let you support me," I teased. "It'll happen, you watch."

This wasn't just me blowing sunshine either... at least, not in terms of Chris's company's success. Back in September, Chris's charcuterie storefront had opened in O'Leary, just a few doors down from Goode's Diner. He not only offered event catering but also sold premium wines, cured meats, cheeses, and custom charcuterie boards he'd sourced from a local woodworker. We'd expected he'd be running the place himself for a while, to save on costs, but in the past month, he'd already had to hire two new employees just to keep up with demand.

I stopped in for lunch almost daily myself, when I wasn't traveling to conduct risk assessments for potential clients once or twice a month. Though, admittedly, I'd have been there even if I hadn't developed a fondness for double-cream brie because I was really inordinately and enduringly fond of a certain charcuterie specialist.

I wasn't the only one who was proud of Chris's success either. Every time Danny emailed or called from... wherever he was... he didn't hesitate to tell Chris how happy he was that Chris was carrying on the family name in the cheese world. And Dolores and Bob, who'd stopped in Copper County twice on their endless RV tour, assured us that Danny was well and happy.

As for Chris's other family member... we didn't hear from him. We'd heard that Nicky had recovered from his injuries, and I knew—because I made it my business to know—that he was still in jail, awaiting trial. As long as I had a single string to pull, there would be no bail for Nicolas Costello.

Ironically, I'd been offered a commendation and a promotion after Nicky's capture and arrest, but I hadn't hesitated to turn it down and hand in my notice, even though Janissey had begged me to stay. The moment I'd kissed Chris in the forest while Danny escaped had been my real resignation from the Division; giving Janissey my letter of resignation was just a formality.

I hadn't regretted it for a single second. And with Chris's warmth pressed against my side and the clean vanilla scent of him in my nose, I knew I never would.

I liked my life. A whole fuck of a lot.

Across the table, Watt peered into the gathering darkness at something beyond the caretaker cabin, and then he froze. "What the hell is that?"

The rest of us turned to look, and I saw something I hadn't seen in the year I'd lived here.

A light in the big house on the hill—the Wrigleys' old house—was on.

"Oh, yeah," Chris said, turning back around to face him. "I meant to ask you about that. There was a moving truck parked by the house this morning. I stopped to say hello, but I didn't see anyone around. Did Mrs. Wrigley's heir finally decide to rent the place? Is the tenant going to be the new campground caretaker since we're leaving?"

Watt shrugged dismissively. "Who the fuck knows? I've given up trying to predict what Jasper Wrigley will do." Though he said the words easily enough, his face looked troubled, and his eyes kept returning to that light in the Wrigleys' window.

Eventually, he stood and clapped his son on the shoulder. "Come on, Der. Let's leave these guys to enjoy their last few nights here. You down for *John Ruffian* on Wednesday, Chris? The usual crew, at my place?"

"Oh. Sure." Chris's lips turned up in a friendly smile. "I'll bring snacks."

"Looking forward to it. Uh... and you can come, too, Reed. If you want."

I rolled my eyes, and Watt shot me a wink. Then, the two men turned on their phone flashlights and made their way home across the field.

"What was that about?" I demanded.

"Hmm?" Chris fluttered his eyelashes. "What was..." He fluttered a hand in the air. "...*what* about?" He stood and stretched. "Gosh, it's getting chilly, huh? We should go inside and—"

I stood, too, only to pull him down on my lap in one of the Adirondack chairs by the fire. "I'll keep you warm. And don't try to wriggle out of this. You said *sure* in the same tone of voice you said *sure* when Gage offered to get you a glass of Boone's Farm apple wine last time we were in the Hollow. You said *sure* like you weren't sure at all. Tell me the truth, baby." I paused to fix his glasses for him. "Are you falling out of love... with John Ruffian?"

Chris snickered. "Bite your tongue. It's just... I worry about Watt sometimes, that's all. He's a good friend. He needs something that's *his*. You know? Something besides a TV show."

I grunted.

He laughed. "Is it weird that I've learned to enjoy your grunts now that I know how to interpret them?"

I rolled my eyes and grunted again.

"See, now *that* grunt means 'No you don't, Chris, because I'm a flipping former Division agent who knows how to do the *click-click* thing with a gun, which means I'm deep and brooding and mysterious and not the sort of person whose grunts *can* be interpreted.'"

I lifted an eyebrow.

"Whereas the *other* grunt, the one about Watt, meant 'Chris is doing his people thing again, and I don't understand what he means because Watt has plenty that's his. An orchard, a kid, a sister, a whole community who loves him. And he'd better keep his moony eyes off what's *mine*.'" Chris grinned up at me smugly. "How'd I do?"

I opened my mouth to protest, but... he'd nailed it, honestly.

I grunted a third time.

Chris pressed a kiss to my jaw and settled his head on my chest. "Yeah. I knew I nailed it even before you grunted," he sighed happily. "The thing is, Watt does have all those things, but they're not all his. They're his right now, maybe. His to care for. But they aren't his the same way I'm yours. They're not *for* him the way you are for me. I hope he finds what we have, that's all."

I frowned. "Wasn't he dating someone recently?"

"You mean Kayla? Yeah, but there was no chemistry. Watt told her they were better off as friends." Chris lifted his head to give me a severe look. "Which is the same way he sees me."

I wrapped my arm around Chris's neck and pulled him in for a long and decidedly passionate kiss before settling him against my chest once more.

I knew, of course, that Watt didn't really have designs on Chris. I also knew that, even if he did, Chris wouldn't be tempted in the slightest because he'd given one thousand percent of his heart into my keeping. I wasn't actually jealous… because there was nothing to be jealous of.

But when you knew someone as well as Chris and I had come to know each other, when you loved someone and saw the truth of them as well as we did… it turned out that sometimes pretending was fun.

"So what I hear you saying is there's *no* good reason Watt keeps putting his moony eyes on my husband," I grumbled.

Chris laughed and shook his head, his fingers toying with the top edge of my Henley. "I'm not your husband anymore, remember?"

"Hmm." I dug my hand into the pocket of my jeans and grabbed the ring I'd stashed there. A ring I'd been carrying around for months, waiting for the perfect moment, forgetting that every moment Chris and I were together was perfect.

"I think you mean not *yet*," I said, sliding the ring onto his finger. And then, as he stared down at it in shock, I added in a whisper, "Marry me, Chris."

When he looked up at me again, his big brown eyes positively glowed with happiness, so bright they outshone the fire, outshone the stars, and made every other damn thing in the world seem dull and unimportant in contrast.

He wrapped his arms around my neck. "Heck. *Yes*," he

whispered. Then he pressed his lips to mine in a kiss that went on for a long, long time.

But when I finally picked him up and carried him to bed a little while later, the light in the house on the hill was still on.

————

Want more Reed and Chris? See what happens when they head back to Little Pippin Hollow (and live out Chris's teenage fantasy) in The Grove, exclusively for newsletter subscribers → https://readerlinks.com/l/4262400

Want more Copper County stories? Check out Watt's single dad, enemies-to-lovers, second-chance romance, The Rivals of Copper County, here → https://readerlinks.com/l/4294420

And if you'd like more O'Leary stories, you can start the series here → https://readerlinks.com/l/4258798

ABOUT MAY ARCHER

May is an M/M author who lives in Boston. She spends her days planning vacations, mainlining diet soda, avoiding the gym, reading M/M romance, and when all other forms of procrastination fail, writing it.

Visit her website at mayarcher.com to sign up for her newsletter to hear about sales and upcoming releases, freebies and behind the scenes info and more! Or join her Facebook group, Club May!

facebook.com/may.archer.author

instagram.com/mayarcherauthor

amazon.com/May-Archer/e/B075JQVGLX

patreon.com/MayArcherRomance

bookbub.com/authors/may-archer

ALSO BY MAY ARCHER

Get my <u>New Release Alerts</u>

Join me on Patreon

Follow me Everywhere Else

<u>Love in O'Leary Series</u>

<u>Whispering Key Series</u>

<u>The Sunday Brothers Series</u>

<u>Copper County Series</u>

<u>The Way Home Series</u>

<u>Licking Thicket Series</u>

(cowritten with Lucy Lennox)

<u>Champion Security Series</u>

(cowritten with Lucy Lennox)

<u>Honeybridge Series</u>

(cowritten with Lucy Lennox)

For a comprehensive list of titles, audio samples, freebies, suggested reading order, and more, visit my website at www.MayArcher.com!